LUNAR

Other titles by Chloe Openshaw

Where Wisteria Falls
Inside the Ballerina
The Shambles

LUNAR

by

CHLOE OPENSHAW

Copyright © 2024 Chloe Openshaw

ISBN 9798335812740 (paperback)
ISBN 9798335813181 (hardback)

All rights reserved. This book or any portion thereof may not be reproduced or used in any manner whatsoever without the express written permission of the publisher except for the use of brief quotations in a book review.

All characters appearing in this work are fictitious. Any resemblance to real persons, living or dead, is purely coincidental.

Edited by Lolli Molyneux
Cover design by Ken Dawson
Typesetting by Book Polishers

*"With freedom, books, flowers, and the moon,
who could not be happy?"*

- Oscar Wilde

1

Yesterday was Thursday.

Shielded by the army of mature sycamore trees that lined the front of his property like a platoon, notorious recluse and ailing pensioner, Lockie Sloan, peered out from behind the grubby curtains of his upstairs bedroom window. With a steely stare, he double-checked that nobody was passing the main road that ran parallel to his house. Confident that he was alone, he savoured the sight of his front garden, particularly the activities of the awakening wildlife. Illuminated by the streetlamps, he admired a bumble of birds as they bounded haphazardly from one branch to another, the early morning charm of finches feasting on a bountiful supply of ruby red berries. After so many years tucked away from the outside world, the sight of the carefree creatures produced pangs of envy in Lockie's wounded heart. Even if it would only last until the sun rose above the nearby Cotswold hills, Lockie yearned to experience a snippet of freedom. His senses longed to once again digest the sights and scents that he associated with the free world. Like the warming, spicy aromatics that ooze with abundance from authentic coffee houses. He wanted to hear the eclectic, mishmash of sounds that act as the soundtrack to a normal existence. Like the fluctuating tones created by excited children playing in a park, or the sound of waves crashing and receding across coastal shorelines. But most of all, Lockie longed for love. He craved to witness subtle shows of human affection. He hungered to experience the sensation of someone's warm skin against his hand. Love was the ingredient that could quench Lockie's greatest thirst. Everything else that he had sacrificed in his life paled in comparison.

Similar to a startled hedgehog, Lockie retreated behind the safety of his curtains the moment he spotted the flashing lights of a cyclist travelling up the main road. His thoughts of freedom flickered out like a candle at the end of its wick.

He peered around his barren bedroom, searching for sources of solace. In a space lacking any traces of love, there was only himself to find. Having lived alone at his double-fronted farmhouse, Lunar, for so long, he couldn't recall the last time he'd spoken to another human being. He cleared his throat in anticipation of speaking, yet failed to mumble a single word. Despite his experience with seclusion, Lockie had always refuted the idea of engaging in conversations with himself, refusing to knock on the door of what he considered would be insanity.

'Sam, are you here?' he suddenly voiced, his words emerging from deep within. Desperate, Lockie repeated the four words and hoped one last time that his prayer had been answered, and that his son was about to come leaping in like an excitable, young gazelle. With his prayer unfulfilled, the house remained still and home to a single, beating heart.

Like clockwork, the moment he heard his astronomical wall clock brush past 06:45 a.m., Lockie headed downstairs and prepared himself for his daily dose of self-punishment. With a mug of weak tea in hand, he walked through to his imposing lounge and, with reluctance, parted each set of pleated curtains. Squinting into the early morning light, he opened the side window that overlooked his rustic barn, a snappy breeze fighting its way into the neglected hideaway. He felt his skin suddenly tingle as goosebumps quickly formed all over. Finding familiarity in the harsh chill, Lockie lingered in the window and forced himself to peer out at his dilapidated barn until the clock struck seven. As always, he remained silent for the full fifteen minutes, stuck to the spot and forcing himself to face the barn as his own form of self-retribution. The day that had continued to haunt him replayed itself in painstaking detail, and for those fifteen minutes each morning, he could see the ribbons of black smoke streaming right in front of his eyes. He could hear screams of terror and the sound of the coroner's van rumbling up the driveway. The pungent stench of the mortuary lingered in his nostrils and rekindled the familiar sense of nausea. He rehashed each moment until the memories stole the air from his lungs, and the feeling of life from his heart.

When the clock struck seven, Lockie allowed himself to turn his back to the barn. He would return to the exact same spot come the following dawn. This morning routine had remained rigid for well over a decade and was more predictable than the rising of the Eastern sun. The only time that the frail, ailing loner had failed to part his lounge curtains was during a bout of bad health a few years previous. A nasty spate of influenza saw him bedridden and for those few days of convalescence, every curtain at Lunar remained closed. Day and night.

Taking care not to spill any tea, Lockie placed down his brimming mug and eased his weary body into the ingrained grooves of his highbacked Chesterfield armchair. He adjusted the footrest and eased off his musty mules. Daylight hadn't yet broken, so with a shaking hand, he reached out and switched on the understated table lamp. The low-wattage bulb did little to illuminate the high-ceilinged room, or the rows of draped, blackened cobwebs. Outside, on the expanse of snow-glistening lawn, a round of robins gathered near Lockie's strategically positioned scraps of stale, seeded bread. From his front-row seat, he relished the sight of the feasting redbreasts, each one ravenous after surviving what had turned out to be a particularly harsh, British winter. Reaching for his drink, Lockie took hold of his mug and pressed the dirty ceramic against his dry, cracked lips. Savouring the moment, he allowed the steaming liquid to trickle down his throat, warming his weak body from the inside out.

Like the robins as they feasted, Lockie relaxed. He relished the unfamiliar feeling of peace that had settled deep within his brittle bones over the past few days. His breathing loosened, and it no longer felt like his lungs were lined with a heaviness, like the clagging mist that usually clung to the peaks and troughs of the Aldebaran terrain. For a moment, the debilitating levels of anxiety that infested every inch of his body felt less suffocating. In his moment of respite, Lockie picked up the biro and notepad that had been resting on the side table for several months, along with his leather-bound copy of the Bible. With his mind and body momentarily still, his private thoughts rose to the surface and caught their first glimpse of daylight.

With a wavering hand, Lockie began to write one word after another. He peered beyond the well of tears threatening to drown his vision and continued to pen his two intended letters. Within minutes, Lockie had written a garland of whispers. Stealing his attention, outside the blush of congregated robins flew the coop. Unable to ignore the feeling that it would soon be his turn to depart the land at Lunar, Lockie continued to pour his heart until his mind was empty and the letters were decorated with words. With hunched shoulders and a scalp scattered with only a few specs of white, wiry hair, Lockie rested his head back and closed his eyes. He pretended that he was sat out on the landing, the expanse of land located at the back of the house, and was once again stargazing with his beloved son and daughter. He held their hands and listened to the resonance of their gentle breathing as they admired the twinkling canopy that stretched as far as they could see. The Bible passages that had underpinned the foundations of his life over the past decade played through his mind with a celestial harmony, wrapping his body in a swaddle of peace.

After relishing the fleeting sense of stillness, his ingrained sense of guilt soon stirred and, like a wake of vultures, swooped in to feast off the fresh scraps of culpability lining the letters. Sobbing harder than an abandoned child, Lockie opened his eyes and scribbled names on each letter, before placing both inside one envelope. He ran his tongue across the seal flap and moistened the tacky glue to seal the envelope closed. The ordeal was over. His dark and sinister past had been regurgitated, allowing Lockie to accept what remained of his future.

With his personal affairs finally in order, Lockie acknowledged his sense of loneliness. He had always welcomed his solitary existence with open arms, but today felt different. Today felt unsettling. Unable to recall the last time that he had come face to face with another human being, Lockie acknowledged the fact that maybe he was destined to end his life the way that he had chosen to live it; alone. His mind and body were exhausted. Had he caught a glimpse of his reflection in a mirror, he wouldn't have recognised the slender, shadowy figure staring back. Every one of his arthritic limbs felt like they were being severed from the socket, and having purposefully stopped taking any medication, the pain felt intolerable. He felt like it was time. He felt like it was his time.

Lockie had already waited fifteen years for a reunion. He didn't want to wait another day, or even another hour. Enough was enough. Alone in his lounge, Lockie shut out the room, bowed his head and locked the fingers on both hands together. He took a moment to pray to the only God he trusted. He pleaded to be freed. He asked for peace. He begged for salvation. But most of all, he prayed to be placed alongside his son. Trusting that his prayers would be answered, Lockie Sloan prepared himself to leave behind his troubled life at Lunar. He kept his eyes closed and tried to imagine Heaven. He could see a lush, green meadow, the carpet of grass interspersed with a collection of vibrant flora. The kaleidoscope of colour beamed with a vibrancy he'd never witnessed. In the distance, he saw Sam chasing a holly blue butterfly, the sound of his laughter so familiar, so comforting. He knew Sam would be there. Heaven wasn't going to disappoint, and he placed all his trust in God.

Today was Friday.

Despite being in his eighties, Arthur Aspey firmly believed that the early bird would catch the worm. He was out of bed before six o'clock each morning, and today was no different. Without looking at his bedside table clock, he already knew the time. The awakening birdsong and snippet of dawn hue seeping beneath the curtains was all the confirmation he required. He swung his legs out of bed and wrapped his fleece over his shoulders. Unable to start the day without a cup of strong brewed tea, he made his way out of the bedroom and onto the upstairs landing of his four-bedroomed Victorian house. Abiding by his daily routine, he paused at the landing window and looked across the rural countryside that epitomised his hometown of Aldebaran. Even after a lifetime spent living in the same village, Arthur still relished the way that the rolling hills tumbled with triumph in the distance. The rugged, peaceful green waves that seemed to sail beyond his window had remained unspoiled for decades. Nothing but a dotting of mighty oaks, pastures of laidback livestock and wrapped haybales ever disturbed nature's best canvas.

Arthur pulled his eyes away from the faraway scenery, allowing his gaze to land on his neighbour's house. He spotted that the lounge curtains at Lunar had already been parted. He checked his watch, momentarily doubting the accuracy of his internal body clock. Confirmation of the early hour suddenly had him unsettled.

'Olive!' he shouted, hoping to rouse his wife, who was still asleep in bed. 'Olive!'

'What's wrong?' she bellowed back. 'It's early,' she added, glancing over at her bedside clock.

'Come here.'

Annoyed and dazed, Olive trundled herself out of bed and

wrapped a cardigan over her nightie. 'Whatever is the matter?' she grumbled, appearing at the bedroom door.

Arthur pointed out of the window. 'Look. Mr Sloan's curtains are already open.'

Olive peered down at her neighbour's imposing house. 'Maybe he woke up early today,' she replied in a nonchalant tone. Feeling cross at her early-morning startle, Olive felt begrudged to acknowledge how strange it was that the curtains were open. 'That house will be the death of you,' she mumbled beneath her breath, heading downstairs. 'I may as well put the kettle on. I'm up now because of you.'

With the sickening sensation gaining momentum in his stomach, Arthur washed and changed before making his way downstairs. 'You can't deny that it's odd,' he said, appearing in the kitchen fifteen minutes later, his body language awkward. 'We both know that those curtains are never opened until bang on six forty-five.'

Having had a bit of time to habituate to the new day, Olive reacted. 'It is unusual,' she commented, reaching in the fridge to return the milk. 'There could be a simple explanation.'

Arthur reached for his tepid cup of tea and took a sip. 'I have a bad feeling,' he announced. His thick-rimmed glasses became covered with mist the moment the warm, kitchen air made contact with them. 'I'm going to wait until quarter to seven,' he said, glancing up at the wall clock. 'And if he's not stood at that window like usual, I'm going over.'

Olive began to empty the dishwasher. 'He won't appreciate your show of concern. He'll probably just ignore you until you go away.'

Arthur peered out of his kitchen window and across his mature garden, the high wall of dividing trees blocking him from seeing too much of Lockie Sloan's house. 'He can slam the door in my face for all I care,' he replied. 'But I can't ignore my instincts. After what we've been through with that house, you of all people should understand.' Feeling unsupported, Arthur stomped out of the kitchen and headed back upstairs, his footsteps louder than usual. Positioning himself once again in front of the landing window, he looked down at the imposing structure that bolted out of the greenery like a Stonehenge monument. Squinting, he tried to detect any signs of movement coming from inside his neighbour's house. The weakened glow of the solitary lounge lamp was the only indication that somebody was home.

Olive showered and changed in the downstairs bathroom, reappearing ten minutes later. 'Any signs?' she asked from the bottom of the stairs.

Arthur looked at his watch, confirming that it was now 06:40 a.m. 'Not yet,' he replied, at which point, Olive disappeared.

With anticipation mounting, Arthur kept his eyes on Lunar's side window, urging his neighbour to appear on cue.

06:45 a.m. came and went.

'Something's wrong,' Arthur muttered to himself. His eyes stung in protest at staring with such intensity.

'Did you say something?' Olive asked, reappearing at the bottom of the stairs, a wooden spoon in her hand and a dusting of flour decorating her chequered pinny.

'I'm going over there,' Arthur announced, making his way downstairs. 'I just have a bad feeling that I can't shake,' he said, grabbing his coat and shoes. 'Are you coming with me?' he asked, looking back at his wife.

Olive reached for her duffle coat and bobble hat off the rack. 'Of course, I'm coming,' she sighed. She placed her hand on Arthur's shoulder, trying to ease her husband's mounting levels of anxiety, the weight of worry dragging down his burly shoulders. 'It's not like last time,' she reassured, knowing what torments would be running through her husband's mind.

'Let's go,' he said, grabbing the house keys and opening the front door. A rush of cold air hit him in the face, forcing his eyes to sting.

Despite springtime being on the cusp of emerging, a dusting

of snow covered the ground. Droplets of ice decorated the leafy canopy of the mature beech, weighing down the branches. Arthur and Olive ducked as they made their way down the slippery garden path, moss and mildew carpeting the paving stones beneath. 'Take hold of my hand,' he encouraged, fearful that his wife might fall.

'He hasn't lit the fire,' Olive commented, spotting the absence of smoke rising from the double chimney pots positioned at the peak of Lunar's slated roof.

Arthur had already clocked the absence of the grey billows, knowing that most days during the winter months, a fire had burnt in the hearth over at Lunar. He remained quiet, trying his best to silence the demons that were screaming at the top of their voice that something was amiss.

Once they had navigated the short walk up the lane, Olive opened Lockie Sloan's gate and headed towards the red-bricked house, her arm linking Arthur's for support. 'It must be years since we last attempted to make friends,' she commented, trying to recall the last encounter with their closest neighbour. 'Are you ringing the bell or knocking?' she asked, her own bundle of nerves now getting the better of her.

Arthur led Olive up the steps of Lunar's wooden veranda, the bold front door now only a few paces away. 'I'll knock,' he replied. 'It's that quiet, he's bound to hear us.' With his arm outstretched, Arthur rattled his knuckles against the wooden front door. He glanced at Olive, sensing her nerves and feeling how tight her arm was wrapped around his.

A few seconds passed. Like a hibernating animal nestled deep within its natural habitat, Lunar remained still and silent, unwilling to awaken.

'Can you hear anything?' Olive asked. Without moving her legs, she tried to peer in through the lounge window, stretching herself like a ballerina on her tiptoes.

'No,' Arthur replied, knocking for a second time.

'What should we do?' she asked, agitated. The unrelenting

chill bit at her skin, sharper than the prick of a needle.

Arthur reached out his hand and twisted the knob. The door eased open. 'It's open,' he said, looking at Olive. 'Should we go in?'

Perturbed, Olive released her arm from her husband's and took a step backwards. 'I'm not sure,' she replied. 'Should we not call someone first?'

Arthur peered through the gap that had appeared in the front door and listened. 'Call who?' he said, turning back to address his wife.

Olive shook her head. 'I don't know,' she snapped. 'But after everything that's happened over the years, we know that Lockie doesn't want us here. He doesn't want anybody here.'

Arthur ignored his wife's suggestion. 'Lockie?' he called out, easing the front door further ajar. Still standing on the veranda, Arthur peered down the long, narrow hallway, listening. 'Lockie, it's Arthur from next door. Am I okay to come in?'

No reply came. Only an eerie silence filtered through the air.

'Did you bring your mobile?' Olive asked, patting down her own pockets.

'No,' he replied. 'I need to make sure he's alright,' he said, following his instincts and taking a bold step over the threshold. 'I can't just do nothing.'

'I'll wait here then,' Olive said, lingering on the veranda with a nervous stance.

Arthur stepped purposefully into his neighbour's property. The air in the house felt cold against his exposed skin. The lounge door to the immediate left was closed, so Arthur headed straight down the hallway and into what he knew was the kitchen at the back of the house. His eyes welled at the upsetting scene. The sink was overflowing with filthy dishes. A cupboard door was falling off its hinges. A musty smell lingered in the air, as pungent as stale milk. The ceiling corners were covered with a concoction of cobwebs and grime. But it was more than just the disarray that upset Arthur. It was the feeling of loneliness that oozed from Lunar's walls that really pained his heart. A lone chair was positioned at the family dining table, more lonesome than a stray lamb. Stacked high, a tower of empty soup cans cluttered the bin, and a pile of unopened post rested on the countertop. Through Arthur's eyes, the room bore no resemblance to the space that he once knew better than the back of his own hand. A room that had once brimmed with love, family, and laughter, was now more akin to a prison cell.

'Are you okay?' Olive asked, teetering with nervousness in the doorway, peering down the hallway herself.

Too lost in his own maze of thoughts, Arthur didn't reply. Touching memories of the Lunar of old resurfaced, and Arthur recalled how he had once felt so welcomed at his neighbours enchanting, family farmhouse. Tears welled in his weathered eyes. He tried to make sense of the sadness that had overturned the home with such a savage hand.

Olive appeared in the kitchen doorway. Her face was stricken by a similar look of shock. 'Oh, Arthur,' she whispered, pressing her hand towards her mouth.

Arthur turned to face his wife, his pained expression reflecting his inner turmoil. 'How on earth has he been living like this?'

Olive peered further into the room. Her heart crumbled. 'Poor Lockie,' she cried. She recalled some of the tenderness that she had once experienced at her neighbour's house when the Sloan family had welcomed her and Arthur into their bustling, family home. With a dab of her tissue, Olive wiped her eyes. 'It doesn't matter what happened in the past. We just need to help him now,' she proclaimed, exiting the room. The stairs creaked beneath Olive's shifting weight as she climbed to the first floor in search of her neighbour. 'Lockie?' she called out, searching aimlessly through the darkness, too scared to switch a light on for fear of what she might uncover.

Tearing himself away from the kitchen, Arthur opened the door to the back room. The dark interior felt equally as barren and hostile as the kitchen. The air was stale with a wintry nip, and once he was satisfied that the room was empty, he eased the wood back into the frame. With a sense of apprehension, Arthur moved to the next room and clasped the handle on the closed door, pushing it gently ajar. After taking a few steps into the room, he yelled. 'Olive! Olive!'

Scrambling as fast as his weary body would permit, Arthur rushed to where Lockie's body was lying slumped in an armchair. 'Lockie, can you hear me?' he asked, shaking his neighbour's unresponsive body. Arthur pressed his hand against Lockie's cold face and witnessed his slightly parted, cloudy eyes, and he knew that his neighbour had passed away. With the pads of his fingers, Arthur pressed against Lockie's neck, the skin rigid. Kneeling, and with a delicate touch, Arthur took hold of his neighbour's hand and cradled it. He closed his eyes and shook his head, struggling to silence the burden of guilt that weighed on his shoulders. He punished himself immediately for not trying harder to reach out in what had been his neighbour's hour of need. 'Oh, Lockie. I'm so sorry, my old friend.'

'Where are you?' Olive shouted, her footsteps stomping down the stairs. The moment she appeared in the lounge doorway and saw the way that Lockie's body was slumped to one side, she knew her neighbour's fate. 'Oh no,' she cried. 'He's not breathing, is he?'

Arthur continued to comfort his neighbour's hand. 'No. He's gone.'

With careful steps, Olive approached her husband and rested her hand on his back.

'Call for an ambulance,' Arthur requested with all the compassion of a pastor.

Olive searched the lounge for a phone before leaving the room, the sound of her voice travelling in through the open door as her call to the emergency services connected. Moments later, she appeared in the lounge doorway. 'They're on their way.'

'Can you go outside and watch for them? I'll stay here. I don't want him to be alone. Not anymore.'

With tears streaming down her face, Olive walked outside and stationed herself on the large wooden veranda. Standing on guard, she waited for the ambulance, watching for flickers of yellow and blue to appear in the distance.

Inside the house, Arthur took the opportunity to say a personal goodbye in private. Remaining by Lockie's side with more purpose than a lifelong companion, Arthur spoke softly. 'It's okay, Lockie. You're with Sam now. He'll look after you from here,' he said with tears in his eyes. 'I'm so sorry, for everything,' he added, continuing to hold Lockie's cold hand. 'I've always blamed myself for what happened that terrible day,' Arthur paused to regain his composure. 'And I know that you blamed me too.' Like spring buds peaking their way through dense soil, dark feelings that Arthur had kept buried for fifteen years began to surface. 'And I don't blame you for avoiding me. I only wish I'd tried harder to make things right between the two of us,' he cried, peering around at the dark, cold room. 'Had I known you were living like this, my dear friend, I would have tried every day until you let me in. I wouldn't have given up on you.'

Arthur noticed an envelope at the side of Lockie's chair, making note of the way it had been carefully propped up on the table, next to a well-thumbed copy of the Bible. Listening for any signs of a commotion outside, Arthur reached out and took hold of the envelope, seeing that his name was scribbled on the front. A sickening sensation stirred deep within his stomach, and his shaking hands struggled to break the seal. Inside the envelope, he found a handwritten letter, along with another, smaller envelope. Fumbling, he opened the letter that was addressed to himself, and read the first line in disbelief.

Dear Arthur,

Hello, my friend. I pray that you aren't offended by me referring to you in this way. Despite everything that has happened between us over the years, I have always thought of you as my friend. Maybe my only friend. Some things in this life can never be broken despite the strain they endure, like the bond we once shared.

I'm so sorry if you are the unfortunate one who has found me, but I suspect that this will be the case. Yourself, and your dearest Olive, will be the only people that would notice something was awry. Take comfort in the fact that I was ready to leave this world behind. I have felt unwell for several weeks, and could feel that my time was approaching. I have waited patiently for so many years to see my Sam, and I am more than ready to be reunited with my boy. Despite knowing that Sam and I will have much to talk about and unravel from the past, I know that he'll be there, waiting for me with nothing but that infectious smile of his.

Going back to the start, let me say how sorry I am, for everything. Although I've never been able to talk to you about the events of that day, please know that I never blamed you for the tragedy that unfolded. I may have spat some unkind words in your direction initially, but none of them were true. You weren't to blame. I can't emphasise that enough.

No matter what I may have said, or how I acted in those first few days and weeks that followed, I don't blame you in any way for what happened to Sam.

I have purposefully locked myself away in this house, this prison, to punish myself. I was to blame that day. Me. Nobody else. I've had to live with the fact that it was my decision that ultimately led to my son's death. I spent a long time blaming everybody else, looking to the outside world for answers, when in fact, I knew deep down that the blame rested only with myself.

I've lost count of how many times I've pictured tearing that bastard barn down with my own hands. But instead, I've made myself face it every single day. That has served as my punishment. I've faced my demons head-on and worked through many feelings of guilt and grief. The life of solitude that I chose to live has enabled me to finally make peace with what happened, and to make peace with myself.

During these years of isolation, I have sought great comfort knowing that each day, you have taken time to look out from your landing window to check up on me. Even after all my unkindness, you still took it upon yourself to watch over me, and for that, I will be forever grateful. After so many years living side by side in silence, I have come to understand that you are a wonderful human being. With that in mind, I have a favour to ask. I don't deserve your kindness, but if you could find it in your heart to do this one last favour for me, I would be so grateful.

My notoriety in the village will no doubt lead to an unpleasant amount of interest after my departure from Lunar. I am therefore fearful of anything going astray. So please, Arthur, could I ask that you place the other letter that I have left into the hands of my daughter, Charlotte? There is so much that I want her to know, things that I have never been able to say to her face. I can't promise that she will take any interest in the news you have to offer, but at least I will have tried.

Thank you, my friend.

Until we meet again,

Lockie Sloan

Arthur heard an approaching ambulance echo in the distance. He stuffed both letters into his pocket and wiped his eyes. With care, he took hold of Lockie's hand and leaned in, whispering into his friend's ear. 'I'll make sure that Charlotte gets your letter. I promise.'

The lights of the ambulance shone in through the lounge window when the vehicle pulled onto Lunar's drive. Seconds later, the lounge door burst open, and dazzling lights illuminated the upsetting scene. Like the fragmented land on which the house stood, the invisible seal that had become wrapped around Lunar had been broken, exposing its hidden secrets.

2

Summer had arrived, unpacked its travel bag, and long since settled over the undulations of the Gloucestershire landscape. A myriad of dormant, winter pastures had successfully shed their hibernation jackets, allowing the wildlife above ground the freedom to breathe and flourish. An army of combines worked in unison to turn the fertile soils, trailed by a parliament of feasting, hungry rooks. As far as the eye could see, rows of steel, sharp blades harvested the corn fields, the hum from the engines rolling in invisible waves across the terrain, the sound only dissipating when it collided with low-lying villages, such as Aldebaran.

Tucked away on the summit of Aldebaran, a quaint hamlet nestled into the gentle slopes of the Cotswolds, a curtain of deciduous, broad-leaved sycamores helped to shield an abandoned property called Lunar. Positioned alongside the main thoroughfare that fed traffic directly into the heart of the charming community, the vacant farmhouse had become an eyesore in the otherwise picturesque village. Grain dust produced by the surrounding combines often floated down off the hills and settled over Lunar's dark-grey slates, lingering as a murky shadow above the house, like a sullied cloud.

Nothing but a tarnished reputation and a ramshackle sign lodged in some overgrown shrubbery gave evidence to the Victorian farmhouse's existence. Bookended by two cannon chimney pots,

Lunar's slated, hotchpotch roof sat above an imposing, central apex. Years' worth of filth lined every window, inside and out, along with pairs of stained, net curtains. The dated window dressings and dirt served as a shield, hiding the remnants of the life that once lurked behind the bold front door. A shabby, wooden barn, infested with a jumble of climbing weeds, completed Lunar's estate.

Taking inspiration from the American South, a spacious, wooden veranda swept across the front of the property, enclosed by cream, wooden railings. A threadbare doormat was in place to welcome anyone who dared cross the threshold of the notorious house on the hill. The vast amount of land that surrounded Lunar formed a fortress to the property closing it off from the outside world. The mature garden bloomed in all corners of the compass, acting as a sweeping veil. Clusters of voluminous hydrangea added bursts of colour to the garden, the pink and purple flowers adding life to the garden's more secluded, shady spots. The burnished, bronze-red flush of other shrubs stood tall, reaching for the sun. Carpeting perennials covered the low-lying rockeries and borders, the royal-blue, star-shaped flowers shining as bright as the summer sky. The neglected farmhouse was reminiscent of a diseased sparrow amongst a nest of flourishing hatchlings, with the landscape surrounding Lunar its crowning glory.

Since Lunar had become unoccupied, the vacant, lacklustre appearance of the house had begun to attract an increasing amount of attention from passing locals, today being no exception. On foot, two pedestrians stopped at the driveway entrance and arched their necks to try and gain a better view of what, or who, might still be lurking behind the olive-coloured front door.

'It still looks empty to me,' one of the passing ladies commented, unapologetically staring directly towards the house. 'I wonder who lived there?' she asked her friend, straining her eyes to try and see beyond the faded net curtains. 'I've lived in Aldebaran for almost two years now, and I've never seen anyone coming, or going,' she commented. 'During winter, or just when I've been passing at night, I used to see a light shining behind the curtains. That's how I know that somebody actually used to live there. But I haven't seen that light on for months now.' The lady continued to stare, searching for something that she may have previously failed to spot, her speculation growing like the fungus that covered parts of the moist rockery. 'I overheard a woman talking in the post office. She said that an elderly man had lived here alone, and one day when she happened to be passing, she heard strange noises coming from inside the house.' The nosey lady turned to her friend before continuing. 'I wonder what was going on?' she asked, her eyebrows arched with suspicion.

In recent weeks, a series of whispers had spread amongst the close-knit Aldebaran community. The rumours only lost momentum the moment they landed on the ears of those select few who knew the truth, but who maintained a dignified silence. Only a handful of villagers had been privy to the secrets that former Lunar owner, Mr Sloan, had now taken to his grave.

'I know I wouldn't want to live here, and not even this wonderful garden could tempt me,' the woman's friend replied. 'Come on, let's keep walking,' she added, an eagerness in her voice. Despite the women's best efforts, and just like all the other curious folk that had gone before them, each person had failed to notice a clue pertaining to Lunar's secrets lurking in an upstairs window. A teeny collection of faded children's stickers remained stuck to the glass in the small bedroom window, and there were what looked to be a few toys resting on the windowsill.

Only a few moments after the two women had continued their way up the main road, leaving Lunar in their shadows, someone else approached the remote farmhouse. Treading carefully through a secret hollow that she had previously created, Charlotte lingered amongst the peripheral shrubbery of Lunar's private grounds. As the house came into view, her eyes welled and a thick lump of emotion became wedged in her throat. Akin to how the local, nesting robins knew each individual tree located in Lunar's garden, every contour of the land felt familiar beneath Charlotte's feet.

'Don't cry,' she told herself, pulling her attention away from the house and wiping her eyes with her sleeve, just like she used to do as a child whenever she had fallen and hurt herself. Taking a moment to steady her heightened nerves and erratic breathing, she took a step forward and revealed her slender figure to the house. Leaving behind the safety offered by the dense undergrowth, Charlotte dashed across the patch of open land that separated the shrubbery border from the barn. She pressed her body against the exterior wall of the outbuilding, ensuring that her shadow remained undetected to anyone who happened to be passing.

'I'm coming, Sam,' she muttered to herself, admiring the handful of flowers she held in her hand. Beads of sweat dotted Charlotte's forehead as the late summer heat continued to cast ribbons of warmth. Beneath her Greek, leather sandals, Lunar's waves and folds felt so familiar, and the sound of the combines in the distance stirred up forgotten memories of how the farming brutes had always patrolled the surrounding land. Like delicate kitten whiskers, individual blades of grass tickled the exposed skin at the bottom of her floral maxi dress, Lunar's way of reminding her where she was. Charlotte had returned home.

Just as she remembered, the lawns at Lunar were lush. The manes of grass displayed every colour of green available on the spectrum. With fumbling fingers, she took out a keyring and with one of the keys, unlocked the barn, seeking refuge inside the rustic outbuilding and closing the door behind her.

'I'm back, Sam. I'm here,' she announced to the emptiness that confronted her. Only flecks of natural light managed to penetrate the cracks that had appeared over time in the shabby, wooden slats. Treading with caution, Charlotte navigated the gloomy interior with a comforting sense of familiarity.

Once hidden in the depths of the barn's warm embrace, she removed the handful of wilted flowers left from a previous visit, and replaced them with the fresh selection of handpicked wildflowers. 'I miss you so much, Sam,' she whispered, kneeling in the far corner, adjusting the organic arrangement of stems. Just above where the flowers were resting, a collection of markings had been ingrained into the wood, rudimentary designs scratched by a child's hand. Through glossy eyes, Charlotte rose to her feet and admired the innocent form of graffiti, allowing her fingers to glide across the etched wood. With her thoughts becoming lost in the drawings, a deep-rooted pain soared through her grieving heart. 'Why did you have to leave me? It wasn't your time to go.'

As she'd done so many times before, Charlotte seated herself on a pile of wooden planks that had been stacked together, an old jumper used as a makeshift cushion. Since the very first day that she had become aware that the house was now unoccupied, Lunar had become Charlotte's favourite place to pause, and reflect. It felt easier for her to take a breath at Lunar, and she savoured the feeling of the fresh air seeping into her thirsty lungs. She found it easier to muse at Lunar, her mind becoming still, like the shimmering surface of a lake on a tranquil day. It felt easy for her to love at Lunar, and deep within her bones, she felt the love was reciprocated.

Once sitting comfortably, she stretched out her legs and wiped the moisture off her clammy brow. 'This hot weather reminds me of all those water fights we had in the garden,' she mumbled, a genuine sense of sentiment sparkling in her eyes. She took out her phone and opened the gallery, the light emanating from the screen shining through the darkness. Each vibrant photo evoked a particular memory and emotion, her pain replaced by swathes of love. Closing her eyes, Charlotte travelled back in time, picturing the moment that life had once felt so complete.

Safe in the knowledge that the house itself remained empty, Charlotte released a gentle exhale and rested her head against the wall, relishing the sense of familiarity. 'I love you so much, Sam, and I'm sorry if I didn't tell you enough,' she whispered, a calming sensation filling her body. The soothing aroma of the barn served to awaken some of her dormant memories, a beam appearing on her face when certain childhood recollections popped in and out of her mind in a welcome montage. 'Remember that day when you ate so much ice cream that you puked all over the kitchen floor?' She released a trickle of giggles which echoed through the barn, the sound soon dissipating into the ether.

Outside, heading up the main road that ran parallel to Lunar, the sound of screeching brakes interrupted the peace. A few seconds later the vehicle in question slowed down and turned onto the driveway. Peering beneath her sun visor as her mum pulled the racing green Mini Cooper onto Lunar's deserted driveway, Jessie looked beyond the petals that had come to land on the windscreen, spotting the house set back in the distance. Even from her distant vantage point, Jessie noticed the discoloured net curtains that covered the filthy windows. But it was the unsightly scattering of rubbish and abandoned glass milk bottles on the veranda that downturned Jessie's smile. 'It doesn't have much curb appeal,' she commented, a scrunched expression evident on her face. In the driving seat, Jessie's mum, Fern, continued to make her way up Lunar's dusty, winding drive.

'The house does need a lot of work. But just look at the garden,' Fern beamed, admiring the way that every inch of the garden had something wonderful to offer. 'Once I've hung some hanging baskets and run a mower over the lawns, this place will be transformed,' she replied.

Jessie turned to her mum. 'You're going to use a lawnmower?' she questioned. 'That's always been Dad's job.'

In a decisive tone, Fern replied. 'Every job is going to be mine from now on, and I'm confident that I'll be able to figure out how to mow a lawn.'

Jessie took another glance towards the house. 'I hope it looks better on the inside.'

Having bought Lunar over eight weeks ago, Fern knew that

the level of neglect ran much deeper than the surface. 'I'm sure you'll tell me the truth once you've seen it for yourself.'

Jessie turned to face her mum. 'If you bought this place months ago, I don't understand why you're bothered what I think. You've already made up your mind.'

'I couldn't stay at home any longer,' Fern revealed. 'And this place was in my price range with no onward chain. All I'm trying to do is make the best of my situation,' Fern sighed, internally grappling with the fact that not only had she just turned fifty, but she was now single. 'If I'm being honest with you, Jess, I agree with everything that you're saying. From the outside, the house looks awful,' she confessed. 'And inside isn't any better.' The warm, sunny rays shone like a torch through the driver's window, causing Fern's already prickly skin to feel like it was on fire. She drew in a long, deep breath that filled her lungs to capacity, forcing away her jumbled feelings. 'But you start college in a few weeks, so I needed to move fast. Get us settled,' she explained in an upbeat tone. 'If I work at it, we can have some of our things hanging on the freshly painted walls by the start of term. All I want is some stability, and a place for you to call home, with me.'

For Jessie, seeing the house for the first time made everything feel more tangible. 'You and Dad are over, aren't you?' she asked, facing away from her mum. She searched for something that might offer some form of comfort, and her gaze fell on a cloud of buoyant, pollinating bees.

'Yes,' Fern confirmed, placing her hand over Jessie's. 'But this can be our new home. Mine and yours.'

Jessie took another glance up at Lunar, trying to look past the grim exterior and catch a positive vibe in one of the dreamcatchers she pictured would look nice hung on the porch. 'It could look nice once it's been done up,' she said, peering beyond the house. 'But it's still in the middle of nowhere,' she commented, trying to ignore the feeling of loneliness that crept up on her like a playful, pouncing cat. 'If the inside is as awful as the outside, I don't think

I can stay here, Mum, at least not yet,' she revealed in a moment of honesty. A pang of guilt emerged the moment she witnessed her mum's look of rejection. 'If it's okay with you, I'll stay at home for now. Just until we can get this place feeling more like ours,' she added, uncomfortable at the idea that she was already picking sides in her parents' messy divorce.

After wiping away what felt like the hundredth tear to have fallen from her eyes in the past month alone, Fern turned off the engine, parking in front of the property. With a slow turn of the head, she looked up in wonder at the house, like a lone hare peering up at the moon. 'Of course, it's okay. If I could go back in time, maybe I wouldn't have bought a place like this. But, I'm going to work hard to make sure that this house will become my new forever home,' she cried, placing her hands over her face before releasing them and turning to Jessie.

'Please don't cry, Mum,' she said, hating seeing her mum upset.

Fern forced a smile through her heartache. 'An offer had already been accepted when I enquired about this place. I should have taken that as a sign to walk away. But instead of listening to my instincts, I placed a higher offer, and asked if it would be considered. And it was,' she shrugged. 'So here I am, or here we are.'

Jessie felt upset when she saw the look of hopelessness spread across her mum's face. 'Empty houses never look inviting,' she said, trying her best to remain positive and keep a firm grip on her positivity. 'Once we move all your shoes in, it'll soon feel like home,' she joked.

Fern appreciated Jessie's compassion. 'The rooms that I've seen are worse than the outside, if that's even possible.'

'What do you mean the rooms you've seen?'

'When I came to the original viewing, there were loads of people viewing that day. People were crammed like sardines, so it was difficult to see every corner and crevice.'

With a shaky voice, Jessie replied. 'I can't believe you've bought a house without seeing every room. Who does that, Mum?'

Fern had nothing else to say, her actions feeling reckless upon reflection.

'It makes me sad that you were so unhappy at home, that you thought this was a better option.' Jessie watched how the carefree birds bounced from one branch to another and wished that she felt the same sense of freedom.

Fern looked up at the derelict house, trying to use nature's palette to paint it in a better light. 'I wasn't unhappy at home with you. I just needed to be away from your dad,' she replied. Fern lowered her head, her hands fiddling with a tissue nestled in her palm. 'I knew I should have arranged a second viewing. I should have involved you from the start. I should have stuck to my original figure instead of raising my bid. I should have done a lot of things,' she confessed, 'but I didn't. I was too upset and too angry to think rationally about the decisions I was making.' Fern made herself look up and face her future, knowing the grim state of the interior that awaited.

Jessie reached out her hand and pressed it against her mum's in a show of support. 'I'll help as much as I can. It's going to be okay, Mum.'

Fern kissed the back of her daughter's hand. 'Thanks, Jess.' She unbuckled her seatbelt and looked over her shoulder. 'I've got a suitcase in the back filled with all my essential stuff, plus a nice new air bed to sleep on until my things get delivered. It's going to be an adventure, if nothing else,' she said.

'You're staying here tonight?' Jessie questioned in shock.

Fern nodded. 'I'd rather stay here, alone, than spend one more night at home.' Taking a deep breath, Fern continued. 'I'm going to transform this place, and then we'll see whose shoe collection is lining the floor,' she smiled, lightening the tone of the conversation.

'Why won't you tell me what really happened between you and Dad? I'm old enough to understand and I'm old enough to see that it wasn't a mutual decision,' she said, maintaining strong eye contact.

Fern tucked a few wispy strands of Jessie's hair behind her ear. 'This new pixie cut makes you look so grown up,' she said, seeing through fresh eyes the beautiful, astute young woman her daughter was developing into. 'I'm not sure how I have a seventeen-year-old. I'm sure you were only eight the last time I checked.'

Jessie turned away. 'I know it's Dad who messed up,' she declared, keeping her broken expression hidden. 'You're moving here because of him,' she concluded, peering up at Lunar. 'And I deserve to know the truth.'

Fern spotted a grey Kia in the rear-view mirror. 'The estate agent is here with the keys. Let's talk about this later,' she concluded, pulling on the handle, and stepping out onto the land at Lunar for the first time as the new custodian.

Startled by the sound of car doors slamming in the distance, inside the barn, Charlotte scrambled to her feet when the sound of voices travelled in through the gaps in the wooden panels. Peering through a crack, she panicked at the sight of people gathering on Lunar's sweeping porch. 'What's going on?' she mouthed. Leaving the flowers behind in the panic, she headed towards the barn's exit, easing the door open and peering through the crack that presented. With the gathering of people preoccupied in conversation, Charlotte made a dash towards the rear of the property, hiding behind the south-facing wall. Panting for breath, the heat of the day added to the perspiration sitting heavily on her skin.

Unable to hear the unfolding conversation with clarity, like a spy, Charlotte crept to the front of the house. From her hidden position, she watched as one of the people on the porch removed the sold sign that had been resting on the veranda. A sinking feeling brewed in her stomach at the realisation that her worst fear had come true. A new family was moving into Lunar. Unable to watch any longer, Charlotte turned away and scurried back towards the rear of the property, scarpering like a frightened fox. She escaped from sight back through the secluded hollow, her initial feeling of surprise already morphing into a debilitating bout of sadness.

Fern, Jessie and Carly, the estate agent, remained congregated on the porch.

'The contracts have been signed and exchanged. The funds have been processed. So, here you go. It's all yours, Fern,' Carly announced, holding out the keys. With a clipboard wedged under her arm, she waited for Fern to reach out and take the keys. 'This place has so much potential, doesn't it?' she beamed, turning back to admire the wealth of plants that surrounded the property. 'And these views are priceless,' she commented, standing on tiptoes and arching her neck so that she could digest the scenery that seemed to stretch to the end of the world.

When her mum didn't take hold of the keys, leaving Carly a little perplexed, Jessie reached out her hand and took hold of them. 'I haven't looked inside yet, but if my mum likes it, then I'm sure I'll love it too,' she commented, aptly filling the awkward moment of silence.

Carly stepped back, ready to leave. 'Wonderful. Well, congratulations on your new home. I hope you'll both be super happy here,' she said, turning to walk away, already thinking about her next appointment.

'Actually, could you stay for a few moments? I've thought of a couple of questions that you might be able to answer,' Fern asked, pausing the narrative on her internal dilemma.

'Sure,' Carly replied, looking at her watch. 'I have a few minutes before I'll need to get back to the office in time for my next meeting.'

'Great,' Fern smiled. 'Jessie, why don't you go inside and take a quick look around without me? I'll just go through a few bits with Carly.'

With reluctance, Jessie approached the front door, unlocked it and eased the wood from its frame. As the door was eased open, a cloud of stagnated dust became dislodged and scattered amid the incoming breeze, encouraging Jessie to cover her mouth and nose with the crease of her elbow. She wafted her free arm in front of her face to fan away the dirt that was now airborne. The drop in temperature instantly brought goosebumps to her skin. Nervous to enter alone, she lingered in the doorway. She absorbed the internal state of the house, taken aback by the neglect. With her face scrunched, Jessie took a tentative step forward and paused on the doormat, cowering when she caught sight of a thick, low-lying knot of cobwebs. The gloomy hallway, the peeling, dated wallpaper, the worn, unkempt floorboards, and the stale stench that hung in the air gave Jessie the impression that the house had been empty for years. 'Mum? Are you coming?' she asked without turning to check her mum's whereabouts.

Unawares, Fern remained locked in conversation with Carly.

Without waiting for her mum's reassuring guidance, Jessie took another step inside and pushed her hand against the door to her immediate left. Jessie remained still, confined to the lounge doorway, her feet feeling trapped like the insects encased in the tangle of webs. A lump rose in her throat at the sight of the barren, dark and desolate room. The moment she spotted some personal items that had been left behind, an unexpected tidal wave of sadness rolled over her like the harvest dust descending over the hills. She saw a pair of reading glasses and a tattered cardigan, left like the previous owner had just nipped out of the room to put the kettle on. There was a child's scrunched up blanket draped over the faded sofa, dinosaurs sewn into the grey and white whimsical design. The moving scene was unlike anything she had witnessed before, and she tried to picture who might have lived in the house previously.

Out on the porch, and out of earshot from Jessie, Fern asked Carly the only question plaguing her mind. 'This is going to sound odd, but I don't suppose you know who else was interested in buying this place?' she asked, expanding on her question when Carly didn't reply. 'I know that an offer had already been accepted before mine, and I thought if I contacted that person, they might still be interested in buying this place,' she said, a hopeless look drowning her vibrant, hazel eyes. 'I'm having second thoughts and I just want to know what my options are.' Fern's usual pale complexion flushed, signalling the anxiety that was scratching beneath her skin.

Carly appeared shocked. 'Honestly, your options at this point are limited. We wouldn't be able to share that type of personal information, so the only thing you can realistically do is place the property back on the market and try to resell.'

Fern's deflated body language conveyed her disappointment. 'I thought so,' she admitted. 'Then do you know much about the previous owner?' she asked. 'I recall on the paperwork you emailed through, the deeds are listed under Mr L Sloan.'

'Well,' Carly began in a more positive tone of voice, studying the notes that were attached to her clipboard. 'It's a bit of a sad story because the gentleman who lived here did so alone, and he passed away,' she read aloud from her stack of papers. 'A solicitor in town has been dealing with the estate. That's all I know.' Carly witnessed the look of despair on Fern's face. 'I'm guessing none of this has helped,' she said, extending her arm and handing Fern a tissue.

Fern thought back to her very first viewing of Lunar. 'From what I remember, some things in the house had been removed,' she explained, recalling the faded areas on the floor where pieces of furniture had once sat. 'Has everything else now been sorted?'

Carly shook her head. 'No, not everything,' she clarified. 'But that was all outlined in the contract that you signed.'

'Yes, I understand, and I'm fine with clearing out the house myself,' she clarified. 'It just won't seem right to throw everything away like it doesn't mean anything to anybody.'

Carly peered back at the house and pictured some of the personal items that she knew had been left behind. 'It's so sad. I can't imagine having nobody to sort through my things with a little care and compassion when it's my turn to go.' Carly changed the tone of the conversation and pointed towards the house. 'This place could be lovely, and your forever home, once it's sorted.'

'Maybe,' Fern replied, offering up some semblance of a smile. 'Well, thanks for all your help, Carly,' she added. 'Stop by in a few months and hopefully you won't recognise the place.'

Carly gave Fern a quick hug before getting into her car and driving back down the driveway, the sound of the engine revving along the main road. With all the combine harvester engines switched off for the day, a piercing stillness once again hung above the remote house on the hill. Fern checked that her rings were no longer secured around her wedding finger, something she had caught herself doing multiple times in the last few months. For the first time, she came to terms with the fact that she no longer had a husband to share her life with, and she hated herself for missing the very man who had turned her life on its head.

For a brief moment whilst she continued to linger on her veranda, the silence allowed Fern to face her fears of loneliness head-on. With no passing pedestrians or adjoining neighbours to distract her attention, Fern gazed out at the scenic views that surrounded her new home like a tight-knitted jumper. The longer she lingered with her thoughts, the more Fern could feel the wind strength increasing off the hills, the gusts encouraging heavy clusters of clouds to descend over the house. Grey billows lingered above the roof slates. A trickle of rain began to fall, encouraging the host of garden sparrows into hiding, the nimble birds seeking shelter deep within the tangle of surrounding bushes. The sudden shift in weather also nudged Fern to seek shelter. Even if she didn't feel ready to face her future, it was time to embrace all that was waiting for her at Lunar.

5

'Mum!' Jessie shouted from the kitchen.

Fern closed the front door behind her. 'Jess? Where are you?'

'I'm in here,' she replied from the kitchen. 'I can't believe the state of this place,' she said. 'You can't run your baking business from here.' Fern appeared by her daughter's side, both standing in silence, digesting the sombre scene.

'I feel sorry for whoever lived here, Mum,' Jessie announced, an empathetic look in her eyes. 'When you viewed the house, were you not surprised by all of this?' she asked, pulling her shirt sleeves down, her skin feeling like it was scattered with a layer of fidgeting dust mites. 'I wouldn't want my worst enemy to live somewhere as dingy as this,' she said.

Fern replied without hesitation. 'I was surprised because when I saw the property advertised online, the majority of the photos were of the garden,' she explained. 'And the estate agent's description of the property just stated in need of modernisation.'

Jessie peered around the grim interior, trying to imagine the kind of family that had once sheltered beneath Lunar's roof. She tried to make sense of the imposing, dark, wood-clad walls, the damaged bits of old-fashioned mahogany furniture left behind, and the random collection of belongings that were sealed into the room like some sort of time capsule. 'How did anybody live here, Mum?'

'I don't know, Jess.' Fern paced around the room, trying to picture for herself the type of person who could have lived in such a place. 'I wonder how he made his meals?' she questioned, noticing the damaged worktops, and the way the splashback tiles were falling off the wall. She opened a few of the cupboards, the insides empty apart from bits of rubbish. 'It would've looked more homely before the majority of his belongings were removed, and I guess whenever a house is stripped of its contents, even the homeliest of homes can look pretty unloved. You said it yourself.'

'*His* belongings?' Jessie questioned.

'The previous owner was a man called Mr Sloan.'

Jessie walked around the central table, the tiled floor feeling harsh beneath the soles of her Converse. She eased the kitchen door away from the wall, revealing a picture taped to the paintwork. 'Look at this,' she said, intrigued. 'Maybe this is Mr Sloan with his wife and two children.'

'Let me see,' said Fern, nestling in next to Jessie. 'If Mr Sloan had a family, why would he have been living here alone, and like this? It makes no sense.'

Jessie wandered back over to the other side of the room. 'This is odd,' she announced, picking up a bedraggled, brown cow soft toy that was sitting on the windowsill, shaking off the dirt. 'It's sad that something like this was left behind because it looks well loved,' she stated.

'I'm going to keep stuff like this to one side, just in case I can trace some of Mr Sloan's relatives.'

Jessie scrunched her face. 'If he had any relatives, wouldn't they have already taken what they wanted?'

Fern opened one of the kitchen windows, allowing a bout of fresh air to breathe new life into the lacklustre space. 'When I show you what's been left behind upstairs, you might understand why I'll take the time to track down any family.'

Fern walked over to the window. 'I've already tried to get some information about Mr Sloan, but didn't get very far,' she explained, looking around the room, spotting other personal items that had been left. 'He lived here alone, and recently passed away. That's all I know,' she sighed. 'There's just so much to do,' she commented, gazing around the bedraggled room.

A look of dread crept its way onto Jessie's face. 'There's more?' she asked. 'It's impossible for it to be worse than this upstairs,' she added, gesturing to the room.

'I'll let you decide that for yourself.'

Fern and Jessie made their way back down the narrow hallway, a single, exposed lightbulb clinging by a thread from the towering ceiling.

'Did you have a look in there?' Fern asked, indicating to the lounge.

'I did,' she replied. 'There's a blanket on the sofa that looks like it belonged to a child, which at first I thought was odd. But now that I've seen the kitchen, I guess it's not so shocking.'

Fern didn't reply, knowing what was to come in one of the bedrooms.

'What's through here?' Jessie questioned, opening the door to the right that led down to the basement. A cool draft washed over her face the moment the steps to the bottom of the house were presented.

'It's the basement, or the cellar. I'm not sure which word I prefer,' Fern replied. 'I only quickly bobbed my head down there during the viewing,' she explained, crossing her arms over her stomach. 'It's dark, cold, full of crawly things and goodness knows what else,' she said, stepping away.

Jessie closed the door. 'Obviously this house has a creepy basement. Why wouldn't it?' she said, rolling her eyes. 'Right then, show me upstairs.'

Fern led Jessie up the dark, steep staircase, the floorboards creaking beneath their weight. The spindles running the length of the staircase looked worn, and flaking bits of paint dotted the incline. In places, the carpet covering the steps was threadbare, evidence of a former stampede. 'Watch your step,' Fern warned, indicating to the damaged stairs.

The cavernous ceilings made the space feel vast, and the lack of soft furnishings caused any noise to echo. Faded outlines on the walls gave further evidence to the lives of those who had gone before. 'I wonder if family photos were here,' Jessie pondered. There were dirty finger marks and scratches ingrained into the wallpaper, every mark contributing to the history of the house. 'Look, there's little doodles,' she commented, spotting where someone had crayoned directly onto the wall.

Fern pulled down the net curtain that was covering the landing window. 'This whole house just needs some light letting in. I've never seen such a dark home before.' She flicked the light switch, the dim bulb doing little to illuminate the cavern. 'Right, let me show you the two biggest bedrooms first,' Fern announced, the doors leading to the two larger rooms already ajar. 'This room has the best views of the rear,' she explained, stepping into the back master bedroom.

'It's a nice size,' Jessie commented, admiring the space, trying her best to imagine it as her mum's new bedroom.

Fern stepped towards the window. 'And look, we even have a barn,' she laughed, peering down over the spacious garden that looked vibrant from any angle. She admired how a necklace of cherry trees cradled the rear south-facing perimeter of the property with perfection. During springtime, she imagined how the lineup of pink, cotton candy foliage would provide a delicate barrier against the expanse of fields that appeared to stretch to the edge of the horizon like the open canopy of a savanna.

Although she couldn't quite see the image with as much excitement as her mum, Jessie agreed. 'The trees do look nice. They distract you from looking at the house,' she joked, walking out of the room and back onto the landing, peering into the front bedroom.

'I thought this could be your room,' Fern suggested, praying that Jessie could see the potential.

'It's a big space,' Jess concurred, whilst secretly thinking that it could never be as nice as her bedroom at home. 'It really isn't as bad as I thought it was going to be up here,' Jess commented, her initial jumble of emotions beginning to calm. 'You made it sound much worse.'

The door to the smallest bedroom located at the front of the house remained closed. 'That's because I haven't shown you in here yet,' Fern said with hesitation. The rusting hinges on the door creaked when Fern pushed. 'Brace yourself,' she warned.

Jessie pressed her hand to her mouth when the room was revealed. 'Oh my God.'

A tightness developed in Fern's throat when she stepped into the room. 'This was obviously a child's bedroom at some point,' she explained, drawing in a deep, sobering breath.

Without thinking, Jessie reached out and took hold of Fern's hand for reassurance, just like she had done as a child. 'Oh, Mum,' she muttered, her eyes teary.

With an ache to their hearts, Jessie and Fern stood still, staring at the contents of the room that remained concealed beneath a dense, dusty shell.

'Now do you understand why I can't just throw everything away?' Fern asked, her voice choked with tears. 'Look at the soft toys under the duvet, and the way that things are still scattered over the floor,' she explained, pointing. 'It looks like a child had been playing, and for whatever reason, he or she never came back. And the room hasn't been touched since.'

'I knew a child had lived here,' Jessie whimpered. 'The drawings on the walls, the soft toy, the blanket. And now all of this.' She noticed a petite, red t-shirt and a pair of worn combat shorts lying scrunched up on a chair. 'Age 6-7,' she confirmed, inspecting the label. 'Why has it all been left like this?' she questioned. 'I don't understand.'

'I don't understand either.'

'It looks like there's something under the duvet. Should we have a look?' Jessie asked, turning to her mum for confirmation.

Fern shook her head and guided Jessie out of the room. 'I'm going to be moving everything soon enough. But let's leave it for today. I'm not sure I can face it right now.'

'Are you okay?' Jess asked.

On the landing, Fern wrapped both arms around her daughter, relishing their moment of closeness. 'I'm just grateful to have you in my life.'

Jessie savoured the moment of tenderness, knowing that for the first time, they wouldn't be sleeping under the same roof. 'Did you hear a noise?' she asked, pulling away from the embrace.

Fern listened before replying. 'We're in the countryside. I bet we'll start to hear all sorts of unfamiliar sounds.'

'I feel like these walls have eyes,' Jessie commented, the obscurities of the house making her feel unnerved. Piercing the silence, Jessie's phone buzzed in her pocket.

'Blimey, that made me jump,' Fern laughed, her nerves shaky.

Jessie stood and read the message. 'It's Charlie. He wants to know if I'm free tonight at six.'

Fern released a weighted sigh. 'Don't rush things with Charlie,' she warned. 'I know you love him. But you've got so much to experience before you can understand what love is.' Fern caught sight of the back of her hands, always slightly surprised by the increasing number of creases and veins that she found there. 'I'm fifty and I'm still not sure what love means.'

'When are you going to tell me what happened between you and Dad?' Jessie asked, craving to learn the truth.

'Soon,' Fern smiled. 'I just need to get myself sorted. Then me and you will have a heart-to-heart. I promise. If I start talking about it now, I might never stop crying,' she revealed, half smiling, half crumbling beneath the weight of her tattered emotions.

'Okay,' Jessie agreed. 'But I'm not loving the idea of you staying here alone.'

'I'll be fine,' she reassured. 'I'm moving my things out of Dad's place tomorrow, and then a team of workers will start the transformation on this place,' she smiled.

Jessie felt emotional at hearing her mum call the family home Dad's place. 'I'll come and visit you all the time,' she said, wrapping her arms around her mum again. 'I heard a noise again,' Jessie announced, peering over the banister. 'It sounded like someone knocking.'

Fern shook her head. 'Nobody knows that I'm here. Apart from you, and Dad.'

The pair looked at each other when the noise echoed up the stairs.

'Oh,' said Fern, surprised at hearing a knock at the door. 'I guess somebody does know I'm here,' she added, making her way down the stairs with Jessie in tow.

'Hi, Auntie Flo!' Jessie beamed the moment her mum pulled open the door. 'I haven't seen you in ages,' she gushed, stepping onto the porch and welcoming Flo with a generous, warm hug.

'Hi, Jess,' Flo replied. 'Work has been keeping me busy, and anyway, I'm sure you've got better things to do than hang around with me. Don't you start college soon?' she asked, kissing Jessie on the head before pulling away from the embrace.

'Yeah, not long to wait now,' Jessie replied.

Fern remained inside. 'Why don't you go and call Charlie?' she suggested, her arms crossed in a tight knot over her chest. 'Once we're finished here, I'll take you home, or you could borrow my car now that you've officially passed your test.'

'Sure,' Jessie agreed.

Jessie paused halfway up the stairs. 'Wait until you see this place, Auntie Flo,' she said. 'I think my mum has finally lost her mind,' she added, before disappearing.

Fern addressed her visitor. 'What are you doing here?' she asked, her stare challenging and brimming with judgement. 'And how did you know where to find me?' she quizzed, her sense of annoyance spread liberally over her face. With a roll of her eyes, Fern laughed at her own naivety. 'Cooper told you. Obviously.'

Flo held her hands out in an expression of helpless surrender. 'You won't answer my calls. You won't reply to my messages,' she said, exasperated. 'I didn't know what else to do.'

Fern glanced up the stairs when she heard the creaking sound of warped floorboards. 'Let's talk outside. I don't want Jessie hearing us,' she ordered, closing the front door and walking past her best friend.

Flo followed Fern down to the front garden, the pair pausing near the driveway.

'I'm not answering your calls because I don't want to talk to you. What part of that is difficult to understand?' Fern spat, finding it hard to look at Flo.

'I made a mistake, Fern,' Flo began, stepping forward to bridge the gap that separated the once kindred spirits. 'And I want you to know how sorry I am.' She lowered her head and searched the foliage, hoping to find the perfect choice of words. 'You're my best friend. I'm lost without you in my life,' she cried, unable to control her overflowing sense of regret. She looked up at Fern. 'These past few months have been awful,' she sobbed. 'I can't eat. I can't sleep. All I do is think about you,' she explained, wiping her face. 'And I know that this is my fault. I'm not denying that. I'm just trying to make things right,' she said, gazing at Fern through her wide, saturated eyes.

Although she hated herself for it, deep down, it broke Fern's heart to see her best friend distraught. She cast her gaze to the sky, seeking composure, before turning back and looking Flo straight in the eye. 'You slept with my husband, Florence, and now my marriage to Cooper is over,' she spat, her words firing through the air with intent. Fern felt her courage rising to the surface after months of evading confrontation. 'And even now, two months later, when I say those words aloud, I can't believe what I'm hearing,' Fern continued. 'Out of *everybody*, Florence, I never thought that you would intentionally hurt me.' Fern felt a protest occurring in her heart, and for a moment, she contemplated the notion that she could die heartbroken. She placed her hand over her chest, and tried to save her wounded heart the only way she knew how.

Creeping in above Lunar, a fresh batch of heavy clouds clogged the sky, casting a downpour over the bickering friends. 'Can I come inside and talk?' Flo asked, unable to recall the last time that her bestie had called her by her full name.

Fern ignored the request and allowed the rain to drench them both. 'I've lost my husband. I've lost my home. I've lost my best friend. Do you know how that feels? You've ruined my life. So, no, you can't come in and talk. I don't want to see you ever again. I don't want anything to do with you,' she cried, shaking her head in disgust, her innermost feelings released with the downpour. She took a few defiant steps back towards the house and scooped her wavy, copper hair to one side, wiping the tears and raindrops from her face.

'I'm not going to give up. I want to make things right between us,' Flo mumbled, desperation drowning her words.

Fern paused, but didn't turn her head to acknowledge the comment.

'We've been best friends for nearly thirty years. I know you better than I know anybody,' Flo continued, desperate to keep her friend from walking away. 'And I'm Jessie's godparent. So, I don't care how long it takes, or what it takes. I'll do anything. I just need to know that there's hope for some kind of relationship.'

Fern turned her head and maintained eye contact. 'You *were* my best friend before you destroyed my marriage. And for what? What exactly was it that was so appealing?' she asked, her eyebrows pulling together, her anger pooling in the rivers running down her face. 'Cooper refuses to go into the nitty-gritty. So, maybe you'll have the decency to tell me exactly what happened. I think I deserve that much,' she said, demanding a reply. 'Who crossed the line first?'

When Flo refused to answer, Fern turned back around and marched towards the house.

'He sent me a message. The night you went away with Jessie to Edinburgh.'

Fern paused and her mind raced to remember dates and times. 'Edinburgh? That was over six months ago. *That's* how long this has been going on?' she exclaimed, turning to face Flo, her lips pinched to a point.

Flo could feel her heart beating in her throat. 'I regret it all,' she confessed. 'I thought I was falling in love with him. I thought he was falling in love with me. But I knew deep down that he'd never love me the way that he loves you.' Flo took a few steps closer to Fern.

Fern edged away, maintaining what felt like a safe distance. 'I've never felt so lonely in my entire life,' she cried. 'You've taken everything from me,' she sobbed, wiping her face with her sleeve. 'So now I want you to leave me alone.' Fern marched towards the front door and closed it behind her, refusing to look back at the friend she had once treasured like family. Fern waited behind the front door, crying. She listened, wondering if Florence would indeed drive away. The sound of a car door closing made Fern cry harder. She turned her head and spied out of the window, watching as her best friend disappeared into the distance.

Having confirmed plans with Charlie, Jessie remained seated at the top of the stairs. 'I heard you arguing, so I stayed up here,' she said when Fern turned around and spotted her.

Fern walked up the stairs and sat beside her daughter, resting her wet head against Jessie's shoulder.

'Why were you fighting?'

Fern took hold of Jessie's hand and scooped it into hers, kissing it with a gentle touch and relishing how soft her daughter's skin felt against hers.

'Is Auntie Flo the reason you and Dad aren't together?' she asked, recalling snippets of the argument, taking hold of her mum's drenched, cold hand.

With a heavy heart, Fern gave a slow, disparaging nod.

Without saying a word, Jessie released the grip she had on her mum's hand and scurried down the stairs, pulling open the front door and escaping to the porch.

Fern chased after her. 'Jessie, stop!' she shouted, almost tripping over an uneven floorboard. 'It's okay to be upset,' she said, grabbing hold of Jessie and pulling her into a tight embrace. 'We'll be okay,' she whispered into her daughter's ear, cupping Jessie's face with her hands. 'Let me take you home. We don't want to keep your Charlie waiting.'

Jessie felt ready to leave Lunar, the new home she already despised. 'How can I face Dad now?'

'Dad still loves you. That will never change,' she explained, trying to be the bigger person and wrap the close father-daughter relationship with cotton wool. 'We all make mistakes.' Fern delivered another hug to her daughter as they savoured the shelter offered by the porch. Treasuring their private moment, both Fern and Jessie remained unawares that they weren't alone. The lurking eyes that Jessie had sensed earlier had now opened.

Behind the wall of trees, a light had been switched on in Nebula, the house to their right. A lone figure stood staring out of an upstairs window, peering down on the unfolding scene at Lunar. As Fern and Jessie got into their car and drove off down the main road, the watchman moved away from the window, leaving it ajar so he'd be able to hear them when they returned.

4

With only the sunken echoes of heartache for company, Fern approached Aldebaran having dropped Jessie off at home. Her tired eyes stung. The delicate skin framing her eyes felt chapped where too many tears had fallen, the moisture lingering with a laziness in the delicate crevices. Whilst navigating the winding, country roads, she noticed how the late summer sun had tucked itself into the Cotswold hills like a burrowing badger cub. Distracted by the scenic views that formed the background tapestry to the place she would come to call home, Fern admired the haziness that hung in threads above the village, the dangling, white vapours reminiscent of a baby's mobile. Amid the undulations that were carved into the landscape of the unfamiliar village, Fern heard the hills whispering her name. The metaphorical welcome felt like the perfect homecoming tonic to wash away the sadness she was struggling to surrender.

The stones crunched beneath Fern's car tyres the moment she pulled onto the driveway at Lunar, the noise echoing through the otherwise quiet, night-time ambience. Having fallen asleep in his favourite armchair, with his house drenched in darkness, Fern's next-door neighbour, Arthur Aspey, opened his eyes upon hearing the disturbance. 'They're back,' he said to himself, pulling himself up and making his way out of his cosy snug. With slow, steady steps, the elderly gentleman made his way upstairs and switched on a modest light. Pausing at the landing window, he peered down over the land at Lunar. He watched Fern get out of her vehicle, noticing in the background how the incoming dusky conditions had settled over the flower-rich limestone grasslands, the dimming light eating away at any remaining specs of pearlescent mist. Arthur rested his hand on the windowsill for balance, the paintwork worn from years of use. 'She's alone,' he mumbled, a pensive look on his face. 'It'll be different this time around,' he added, offering himself a slice of reassurance. Still to come to terms with the fate of Lunar's previous occupants, Arthur felt daunted as he witnessed new life entering the infamous farmhouse. 'Please let it be different this time,' he prayed, bowing his head like he was kneeling before a church altar.

When Fern stepped foot onto her porch and disappeared inside the house, Arthur felt his body brace itself for battle. With a heavy heart, the elderly man gazed at the single photo that hung on his wall. He admired the way that the fair-haired young boy beamed with excitement while climbing a towering tree, the same tree that was displaying the glory of its full bloom in Lunar's front garden. Arthur turned off the landing light and dragged his ailing body to bed, careful not to disturb his sleeping wife, Olive. As he rested his head and closed his eyes, historical memories of Lunar charged through his mind. Within seconds, a stream of warm tears escaped onto his cotton pillowcase. He repeated the words *'I'm sorry, Sam,'* until his mind and body succumbed to sleep, a ritual that over the years, he performed religiously beneath the privacy of darkness.

Behind the dividing wall of trees that separated Fern's property from her closest neighbour, a sense of vulnerability edged its way under her skin the moment she stepped foot inside her home. The background chanting emanating from the hills had silenced, leaving Fern alone with nothing but her thoughts for company. She stood still, trying to acclimatise to the hostility. The structure of her new home felt bold and imposing as it sat under a descending shield of darkness. A chilling coldness crawled its way out of all the cracks like an intrusion of cockroaches. 'I'm home,' she said to herself, sighing at the silence. After nearly thirty years of marriage, the crux of loneliness emphasised her vulnerability. 'You can do this,' she told herself, pressing her back against the front door. The house felt eerily quiet. The longer she stood, the more she noticed the lack of familiar, ambient sounds that had once offered her a sense of comfort. There was no noise of nearby front doors being banged by heavy-handed neighbours, or the sound of people chatting as they passed the house. There was little vehicle traffic to be heard, and even the hum of the combines had been put to bed. There was nothing. Just silence.

Down the long, narrow hallway, Fern spotted the moon's reflection as it shone through the exposed windows. A collection of confusing shadows climbed the walls and danced across the floor. Reaching out to switch on the hallway light, the single, exposed ceiling bulb did little to illuminate the darkness.

Beathing deeply, Fern attempted to cast her feelings of loneliness aside. She threw her jacket over the banister and grabbed a stash of bin bags. 'Don't cry. Just bloody well get on with it.' Illuminating the ground floor, Fern walked from one room to another and switched on all the lights, turning Lunar into a lighthouse at Aldebaran's summit. Starting in the kitchen, she grabbed handfuls of rubbish that'd been left by Mr Sloan. 'You can do this,' she encouraged herself when a bag felt too heavy to lift, resulting in her dragging it down the hallway and casting it out onto the porch.

Outside, hidden beneath the darkness, an ambiguous noise startled Fern, causing her to pause on the porch. As far as she could see, the main road and pavement were deserted. The hidden corners of her garden remained concealed by shadows, and she couldn't help but feel like she was being watched. Her face turned pallid with fear, her exposed silhouette more vulnerable than one of the lonesome scarecrows that had been staked out in a nearby field. A change in wind direction caused the clouds to part, allowing the reflection of the moon to shine down over Fern's dilated pupils. A rustling noise echoed in the distance, making her body flinch and her heart pound. The swirling breeze made it difficult to decipher where the noise was coming from, or who was making it, and her palms were now clammy with fright.

She turned to scurry back inside and closed the door. Almost as though it had never happened, the dubious noise disappeared, and the silence Fern had come to know returned. She paced through to the lounge and switched off all the main lights to continue her surveillance of the garden. Hovering in the lounge window, she peered through the net curtains. Her body flinched in response to the eclectic sounds she deciphered as burrowing wildlife. To get a better view, with one quick tug, she pulled the curtains away from the railing, the material disintegrating like snow in her hands. The main road still appeared quiet, the pavement nothing but a barren walkway. The glow from the streetlamps only just illuminated the entrance to her driveway. 'You're being paranoid,' she told herself just as her phone buzzed in her pocket.

'Hi Jess. Is everything okay?' she asked, pulling herself away from the window and continuing to clear out more rubbish.

'Yeah, I'm back at home. I wasn't really in the mood for going out tonight,' Jessie replied.

'I'm sure Charlie understands. You've got a lot going on.' Distracted by the conversation, Fern failed to hear the faint sound of footsteps as someone crept beneath one of the lounge windowsills.

'I'm worried about you,' Jessie confessed. 'I don't like the thought of you alone at the house.'

'Don't worry about me. I'm getting stuck in already. I've filled dozens of bin bags and I'm stacking them up outside ready to throw in the skip when it arrives.'

The cheery, upbeat sound of her mum's voice eased Jessie's concerns. 'That's good. Have you found any other weird stuff?'

'Nope. So far, it's just been things that you'd find in any house clearance. Tattered old shoes, broken mugs, piles of old papers and circulars, that sort of thing.' Fern held the phone in place with her shoulder, using both hands to haul the next black sack towards the front door. She dumped it on the porch along with the others before heading back inside, leaving the door ajar for ease.

'I can't stop thinking about the little bedroom upstairs,' Jessie revealed. 'And why it was left that way.'

Fern grabbed another bag and began to heave it towards the front door. 'I know it looks odd, and we're expecting there to be some awful story to go with it. But there could be a simple explanation.'

Jessie went quiet.

'I feel like you want to say something,' Fern quizzed, sensing her daughter's apprehension.

'Would you go and look what's under the duvet? Remember it looked like there was something under the covers? I can't stop thinking about what it might be.'

Fern released the heavy bin liner clenched in her hands and left it near the doormat, closing the front door. 'If it'll make you feel better, I'll go and look now,' she replied, making her way up the stairs. 'I really need to think about pumping up my air bed,' she added, her heavy eyes an indication of the approaching late hour.

Downstairs, having been spying through the side window, Charlotte eased the front door open the moment that she saw Fern disappear upstairs. With a gentle foot, she stepped over the discarded bin bag, and paused on the threshold. 'I'm home,' she mumbled into her palms, both hands pressed to her face. Her eyes filled with bulbous tears when she felt the familiarity of Lunar's loving embrace wrap itself around her nervous frame. For so long, Charlotte had longed to visit Lunar and allow the familiar voices that she associated with the house to land on her ears. But when the neglected, gloomy interior presented itself like an unwelcome ghost, waves of disappointment poured from her heavy eyes.

Deep down, Charlotte knew that inevitably, the house would

have changed with the passing of time. But she never imagined that the once loving family home could be filled with such emptiness. With her hands cradling her face, she took a moment to digest the scene. Knowing the house had been empty, she presumed that all the previous owner's belongings would have already been removed, and yet items of familiarity remained, like an oval hallway mirror. Forcefully, she took a deep swallow to try and dislodge her internal pain. She searched for traces of warmth yet failed to find any form of comfort in the cold, prickly hollow. Struggling to fathom that it could be the same house that she had once held so close, the moment that she heard the familiar sound of the creaking floorboards above, she had to accept the fact that the passing of time had been particularly cruel. With no concern about being caught, brazen as a boar, she continued to linger with a steely sense of entitlement.

Charlotte closed her eyes to evoke the sounds and smells once so synonymous with the mighty farmhouse. A smile crept onto her face when Lunar came alive in her mind, a cornucopia of simple pleasures. She could visualise the house in its prime, brimming with love, laughter, and family. The smell of simmering ratatouille drifted through her nostrils and reinvigorated her appetite. The sound of chattering voices made her want to jump in on the conversation and add her two pennies' worth. The sight of broad, wide smiles filled her heart with some of the love that it had recently haemorrhaged.

Drinking in deep breaths, she inhaled the magical nostalgia. Unable to resist the temptation to experience more of Lunar, she took another step inside the house. With her arm extended to guide her forwards, she allowed her fingers to glide across the wall where three nails were still embedded into the plaster, and she recalled the cheeky family photo that was once on display. Becoming lost in her wishing well of memories, Charlotte released her attachment to the wider world. Unable to ignore her craving, she stepped further down the hallway, walking past the lounge and towards the kitchen, lingering in the archway. Navigating the internal maze brought back so many cherished recollections, and for a moment, it was like she had never left.

The sound of Fern's voice came trickling down the stairs and interrupted her moment of solace, silencing the familiar voices that had begun to echo in harmony through her mind like a prairie soundscape. Panicked, Charlotte froze. She listened as Fern's voice became louder as she made her way downstairs. Without thought, Charlotte opened the door that concealed the cupboard under the stairs and sheltered herself in the hideaway.

'Are you happy now that I've checked?' Fern asked, walking back down the stairs with a cuddly toy wrapped in her arms. 'This little fella gives us another clue to the family who lived here,' she explained to Jess down the phone, looking at the four words stitched onto the bear's stomach: *I love my sister*. 'And I'm sure that when I clear that room out properly, we'll uncover more clues.'

When Fern reached the bottom of the stairs and spotted the front door was ajar, her heart leapt into her mouth. She bobbed her head into the empty lounge, questioning her actions. 'I'm sure that I closed the front door,' she said to Jessie. 'I mustn't have done,' she added, shaking her head and grabbing the last bin bag, casting it outside. 'I think I'm losing my mind. It's late and it's been a *really* long day.'

'Before you go to bed, please make sure you lock all the doors,' Jessie urged, rolling her eyes at her mum's nonchalant approach to safety. 'Dad has always done the locking up at night but it's your job now.'

Fern closed the front door and locked it, removing the key and placing it in her pocket. 'Try not to worry. I'm absolutely fine here. I've locked the door and I'm not going back outside tonight. I'm calling it a day and heading straight to bed,' she said, exasperated. 'I think I've done enough for one day.' Fern pottered down the hallway and into the kitchen, checking that the windows and door were all secured. 'The back door is locked too, so you don't need to worry about me, okay?'

'I think you're amazing,' Jessie said, the heartfelt words bringing instant tears to Fern's eyes.

Taken aback by her daughter's sentiment, Fern paused in the hallway, right next to the cupboard under the stairs, the bear still wrapped in her arms. 'I'm not amazing enough,' she blurted, unable to hold back how she really felt about the breakdown of her marriage. 'But, my amazingness will return. I just need to find my hairbrush, some clean clothes, and a mirror,' she joked, brushing off her moment of vulnerability.

'What are you going to do now that you're by yourself?' Jessie asked, knowing that her mum and dad had always enjoyed doing life together.

Fern tried to think of an answer to the question that she had thus far avoided asking herself. 'Well, I'm obviously going to turn this amazing house into a home for me and you,' she replied, her words bypassing the undercurrent of uncertainty chiming to a steady beat through her body.

'I mean, are you going to date?' Jessie clarified with hesitance.

Fern shook her head and laughed. 'No way,' she confirmed with certainty. 'I'm going to have the sofa all to myself for a change.' Fern tried to dispel her tears in silence. 'Anyway, it's getting late and I still need to sort out my air mattress thingy. So, I'll say goodnight and speak to you tomorrow, okay?'

'I love you, Mum. I'll call you in the morning.'

'Okay. Love you, Jessie.' Placing the bear in her lap, Fern sat herself on the floor in the hallway, allowing herself, for the very first time, to mourn the end of her marriage.

On the other side of the cupboard door, like a gag, Charlotte secured her hand over her nose and mouth, trapping any sounds that threatened to escape. Fern's sobs reminded Charlotte of the time she had once hidden in the very same spot as a child, frightened and trying to find a place where she couldn't hear the sound of her own mum crying.

Blinking in rapid succession within the darkness, Charlotte

held her breath and prayed, waiting for Fern to stop crying. She urged Lunar's new custodian to find her, and then they could both cry together, sharing in their sense of sadness and her ordeal would finally be drawn to an end. But the door didn't open, and Charlotte failed to savour the rescue she had always longed to experience. Instead, she heard footsteps echoing above her head, indicating that Fern had retreated to the first floor. She heard the door to the small bedroom creak open, and for a moment, she anticipated the sound of excitable feet to come trundling down the stairs.

Upstairs, Fern couldn't explain her behaviour, but she felt the need to tuck the two soft toys that she'd found back into bed, where, at least for now, she felt they belonged. The little brown cow rested alongside the bear, and she tried to imagine what the child looked like that they had belonged to. To alleviate the loneliness that was closing in around her, she sat for a moment on the child's single mattress. She recalled all the nights that she had whispered nursery rhymes to Jessie, and she wondered if Lunar's walls had ever been privy to such soothing melodies.

After a few moments of silence, downstairs, Charlotte eased the cubbyhole door open to reveal a slight gap, and listened. She heard Fern mooching around in the back bedroom upstairs, the innocuous sound of a foot pump breaking the otherwise silent night. Taking care not to make any noise, Charlotte stepped out into the hallway and eased the cupboard door back into its frame. With bated breath, she tiptoed towards the exit, removed her keys from her pocket, and unlocked the front door.

'I'll come and visit again soon,' she whispered. Charlotte turned her back on Lunar and walked away, disappearing into the shadows offered by the secluded, shrubbery garden nooks. Curious to know what was in the collection of bin bags stacked on the porch, she nuzzled herself into the garden's shadowy embrace, and waited. With her heart galloping, she hoped that Lunar's lights would soon be switched off for the night, leaving her a window of opportunity to explore. The longer she waited, the more she grappled with feelings of guilt for having made such an out-of-character, intrusive move and entering someone's home without invitation. But it was the way that her heart ached in time with the tears trickling off her cheeks that revealed her deepest feelings.

Just as she was about to give up, the house fell into near complete darkness, with only brief illumination provided by the light of the moon. Stealthily, she snuck back over to the porch, and crouched amongst the discarded bags. Untying the knots, one by one Charlotte opened the bags, rummaging through a lifetime of memories. Her hands landed upon something soft and she pulled out a pair of tattered, dirty mules. Her frame collapsed onto the floor, and she shook her head in disbelief, recalling the slippers with fondness. With delicate, slow movements, she cradled the worn sliders, easing her hands into the grooves, feeling where someone's feet had once been positioned, warm and snug. Like a scavenging fox, she sifted through the other bags. Her tears fell harder each time she came across another empty soup can, the empty tins telling a heartbreaking tale of someone who was not only completely alone, but who had given up on themselves, and given up on life.

With the slippers tucked under her arm, Charlotte skulked away from Lunar dejected, internally punishing herself. Had she known Lunar's interior was in such a state of dire neglect, she would have approached the lonesome house sooner. She would have banged on the olive front door and refused to leave until someone had let her back in. Her tears fell harder at the thought that she could have helped, or even saved a life. In addition to the toxic concoction of emotions already seeping through her conscience, Charlotte scolded herself further. Now that she had successfully entered the house unlawfully, and without detection, she knew she would be returning to the centre of Lunar's dark embrace. Guided by her vulnerable mind, she wasn't ready to release herself from the pitfalls of her past. She craved the love the old farmhouse had once provided, and with more determination than a mother protecting her young, Charlotte felt like she had to safeguard her past before her cherished memories became erased forever.

5

As Fern made the journey back to the family home she had once shared with her husband, she began to feel jarred. She couldn't help but notice all the imposing, concrete structures protruding out of the ground. More than she realised, in the blink of an eye, the Cotswold countryside had begun a process of personal transformation. Fern found herself craving the softness that surrounded what she had come to view as her new hideaway retreat.

The moment she turned onto the driveway of her marital home, she felt nauseous. The spacious, four-bedroomed cottage was located about thirty miles west of Aldebaran as the crow flies. The mere sight of the house caused her stomach to twist into knots, and a deep breath failed to fend off the tightness constraining her chest. She turned off the ignition and took a quick glance in the rear-view mirror. 'Pull yourself together,' she insisted of herself. Touching up her reflection, Fern wanted to look nothing other than perfect before confronting her cheating husband. 'Your life is a mess. But for heaven's sake, don't show him that.' With a generous hand, Fern applied a fresh layer of crimson lipstick to her poised pout, a new shade that she knew Cooper would find attractive.

Fumbling with her handbag on the passenger seat, Fern felt unsure if she should knock, or use her own set of keys. Then, like a moment of joy that brought life back into her world, she caught sight of Jessie opening the front door, her daughter waving at her with both hands.

'Hi Mum. How was it last night?' Jessie asked before she'd even reached her mum's car, opening the door like an efficient hotel valet. 'Did you get much sleep?'

Fern stepped out and inhaled the smog-infused air and plastered on her best smile, just in case Cooper appeared. 'I did thanks,' she replied, hugging her daughter like she hadn't seen her in months. 'Is Dad in?' she asked, hoping that he'd respected her wish and stayed away.

Jessie nodded. 'Are you really taking the rest of your things today?' she questioned, hoping to delay what she knew was inevitable.

With more beauty than a blossoming sunflower facing the sun, Fern drew her posture up to full height, and beamed with satisfaction. 'I sure am. The van will be here any minute,' she said, looking at the time, urging the removal company to be timely. 'I just want this bit over with.' With a slow turn of the head, Fern took a moment to admire the home that she had created, and it felt like all her treasured memories were fluttering away like the parts of a dandelion clock caught in a brisk breeze.

'Did you talk to Dad last night about him and Auntie Flo?'

Jessie shook her head. 'I didn't know what to say, so I stayed in my bedroom all night,' she confessed. 'I told him I was tired and he bought it.'

In her periphery, Fern saw Cooper approaching and felt her body stiffen. 'You go inside. Give us a minute to talk,' she requested, kissing Jessie on the head before releasing her grip.

In a manner that she couldn't control, Fern pined for Cooper the moment she spotted his familiar features. She hated herself for longing to be the one on the receiving end of his affections. In her mind, he had been her forever person, until he chose to break his vows. 'I asked you politely to stay away today,' she began, watching as her husband approached from the side of the house, her hair wafting in front of her face, helping to conceal her blushing cheeks.

Cooper held his hand out in a show of peace. 'I've been respectful this whole time and stayed away as much as I could, just like you asked. But I wanted to see you before you leave,' he explained, remaining a handful of paces away. 'I know that you're moving on. But I wouldn't forgive myself if I didn't give this one last try.' Cooper's dark features remained downturned, all the natural charm that he usually exuded was now masked by ripples of regret. 'You've never even given me an opportunity to explain.' Cooper spotted his wife's new shade of lipstick, and the way that it accentuated the natural features that he adored.

Fern let out a forceful breath and threw Cooper an intense, cold stare. 'Why should I give you anything? You slept with my best friend. What else needs to be explained?' Fern nipped her new denim jacket in around her waist, showing off the contours of her hourglass figure. 'Anyway, it's too late for any of this,' she sighed.

'It's never too late to try and save our marriage. Thirty years is worth fighting for,' Cooper protested. 'I love you, Fern. I always have done.' For the first time since the day they met, his wife presented as a stranger. The way that Fern held herself seemed different. Her shoulders were pulled back and her chest proud, exuding a level of confidence he had seldom witnessed. He couldn't help but admire his wife's new selection of clothes and the way that her makeup glistened. Through his eyes, everything appeared different, and he didn't like the feeling that he was losing his wife. 'I made a mistake, a stupid mistake, and I want you back. I *need* you in my life.'

Fern stepped back, maintaining the space between them both. 'You only want me back because Florence doesn't want you.'

Cooper looked surprised, his eyebrows raised. 'You've spoken to Flo?'

Hearing Cooper say Flo's name hurt more than Fern could have imagined. 'I have, and I know the affair started when I took

Jessie to Edinburgh for that long weekend. Over six months ago!' she exclaimed. Fern couldn't help but drink in the smell of Cooper's aftershave, the familiar scent seducing her senses and evoking buried memories. She craved to savour his touch, and to be held close to his chest, a place she had once felt protected. 'And that's the reason that I'll never love you again,' she said. 'All I see in my mind is you and her together,' she cried. 'Do you know how hard that is?' Fern covered her face, using her hands as a shield. 'When did it end? Or are you two still together?' she asked, desperate to know every detail so that she could silence her cruel imagination.

'It's over,' Cooper confirmed, moving closer.

'Is it only over because I found out?'

Cooper shook his head. 'I never loved her, not the way that I love you.'

She found herself surprised at how irrelevant his words had become to her. 'I thought I would love you forever,' Fern announced, working hard to prevent more tears from falling. 'But I don't. Not anymore,' she continued. 'Once the van arrives, that's me done. I'll be out of here,' she explained, hiding the fact that, deep down, it felt so painful to let go of the only life that she had ever known. 'We'll communicate like adults because of Jessie. But that's it as far as I'm concerned.' Fern diverted her gaze, drawing in a fresh bout of strength that was spinning in off the concrete. 'I think she's going to be staying here for a while. My new place is a project because that's all my budget would stretch to in Aldebaran,' she began. 'But it'll be worth it in the end because it's far enough away from you, but it's close enough to college for Jessie,' she confirmed with conviction.

Cooper detested the feeling that he was now on the fringe of Fern's life, stirring intense feelings of jealousy and anger. He wanted Fern back. She was still his wife, and he couldn't bear the thought of her with another man. 'I've heard some grim rumours about your new place, Lunar,' he commented, a pitiful sense of desperation fuelling his actions. 'And I think you should know what you're getting yourself into.'

The snide comment irritated Fern more than she wanted to admit. 'Why are you getting involved in my business? Why do you even care?' Fern questioned. 'You're just jealous,' she replied, resisting the urge to ask everything he knew. 'And I don't trust anything that you say anymore.'

'I'm just trying to protect you,' he defended, reaching out to touch her arm.

Fern deflected his offer of physical affection. 'I don't need protecting,' she retaliated, retracting her arm. 'I can look after myself.'

Cooper displayed a pinched expression, and his face reddened the more he felt his demeanour crumbling.

'I've contacted a solicitor about getting a divorce,' Fern announced in the moment of silence that presented. 'I've obviously taken all the money from our savings account to buy my new place,' she confirmed. 'It's not our south of France retirement dream, but I guess it's my new dream,' she said, recalling her and Cooper's plans to purchase a quaint, French gite ready for the next stage in their lives together. 'I don't want anything else. You can keep the house, keep your pension, keep all of it for all I care. I don't want anything from you.'

'Divorce?' Cooper replied with a sullen look.

Fern looked puzzled, like it was obvious. 'Yes, a divorce. What did you expect? You've had an affair, Cooper. And on top of that, it was with my best friend,' she cried. 'We were never going to be able to overcome that, or at least I wasn't. And no matter how hard it is for me to admit, this is over. Our marriage is over.' Fern felt heartbroken, and she no longer cared who bore witness, her perfectly presented demeanour crumbling faster than her marriage.

When he saw her cry, Cooper reached out once again to console his wife. 'We can make this work. We can go to counselling. I just can't let you go.'

Fern pulled her jacket tight around her body again, folding her arms in defence. 'Don't touch me,' she protested when he tried to offer an embrace. 'Don't *ever* touch me,' she begged, her skin crawling at the thought of any physical intimacy. 'Please, just leave. This is hard enough. Don't make it any worse.'

Cooper backed away, thrashing his leg and kicking over a ceramic flowerpot. 'You've made a massive mistake buying that house,' he said, heading towards his car, 'and when it all goes wrong, don't say that I didn't try to warn you.'

Fern raised her head, her face awash with streaks of black, smudged mascara. In a moment of spite, and in retaliation for his snide comments, Fern replied. 'Jess knows everything, by the way,' she admitted, her words stopping Cooper from taking another step. 'She heard me and Florence talking. I couldn't keep it from her any longer. And why the hell should I?' she said, walking away when she spotted the removal van pulling onto the stretched driveway. 'I'd talk to her if I were you, otherwise you'll end up losing both of us.'

Angered by the revelation, Cooper got into his car and sped away, his spinning tyres leaving behind a cloud of dust. He watched Fern in his rear-view mirror before pulling out onto the main road, and in that moment, he knew that he'd destroyed his marriage and lost the true love of his life.

Back on the driveway, the two guys in the removal van jumped down from the cabin. 'Mrs Jones?' the driver asked, checking the name on his paperwork. 'I'm Gareth. I think we spoke over the phone.'

Fern held her hand out. 'That's me, but not for too much longer,' she laughed, wiping away her blackened makeup and pulling out a tube of lip balm from her pocket, applying a fresh layer to her full lips.

'Oh, it's like that is it?' the driver commented. 'We deal with lots of breakups, but we're not complaining. It's kept me in business all these years,' Gareth added, looking at his son, Daniel, and laughing. He then looked at his paperwork again, checking the onward delivery address. 'Lunar. Aldebaran?' he read aloud in a questioning tone. 'That's the old farmhouse at the top of the hill, isn't it?' he asked Fern, the smile falling off his face like a landslide.

'That's the one,' she replied, catching the strange look that had appeared on his face. 'Don't be telling me that it's built on a mine, or a cemetery,' she mocked, laughing off her nervousness. 'Do you know the property well?' she probed when her attempt at humour seemed to fall flat.

'I've been in this business more years than I care to remember. Most places sound familiar to me,' Gareth brushed off, unwilling to reveal his true connection to the property. 'Why don't you show us what we're loading, and we'll make a start?'

'Great, this way,' Fern said, showing the guys through to the heart of the house, pointing out everything that she wanted removing. 'I'm not taking that much,' she smiled, her eyes glossing over at the sight of her life packed up in boxes. 'Is this how all your divorced customers act?' she asked, trying to prevent herself from crying.

'You'd be amazed how many couples fight over the stupidest of things,' Gareth replied, trying to shoo memories of Lunar out of his mind. He looked around at all the boxes and adjusted his cap. 'We'll start with the few bits of bigger furniture. Then we'll pack the van around those,' he said, nodding at Fern to confirm the plan.

'Great, let me know if you need anything,' she said, standing back and watching the father-and-son team move all her belongings into the modest removal van, possessions that once felt so important, but now seemed irrelevant to her new life in the hills.

'Are you okay?' a voice asked from behind, and Jessie appeared at her mum's side like a faithful lamb.

'Yep, all good,' Fern reassured, producing a smile to back up her statement. 'They won't be long packing up all the stuff, and then that's it. I'll be gone,' she confirmed. 'Dad's left for work.'

'Good. I don't want to talk to him anyway,' she groaned. 'The thought of him going behind your back makes me feel sick, and with Auntie Flo makes it even worse. How could they, Mum?' she added, her facial expression reflecting her own sense of personal betrayal.

'He's still your dad. Just talk to him,' Fern encouraged. 'This is your home and you're both going to be living here together. You need to get along.'

'And what if *she* comes over? Are they still together?'

Fern scratched her neck, feeling restless. 'I don't think they're together, but who knows what the truth is,' she admitted. 'They can do whatever they like from now on,' she smiled, lifting her head at the realisation that she was nearly a free woman. 'Give me a hug,' she said, wrapping her arms around Jessie. 'Promise that you'll come and visit,' she whispered in her ear.

'I will,' Jessie replied. 'And as soon as the house starts to look more like a home, I'll definitely want to be with you.'

'Brilliant,' Fern beamed.

'I'll text you later,' Jessie said. 'I'm off into town. Will you be okay?'

Fern nodded, her eyes glowing. 'Absolutely. I'm fine, honestly. I'll talk to you later,' she said, blowing Jessie a kiss as she walked out of the door.

Fern lingered in the hallway for a few moments, watching as, one by one, her belongings were loaded into the van. Like a stranger visiting for the first time, she wandered aimlessly from room to room. In her mind, she pictured Cooper and Flo together, and in that moment, she knew that she'd made the right decision to leave.

Outside on the driveway, just as the removal guys loaded the last box, Gareth prepared himself to make the drive up to Lunar. 'Would you just double-check that we have everything? I just need to take a minute and get a drink,' he asked his son, Daniel.

In that moment of pause, Gareth could see the image of smoke rising like an erupting volcano at the top of the hill in Aldebaran village. He felt like he could smell the embers of a raging fire, and in his mind, he could see the haunting sight of smoke drifting across the landscape like a pocket of poisoned clouds. But it was the piercing sound of a woman's incessant screaming that made him weep, and he pulled his arm over his eyes to shield his moment of sadness. With one of his senses momentarily removed, the screams tearing through his ears became louder. The smell of smoke overwhelmed his composure, and he shook his head, trying to dislodge the painful, historical images firing through his mind like targeted missiles.

'That's it. We're ready, Dad,' Daniel confirmed, interrupting Gareth's moment of turmoil.

Gareth finished his drink and took out his keys. 'Let's get going then.'

Fern appeared on the driveway. 'You go on ahead. I'll follow in a few minutes once I've locked up,' she announced, signalling with a thumbs-up.

Gareth nodded in acknowledgement and eased the van off the driveway. He made his way along the main arterial road that fed directly into Aldebaran, his palms holding tight to the steering wheel until his knuckles turned white. With a sense of apprehension stirring in his stomach, Gareth's nerves bubbled beneath the surface, and he grew unusually quiet. Half an hour into the trip, Daniel couldn't help but acknowledge the strange silence.

'You're quiet, Dad. You okay?' he asked, unable to recall a time when his dad hadn't sung along with the radio.

Gareth didn't reply. His attention was drawn to Lunar's two towering cannon chimneys as the house came into view in the distance. A twitch developed in his eyelid and his pupils dilated.

Unfamiliar with the address, Daniel checked the paperwork. 'That's the house there, Dad,' he said, pointing to the right.

'I know,' Gareth finally replied. 'A long time ago, I told myself that I'd never come back here,' he revealed, pulling the van to a halt on the main road.

Daniel looked around, confused that his dad hadn't driven the van onto the driveway like he usually did. 'Why?'

The sight of the house washed Gareth's memories onto the shore, memories he had worked hard to erase. His grip on the steering wheel loosened, and he pressed his palms over his face before letting his fingers fall away, like a flurry of autumn leaves. 'There was an accident here. Ten, maybe fifteen years ago,' he began, turning to face the house that still sporadically haunted his dreams. 'And on that day, I just happened to be travelling past this stretch of road,' he continued.

Gareth looked over at the barn with hatred in his eyes. His stomach fell to his feet as one memory after another unwrapped itself. 'I just remember seeing smoke from the main road,' he muttered. 'But nasty stuff. It was a thick, toxic smog, and I knew something wasn't right.' The feeling of dread Gareth had experienced fifteen years ago sprang back into life like a haunted Jack-in-the-box. 'Within a few seconds of me arriving, the fire brigade came charging up the hill at a rate of knots — two, maybe three engines,' he recalled. 'And from where I'd stopped on the road, I just remember seeing this young lad standing by himself at the front of the house, crying his eyes out,' Gareth described, still able to recall the colour of the boy's tie-dyed t-shirt. 'The boy's friend was trapped inside the barn.' Gareth turned his face away from Lunar, the memories too painful to square up to.

'What happened?' Daniel asked, already anticipating his dad's reply.

'The fire brigade tried their best to get the lad out, but they were too late,' he recalled, picturing the police tarpaulin that was erected at the side of the barn. 'And when his parents arrived back home, a police officer escorted them inside. That's when I knew that something terrible must have happened,' he recalled. 'The thing I've never been able to forget was the sound of a woman screaming. It was such a haunting, terrifying sound. Something I've never heard before and hope to God I never have to hear again.'

Daniel turned to look at the house. 'Did someone lose their life?'

Gareth looked up at the sky, hoping that by diverting his gaze, his internal pain would escape with the wind. 'A young lad died. He was only six or seven, and this was his home.' Turning to shield his face, Gareth wiped away the tears. 'I wanted to help, but I didn't know what to do,' he confessed through a crippling sense of shame. 'I should have asked if they needed help. I should have volunteered. I should have done something. But I didn't. I was in shock. I just sat and watched them struggle to get the flames under control. It felt like a lifetime,' he revealed, expressing the feelings of guilt that he had never been able to shake.

'The firefighters wouldn't have wanted people getting in their way,' Daniel reassured.

'I could tell that they were struggling. There was a look of panic that I could see on their faces,' Gareth explained. 'The smoke was thick and black, and when it caught in the back of my throat it was almost too much to bear. The little lad didn't stand a chance,' he added, a pained expression clawing its way back onto his face. 'Later that night, when I got home and showered, I could still smell the smoke on my skin. It was such a sickening smell. It stayed with me for days.'

Having rarely witnessed his dad so emotional, Daniel reached out and placed his hand on his dad's shoulder. 'There was nothing that you could have done.'

Gareth lowered his head. 'I've always felt guilty about not coming back here. I acted like the tragedy never happened because it was too hard to talk about. You were just about to turn seven, roughly the same age as the lad that died. I don't even know what his name was.' Gareth noticed the vibrancy of the mature garden, something that had been masked by flecks of ash and ripples of smoke during the day of the fire. He then turned to look at the barn, noticing the sections that had undergone repair. He wished that someone had just been done with it and bulldozed the bastard building.

'Are you going to be alright finishing this job?' Daniel asked, spotting Fern's car approaching in the distance. 'I can do most of the lifting by myself. You stay here in the van if you need to.'

Gareth took a deep breath, the smoke-free Aldebaran air inflating his lungs. 'I'll be fine,' he confirmed. 'I get the impression she doesn't know about the fire. Let's keep it that way. It's not our place to tell her,' he insisted.

'Okay,' Daniel agreed, slipping the paperwork back into his pocket.

Gareth manoeuvred the van onto Lunar's driveway, turned off the ignition and stepped onto the gravel. 'You tell us where you want everything going, and we'll follow your lead,' he said the moment that Fern got out of her car.

Fern no longer felt hesitant to start the next chapter of her life, and a lightness could be seen in her footing as she stepped out of the car. Her return to Lunar felt victorious, the war with Cooper buried. Her radiance couldn't be hidden, her face aglow with feelings of freedom. The melodic echoes coming from a nearby skein of thrushes served as a welcome chorus. With a tilt of her head, she cast her gaze to the horizon, the craggy hills elevated with additional prowess, crumbling the concrete giants now confined to her past.

'Most of the stuff can go straight into the barn,' she replied to Gareth. 'Until the house is decorated, there's no point filling the rooms with all of my junk.' Fern walked over to the barn and unlocked the door. 'I haven't even been in here properly,' she confessed, taking a quick glance inside the gloomy interior, failing to spot the cluster of freshly picked flowers at the far end. 'It's a bit grotty, but it'll be fine for storage in the short term. Just dump the stuff at this end so it's more accessible for me to shift later. The main things I need in the house are my bed, and boxes I've labelled as essential.'

Daniel and his dad followed Fern to the barn, her reply sending a wave of shivers coursing over Gareth's skin.

'No problem,' Daniel replied when his dad failed to respond. 'Let's get started.' Walking back towards the van, Daniel once again placed his arm over his dad's shoulders. 'Just let me know if it's too much.'

'I just need a minute,' he said. 'Can you take her to the house and get her to sign the paperwork.'

With Fern distracted and out of the way, Gareth stepped over the barn's threshold, balancing a box in his arms. His body felt sweltering, like he was stuck in the middle of a blazing wildfire. In rebellion, the surface of his skin prickled and itched beneath his clothes. Through saturated eyes, he gazed around the space, wondering exactly where the young boy had been trapped. His tears fell harder knowing that the boy would have been terrified and alone, waiting for help that never arrived. Uncomfortable, Gareth felt his chest tighten, and for a moment, he placed himself in the boy's shoes, experiencing for himself what it would have felt like to gasp for every breath when the air was polluted with deadly vapours strong enough to kill. Placing the box on the floor, he lowered to his knees and bowed his head. With his eyes closed, he prayed for peace, savouring an unexpected moment of serenity that ignited his heart, like a lighthouse during a storm.

6

Lunar's internal maze of dated copper pipes filled with boiling water, causing the expanding metal to creak loudly. The early boost of warmth removed the morning chill lingering inside the heart of Lunar. The gurgling noises did little to rouse Fern, who had already slept through two alarms and three missed phone calls from Jessie. It was the second thud against the front door that dragged her out of the state of slumber that was holding her exhausted body captive.

Dazed, Fern ripped the duvet back in one swift motion and grabbed her phone. Through blurred vision, panic set in when she realised that she'd slept through her alarms. Still wearing a mismatch of pyjama shorts and a t-shirt, she side-stepped the scattering of boxes, and stumbled downstairs. 'I'm coming!' she shouted to the person hollering with impatience on her front doorstep. Fumbling with her keys and still sleepy, Fern failed to realise that the door was already unlocked. 'I'm so sorry,' she apologised, sweeping her hair into a messy bun. 'I slept through my alarms,' she explained upon opening the door.

The man's scrunched forehead conveyed his annoyance at the delay. 'Where do you want it?' the burly skip driver asked.

Fern stepped outside. 'Here. As close as possible, please,' she requested, moving out onto the sweeping porch.

The driver got back into his van and positioned the skip as

instructed. 'Here, ok?' he shouted, having swung the empty vessel into place with ease.

'Yep, great. Thanks very much,' Fern replied, giving him the thumbs up whilst trying not to look too disgruntled about the bed of peony and foxglove that he'd inadvertently trampled.

'I never thought someone would buy this place,' the driver commented, looking up at the house, admiring the bold, central apex.

'Oh? Why's that?' she asked, most of her attention still with the slayed foliage.

'You're not local, are you?'

Fern shook her head. 'No. I'm not.'

The driver's phone rang, and he jumped up to grab it from where it was resting on his seat. 'No time to chat. The boss is already on my back,' he moaned, starting the truck's ignition, holding his hand up to acknowledge his swift exit.

'Thanks for that,' Fern mumbled to herself with sarcasm. She watched the man drive away, his odd comment sticking like sap in her mind. Unnerved, she headed back inside and paused in the hallway, the collection of bags and boxes waiting to be unpacked hiding the fact that the cupboard under the stairs had been opened, the door still ajar from where Charlotte previously hidden, and escaped.

Taking out her phone, Fern pressed on her daughter's icon in her call log. 'Morning,' she announced when Jessie answered her phone. 'Sorry I missed your calls,' she apologised. 'For some reason my phone was on silent.' With nowhere else to sit, Fern perched herself on the bottom of the stairs, unable to stop thinking about the man's statement.

'I was about to come over and check on you,' Jessie replied, annoyed. 'Where have you been? Are you okay?'

Fern got up and pottered through to the kitchen, unpacking a box of cleaning products. 'I'm fine. I was just that exhausted after a long day of moving stuff out, then moving stuff in, that I slept through my alarms.'

Jessie removed her jacket and fell onto her bed. 'I was worried, Mum, and I was about to come and check on you. Anyway, now that I know you're okay, how's the house looking?'

Fern sighed. 'I'm still de-cluttering stuff that was left behind, and now I have some of my own stuff in here too,' she explained, pinning her phone to her ear with her shoulder while grabbing two bin bags of rubbish and heading out onto the porch. She plunged them into the skip, failing to spot that the pile of bags she'd already left outside had been opened, and resealed, some of the contents missing. 'It's amazing what you can achieve when you don't have a TV for distraction.'

'I thought you were keeping some stuff, not chucking everything away?' Jessie asked, recalling an earlier conversation.

'I am, but only sentimental items that might have meant something to someone, not all the other clutter that this house seems to have been filled with,' she explained, walking through to the back of the house. The morning sunshine splashed in through the kitchen windows and bounced off Fern's face. She took a moment to relish the feeling of warmth on her skin, and she wondered if she would ever get to experience the type of tropical heat offered by more exotic climates, wondering what it would be like to holiday alone.

'Mum? Are you still there?' Jessie asked when the line fell silent.

There was a knock at the door. 'Hello?' Fern heard someone shout.

'Jess, I've got to go. Someone's here. I'll chat to you later.' Fern stuffed her phone in her shorts pocket and scurried to the door.

'Hello,' she replied, spotting someone lingering on the porch.

The woman standing on the porch turned to look at Fern. 'Oh, hi. My name is Edith. Edith Preston,' she began with a smile and friendly, meek wave. 'I was just walking past so I thought I'd bob my head in and introduce myself, welcome you to the village,' she explained. 'I walk past here every day on my way to work and it's so nice to see that someone's finally moved into this wonderful house.'

Fern burst into tears upon actually hearing someone refer to her house as wonderful.

A pained expression appeared on Edith's face. 'I'm so sorry,' she apologised. 'I didn't mean to upset you. I've obviously called at a bad time,' she continued, turning to walk away, regretting having not just walked past in the first place.

Fern shook her head and stepped outside. 'No, please. You don't have to leave,' she said through a shaky voice. 'I'm so sorry. I'm not usually such an emotional mess,' she smiled, encouraging Edith to step back onto the porch. 'I've only just moved in,' Fern explained. 'And although I hate to admit it, I've never felt so overwhelmed in my entire life. Your kind gesture to stop by and say hello really means a lot to me.'

Edith fiddled with one of her effortlessly stacked gold necklaces as she spoke, her aqua blue eyes accentuated by the vibrant shade of her long, blonde hair. 'Whenever I'm feeling overwhelmed, I just jump in with both feet. Then, once you get going, the mountain that you're standing at the bottom of doesn't seem so steep.'

Fern immediately warmed to Edith's youthful take on life. 'I think whether I wanted to or not, I'm definitely jumping in with both feet. This house is wonderful. But there's so much work to do and I'm not sure that I'm the right person for the challenge.'

'Well, if you ever need a refreshment break, I own a café in the village. I'm trying to promote a new event that I'm starting this Wednesday called Coffee Mates,' she explained, pulling out a leaflet from her bag. 'I've been posting these through letterboxes in the local area, but missed out this house because I could see that it was empty. But, now you're here,' she welcomed with yet another wide beam that shone brighter than a rainbow.

Fern took hold of the flyer and scanned the details.

'If you decide to come along, you'll see some yellow tables at the back of the café. The idea is that if you sit at one of those, it means that you're interested in socialising,' she smiled. 'It's a way to encourage people to make new friends, and hopefully feel less lonely.'

Fern offered up a broad smile of her own. 'Sounds like a great idea.'

'Feel free to bring along any family, or friends,' Edith suggested.

Fern shook her head. 'There's actually just me here at the moment,' she revealed. 'I have a daughter, Jessie. She's seventeen and starting college in September,' Fern explained, turning back to look at the house. 'She's decided not to move in with me until some of the work is done. And who can blame her. This place is far from cool for a seventeen-year-old with an image to uphold.'

'When a house is a project, it just means that you can make it your own. Inject some of your own personality,' Edith replied with enthusiasm.

Fern tried to absorb some of Edith's positivity. 'I make celebration cakes for a living. So, I'm excited to create the kitchen of my dreams,' she smiled. 'I'm talking a lot, aren't I? I've only been on my own for a few days and I'm already acting like I haven't spoken to another human being in months.'

Edith warmed to Fern, finding her quirky personality endearing. 'There's nothing wrong with being a chatterbox,' she grinned. 'I sell cakes at the café, and people are *always* asking if I cater for special occasions, which I don't. You should leave me some business cards. I'd be happy to hand them out.'

'Really? That would be great, thank you so much. I'm hoping to drum up some new business in this area, so that would really help me out. Do you have a few minutes now? I could go and find some to give you.'

Edith glanced at her watch. 'Of course,' she nodded, secretly thrilled at the unexpected invitation. Having passed the house with frequency over the years, sometimes making an excuse to pass twice in the same day, for some reason, she held a part of Lunar in her heart. On her way to work, Edith would admire the fullness of Lunar's front garden, savouring the floral, seasonal changes. She watched for the pockets of vibrant daffodils to appear in spring, along with the sweeping row of peeking cherry blossom, the trees hiding in the background like a child cowering behind the protective coattails of an elder. The flourishing sprawls of dahlias, foxglove and delphiniums was Lunar's way of letting Edith know that the warm, summer months were in full swing. The carpet of copper, amber leaves beneath her feet was an indication that winter was beckoning. And yet despite her secret love affair with the property, for a number of years the heart of the house had remained elusive. Edith's bouncing nerves confirmed her trepidation, scared that the internal charm wouldn't match what she viewed as the exterior magic.

'Perfect, come in. Just watch your step. It's crazy in here at the moment,' Fern apologised. 'I'm eager to start decorating.'

With a tentative step, Edith followed Fern to the front door and stepped inside, where Lunar's interior presented itself like a dying, weeping willow. When her curious gaze landed on Lunar's hidden heart, her eyes welled in the knowledge that before the property had been put up for sale, the house had actually been someone's home.

'I'd offer you a seat, but I obviously don't have any yet,' Fern apologised. 'So, if you wouldn't mind waiting, I'll just nip upstairs and rummage in my bag for some of my business cards. Hopefully they're not in the barn with all my other belongings.'

'No rush,' Edith smiled.

Fern dashed upstairs, leaving her visitor alone.

A sense of morbid curiosity drew Edith into the heart of the house and with tentative steps, she pottered further down the hallway. She caught sight of the rear end of the barn through one of the side windows, and witnessed how the rotten wood had become overgrown with a tangle of unsightly weeds. Wrapping her Boho-chic, chunky knit cardigan around her body, Edith took a few more paces and lingered at the end of the hallway. The high walls were infested with specs of black mould, which made the space feel imposing and grubby. The intricate, Victorian coving and ceiling rose added to the dated aesthetic. A single oval mirror was the only accessory adorning the walls, and Edith pictured who the fingerprints might have belonged to that were scattered like a ghostly mosaic over the dusty glass.

With the kitchen door ajar, she peered her head in, witnessing nothing but a derelict, shabby shell. Failing to see any evidence pertaining to the previous family, Edith's heart ached for the person who had once called Lunar their home. The sight of the single dining table chair filled her with regret, and through her fresh eyes, she understood that Lunar was a house unloved. Abandoned. It was a feeling that sent shivers across her skin and caused a furrow to appear on her brow. Deep down, she had always suspected that whoever had lived at the property was lonely, possibly in need of help, and yet each day when she walked past, she avoided approaching the door.

'Oh, please don't look too closely. It's bad enough when you look at it all from a distance,' Fern joked, spotting her visitor at the end of the hallway, leaning against the wall and peering into the kitchen.

'Was the house like this when you bought it?' Edith questioned. 'So run down and neglected?'

Fern clenched her teeth. 'It was,' she revealed, shaking her head, her facial expression downturned. Fern spotted a look of sadness burrowing deep within Edith's eyes. 'You're wondering who could have lived here like this, aren't you?'

Edith pulled herself away from the wall that was supporting her frame. 'I was,' she replied. 'I just don't know how someone could have been happy living here, in these conditions.'

'I'm not sure how long it's been empty but even so, whoever lived here previously was clearly struggling with their mental, and possibly physical, health. This isn't normal, is it?' she asked, seeking confirmation. 'Even though some things must've been removed before I got the keys, it doesn't take away from the feeling of neglect.' Fern thought about showing Edith the small bedroom upstairs, but witnessing how upset she was, she changed her mind. 'I've found some things in the house that I'm going to keep. Things that I think should be returned to the family, that's if the person who died has any living relatives, and if I can track them down.'

'I think it was an elderly man who lived here,' Edith revealed. 'I always walk past this stretch of road on my way to work, and maybe only once or twice, I caught sight of a gentleman behind the net curtains.'

'Did you ever speak to him?'

Edith shook her head. 'Early on, we're talking years ago now, when I knew that someone actually lived here, I would knock on the door,' she recalled. 'I was going to pretend that I was promoting the café, but really, my intention was just to say hello. I wanted to introduce myself and let him know that somebody cared, he just appeared to be so isolated from the world.'

'And what happened?' Fern asked, intrigued.

With a heavy sigh and shake of the head, Edith replied. 'He never answered the door. Not once,' she explained, a look of failure in her eyes. 'So, one day, I just stopped trying, and instead, I would push little notes or postcards through the letterbox wishing him a nice day or inviting him to the café. I'd leave my phone number, just in case he wanted to talk to someone.'

'And did he ever call?'

Edith spoke in a soft tone. 'No, he never did.' With a slow walk, Edith strolled further into the kitchen. 'Had I known that he was living like this, I would have knocked every day, and I wouldn't have stopped trying. Someone like this needed help, and it looks like he had nobody for support.'

Delving in her pocket, Fern pulled a tissue out and handed it to Edith. 'It's not your fault. You didn't even know this man.' She placed a hand on Edith's shoulder. 'You went out of your way to try and help a stranger. Not many people would have done that much.'

Becoming lost in the history of the room, Edith pictured the man sitting at the dining table, alone. She imagined how he might have lived, peering at well-worn touch points. 'He must've liked sitting here,' Edith commented, spotting that the floor was well scuffed, and the tabletop above was particularly scratched in one isolated area. 'The seat would have been facing whatever picture was here,' she explained, walking towards the opposite wall, and pointing to a faded patch where a frame was once hung.

'That picture had already been removed when I got the keys,' Fern replied, herself having wondered what was hung in such a prime spot. 'There's another spot in the house that looks well worn, like Mr Sloan had enjoyed standing there, and I can't work out what he would have been looking at,' Fern revealed.

'Oh, where's that?' Edith asked, intrigued.

Fern made her way into the back room and walked towards the patio doors that offered uninterrupted views out over the garden. 'If you look here,' she explained, indicating with her foot, 'the carpet just here is completely threadbare where someone has stood for long periods of time.' Fern looked up and tried to establish what Mr Sloan had been looking at. 'I mean, he could have just been admiring his garden, but why would he stand?'

Edith slid her feet into the ingrained footprints nestled into the carpet, and looked up, imagining it was a dark, cloudless night. 'Maybe he liked to stargaze. This area is known to be great for astronomers and if you look up, I bet this view is one of the best in the village,' she speculated, spotting that there weren't any obvious sources of light pollution, or towering infrastructures as far as the eye could see. Out of practice, she searched the sky for traces of familiarity, recalling how once darkness descended, she once loved joining the twinkling dots together in a way that formed a constellation.

'I didn't know that about the village. Have you always lived in Aldebaran?' Fern quizzed, wondering if Edith might know any more history about the house.

Edith pulled her attention away from the sky. 'I've only been here for a few years. I only know about this house because I pass it every day, and it kind of stands out with it being on top of the hill. And I overhear conversations in the café, people who have travelled to the area just to stargaze.'

'Well, Mr Sloan, that was the man's name, might not have wanted to open the door to you, but I'm so grateful that you took the time to introduce yourself and say hello to me,' Fern said, a relaxed smile landing on her face with more grace than a butterfly coming to rest on a petal. 'You'll have to come back once I've done some of the work so that you can appreciate the before and after,' Fern invited. 'Here are some of my business cards, and thanks again,' she said. 'I hope I haven't made you too late for work,' she commented, the pair walking back towards the front door.

Edith stepped out onto the porch. 'Not at all. It was lovely to meet you and I'll hopefully see you soon,' she said, walking down the steps.

'I'll come and visit the café the moment I get my hands on some fresh clothes and a hairbrush,' Fern joked, waving just as Edith stepped out onto the main road.

Fern walked back inside and eased the door into its frame. Alone and with no distractions, she could think of no better time than to tackle the small bedroom. With an empty box and some bin liners in her hands, she headed upstairs and paused on the landing. She placed the things on the floor and took a deep breath. For reasons she couldn't explain, she felt herself having to resist the urge to knock before entering. She understood that the house now legally belonged to her and that the deeds reflected her name, and yet she felt like the small bedroom was still in some way occupied.

With a slow, cautious movement, she turned the handle and pushed the door ajar. An oppressive force greeted Fern as she lingered in the doorway with hesitance. A dark, cold front prevented her from stepping forward. She found herself waiting for an invitation that was never going to materialise. With a pounding heart, she could feel a cutting level of despondency seeping its way through the darkness like an eclipse of dormant moths.

She reached out her hand and switched on the light, the single bulb doing little to deflect the intangible sense of gloom that touched every corner. On tiptoes and taking care not to tread on any of the items scattered over the floor, Fern stepped into the room and with one gentle swoop, drew back the curtains. Decades' worth of dust trickled through the air in a slow and steady stream, like falling pockets of pollen captured in a summer downpour. Her senses rebelled against the irritation, and she released a cluster of irritable sneezes. The sudden influx of natural light illuminated the room and showcased the contents in their true light for the first time. Unable to fend off her emotional reaction, the touching scene brought Fern to tears, like she herself had lost a loved one and was faced with the grim task of sorting through a lifetime of personal belongings.

Her internal body temperature rose faster than a garden thermometer facing midday sun. She wilted beneath the hot flush, her chest clammy beneath her clothes, and it felt like her skin was scorching. Gasping for relief, she reached out her arm and swung open the window, plunging her face into the welcome breeze. With her face resting against the window frame, she savoured the feeling of natural light resting on her eyes, and the sensation of cool, fresh air inflating her lungs.

Feeling composed, she took out her phone and faced the room with a fresh bout of resilience. She opened her camera and began a video. 'I want to capture this moment,' she continued like a narrator. 'Out of every room in this house, I feel like this one is the most heartbreaking,' she explained, 'and that's why I want to document everything before I disturb the contents.' She strategically positioned herself like a videographer and started filming in one area.

'So, this is the tiny box room here at Lunar,' she began in a more upbeat tone. 'Unlike the rest of the house, this room looks like it was once cared for,' she continued. 'It feels like I'm invading someone's privacy, someone safe space.' She hovered the camera over the huddle of teddies that were tucked underneath the child's duvet. She held her phone over the bear embossed with the words *I love my sister*. 'You can tell that somebody really loved this teddy because it's been cuddled a lot. Look here, the fur is all worn,' she described, zooming in.

Fern then pointed the camera towards the floor and nestled herself amongst the clutter. Shivers swept through her body when she filmed the part-built train track that still covered the carpet. 'Someone had obviously been playing with this, but for whatever reason, they never came back,' she explained. 'You can tell that all this stuff hasn't been moved in a long time because if I move this tiny section of track,' she continued, removing a piece with her free hand, 'the carpet underneath has been protected.'

With care, Fern rose to her feet and walked towards the end of the bed, stepping over the toys and pointing her phone towards the far wall. 'There are so many lovely little pictures and paintings,' she explained, allowing the camera to film each photo that was displayed on the wall. 'These drawings here look like monsters or aliens,' she said, her voice choked with emotion. An incoming breeze swept through the room, the wind causing the drawings to flutter, the paper monsters coming alive amid the movement. She followed the sun's trajectory. 'Oh, my goodness, look at this,' she whispered, sniffling. Fern held her phone over a tiny, painted handprint that had been pressed directly against the wall. With the video still recording, she held out her free hand and pressed it alongside, illustrating the scale of the child's handprint. 'Such a little hand,' she described, trying to recall what age Jessie's hands had felt so tiny. 'There's a date here,' she said, moving closer so that she could read the squiggle, doing the maths in her head. 'It really does feel like this room could have been like this for fifteen years.'

Sitting on the edge of the bed, Fern took hold of one of the soft toys. She held it in her hand and released an expansive breath, turning the camera to face herself. 'I feel silly getting emotional,' she sobbed, crying into the camera. 'But there's just something fundamentally upsetting about this house, and maybe that's why the skip driver, and the removal guy, both seemed a little perturbed that I have chosen to buy this place. Maybe they know something I don't know.' Fern wiped her face with the back of her hand. 'I feel like I need to find out what happened to the family who lived here. I *want* to know what happened. I want to know why this child's room hasn't been touched. I want to know who used to sleep in this bed, and where they are now. I want to know everything.' The sound of voices travelled in through the open window. Fern peered out and saw a group of excitable children passing with their parents, an array of laughs and screams bouncing in the air. Like a modern-day maiden trapped in a tower, Fern looked down and longed to experience a fraction of the happiness that was painted with a liberal hand across the stranger's faces. She couldn't remember when she had last felt so happy, and she wondered if she had already experienced her quota of happiness.

Tearing herself away from the distractions, Fern got off the bed and propped her phone up against the wall so that it continued to film without her assistance. She opened the wardrobe that was positioned in the corner of the room, the hinges creaking when she pulled apart the doors. On her knees, she reached inside and grabbed hold of some of the clothes that had fallen to the bottom, the style and shape indicating that the room had probably belonged to a little boy. Towards the back of the wardrobe, she took hold of a picture frame, the photo inside of a mother cradling a baby deep in her arms. 'She looks so happy,' Fern described, spotting that the photo had been taken downstairs on Lunar's porch. She held the photo close to her camera. 'You can just about see another pair of feet lurking in the background, maybe an older sibling, and you can see a red bike and collection of shoes. This picture proves that a family of sorts did live here at some point. I just don't know what happened to them.' With one click, she concluded the video, unwilling to record the room's subsequent demise.

Fern got up and took hold of the empty box from the landing.

One item at a time, she began sorting through the contents, deciding what to keep, and what to discard. With the little boy's family in mind, she placed the precious gallery of hand-crafted pictures, along with the *I love my sister* teddy and highland cow in the awaiting plastic box. She also kept some of the well-thumbed reading books that were resting on the bedside table, a handful of colouring books, and what looked to be a few unwashed pairs of shorts that had football trading cards poking out of one of the pockets. With an aching, heavy heart, she placed most of the things into bin bags, the character of the room falling away like leaves caught in the current of an erratic river. Outside, perched in a nearby tree, sat another distraction for Fern to appreciate. She could hear the elaborate melody coming from a lone blackbird, serving as a reminder that even when she felt alone, it was still possible to experience moments of joy in a house that she desperately wanted to feel like home.

With only the birdsong for company, Fern continued to clear out the bedroom until the incoming sunlight could only reflect off the sparseness that remained. She took hold of the last item, a wooden chair situated near the door. With weary arms, she lifted it out onto the landing ready to throw in the skip along with the lineup of brimming bin bags. When she stepped back into the room, she spotted a mahogany box that had been hiding beneath it. The antique box looked out of place in a room that had been filled with nothing but an array of colourful toys. Intrigued, Fern reached down and took hold of the box, inspecting it from every angle. The brass padlock continued to perform its function by ensuring that only the person with the key could gain access, Mr Sloan's precious contents concealed within.

7

Dylan Wallace eased his body out of bed and made his way to the bathroom, stumbling over his own pair of two left feet. A sleepless night combined with a crack-of-dawn start meant that a grogginess clung to his usual youthful demeanour. A quick wash did little to soften the dark circles lingering beneath his eyes, the cold water accentuating the shadows. In preparation for his scheduled business meeting with Fern over at Lunar, he applied a liberal layer of gel to tame his unruly, jet-black hair. To make a positive first impression, he replaced his usual scruffy work clothes with a pair of smart combats and a collared t-shirt. Inked across the full length of both arms, Dylan admired his bold tattoos, seeking comfort and courage from some of the more intricate parts of the memorial motif. 'You need this job,' he told himself, running his fingers over poignant parts of the design. He gazed at the hidden initials, the letters concealed within the collage of a tree, a scattering of leaves appearing like they had been caught in a breeze.

Foregoing his usual breakfast, Dylan took straight to his van and began the short drive up to the top of Aldebaran. The usual bustling roads were less chaotic, school holidays seeing families depart for foreign adventures and tropical vacations. With fewer distractions, Dylan spotted the way that the hills rose like giants in the distance, the view taking him back to his childhood. He recalled one lazy summer day in particular when he and his friend had sat in one of the corn fields, eating ice cream and naming each of the peaks.

Arriving at Lunar ten minutes before his pre-booked appointment, Dylan parked his black transit on the main road that ran parallel to the house and jumped down onto the pavement. The climbing heat of the day combined with his jumble of nerves made him feel like his airway was constricted, so he unfastened a button on his t-shirt and ran his clammy hands down his trousers. Ensuring that he remained out of sight, Dylan paced a small section of street that was located a handful of yards away from the house. He silenced the stubborn voice in his head that was telling him he was about to make a big mistake. Like a bolt of lightning, a fierce flashback ripped through his mind. Dylan had been transported back in time fifteen years, and he now felt like he was standing in the exact same spot, reliving the tragedy. Despite the road being quiet, he could hear the sound of agitated voices bellowing commands. He could see the flames of the fire rising like a volcano out of the barn, the heat landing on his face like he was standing at the foot of a giant bonfire. He could taste the smoke, the vapours seeping in through his nose and mouth until he could no longer breathe. The cyclone of memories caused carnage as it ripped its way through his susceptible mind, leaving Dylan feeling more vulnerable than ever.

Having dealt with the symptoms of his post-traumatic stress disorder before, Dylan fought back and dragged himself out of the blinding daze. 'Pull yourself together,' he muttered, taking a calming breath. Like he had done so many times in the past when grief and anxiety had taken hold of his emotions, Dylan stilled his mind and listened for inspiration. But no matter how hard he tried, all he could hear were the whistles and whines from a murmuration of nearby starlings. On previous occasions, when he had drawn upon the same technique, it had felt like he was hearing the quiet voice of a guiding, spiritual entity, or even the familiar tones of an old friend offering words of encouragement. But today, Dylan felt like he was walking his path alone.

A quick glance at his phone confirmed that it was time to face the house that he had avoided encroaching upon for so many years. A haunting expression hung from his face, the sadness bearing witness to a lingering memory. Like an owl ruffling its feathers, Dylan shook his arms to dislodge the stubborn ghosts clinging to his skin like an unwanted parade of parasites. He paced up the road and approached the front door to Lunar, lingering on the porch. He pressed his finger against the cracked doorbell before his nerves got the better of him and waited, the imposing house dwarfing his frame. An uneasy feeling stirred deep within his stomach, encouraging him to take a step backwards while he continued to wait for someone to appear. He turned back to see if there was anybody passing the spot he knew better than the back of his hand, the pavement and road both deserted. The heat of the morning made his forehead perspire and a sense of discomfort crawled over his skin.

'Hi,' announced Fern upon opening the creaky door. 'You must be Dylan.'

'I am. Are you Mrs Jones?'

'That's me,' she confirmed. 'Please, call me Fern. Come in,' she insisted, indicating for Dylan to enter. 'Please leave your shoes on, it's messy in here and I wouldn't want you to hurt yourself,' she warned, side-stepping the clutter. 'I've been in the house for a few weeks now, and I know that it doesn't look like I've done much, but it's actually looking much better than it was when I first got the keys,' she explained.

Dylan stepped over Lunar's threshold for the first time in over fifteen years and paused. He planted his feet on the exact spot where he had always kicked off his shoes before charging up the stairs. Cradling his nerves in his arms, he couldn't ignore the strange feeling that hit him the moment the house's interior presented itself. Through dilated pupils, Dylan digested the bedraggled state of the hallway. He tried to come to terms with the unexpected level of disarray in a house he had only ever known as a cherished family home. With languid movements, he stepped further into the heart of the property, following Fern as she navigated the long, narrow hallway.

'We'll chat in here, if that's okay?' she asked, making her way towards the end of the hallway and through to the kitchen.

Dylan heard Fern's voice, yet failed to register her question. The appearance of the downtrodden interior enthralled his attention and numbed his senses. With a wandering gaze, he searched for the flickers of familiarity that his heart yearned to experience. He waited for his friend to appear like a whirlwind and jump on his back. He waited to hear his friend's voice, or the sound of the radio humming away like a chime of wrens in the background. He waited to be asked how he was doing today, and if he would like a cool glass of apple juice. When nobody appeared, Dylan frantically searched for other clues, like a family photo, a pair of shoes, or maybe a worn coat or jumper.

When no traces of comfort appeared, Dylan retreated into his own private world. He imagined how the house had once looked and sounded, recalling certain conversations and picturing where he had once stood as a child. A slack expression appeared on his face when another glance around the space presented such a contrasting picture.

'Are you okay?' Fern asked, noting his silence.

'Yes, sorry,' he confirmed. Dylan paced further down the hallway, treading carefully to avoid stumbling over the bits of clutter that were lining the floor.

Having positioned himself further into the house, Dylan began to identify glimmers of sentimentality shining through the darkness. He recognised the layout of the rooms, the floorplan unchanged from how he had remembered it as a child. Peering up, he further noticed how the imposing ceilings were still decorated with the original, intricate coving, a detail of the house that had always caught his attention. His eyes then landed on the cupboard under the stairs, and how the peculiar, slanted door was still fitted with an oversized knob. He could picture himself pulling on the handle as a child and diving into the secluded space during a game of hide and seek.

And yet despite these nuggets of contentment, the substance of the house still felt alien. Peering back towards the front door, Dylan could see that there was no bundle of coats piled on the bottom of the banister, and there was no comforting aroma of a home-cooked stew bubbling away in the oven. He also noticed the derelict nature of the walls, racking his brain to recall the specific family photos that had once hung with more pride than the famous paintings of a prestigious national gallery. Stepping into the blueprint of the kitchen, Dylan could see that the integral structure remained unaltered, and yet the feelings swirling in his heart told him that everything had changed. Through his eyes, the essence of the home had vanished along with the people, and there was no longer any love to be found at Lunar.

'So, what can I help with?' he asked, turning his attention back to Fern before the pause in conversation felt awkward.

Fern rested her hands on the back of a kitchen chair. 'Well, I've rang I don't know how many different trade companies since moving in, and I haven't actually been able to secure a single one,' she began. 'Nobody wants to take on this job and I don't know why,' she explained. 'So, basically it means that I need help with everything,' she joked to mask her vulnerability. 'I need as much help as you're willing to offer,' she said, exhaling.

'Can you be a bit more specific?' Dylan requested, silencing his doubts. 'Then I can get a better feel of what's involved and provide you with a quote for the work.' He peered around the space, shocked at how gloomy, cold, and dingy the interior had become over the years.

A flicker of hope flashed through Fern's heart. 'Of course,' she replied with enthusiasm. 'As you can probably tell, there's lots to be done in here,' she began. 'I've cleared this room out as best as I can, and now I need somebody to paint the walls and fit the new kitchen that I ordered some time ago.'

Dylan took out his tape measure and began to take some rudimentary measurements of the space. Outside, he caught sight of an old piece of rope dangling from a tree, once used as a swing, and felt his emotions waver beneath the surface. 'Do you know anything about the previous owners?' he asked. 'Was the place in this state when you bought it?' he added, trying to remain composed.

'It was worse,' she revealed, her eyebrows squishing together. 'The only thing I know is that an elderly gentleman lived here before me but sadly passed away.'

Dylan released a shallow sigh. 'So, apart from fitting the kitchen, what else are you looking for help with?' he asked, peering back down the hallway, once again becoming lost in his treasure chest of memories. The sombreness that he could feel saturated into the walls of the house made him question how many years had passed since he had last stepped foot onto the land at Lunar.

'Well, luckily nothing structural because I like the size and layout of the rooms. It's just lots of cosmetic work,' she began. 'The kitchen is essential for my business, so I'd like that job completing first,' she explained. 'And then in all of the other rooms, I'd just like the walls reskimming if they need it before painting, and then the floors need replacing,' she concluded.

Fern's heart sank the moment that she caught a look of apprehension appear on Dylan's face. 'If you can help me with *any* of the work, I'd be grateful,' she explained, close to tears when she anticipated him declining the job. 'Literally every tradesperson I have contacted in and around this area has been unable to even come and give me a quote, let alone agree to take on the job. For whatever reason, this house just doesn't seem to be an appealing prospect for a tradie,' she explained, trying to conceal her true feelings. 'So far, you're the only person that has stepped foot through the door.'

The house fell silent as she waited for a reply.

'If I do take on the job, there's something that I think you should know,' Dylan confessed, his arms folded across his body.

Fern's stomach tightened, and she chewed on the inside of her cheek. 'Okay,' she replied with hesitance. 'What is it?'

Dylan's posture became deflated. 'I found myself in the wrong place at the wrong time a good few years ago, and I was arrested,' he began. 'And although I was cleared of all charges, I got a mark against my name, and in this industry, reputation is everything. People in this village see me as trouble, but that's not who I am.'

Fern felt cautious following the revelation, his heavily inked arms pushing her to make a snap judgement based on appearance alone. 'I appreciate your honesty,' she began. 'If I'm being honest with you too, I'm desperate for a workman, so I'd be willing to take a chance on you, if you're interested in the job,' she explained. 'I'll pay you daily, then we both know where we stand.'

Dylan maintained strong eye contact. 'These are my hourly and daily rates,' he explained, handing Fern one of his business cards. 'And then you supply the materials. How does that sound?'

Fern reviewed the fees and produced a wide grin. 'Perfect.'

Dylan unfolded his arms and offered up a warm smile of his own. 'When do I start then?'

'Is now too soon?' Fern asked without thought, anticipating him to mock her bold, unorthodox suggestion.

Dylan held out his hand to seal the arrangement. 'Now is perfect.' He turned his cap backwards and removed the pencil wedged behind his ear before shaking her hand. 'Where should I start?' he asked, eager to make headways.

'Are you able to measure up for the flooring, and then once I get the dimensions, I can order in the raw materials? I've already bought the paint, and I'd like the same shade throughout.'

Dylan took out his tape measure from his pocket. 'Absolutely,' he agreed.

Fern walked out of the kitchen and into the hallway. 'But let me give you a tour of the house first,' she suggested. 'The only places that you don't need to worry about are the basement, and the barn outside. They're both completely different projects that I haven't budgeted for,' she laughed. 'That's the basement,' she explained, opening the door to reveal the dark, cold hollow, and steep steps that led down to the hidden room. 'This is awful to admit but I've only actually ventured down there a few times myself,' she admitted. 'There's another door at the far end that leads up some steps to an external hatch. Neither look like they've been opened for years,' she added. 'Do you want to take a quick look?' she asked, sensing his curiosity.

'Sure,' he replied, stepping forward and, without thought, reaching out his hand to where he knew the light switch was located, before making his way down. Once at the bottom of the stairs, Dylan peered around, the single exposed light bulb highlighting the dishevelled state of the Victorian basement. 'The ceilings are lower than I expected,' he commented, dislodged dust scattering over his head from the exposed beams.

Fern followed him down, surveying the foundations of her house for herself. 'I got a full survey completed before I bought it,' she felt quick to comment, spotting the state of the ceiling. 'Structurally, everything came back sound, but it does look questionable.'

Dylan pressed his hand against the exposed brickwork. 'It's just been neglected,' he replied. 'Once the ceiling joists are covered by drywall, and the walls are plastered and painted, it'll already start to feel like a more useable space.' Dylan spotted rusting hooks nailed to the walls that he knew were once used for bike storage, and the snug alcove that functioned as a perfect hiding spot for a slight ten-year-old. 'I think that's your electric box over there,' he commented, spotting the circuit at the far end of the room. 'I'd probably get an electrician over to give that a once over. It's not my area of expertise, but it looks like it could do with a service.'

Fern felt uncomfortable, a feeling of claustrophobia making

the veins in her neck protrude. 'I hate it down here,' she confessed. 'It just makes me crave fresh air,' she added, her stance wavering.

Dylan spotted the sense of apprehension in her body language. 'Are you okay?' he asked.

Fern looked at the rickety door that led up to the external hatch. 'I just need some air,' she replied, her brow feeling clammy. 'I feel a bit faint.'

Dylan clambered over some boxes and pulled on the external door that led up to the hatch. 'Can we get out here?' he asked when the door didn't open.

'I don't have a key for that door,' Fern confessed, turning to make her way back up the way she came. 'At least I don't think I was given one.'

Dylan followed Fern up the stairs, making sure that she didn't topple backwards. 'Here, get some fresh air,' he suggested when they reached the hallway, opening up the front door. 'It was pretty bad down there,' he sympathised when they were both outside.

He walked over and stood by her side, unsure what to say. 'Are you okay?'

'I don't really know what I'm doing,' she confessed. Fern peered at the mighty house like it was an enemy defeating her in a battle. 'For the past thirty years I've done nothing but be a wife, raise my daughter, and bake cakes. My husband took care of everything else, but now he's out if the picture.' Fern pressed her fingers against her eyes, stemming the flow of tears that were obscuring her vision.

Dylan turned to look at the house, leaning his back against the railings. 'This is a big project, but because there's nothing structural to alter, you'll start to see changes in no time,' he reassured.

Fern rested her back against the railings too, Dylan's words of encouragement halting her tears. 'Are you going to come back tomorrow?' she asked. 'Because I understand if you've already changed your mind. Given the state of my life right now, I can't promise that I won't cry again tomorrow, or the day after that.'

'And I can't promise that I won't cry either,' he joked. 'I was hoping that this job wouldn't involve painting, and yet here I am agreeing to paint a whole house.' More than anything, Dylan wanted to inject life back into Lunar and restore it to its former glory. He felt like he owed the old farmhouse that much. And during their brief meeting, he had already warmed to Fern, feeling like she was a kindred soul.

'I guess its lucky that I'm not asking you to paint the barn too, then,' she joked, peering over at it.

Dylan knew that the time had come. It was time to remove the blinkers that had been acting as his shield and to face his fears through fresh eyes. In the moment of silence that presented like a candle in the darkness, he felt a guiding force infiltrate his heart, and he knew that he was no longer walking the path alone. 'Can I take a look?' he asked, capitalising on his moment of strength.

'Sure,' Fern agreed, walking towards the side of the property. 'When the removal guys came, I got them to put most of my things in here,' she explained. 'So, I can't blame the mess on anybody else but myself,' she added, opening the door. 'What do I need with a barn?' she laughed, shaking her head. 'I don't think I ever stepped foot inside my own shed, or even used a lawn mower, and now look at me.'

'Can I take a look inside?' Dylan asked.

'Sure, go ahead,' Fern replied, taking out her phone and seeing that Jessie was calling. 'I won't be a second.'

When Fern left, Dylan walked into the heart of his nightmare, one slow pace at a time. The moment he was confronted with memories from his past, his eyes welled, and a steady stream of tears fell from his cheeks that he couldn't control. He peered up at the barn's roof, noting the sections that had sustained repairs. With his hand pressed against his breastbone, he allowed his chin to fall to his chest until the thickness in his throat dissipated. 'I'm sorry, Sam,' he mumbled, his voice croaky, the weight of emotion bringing him to his knees. 'I'm sorry.' He closed his eyes and tried to shake away the guilt that had remained by his side for the past fifteen years. 'I feel like I've been guided back here for a reason, and I'm going to do my best to make you proud,' he muttered into the darkness. Through the silence, he could once again hear the sounds of his childhood; the ripples of laughter and the commentary that underpinned their comradery. He quickly rose to his feet and wiped his eyes when he heard the sound of Fern approaching.

'Sorry about that. My daughter is seventeen and she still relies on me to sort out whatever catastrophe is going on.' Fern failed to spot the glossiness lurking in Dylan's eyes.

'You could fit a couple of tractors in here,' he said, walking towards the far end and pretending to look around, giving his eyes time to dry.

'Or I could knock it down and replace it with a lovely orangery.'

'Is that your plan?'

She peered around at the dark, dismal interior, the sight of all her belongings serving as a reminder of the unexpected turn of events in her life. 'It's a nice plan, but it's not a realistic one,' she sighed. 'My plan is to add some life back into the house so that my daughter will want to stay here. Everything else can wait.'

'We better get started then,' Dylan announced. 'I think I'm the one that needs some fresh air now,' he confessed. 'It's stuffy in here, isn't it?'

'Let's go,' Fern suggested, walking back outside. 'That's the external hatch that I showed you down in the basement,' she explained, walking towards the side of the house. Fern and Dylan stepped closer to the unorthodox means of entry. She rummaged in her pocket for all the keys given to her by the solicitor. 'I definitely don't have a key that fits,' she explained. 'Not that it really matters because until the basement is sorted, I have absolutely no intention of using this as a means of entry.' She placed the keys back in her pocket. 'If you happen to come across any keys in the house, let me know,' she added. 'Along with this lock, I also found a locked, wooden box in one of the rooms that also needs a key, so I wouldn't be surprised if there's a bunch knocking about somewhere.'

'Will do. Right, I'll go and start measuring up for the flooring.'

'That would be great. Thanks,' Fern replied. 'Can I get you a cool drink before you start?'

The way that Fern offered him a drink felt comforting, and familiar, serving as a welcome nod to the past that he had longed to experience at Lunar. 'No, I'm okay, thank you.'

'I'll be in shortly,' Fern said as Dylan walked away. She took out her phone and opened her notepad entitled: *Stuff to do on the house*. At the end of the long list, she added three new line entries.

- New lock for external basement door.
- Install security cameras?
- Knock down the barn?

For the first time since moving to the charming village a few weeks previous, Fern made her way into the bustling heart of Aldebaran on foot. Frustrated by the number of times she had caught herself talking to her own reflection, Fern found herself clawing for company. Although she appreciated the friendship that had formed with ease between herself and Dylan, she found herself longing for female company, and the type of bond that she had once shared with Florence. With teary eyes, she took out her phone and scrolled through Flo's messages of apology, resisting the urge to attempt a reconciliation.

Peeking through the oversized sunglasses that she was trying to shield herself behind, Fern strolled into the village and soon arrived at Wildflower Café. She looked up at the sign, checking that she had the right place. A bell jingled the moment she opened the rickety pink door, her attempts at an understated entrance squashed.

'Hi,' greeted Edith when she looked up and spotted Fern lingering in the doorway. 'You decided to stop by after all,' she beamed, preparing a coffee for the customer at the front of the queue.

The lovely greeting was just what Fern needed to make her feel welcome. 'I'm sorry it's taken me so long,' Fern apologised, approaching the counter when the queue dwindled. 'I've been so busy at the house these past few weeks, and time has just passed me by,' she explained. 'But then I found your flyer about the coffee morning, so, here I am,' she said, holding her hands out and removing her shades.

Edith could tell that Fern had been crying; her eyes were reddened, her fair complexion blotchy. 'Well, I'm just glad that you decided to come.'

Fern looked around and admired the quaint, cosy interior of the snug café. The hand-drawn wildlife murals on the wall brought the outside in. 'It's so lovely in here,' she complimented, turning back to look at the oversized chalk board behind the counter. 'So, what would you recommend?' she asked, decoding the raft of options displayed on the menu.

Edith stuffed her tea towel under her apron string. 'The soup is a firm favourite with the lunchtime locals,' she suggested. 'Today it's lentil, cauliflower and cumin.'

'Perfect, I'll have a bowl of that and an espresso, please,' she ordered. 'Oh, and a slice of the lemon drizzle cake, too,' she added, spotting the selection of homemade cakes on display. 'These all look delicious and a bit of something sweet is exactly what I need.'

'Cake should be a staple in everyone's diet,' Edith joked. 'Take a seat and I'll bring it over,' she said after taking payment. 'You can sit on a yellow table over there, which means you're happy to socialise with others who might choose to join you, or anywhere else you fancy.'

Fern produced a slack expression and shook her head slowly. 'I don't think I'd be great company today, so I'll sit over there,' she said, pointing towards the window. She meandered through the café and perched herself on one of the high bar stools in the window, the communal nature of the seating making her feel less self-conscious about eating alone for what felt like the very first time. Placing her sunglasses on the table, she took out her phone and pretended to busy herself.

'Here you are,' announced Edith, placing Fern's order on the bench. 'Is there anything else you need?' she asked, taking a sip from her own mug of tea.

'No, that's fine, thanks so much.'

'Brilliant, enjoy,' Edith replied, walking back behind the counter.

Fern gazed out across the street and admired the row of quaint, hotchpotch shops. She wondered when, and if, Aldebaran would ever come to feel like her home, and she found herself yearning for a sense of familiarity in her new life.

'Nice, isn't it?' the elderly woman at the far end of the bench commented, glancing sideways at Fern in between slurps of her soup.

Fern glided her spoon through the creamy soup and took a taste. 'Delicious,' she replied, making eye contact and engaging in conversation.

'Have you tried the chicken and tarragon chowder?' the lady asked, dunking a crusty wedge of sourdough bread into her bowl. 'It was my late husband's absolute favourite.'

'This is actually my first time here,' Fern replied, turning her body to face the lady, realising after all that her company could be endearing to others. 'I've only just moved to the area.'

'I like it so much that I've lived here all my life,' the lady beamed with a sense of pride. 'Whereabouts have you moved to? I'm familiar with most parts,' she said, relishing the moment to talk to someone, knowing that when she got home, she wouldn't see or speak to another person until her next venture into the village.

Fern placed her spoon down and wiped her mouth with a napkin. 'I've moved into an old farmhouse just up the road from here. It's called Lunar,' she explained, warming to the conversation. Fern caught an odd look on the stranger's face. 'Do you know the property?' she asked.

'How are we doing over here?' Edith interrupted, clearing up the elderly lady's empty bowl. 'Can I get you a slice of your favourite carrot cake now, Iris?'

'Not today, thanks Edith, I'm in a bit of a rush,' the lady replied, seemingly flustered.

Fern watched how the lady struggled to put her coat on, her knuckles inflamed and stiff, making even the simplest of tasks a struggle.

'I'll see you tomorrow then, Iris. Take care,' said Edith, walking back towards the counter.

Iris brushed past Fern's stool on her way out. 'Nice to meet you,' she said politely, nodding her head.

'Can I ask you a quick question before you leave?' Fern asked, placing her hand on Iris's arm, encouraging her to pause. 'If you've lived in Aldebaran all your life, did you know the family that lived at the old farmhouse before me?'

Despite the comfortable temperature, Iris took out a woolly hat and pulled it over her fine strands of white, wispy hair, her composure rattled. 'I knew the family well,' she replied, her eyes glossy. She took out a tissue and dabbed her cheeks, releasing Fern's hand from her arm before stepping outside and walking away.

'How was the soup?' Edith asked, straightening out the vacant stools in the window.

Fern looked up at Edith before looking back out of the window, seeing that the elderly lady had vanished. 'It was super tasty,' she began. 'That lady who just left — Iris, was it?' she asked. 'Do you know her well?'

Edith smiled. 'Iris is a lunchtime regular. I can set my watch by her, she's that punctual.'

'I was asking if she knew the family that lived at Lunar before me, and she seemed a bit... upset, I guess would be the word.' Fern displayed a worrisome look. 'I hope I didn't upset her.'

'The man had a family?' Edith questioned, picking up on Fern's comment.

'I think so,' Fern replied, looking out after the elderly lady before turning back to address Edith. 'I found a photo in the kitchen. It was of two children alongside who I can only assume were their parents, maybe Mr Sloan and his wife, or partner.' She turned and looked back outside. 'I hope Iris is okay.'

Edith perched herself on a stool next to Fern in a relaxed fashion, resting her arms on the bench. 'Iris lost her husband in May this year,' she began to explain. 'I think they'd been married for over fifty years, and even though she says she's fine, you can see in her eyes that she's lonely. So, it's probably nothing that you will have said. In fact, I'm sure she'll have appreciated the little chat.' Edith peered out of the window. 'Can you imagine being married to someone for over fifty years?' she pondered, her thoughts becoming lost in the postcard-worthy scenery. Drawing her attention back inside, Edith spotted a white mark on Fern's wedding finger where a band must have once sat.

'I'm in the process of getting divorced, so no, I can't imagine how fifty years would feel,' Fern blurted in a moment of honesty, looking up. 'My husband cheated on me… with my best friend. We'd been married for nearly thirty years,' she revealed in staggered bursts. 'He was my first love, but hopefully won't be my last.'

The two women sat in silence for a moment. 'I'm so sorry,' Edith replied, rummaging in her pocket for a clean tissue and handing it to Fern.

Fern wiped her eyes, still unable to speak about Cooper without bearing her true emotions. 'The thing that bothers me the most is I really didn't see it coming. I had no idea,' she explained, the hurt evident in her words. 'I've lost my husband, my best friend, and my home,' she said.

Edith fidgeted on her stool, the incoming rays of sunshine accentuating the tones in her golden tan. 'It's probably hard to believe right now, but something better will be on its way to you,' she explained. 'You just have to keep going,' she said, dipping her head to catch Fern's gaze, 'and trust that things will get better.'

Fern locked eyes with Edith and appreciated the morale boost. 'The only thing that has come into my life is the house, and at the moment, it doesn't feel better than what I had before.'

'How's all the decorating coming along?' Edith asked, turning to check that nobody was waiting at the counter to be served.

'I feel like I've made good progress,' Fern laughed, wiping her face again. 'I managed to get a tradesman onboard. He's just a local handyman, but Dylan's been brilliant and he's done so much to help me already. Most rooms have been painted, which has already made such a massive difference. I have a new fully functioning kitchen — well, almost functioning, there are just a few bits to finish. And then the next big job is to fit the new flooring. But all the rooms are feeling more homely, so hopefully my daughter will want to stay over and test the new bed that I've bought her.'

Edith raised her eyebrows. 'Did you say Dylan? Is that Dylan Wallace, by any chance?' she questioned. 'Handsome fella with loads of tattoos covering his arms?'

Fern nodded. 'I know he has a reputation because he was super honest with me before I took him on. But he's been nothing but brilliant. I couldn't have done the work without his help.'

Edith placed her tray down. 'Just be cautious. The regulars that come in here don't have a good word to say about him, and certainly wouldn't want him working in their house.'

'Luckily, there's nothing to steal at my place, if that was his intention,' Fern joked. 'And he'd be welcome to take the stuff that I've got stored in the barn. Most of it reminds me of my husband so he'd be doing me a favour.' Fern's sarcasm reflected her inner turmoil, and despite the steps she'd taken to move on with her life, her thoughts were still firmly planted in the roots of her past.

'Hopefully Dylan will prove everyone wrong,' Edith said. 'Oh, by the way, I've put some of your business cards over there, and I've already had people asking about your cakes,' Edith smiled, pointing towards the counter.

'Great. Thanks. It's so quirky in here, I love it,' Fern commented, spotting all the mason jars that were dotted about, each filled with fresh flowers. 'Is this your own place?'

Edith followed her gaze. 'Yep, I bought it a few years ago, and although it was a struggle at first, financially, it's doing really well now,' she beamed.

'Have you always lived here?' Fern asked, enjoying Edith's company.

'No, I only moved to the area when I bought this place. Wish I'd done it sooner, to be honest.'

Fern gazed out of the window, admiring the way blooming wisteria trees stretched across shop windows, colourful strips of bunting adding to the charm of the village. She watched how strangers smiled at one another as they passed on the pavement, sometimes exchanging a few words as they did, and she hoped to find a little slice of such happiness for herself. 'It does seem like a lovely place.'

'It's officially an area of outstanding natural beauty,' Edith boasted in her best posh accent. 'How could anyone not love these golden-coloured, stone-built houses?' she asked, pointing out of the window. 'And the rolling hills just add to the charm, I guess,' she mused. 'Most of the men seem to be married though,' she laughed, rolling her eyes when a tall, handsome fella walked past the window with his arm wrapped around a stunning young woman.

'Who needs a husband?' Fern mocked. In the distance, across the street, she spotted Iris taking a seat on a bench. 'Anyway, I best get going. The house won't decorate itself,' she said, slipping her hands into her jacket sleeve. 'I'm sure I'll be back. Apparently, your chicken chowder is delicious.'

Edith stood up, too. 'Good luck with the house,' she commented. 'I can't wait to see what you've been up to.'

'Would you like to come over one night after work? My cooker is waiting to be connected, but I can order us some pizzas.'

Edith jumped at the invitation without hesitation. 'That would be great. I'd love to see how you're getting on.'

'Brilliant. You'll be my first official guest.'

'I'm honoured,' Edith smiled. She fixed her collection of gold necklaces that had become caught in her hair, the stack of bangles on her wrist jangling with each move.

'And, I've got something to show you. Something that I found at the house,' Fern revealed.

'Oh?' questioned Edith, looking puzzled.

'When you came over, I couldn't help but to feel saddened by your memories of Mr Sloan, the previous owner. Anyway, I found something that might shed more light on his life and I thought of you.'

'Oh, I'm intrigued,' Edith replied, wondering what Fern had uncovered. 'Just let me know when is best for you, and I'll bring some leftover cake,' she offered, writing her number down and handing it to Fern. 'Or just pop back in. I'm always here.'

'Super. I'll be in touch,' Fern smiled, holding up her hand before opening the door and leaving.

Out on the street, Fern crossed the road, side-stepping a dotting of cars, and hurried to catch up with Iris. 'Hello again,' she announced, walking alongside the frail pensioner. 'I'm so glad that I've bumped into you again,' she said, breathless.

'I'm just on my way home,' Iris replied, struggling to carry her bag of shopping in her arthritic hand, the pint of full-fat milk and carton of eggs weighing heavy on her fingers.

'Here, let me help you,' Fern offered, taking hold of the brimming bag. 'I'll walk with you. I'm going this way too and it's a bit of a steep hill, especially when you're carrying shopping,' she encouraged, walking alongside Iris. 'It's a lovely day, isn't it?' she commented, admiring the way a mixed flock of birds glided through the sky like heavenly gatekeepers.

'I feel the cold no matter what the weather,' Iris replied, adjusting her bobble hat. 'So did my husband, and even right up until the day he died, he was pestering about getting himself a new coat ready for the changing season which, at that time, was months away.'

Fern spotted the collection of gold secured around Iris's wedding finger. 'He must have really loved you,' she smiled, indicating towards the rings.

'I can't get them over my knuckles now, so even if I find myself a new, dashing young man, it looks like I'll always be my Henry's.' Iris paused for a moment, taking a moment to catch her breath, herself admiring what she knew to be a host of locally nesting house sparrows. 'I'm sure this hill gets steeper each time I walk up it,' she groaned, continuing to make slow paces.

The sight of Fern's bookend chimney pots came into view as the pair continued to make their way back up the hill. 'I haven't lived here that long, but in a small way, this is already starting to feel like home,' Fern commented, admiring the sight of her house as it came into view, the sun accentuating the dark blue-grey roof slates.

'Thank you for helping with my bag,' said Iris, taking hold of the carrier. 'This is me,' she said, approaching a gate.

'Oh, we're not far away from each other, are we? You'll have to pop over for a coffee sometime now that we're neighbours.'

Iris didn't reply, and instead, opened her gate.

'You have a lovely house,' Fern commented, admiring the single-storey red brick cottage, an image worthy of a place in a child's picture book. 'Could I ask you a question, Iris?' she asked, just before the elderly lady turned to walk away. When Iris turned around, Fern took her window of opportunity. 'I've come across some personal items that must have been left behind by the previous owner,' she began, her voice shaky. 'I know you mentioned that you knew the family, so I was just wondering if you could tell me anything that you might know that would help me track down any relatives.'

Iris raised her head and gazed out across the horizon in the direction of Lunar, like she had done so many times over the years. 'It was a cruel twist of events that happened over there,' she replied, her eyes fixed on the horizon, her mind lost in a muddle of memories. Her senses played tricks with her, making her believe that, once again, she could smell the embers of a fire and see billows of smoke, the smoulder rising from the rubble.

Fern could see the trauma lurking in her eyes. 'What happened, Iris? Can you tell me?'

The strength of the sun shone directly over Iris's eyes. 'It happened on the third of May, 2007,' Iris began. 'I'll never forget the date because it was my Henry's birthday.' Iris's bottom lip quivered, and her posture loosened, making her unsteady on her feet. She reached out her hand so that she could steady herself against the railing that ran the length of her path.

'I'm sorry for upsetting you,' Fern commented, spotting the glossiness in the old lady's weathered eyes. 'That wasn't my intention.'

'Would you help me inside? I feel a little light-headed,' she said, indicating for Fern to take hold of her shopping bag.

Fern took the bag and held out her arm for Iris to link. 'Yes, of course. Here, take my arm.'

Iris looped her arm around Fern's for stability. 'Thank you. I think I just need to sit down and get a drink.'

Fern helped Iris to unlock her front door. 'Would you like me to come in and make sure that you're alright?' she offered, placing Iris's shopping bags in her hallway.

'No, I'll be fine now, but thank you,' she replied, removing her shoes. 'My Henry always carried the bags for me. I should maybe think about getting one of those old lady shopping trollies,' she laughed. 'Thank you again.'

Fern stepped back outside and scribbled her phone number on a scrap of paper she found in her bag. 'Here, I'll leave my number for you,' she said, handing it to Iris. 'Call me if you ever need anything, or just fancy a chat. I'm only across the road and would appreciate some company myself.'

'Thank you, and bye for now,' Iris said, closing the door.

Fern crossed the road and made the short walk home. She took out her phone and made a note so that she wouldn't forget the date Iris had stated. *3rd May, 2007.*

9

Awoken by the sound of rain bouncing off her bedroom window, Charlotte couldn't sleep. Alone in her bedroom, thoughts of Lunar ran through her mind like an old fashioned, black and white movie reel. She grappled with thoughts of returning home, her instincts and experience telling her that in this weather, Lunar's basement would be leaking. She jumped out of bed, put on a change of clothes, and made a dash to her car, driving the short distance from her flat up to Lunar. Pounded by an unseasonal downpour, the window wipers on her Fiat 500 worked overtime to dispel the torrent of rain, the blades catapulting swathes of water from side to side. Agitated, Charlotte parked her car a few meters down the road from the farmhouse and silenced the engine. With her cagoule zipped right to the top and the toggles fastened around her chin, she made a dash on foot towards the sleeping house.

Side-stepping the pools of water that had already formed on the ground, Charlotte battled her way through the raging weather that continued to sweep across the exposed land at Lunar like a monsoon. The usually active nocturnal wildlife sought shelter and hunkered down, waiting for the eye of the storm to pass. Concealed by darkness, in a bold move, Charlotte walked across the porch and attempted to unlock the front door with a key that had once belonged to her. Wedged in the lock on the inside of the house, Fern's key blocked Charlotte in her attempt to enter.

Unperturbed, Charlotte made a dash to the hatch located at the side of the property, the bombardment of rain striking against her face, causing an irritation to her contact lenses. With fumbling hands, she grabbed hold of the smaller key on her chain, eased it into the lock and twisted, the stiff, unused latch releasing with reluctance. The moment she pulled apart the hatch doors, the overgrown sprawl of weeds parted, permitting entry to the set of descending steps. Keeping her hood wrapped around her face, Charlotte made her way down the cold, concrete flight of stairs, closing the hatch doors behind her.

Buried beneath total darkness, Charlotte's heart raced. She took hold of the remaining key on her chain and slid it into the lock. The internal door mechanism clunked when it was required to open for the first time in decades. With a bit of persuasion, Charlotte eased the door ajar. Before she could shine her phone torch through the darkness, a familiar, ingrained smell greeted her like a warm hug, wrapping around her heart and encouraging it to settle. Recalling the presence of an uneven step, she paced further into the basement, treading with a careful footing over the clutter scattered across the floor. With the torch on her phone switched on, she shone the light through the gloomy interior. A sense of relief and justification for her actions came when she caught sight of dripping water in the far corner. Peering to her left, she felt a pang of emotion when her eyes landed on the rusty, antique coal skuttle that was hung by a nail to the wall. It was exactly where the vessel had always been secured. Taking care to navigate the space, Charlotte reached up and took hold of the skuttle with her free hand, easing it down without any disturbance. Outside, the sound of the howling wind echoed unapologetically through the basement hollow, a perturbing noise that had always scared her as a child, and once again caused her heart to canter.

With a precise hand, drawing upon her years of experience, Charlotte positioned the skuttle in the far corner so that it would capture the leaking rainwater. Once in place and preventing any damage to the electricity box below, she knew that making her way back out was the right thing to do. And yet she didn't leave. Lunar still had hold of her heart. Her whole childhood was ingrained into the foundations of the house, and she didn't know how to sever the ties. In Charlotte's mind, separating herself from Lunar would mean separating herself from Sam.

Despite her best intentions, the lure of the upstairs proved too much, and before she could convince herself otherwise, she had climbed the internal stairs that led to the main house, leaving behind a trail of wet footprints. Maybe this time, her dad would be home, she thought. Maybe this time, things would have gone back to how she remembered. Maybe this time Sam would be home too. Charlotte anticipated how it would feel to see his red coat hung near the front door, and she longed to feel frustrated when she would inevitably trip over his abandoned, tatty trainers. Slowly turning the handle, she eased the basement door open.

All was quiet. All was dark. The subdued ambience that oozed like fungus from the sleepy hollow told Charlotte that Sam still wasn't home. Much to her disappointment, Lunar remained a stranger. Her miracle hadn't materialised and she felt deflated, despite knowing deep down that it never would. The light from her phone confirmed what her heart already knew. Her family were still nowhere to be seen. Dejected, she hung her head and turned to leave, finding herself paused in her tracks at the sound of dripping. It was coming from somewhere inside the house. Wiping her nose across her wet coat, she listened. Upstairs, she heard a bed creaking. In one swift move, she covered the light on her phone, sending Lunar back into complete darkness. She held her breath and lingered in the doorway, her blinking eyes the only movement.

After a few seconds submerged by a reassuring silence, Charlotte followed the sound of the dripping noise. A gust of wind swept across her face when she stepped into the lounge. In the far corner, she spotted an open window, the wind direction causing rain to blow straight in through the narrow gap. Without thinking, she dashed across the room and closed the window, preventing any more damage to the fresh paintwork that she could tell had been applied to the windowsill below. The moment the air tunnel had been sealed, one of the upstairs doors banged shut, the noise resonating through the entire house. Like a bullet, Charlotte made a dart for the basement door, scurrying back the way she came like a burrowing mole.

Upstairs, Fern checked the time. After being startled awake, she raised her head off the pillow. Dazed and bathed in darkness, she managed to convince herself that the noise would just be Jessie returning home from a night out. She settled herself again and prepared for sleep.

Suddenly, the noise came again. This time, her eyes opened wide, and she sat up in bed.

The glow of the full moon filtered in on her bedroom, offering only a glimmer of light to illuminate her lone silhouette. She reached out for her phone and, upon witnessing the time, spotted a message from Jessie confirming she had decided once again to stay with her dad.

I'm alone, Fern thought, slowly turning her head towards the bedroom door, listening. After a few moments of silence, the noise echoed through the house again, only this time it sounded closer. A surge of panic made Fern feel nauseous. Scared and alone, a feeling of vulnerability ate away at her bravery. She crept out of bed and peered out of the bedroom window, the storm clattering against the glass.

The ambiguous noise rattled again.

Fern grabbed her jumper and phone before cowering into the corner of the room, her back pressed into the crease. She held her breath and listened. The second the noise resonated again she scrolled through her list of contacts, her fingers shaking. Her eyes welled at the realisation that she no longer had an emergency contact. The noise echoed up the stairs, making her cry harder. She peered across the room towards her closed bedroom door, wondering who was on the other side.

With the phone still clenched in her hand, she scurried towards the door and pressed her ear against the wood, standing back when she heard a sound. Fumbling, she pressed her emergency contact icon and urged the call to connect. 'Cooper,' she whispered when it went straight to voicemail. 'I'm at home,' she cried 'and I'm scared.' Her eyes blinked in rapid succession through the nighttime gloom, her breathing laboured. 'I think someone's in the house, and I don't know what to do,' she said, her voice filled with fear.

After a few moments of silence, and with the phone still pressed to her ear, she placed her hand on the doorknob and pulled it open. Peering around the crack, the glow from the screen shed a flicker of light out onto the darkness covering the landing.

The voicemail to Cooper ended. She hid back behind the door and clicked onto her messages, noticing that the person she'd last sent a message to, Dylan, happened to be online. *I think someone's in the house*, she wrote, before hitting send. *I'm scared. Can you come over?* read her second cry for help.

Within seconds, her phone buzzed, and a reply came. The sound pierced the silence, and she fumbled to put her phone on mute. She read the message on the screen, *On my way.*

With a tentative step, Fern headed out onto the landing and slowly reached down to grab hold of a hammer out of Dylan's toolbox. Holding it aloft, she tiptoed across the first floor, illuminating each empty room with her phone. She leaned over the banister and listened. When no sound came, she paced down the stairs, her heart in her mouth. The hammer felt heavy in her hand the longer her fingers gripped the handle, her knuckles white.

The moment her feet landed on the bottom step, her gaze darted towards the back of the house. 'Who's there?' she shouted, hearing a noise. She pressed the side button on her phone so that it illuminated and directed the screen towards the kitchen.

Outside, the wind continued to rage, causing shadows to reflect in through the exposed windows. With the hammer gripped in her palm, Fern stepped into the hallway, her body weight making the floorboards creak. She pushed open the lounge door until it pressed against the wall. With slow steps, she moved into the lounge. The chill in the room sent a rush of goosebumps over her entire body, her limbs trembling. Stepping across the footprint of the room, she pressed her body against the wall and peered out through the small side window.

Across the house, a noise rattled again, making Fern's head turn back towards the hallway. Holding her breath, she followed the sound. Taking a few more paces down the hallway, she paused and pushed the dining room door open until it touched the wall. The room was empty, and all she could hear was the sound of the wind howling down the chimney breast.

A loud banging noise rattled from the back of the house causing Fern to jump and drop her phone. She scurried into the corner of the hallway and crouched, pressing her legs towards her chest. With an outstretched arm, she reached out and grabbed her phone before tightening her grip on the hammer.

A clatter rattled again in the kitchen. Tears trickled down Fern's cheeks when she heard a noise at the back door. She rose to her feet and with the hammer in front of her, she burst into the empty kitchen. She flicked the kitchen light on, catching sight of the old washing line that had come loose in the storm, the dangling wire clattering against the back door each time the wind howled in a northerly direction. Fern burst into tears as she stood and listened to the ambiguous noise that had echoed through the house, relief flooding from her eyes. *Oh thank God.* She released the hammer and pressed her hands against her face, trying to calm herself.

Fern heard a car engine and then the crunching of her driveway stones. She stepped into the hallway to see the approaching headlamps, light flooding in through the panes of glass sandwiched at either side of the front door. She grabbed a jumper that was hanging on the end of the banister before unlocking the front door.

'Are you okay?' Dylan asked, running towards the house when Fern appeared.

The moment he stepped onto the porch, Fern wrapped her arms around his body, pressing her face to his chest. He could feel her sobbing, her whole body shaking. 'Did you see anybody?' he asked when she pulled away. 'Are you hurt?'

She shook her head. 'No,' she began, looking back at the house. 'I was asleep and heard a noise. I thought someone was here. I thought someone was in the house.'

Dylan glanced in through the open entrance, an internal door slamming against the wind, making them both jump.

Fern wrapped her arms across her chest. 'And I heard a noise at the back, but I think it was all just the wind. The washing line has come loose, and it was banging against the glass.'

Dylan backed away and walked towards his car. He rummaged in his boot and took hold of a crowbar and a torch. 'I'll go and take a look around, just to make sure,' he said, closing the car door behind him. 'You go inside and keep warm. I'll be back in a minute.'

Dylan made his way to the barn, pulling on the door and checking that it was locked. Through the pouring rain, he shone his torch and surveyed the land surrounding Lunar. The wind blew through his hair, the rain causing it to stick against his face and partially cover his eyes. He shone the torch over the external hatch as he passed the side of the house. In his haste, he failed to see that the overarching weeds had been disturbed by hand, some of the weed stems torn and uprooted. Dashing through the wind and rain, he continued his sweep of the garden, confident that all doors and windows were secure.

Inside, Fern sat herself at the bottom of the stairs. She spotted flickers of light shining in through the windows as Dylan made his way around the house perimeter. She released her clenched jaw and, with deep breaths, tried to calm herself.

'Everything looks secure,' Dylan confirmed when he opened the front door, shaking off his wet clothes. 'I've checked all around and you're right, the washing line was flapping against the back door, and one of your bins had toppled over.' He closed the door and crouched besides Fern on the bottom step, resting his arms on his damp legs. 'Are you okay?'

'I am now,' she reassured, looking at Dylan. 'I think I just panicked.'

'I would have done the same,' he said. 'This is a big house, and it's exposed, especially in weather like this. But, we can make the outside more secure, and maybe you should look at getting some security lights installed.'

'That's a great idea,' she smiled, appreciating Dylan's support and friendship. 'I'm sorry I made you come all the way over here,' she apologised, embarrassed.

'It's no bother,' he replied, standing. 'As long as you're alright.'

'I'm fine, honestly.'

Dylan bobbed his head into the lounge. 'Should I quickly check inside too, just to make sure everything's secure?'

Fern stood up and walked into the lounge, turning on the light. She fell silent. Her face turned white, and she shook her head in a slow act of denial, like she had seen a ghost.

Confused, Dylan also peered into the room, following her gaze. 'What's wrong?' he asked, spotting the bits of furniture and soft furnishings that Fern had now moved into the room.

'Someone's been in here,' she declared the moment her gaze landed on the window.

'What? How do you know?'

Fern walked over to the bay window. 'When I went to bed, I left this window open,' she explained, pointing to the smaller, side window.

'Are you sure?' he questioned, seeing that it was now closed.

She walked across the room. 'I left it open to try and help dissipate the smell of paint. The fumes are so strong, and it makes me feel sick, so I thought if I left it open, it would help to aerate,' she explained, her voice shaky.

Dylan scanned the room, checking that the windows were closed. 'I'll go and check the whole house,' he said, leaving the room.

Fern remained in the lounge, curling herself up in the single chair. Upstairs, she heard Dylan's footsteps as he systematically made his way into each room. She peered over at the damp windowsill, questioning her sanity, and going over the previous night in her mind.

Moving downstairs, Dylan opened the door to the basement, and without heading down the steps, shone his torch down into the darkness. He could see that the external door was still closed, and seemingly undisturbed. The wet footprints went undetected as he closed the door and secured it into the frame.

'All the windows and doors are locked,' he confirmed upon entering the room. 'And I've popped my head into the basement, the door is closed, and we know that it's definitely secure because you still haven't got a key, have you?'

'No, I haven't.'

'I don't understand why someone would break into a house just to close a window. But more than that, I can't see how they got in either,' he said, checking the lock on the front door.

Fern felt a heaviness in her limbs, the ungodly hour catching up with her. 'Maybe you're right. Maybe I did close it after all. I'm exhausted so it's possible that I'm losing my mind and just forgot.'

'Well, there's definitely nobody here now, and everywhere is secured,' he said, trying to offer some more reassurance. 'I can spend the night in my car on the drive, if you want?' he offered.

Fern shook her head. 'I'll be fine. I'm sure in the morning all this will make sense,' she laughed. 'Thank you so much for coming over,' she said. 'And you got here so quick.'

Dylan looked at his phone, noting that the night was passing him by. 'If you need me again, I can come back, it's no bother at all,' he replied, opening the front door and heading out onto the porch. 'Anyway, I'll be back soon,' he joked, getting into his car and driving away.

Fern locked the front door, and triple checked it was secure before reaching to turn off the light. With heavy feet, she walked back upstairs and dived beneath the duvet, listening for ambiguous sounds until she fell asleep, her phone still clenched in her hand. Outside, the glow of the moon continued to cast shadows over the old farmhouse. Once quietness descended, a misty grey cat that had been lurking in Lunar's thick shrubbery returned to its original resting place having been disturbed earlier on in the night. The feline scratched around in the broken soil and, in a similar vain to Charlotte, who had walked the land only moments earlier, tried to reclaim its territory. Even after Fern had fallen asleep, there were still eyes wide open on the land at Lunar.

10

Hungover and having slept through his alarm, as soon as Cooper spotted a missed call from Fern he listened to her voicemail, dialling her number before it had even finished. 'Are you okay?' he asked, relieved when his wife answered his call.

Fern opened her door and meandered down the front garden in a pair of old wellies, the grass saturated from all the rain that had fallen during the night. 'I'm good, thanks,' she replied, her heart somersaulting when she saw his name appear on the screen.

'I've just picked up your message from last night. What happened? Are you okay? Can I come over?'

Fern wedged her phone between her ear and shoulder, and crouched down. 'It was all just a mix-up. There was nobody here, it was just the wind causing havoc outside,' she explained. 'Sorry I called you. I hadn't updated my emergency contact person in my phone, so I dialled you by mistake. But that's all sorted now. It won't happen again.' She snipped a few stems from her flower patch, the shrubbery blooming with an abundance of late summer offerings. The morning sun shone over Fern's face, making her squint. Her senses relished the breeze that whipped round her face like a coastal summer swell.

'I'm glad you called me,' Cooper revealed. 'I would've come over had I heard my phone.'

Fern secured the delicate bunch of flowers with some simple

string and looked back at the house. 'A friend of mine came over, so I was absolutely fine.'

The line went silent as Cooper tried to come to terms with the fact that his wife was making new connections. 'What friend?' Cooper couldn't refrain from asking, his tone snappy.

Fern replied with a sense of coyness. 'Just a friend. His name is Dylan, but you won't know him.'

'Oh, right,' Cooper replied, his feelings of jealousy soaring. 'Have you told this friend that you're married?'

'It's not like that. And anyway, I'm technically separated and soon to be divorced,' she corrected, walking back towards the house.

'Should I put the kettle on?' Dylan shouted from the porch, looking out over the garden, failing to see that Fern was on the phone. 'Sorry,' he mouthed upon realising.

Fern gave him the thumbs-up, secretly loving the timing of his loud comment, knowing that down the line, Cooper would have heard a man's voice.

'Technically, you're still my wife,' Cooper snapped. 'And I know where you live so if I ever need to, I can just stop by,' he asserted, his tone conveying his unease at the thought that his wife was moving on with her life without him.

'You didn't just happen to stop by last night, did you?' she questioned in a suspicious tone. 'Because if that's your trick, if that's the game you're playing to try and scare me so that I'll change my mind and come back to you, it won't work,' she replied, terminating the call and pausing on the porch. 'Dylan, I won't be long. I'm just nipping next door,' she shouted down the hallway.

As Fern made the short walk along the main road to her closest neighbour, she tried to dislodge all thoughts of Cooper. Her husband's snide comments wriggled their way under her skin and burrowed. She could feel herself seething at the thought that he might be purposefully sabotaging the new life she was trying to forge for herself in the Cotswolds. With a primitive bundle of flowers clenched in her hand, she approached her neighbour's house, Nebula, and put Cooper to the back of her mind.

Tired and dishevelled from her disturbed night's sleep, Fern straightened out her shirt and ran her hand through her unruly hair. Standing before her neighbour's enclosed private plot, she felt intimidated. The bold property remained hidden behind a brick boundary wall and array of mature trees and shrubbery.

Fern pushed open the decorative, wrought iron gates, and slipped her body through a narrow gap that unwillingly presented itself. She admired the red brick elevations and spacious garden that the house boasted as she snaked her way up the garden path and to the front door. Reaching out her hand, Fern pressed the bell. She could see that there were no lights on in the front room, the house eerily quiet. Peering over her shoulder, the overgrown garden appeared dark and imposing, only specs of daylight seeping through the dense canopy. Rather than the space feeling vibrant and inviting, it felt like the garden was acting as a barrier between the house and the outside world. Quicker than a hare, a grey cat jumped onto the windowsill, the sudden jerky movement making Fern jump. Feeling perturbed and following her instincts, she turned to walk away, at which point an elderly lady appeared behind a crack that presented in the door.

'Hello,' the lady mumbled, her back hunched and her hand clutching a walking aid. 'Can I help you?' she asked, glancing around uneasily, trying to gauge if there were any other strangers lingering at her front door.

'Oh, hi,' Fern replied in an upbeat tone, trying to conceal her sense of unease. 'I'm Fern Jones. I've moved in next door, and I just wanted to come and introduce myself,' she greeted, stumbling over her words. From the other side of the trees, the sound of Dylan's electric saw penetrated the thick shrubbery that separated the two houses, and Fern's features flushed with embarrassment, unawares of exactly how much noise she'd been making during the renovation. 'I brought you some flowers,' added Fern, holding up her offering.

The elderly lady failed to make eye contact and her eyebrows remained squeezed together, making her appear disgruntled. After an awkward pause and with some hesitation, the lady released the chain securing the door, and allowed it to open fully. 'I'm Olive. Come in,' she invited, holding the door further ajar, struggling on her feet and dropping her stick.

'Oh, here, let me get that for you,' Fern offered, reaching down and grabbing the stick, placing it back in the lady's wrinkled hand.

With hesitant steps, the lady turned to walk back through the house. 'Thank you. I'm nothing but a dithering old woman these days,' she explained, slowly making her way to the back of the house. 'And that's why I'm not keen on opening the door to strangers. You never know what you're going to be greeted with.' The lady shifted her weight from one foot to the other. 'I broke my left leg a few weeks ago and now everything just feels like a struggle.'

Fern followed the lady inside. The interior of the house felt dark, yet cosy, the type of setting you'd expect from a rural retreat. 'You have a lovely house,' she commented, recalling a time when her home had once felt so inviting. Full of knick-knacks, Fern could tell that the house was a loving home, full of character and personality once you broke through the intimidating exterior shell. On a side table that housed an old-fashioned rotary phone, she spotted a vibrant photo of a young boy, bundles of blond hair blowing in the breeze.

'If you follow me, I'll show you through to Arthur. That's my husband,' Olive smiled, permitting Fern no time to linger. 'He's watching the birds.' Olive pushed open the door at the end of her hallway. 'Arthur, this is our new neighbour, Fern. She's just moved in and wanted to come and say hello to us. Isn't that nice of her?' she announced. 'Take a seat,' she invited, pointing to the two-seater sofa next to Arthur's chair. 'Can I get you a drink. Tea? Coffee?'

'A tea would be lovely, if it's not too much trouble,' Fern replied, taking a seat and placing the flowers on her lap.

'Not at all,' replied Olive, turning to leave the room and closing the door.

Arthur turned to look at Fern, reaching for the hearing aids that were sitting on his cluttered side table, his thick-rimmed glasses sat squidged on the end of his button nose. 'This daft cat always tries to catch a bird,' he smiled, pointing outside. 'Every morning he tries his luck once I've topped up the bird seed,' Arthur explained with enthusiasm. 'And never once in all the years has it caught even a dickie.'

Fern made herself comfortable on the sofa. 'You have a lovely garden,' she commented, herself intrigued by the mischievous grey cat that had already caught her out. 'Once I have completed all the internal work next door, I'll start on my garden,' she explained. Out of the corner of her eye, acting discreet, Fern glanced at Arthur. His slight frame was hidden beneath a few layers of warm clothes, yet there was no hiding the signs of fragility that were scattered over his hands. Arthur's skin looked wafer thin, his bulging veins surrounded by a sea of age spots. 'I just want to apologise for any noise I've been making,' Fern said, still able to hear Dylan's machinery in the distance. 'I'm having a new kitchen installed and new flooring fitted, and I had no idea how much the noise travelled.'

Arthur fiddled with his hearing aids until one made a whistling noise.

'Have you lived here long, Arthur?' Fern asked in a bid to make conversation. Next to Arthur's chair, she spotted the same photo that she'd seen in the hallway. The little boy, who she guessed to be around age six or seven, was climbing a tree. It looked to be summertime; the blue sky only interrupted by a splash of wispy cloud. 'Did you know the previous owner who lived next door?' she added when no response came. Feeling awkward and unwelcome, Fern contemplated making an excuse and leaving. She caught Arthur looking at the photo next to his chair, a series of wrinkles appearing on his forehead.

'In recent years, I never saw much of Mr Sloan,' he revealed, just as Fern was about to make her exit. 'I don't get out much anymore.'

Fern reached into her pocket and took out the family photo that Jessie had found behind the kitchen door at Lunar. 'Is this Mr Sloan with his family?' she asked, reaching over and holding it out so that Arthur could look.

The moment that Arthur's eyes landed on the photo, his heart ached with an intensity he found hard to conceal. His eyes widened, and he appeared restless in his chair, the pain in his chest relentless. He allowed his eyes to admire the faces in the photo, and the way in which their smiles jumped off the page. 'It is,' he confirmed, his voice soft yet elusive.

Fern spotted the way Arthur's body winced, and his lips pressed together. She gazed around the room, spotting an array of pictures on the walls, noticing that some were of Lunar, the two cannon chimney pots easily identifiable. She squinted, trying to see if she could spot a date, or any other clues why Arthur would have them on display, but the picture quality was too grainy. 'Can you tell me what you know about Mr Sloan and his family?' she asked, sensing that there was a story to be told and a history to be aired.

A vacant expression spread across Arthur's face and Fern noticed the sense of sadness that washed over his eyes like a muddied wave. An unnatural stillness crippled his demeanour, and he appeared dejected, lost in his own world. With the old, crumpled photo still gripped in her hand, Fern spotted the boy's unruly mop of blond hair. She looked up and compared the child with the photo sitting next to Arthur, realising that it was the same boy. Just at that moment, the lounge door swung open. Olive entered the room, a mug of tea gripped in her hand. 'Here we are,' she announced. 'I forgot to ask about sugar, so I put one in.'

Fern jumped up and took hold of the hot mug. 'Perfect, thank you so much.' She placed the photo back in her pocket, fearful of pressing Arthur any further. 'We've been watching the naughty cat,' she commented, eager to change the subject. 'And Arthur is right, it is a playful little fella.'

Arthur remained silent, and without having to ask if her husband was okay, Olive reached out her arm and rested her hand on his shoulder, applying a little pressure so that he knew she was there, by his side. 'Thank you for the flowers,' she smiled, looking at Fern. 'Would you mind helping me to put them in water? Everything feels like an effort with this blinking stick, even the simplest of tasks.'

'Of course,' Fern agreed, following Olive out of the room. Just before she closed the door, Fern caught Arthur wiping his eyes. His gaze was directed at the photos of Lunar on his wall, and in that moment, Fern knew that the frail gentleman had been crying.

'There should be a vase in here,' Olive suggested, leading Fern through to the kitchen, taking hold of a glass jug and placing it on the central island. 'Would you mind doing it for me? I've never mastered the art of flower arranging,' Olive requested as she took a seat.

'This is a lovely room,' Fern complimented as she arranged the flowers. 'These are all from my garden' she explained. 'I'm no horticultural expert either, so I don't know the names. I just know they look pretty bunched up together.' On the island, stood in a decorative frame, Fern noticed another copy of the exact same photo that was in the lounge and hallway, the picture positioned strategically, taking pride of place. 'Is this your grandson?' she asked, taking the opportunity to have a closer look.

Olive didn't need to look to know which photo Fern was talking about, it was the exact same picture that could be found in every room of the house. 'No. We never had children of our own. I'm not sure if it was because we couldn't, or if it just wasn't meant to be. Either way, we've always been happy with it being just the two of us.'

Fern's closer inspection revealed that, just like those in the lounge, the picture had been taken next door. Her keen eye noticed that the tree the boy was climbing still stood in her own front garden at Lunar. Fern felt a rush of adrenaline surge through her body. She felt desperate to ask about the boy and to learn what Olive and Arthur's connection was to the farmhouse. And yet, something held her back. 'It's a lovely photo,' she complimented, admiring the professional photography that had captured the moment.

'Arthur worked as a photographer for most of his career. He's taken all the photos in this house,' she explained. 'Lots of the night sky, with this being a perfect stargazing area, and more recently, he specialised in wildlife photography, particularly birds.'

In a moment of bravery, Fern turned to address Olive. 'I asked your husband about Mr Sloan and his family, the previous owners of Lunar. And I feel like I might have upset him. And that was never my intention, so I just wanted to apologise. I'm keen to make this my forever home, and it would mean the world to me if I formed great relationships with my closest neighbours.'

Olive released a weighted sigh. 'Given our age, we weren't sure this day would ever come,' she revealed. 'And yet here you are,' she continued, a similar look of sadness in her eyes.

'Would you mind if I asked you about Mr Sloan?' Fern asked in a tentative tone. 'I'm just trying to find out if he had any family. There were some things left behind in the house that I feel belong to someone. I don't want to upset anyone or cause trouble, that's not my intention. I'm just trying to do the right thing.'

Olive could see the sincerity on Fern's face, and all she wanted to do was sit her neighbour down and, for the first time, talk about Lunar's past. 'I was hoping that Arthur might have broached the subject himself,' Olive revealed. 'What he has to say is his story. Not mine. And for that reason, right now, I don't feel like it's appropriate to talk about Mr Sloan. I do hope you understand.' Olive recalled the day that she and Arthur had discovered Lockie Sloan's body slumped in his chair. Despite telling herself that it wasn't her fault, Olive still hadn't come to terms with the way in which her closest neighbour had passed away, desperate and alone. And despite her innocence, Olive felt like Lockie's blood was on her hands.

Fern's arms hung by her side, her posture hunched and deflated. For a moment, it had felt like Lunar's history was finally going to land neatly into the palm of her hands, only for a sudden wind to dispel the opportunity. She knew there was a story to be told, and from day one, her instincts had screamed as much. Discouraged, she tried to mask her disappointment and produced a reassuring smile. 'Of course, I totally understand.' She finished her tea and placed the mug in the sink. 'It's been nice just meeting you both, and now I know who I'm living next door to. It can get a little lonely up here by myself.'

'The seclusion can take a little getting used to. But there's nothing quite like these views,' Olive commented, pointing towards her patio doors and out across the stretching scenery. 'And the peace and quiet is priceless.' Olive eased herself out of the chair to place her mug in the sink, her back momentarily to her visitor.

Without thinking, Fern took the opportunity to take a copy of Arthur's photograph with her phone. 'Oh, it looks like I'm needed back home,' she said, gesturing to her phone when Olive turned around. Fern made her way towards the door. 'My builder needs me to make a decision,' she lied, placing the phone back in her pocket.

'It was nice meeting you,' Olive said, opening the door for Fern.

'You, too,' Fern replied. 'And thanks for the tea. I hope to see you soon,' she added, making her way back down the path and out onto the main road. Sensing that Olive was watching her, Fern felt ruffled. She walked back to her house and, once in the safety of her garden, she veered to the left. Ambling through the shrubbery and trees, she ducked and dived to try and figure out from which direction Olive and Arthur's photo had been taken.

She could hear a rustling noise and looked around for the menacing cat from next door, expecting the feline to have followed her home. Jittery, with thoughts of last night's disturbance still plaguing her mind, Fern stopped and listened. With the grey cat nowhere to be seen, Fern followed the noise and dived into the tangle of undergrowth that separated her house from her neighbours. The leaves and ground were still drenched from the storm, nothing to be seen or heard apart from a scattering of dragonflies and fleet of ferreting beetles lurking in the shadows. Telling herself that she was being paranoid, just as Fern turned to retrace her steps, she spotted an area of flattened undergrowth. Clambering over a fallen tree branch, she inspected the ground, noticing that the weeds and shrubbery had been purposefully flattened by someone's footing or handywork. She could tell that the clearing had been created recently, a footprint still evident in the wet soil.

In the distance, Fern heard the sound coming from Dylan's electric saw as he sliced through floorboard panels. When she turned to look towards her house, she could see Lunar through another clearing that had been created in the trees. A tingling sensation developed deep within her chest, and her muscles tightened at the thought that she wasn't alone. She stepped closer and peered through the gap, spotting Dylan in the lounge. In that moment, she knew that someone had recently stood in exactly the same spot, watching her from afar.

11

Wrapped in her dusky pink gilet and bobble hat, Fern got in her car and drove towards the far end of Aldebaran, part of the village she still hadn't ventured to or explored. The warmth provided by the long summer days began to drift away over the tumbling Cotswold hills, leaving behind a sense that autumn had landed. In the distance, she spotted a flight of swallows migrating to warmer shores. The poignant show of freedom momentarily made Fern wish that she could just leave behind the tattered parts of her life and make a fresh start on a secluded shoreline, one impossible for Cooper to reach.

The subtle change in temperature made Fern contemplate the seasons ahead, and in particular, what her first Christmas at Lunar would look like. Where would she position her traditional, twinkling, Nordmann Fir? How would she manage to decorate the outside single-handedly? Who would Jessie choose to spend the special day with? The thought that she could end up alone with nothing but a microwave meal for one brought tears to Fern's eyes. Overwhelmed with the various gloomy scenarios, Fern parked her car in front of Shelby Central Library and turned off the engine. She took out her phone and checked the time before dialling. 'Morning, Jess. I just wanted to wish you luck for your first day,' she said in the best jolly tone she could muster.

'I'm on the bus, Mum,' Jessie whispered through gritted teeth, self-conscious about which of her peers could hear.

'I'll be thinking about you all day.'

'I'll call you tonight and we can have a proper chat, okay?'

'Okay. Love you.' The phone went silent, and Fern took a deep breath, trying to come to terms with the fact that her daughter was now of college age. She got out of the car and paced towards the library entrance, stuffing her phone in her pocket. 'Hi. My name is Fern Jones. I spoke with someone on the phone yesterday about using the microfiche,' she said, placing her hands on the counter, the fingers on her left hand drumming.

The young assistant produced a blank expression.

'The lady I spoke to was called Pippa, if that's any help,' Fern added, raising her eyebrows.

'Pippa is the manager. I'll just go and get her,' the assistant replied, walking off into a back office and leaving Fern lingering at the counter.

Fern thought back to the last time she recalled having stepped foot inside a library, and her heart landed on memories of Cooper. They'd met in the university library while they were both studying for a degree in Chemistry. As she continued to wait, Fern admired the high ceilings. She loved the way the first floor of the building wrapped itself around the central desk below like a sweeping cloak.

'Hi. Can I help at all?' a brunette lady asked, appearing behind the desk and taking Fern by surprise.

'I'm Fern. I think I spoke with you yesterday about using the microfiche,' she replied, her feet shuffling.

The lady nodded. 'Yes, I remember. Did you say you were interested in looking at historical editions of the Aldebaran Advertiser?' she asked, pulling open a drawer and grabbing a single brass key.

'Yes, that's right,' Fern agreed. 'Specifically, early May, 2007, if you have that edition,' she added.

'Great. Just follow me and I'll show you up to the room,' Pippa advised, walking towards the main, central staircase that led up to the first floor. 'We don't get many requests for the microfiche anymore. I guess most things can be found online these days.'

Guided by her hand, Fern made her way up the stairs, following Pippa. 'I've searched online already, but I was struggling to find what I was looking for, and it was only when I thought back to my time at college, I remembered using the microfiche machines to complete a study I was doing on the history of my local village.' Fern's attention was drawn towards the vast collection of antique books, journals, and other reading material that lined the swooping bookcases.

'We have one of the best local history collections in the county,' Pippa boasted, catching Fern's reaction to the stock. 'Most people are amazed when they visit for the first time.' Pippa moved aside a partition that prevented members of the public from accessing some of the private rooms, and then unlocked one of the cubicles that was located at the back of the first floor. 'Here we are,' she said, opening the door and inviting Fern to enter first. 'It'll be nice and quiet because nobody is allowed back here unless by appointment, so you won't be disturbed.'

In the small room, the microfiche reader was located on the back wall, and rows of cabinets lined the walls at either side. 'All the films are in here,' Pippa explained, unlocking a cabinet to reveal the boxes. 'The one you're after should be in here,' she said, rummaging through the drawer until locating the specific date in question. 'Yep, here we are. The Aldebaran Advertiser. This one is for May the first to May the tenth, 2007.'

With a sense of impatience, Fern watched Pippa load the film into the machine. 'You said that you've used the machine before?' the library manager questioned.

'It was a long time ago, so a quick refresh would be great, if that's alright?' Fern requested, watching what Pippa was doing.

'No problem. So, you use this dial to flick to the next slide, and then these buttons to enlarge, move around the page, et cetera,' she said, providing Fern with a quick demonstration. 'You sit down and have a go before I leave you to it,' Pippa suggested, standing back.

'Okay,' Fern replied, taking a seat and positioning herself in front of the machine. 'So, I turn the dial to flick to another slide, and then these are for finer details once I've found a page of interest?' she questioned, having a go at using the various functions.

'Perfect, looks like you know what you're doing, so I'll leave you to it,' Pippa said, pulling open the door. 'If you could let me know once you're finished, I'll come back up and lock the room.'

When the door closed, Fern turned back to face the machine, her eyes adjusting to the dim lighting of the snug interior. She pulled her seat closer to the machine, 'Please be here,' she whispered to herself, scanning the first screen of text, noting the date at the top of the page was May 2nd, 2007. With a scrutinising eye, Fern kept flicking the microfiche dial, moving the slides along when she didn't find what she was searching for. And then, just as she loaded the next slide, there on the cover of the newspaper was a photo of Lunar, a bold caption framing the picture, *The Boy in the Blaze*. Her insides knotted when she saw a photo of her house, dark billows of smoke rising like an inferno. She drew her hand towards her face. Sitting limply, Fern blinked slowly as she tried to digest the shock. Her eyes became dull, her stare flat the longer the image lingered in her view.

Fern leaned away from the machine, her back pressing against the chair, and she burst into tears. She momentarily placed both hands over her face to block out the screen, preventing the haunting image staring back. She hoped that she'd made a mistake. Maybe it was a similar house, not hers. Or maybe the story wouldn't be as haunting as she expected. Moving slowly, she peeled her fingers away from her eyes and brought the screen back into focus.

After a few quick blinks to dispel her tears, Fern studied the screen, peering closely at the photo of her house. She saw that the barn was on fire, flames pouring out from one corner at the far end. Despite the cool temperature of the room, Fern's skin felt like it was inflamed, burning to the touch, and a tightness took grip inside her chest.

The door lunged open, making Fern physically jump. 'Oh, I'm sorry. I didn't mean to scare you. I just wanted to check that you'd found what you were looking for,' Pippa asked, appearing in the gap.

Fern calmed herself. 'Yes, thank you. I shouldn't be too much longer.'

'Take your time. There's no rush.'

Fern looked back, releasing an exaggerated sigh. She focused her attention on the inset picture of a child on the screen, the churning sensation brewing in her stomach. She knew that the boy's face was familiar; his blue, piercing eyes that beamed with happiness. Fumbling, she quickly took out her phone, and compared the boy on the screen with the boy that Arthur and Olive had displayed in several places in their house, realising instantly that it was the same child.

Locked in a state of shock, Fern read the news article word for word. She digested the facts and swallowed the grim truth like a spoonful of distasteful medicine. With nobody else to call, knowing that Jessie was at college, she dialled Dylan's number.

'Hi, it's Fern,' she whispered when he answered.

'Hi. Is everything okay? Why are you talking so quiet?' he asked, peering out to the front of the house after thinking that he heard a car on the driveway.

'I'm at the library,' she replied. 'And guess what?' she said, her voice unstable with emotion.

Dylan downed his tools. 'What?'

'There was a fire at the house,' she revealed, her heart beating. 'I knew something had happened. I just knew it. Cooper was right all along. I should have listened to him.'

'A fire? What? Here? At your place?' he questioned.

'Yep. Back in May 2007. A fire broke out in the barn.'

'Blimey,' Dylan replied, hanging his head with remorse. In that moment, he wanted to tell Fern the truth about what he knew. He wanted to tell his new friend everything and explain his side of the story, and yet he didn't know how to begin. He sat on the porch floor and pulled his knees to his chest, a feeling of heaviness weighing down on his shoulders that, for over a decade, had never eased.

'The owners at the time, Mr and Mrs Sloan, were out when the fire started,' she relayed, scanning the text to ensure that she was explaining the story with accuracy.

Dylan could hear that Fern was crying at the other end of the line. 'Are you okay?' he asked, feeling uncomfortable.

'It's such a heartbreaking story,' she revealed.

Dylan lowered his head, knowing that he was about to relive that frightful day all over again. 'Was anybody home?' he asked.

The sound of Fern bursting into a fresh flood of tears travelled down the phone. 'Their son,' she cried.

For a few seconds, Dylan and Fern kept their phones pressed to their ears, and yet neither one spoke, the sound of their breathing the only indicator that the other person was still there.

'The little boy died in the fire,' Fern revealed.

Dylan raised his head and couldn't take his eyes off the barn, tears welling in his eyes.

'He was only seven,' Fern added, her face awash with streams of sadness.

'Are you okay?' Dylan asked after a few seconds, not knowing what else to say.

Fern's downturned features and shaking head denoted her reply. 'No,' she mumbled.

'What can I do to help?' he asked. 'Anything, just name it.'

'I don't know what I want right now,' she replied, her eyes fixated on the image of the burning barn, and in her mind, she could hear the harrowing screams of a terrified child trapped inside. 'The fire fighters didn't get there in time to save him.' Fern wiped her face with her sleeve. 'Apparently, some eyewitnesses stated that they heard screaming, and others just saw the flames rising in the distance.'

Dylan hid his face in the crease of his arm. 'That's terrible,' he said, trying to ignore the memories that were tearing through his mind with all the might of a gale-force storm.

'Mr and Mrs Sloan had a daughter, but she was also out at the time.'

'What a tragedy.'

'An older lad was seen running away from the house.'

'Running to get help?' Dylan questioned.

'I'm not sure. The article just says running away.'

Dylan shook his head, shaking away all the emotions that had risen to the surface like a clew of earthworms after a heavy downpour. 'Does it tell you the names of anybody involved?' he asked, preparing himself for Fern's response.

'Nobody could be named for legal reasons. It was an ongoing investigation at the time. But in the article, it refers to the boy that died as James, after the firefighter who found his body.' Fern pushed her seat away from the machine, and took a moment to savour the darkness and sanctuary provided by the room.

'Are you still there?' Dylan asked, looking at his screen to see if the call was still connected.

Fern couldn't help but think about the little boy's room that she had unearthed at Lunar, the contents now taking on new meaning. She now knew that the boy named as James had been building the train track, and that he had drawn the monster pictures. She knew how little James's hand had been, and that he loved his sister, recalling the teddy that she'd found tucked beneath his bed. 'I'm here,' she muttered.

'Do you want me to come and get you? You don't sound fit to drive.'

'Thanks for the offer, but I'll be okay,' she said, appreciating the friendship that she felt blooming between her and Dylan. 'I wonder what he was like,' she mumbled.

'Who?'

'James.'

Dylan couldn't help but produce a wry smile, fond memories finding their way to the surface amongst his layers of grief. 'From what you told me about his bedroom, he was a good little drawer who liked trains.' Dylan wiped his eyes and drew in a breath, pushing away his emotions and bracing himself to tell the truth.

'I need to return his things to family members, or at least someone who was close to him. It's just not right otherwise,' she said, getting up and walking towards the door. 'Is it okay if we chat in a bit, there's something I need to do.'

'Sure, I'll see you later' Dylan replied before ending the call, knowing he'd missed another opportunity to out his grief.

Fern zipped up her gilet and made her way out. 'Thanks for letting me use the room,' she said, leaving the keys on the desk before making her way outside.

The brightness of the day made her squint as she got into her car and headed towards Aldebaran's only church, St Mary's. She turned the radio off, leaving her with thoughts about James swirling through her mind. With her foot pressed against the accelerator, she sped through the winding country lanes. The quaint church came into view just ahead in the distance, the spire acting as a guide as it protruded high into the sky. Once she had parked her car, she grabbed her phone and called Dylan back.

'Hi,' he answered after only a few rings.

'I'm sorry for dashing off like that,' she apologised, getting out of the car. 'I just needed to get here before I changed my mind,' she explained.

'Get where?' he asked, walking towards Lunar's front door, expecting to see Fern's car pull onto the driveway.

'I'm at St. Mary's.'

'St. Mary's church?' he questioned.

Fern walked towards the graves located towards the back of the cemetery. 'Yes,' she confirmed. 'After finding out about the fire, and finding out about James, I just felt like I needed to come and, I don't know, maybe see if I can find his grave,' she said. 'I feel like I've come to know him, Dylan. This little boy lost his life at Lunar, at my house.'

'How do you know that he's even buried there?'

'I don't. But this is the only church in the village, so there's a pretty good chance.'

Dylan downed his tools once again and removed the safety goggles that he'd been wearing. He pictured Fern's location and knew that his friend's assumptions were correct. 'Do you want me to come and meet you?' he asked.

Fern made her way further into the cemetery, and with her arms folded across her body, she began to inspect each gravestone. 'No, it's okay. I'm already here.' She caught the solemn faces of people who were congregated around one particular grave, muffled cries drifting on the breeze. 'I haven't been to a cemetery in a long time,' she confessed, the sight of all the stones overwhelming.

Familiar with St Mary's, Dylan tried to picture where Fern was walking. 'Whereabouts are you?'

Fern reached the end of the particular row that she was inspecting, noting that all the graves she had passed looked undisturbed, unloved and uncared for. 'Are you familiar with the layout?' she asked, unsure if Dylan knew the church.

'My grandparents are buried there,' he revealed. 'Towards the side where all the benches are located.

Fern peered around, looking for Dylan's point of reference. 'Oh, I see the benches,' she replied. 'I'm a few rows closer to the church.'

Dylan could picture Fern's location. 'If there is such a thing as a nice graveyard, St. Mary's is a nice place to visit. It's peaceful,' he said, recalling his own experiences.

Fern treaded over the shrubbery that had entwined itself in

and around some of the older graves. 'It's so upsetting because some of these headstones look like they haven't been tended to in years, decades maybe.'

Dylan could picture the cluster of graves that Fern was referring to. 'Not everybody has someone.'

Fern continued to walk past each grave, reading the names etched into the headstones.

'You've gone quiet,' Dylan commented.

'I've found it,' she announced. Fern paused in front of a granite headstone that displayed a pair of little white feet and a dandelion clock caught in the wind. Her eyes glossed over when they landed on the name etched into the centre of the headstone. 'Sam Sloan,' she mouthed. With each blink, a tumble of tears rolled off Fern's cheeks, and she crouched.

'Did you say something?' he asked, bracing himself for Fern's reaction.

With her knees embedded into the moist grass, Fern wiped her face with her free hand so that she could read the gravestone inscription out loud. '*So little, yet so loved. Sam Sloan. 11th June 2000 - 3rd May, 2007. Forever in his parent's hearts, Lizzie and Lockie Sloan.*' Fern's gaze became unfocused, the letters on the stone merging until they became illegible, and she tried to blink away the fuzziness. Through the tingling sensation mounting in her chest, she took small breaths, gasps that Dylan could hear at the end of the line.

'Are you okay, Fern?' he asked.

'It's just so sad,' she cried, unable to hold her emotion. 'As soon as I set eyes on Sam's room back at the house, and the way it had been left, I knew something terrible must have happened. I could just feel it.' Fern read the words over and over, picturing what she now knew was Sam's blond hair and broad smile. 'Being a mum myself, I can't imagine how his parents must have felt. Leaving all Sam's things the way they did tells me that they never got over it. It's like life at Lunar stopped after the fire.'

Dylan made his way up the stairs, and into the small bedroom. He crouched down to where the little painted handprint had been pressed against the wall, and he placed his alongside. 'It shows how much Sam was loved,' he commented, trying to mask the sound of his own emotions. He sat on the floor, feeling ready to tell Fern about his connection to Sam. 'There's something I need to—'

'Oh, there's a card,' Fern interrupted, spotting what looked like a handwritten note that had fallen to one side in the wind. She opened it up, reading the words scrolled inside:

Happy Birthday! Thinking about you more than ever today. Miss you more than ever before. Much love now and always xx

'This card has been put here recently,' she announced, reading the words again. Unnerved, Fern looked around, still unable to shake the feeling that she was being watched. The eerie, cemetery silence added to her mounting suspicions, and she could feel her body trembling beneath her clothes. Perched high up on the ornate cross spire, she spotted a conspiracy of ravens. The jet-black birds croaked in unison and the rising pitch echoed through the cemetery. 'I need to find out who wrote this card,' she concluded before hanging up.

12

The sounds and scents of autumn settled over Aldebaran like a warm, knitted blanket. From the vantagepoint at her kitchen window, Fern wrapped a tartan shawl around her shoulders and gazed out across the dusky landscape that was framed by her newly painted casement windows. In the surrounding fields, she watched as the farmers worked tirelessly to harvest the rows of sugar beet, whilst in another direction, a frantic canine was being put to work. She admired how the sheepdog gathered a roaming flock and eased the herd down towards the barns before the temperature dropped too far. The farmers had come to feel like friends, the sights and sounds of their machinery a welcome hum that was now woven into the background tapestry of her new life. In anticipation of welcoming her first official guest, Fern set about making a fire in the lounge grate. After following some rudimentary instructions, her face lit up when the paper, kindling and coal began to burn in earnest.

Just as the flames became established and matured, she heard a knock at the front door. A wave of excitement made her dash like a child down the hallway. 'Hi,' she beamed, opening the door to greet Edith. 'Come in and keep warm,' she encouraged, shutting out the wind that was swooping around the garden.

When the hallway revealed itself like an unfolding peacock's tail, Edith did a double-take, feeling like she'd knocked on the wrong house. 'This is amazing,' she complimented. With wide eyes and a gaping jaw, she admired the internal transformation. 'I've brought these for you. Just a little housewarming gift.'

Fern took hold of the generous bunch of dusty pink lillies and selection of boxed cakes Edith had brought, touched by the gesture. 'Thank you so much. These look lovely, and these look delicious.' She closed the front door and switched on the candle-style chandelier, the five lights highlighting the subtle tones in the freshly painted walls.

'It really does look amazing in here,' Edith complimented, taking a moment to admire the decor. 'Very homely and inviting.'

Fern strolled towards the kitchen. 'Come and have a look in here. I think this is my favourite room in the entire house,' she explained, flicking on the spotlights to illuminate the heart of the old farmhouse. 'Dylan's done such a great job.'

Edith could smell the faint scent of home baking, like something sweet had not long since been rising in the oven. 'It doesn't even look like the same room,' she commented, running her hand along the copper-speckled ceramic worktops, spotting a stack of blueberry muffins near the windowsill. 'You must be so pleased with how it's all turned out,' she said, recalling how the dingy interior had once felt so cold and oppressive.

'It's definitely starting to feel like my home,' Fern replied, opening the fridge. 'Can I get you a drink? Wine? Prosecco? Gin? I wasn't sure what you like, so I bought a bit of everything.'

'A glass of white wine would be lovely, thanks, and I'm sorry I couldn't come for pizza like we'd planned. Things at work were so busy and I couldn't help but stay late.' Edith removed her chic black biker jacket and took a seat at the central island.

'Who needs pizza when we have cake and wine?' Fern joked.

Edith sat back and admired the new feel of the room. 'I have to be honest, when you first showed me around this place, I thought you were crazy for taking on such a *huge* project.'

'I thought I was crazy, too.' Fern placed the glasses on the island and took a seat. 'Cheers to new friendships,' she toasted, holding her glass aloft, 'and to new beginnings.'

Edith raised her glass. 'Cheers to that,' she toasted, taking a sip of her wine. 'It's like Mr Sloan was never here. Have you managed to track down his family yet? I know you were hoping to return some things that you've come across.'

Fern sighed and slumped herself in her seat. 'No, not yet,' she replied. 'But I do know that there was a fire here about fifteen years ago,' she revealed. 'It was outside, in the barn. A little boy lost his life.' Fern couldn't mask her sadness when vivid images of Sam popped into her mind.

With sadness evident on her face, Edith responded to the news. 'Oh, how awful.' She took a sip of her drink, her stack of gold bangles rattling with each arm movement.

'The little boy was only seven at the time.' Fern savoured the taste of the chilled wine. 'I just knew this house had a story to tell. When I first moved in, the small bedroom upstairs looked like it hadn't been touched in years. I was going to show you that first day when you came over, but you seemed so saddened by how Mr Sloan had been living that I changed my mind.' Fern peered into her glass, the punchy alcohol awakening her senses. 'There was a child's bed that was still made, toys on the floor, paintings stuck to the walls, clothes scattered across the floor. It was just how my Jessie used to leave her bedroom when she was that age, so I'm guessing that the bedroom must've belonged to Sam.'

'Sam?' Edith questioned.

'Sam Sloan. That was the name of the boy who died in the fire.'

Edith put her glass down. 'And you think that his room hadn't been touched since he passed away? How long ago did you say the fire was?' she questioned, finding the notion hard to swallow.

'Fifteen years ago, and I bet the room hasn't been touched in all that time.'

Edith took a long sip of her wine. 'I suppose that could explain why Mr Sloan was such a reclusive character. I don't think any parent would get over losing a child, especially in such tragic circumstances.'

'I read in a newspaper that Sam's mum and dad, they were called Lockie and Elizabeth Sloan, had gone out that day and left Sam at home. He had an older sister who was also out at the time of the accident.'

Edith's eyes glossed over, and she momentarily fell silent. 'Oh gosh, that's terrible. I don't know how any family would get over something so tragic.'

'It must be every parent's worst nightmare.' Fern topped up Edith's glass, noting it was already empty. 'I went and searched the electoral register for an Elizabeth Sloan. But it's only arranged by polling districts, and not alphabetically by person, which wasn't helpful at all. And there wasn't an entry for her in this area.'

'Have you tried searching for her online?'

'I did. But there were over 100 results for Elizabeth Sloan in England on the electronic register, and it included names like Lisa, Lizzie, Libby, Liz, Beth. Without knowing where she might be living, it was impossible.'

'You need more information,' Edith said, pulling down the sleeves on her jumper to try and warm her hands.

'Let's go and sit in the lounge. It's warmer and cosier in there,' she said, jumping down off the stool and grabbing the wine bottle. 'I know it's still September, but I lit the fire this afternoon. I just couldn't get myself warm.'

Edith took hold of her glass and followed Fern down the hallway. 'Oh, it's so cosy in here,' she complimented, the warmth from the real fire landing with a soft touch on her cool cheeks. The sound of the crackling coals and the sight of the dancing, deep-orange flames reminded Edith of her childhood. She could picture herself huddled around a roaring fire with her family, all keeping warm during the depths of winter. An aggressive, stubborn lump appeared in her throat that she had experienced before. She took a seat on the sofa alongside Fern, trying to dislodge her own painful childhood memories.

The glow from the fire was reflected in Fern's eyes. 'On wet, wintery nights, I think I'll really feel the benefit of this room.' She placed her glass on the floor and spotted the wooden box that she'd still been unable to find a key for. 'Oh, this is what I wanted to show you.'

'What is it?' Edith asked, also placing her glass down.

'It's a box that I found in the small bedroom.'

'What's in it?' Edith asked, intrigued.

'I don't know,' Fern giggled, the alcohol starting to seep into her bloodstream. 'I haven't been able to find a key.'

'Why don't you just break the lock?' Edith asked like it was the obvious solution.

'Well, I had thought of doing that,' Fern laughed. 'But it felt wrong breaking into something that doesn't belong to me.'

'There could be something in there that'll help you track down Mr Sloan's family.'

Fern raised her eyebrows. 'You're right! That's the perfect excuse to open it,' she said, standing. 'I'll go and get a hammer. I know there's one in the back room.' Moments later, Fern returned and crouched on the floor in front of the fire. With the box resting in front of her, she raised the mallet ready to thrash it against the lock. 'Here goes,' she announced, squinting. The moment the hammer struck the lock, the brass fixture shattered. 'Well, that was easier than I thought.'

'Take a look inside,' Edith encouraged, getting up and sitting alongside Fern on the floor. 'If it's full of money, what would you do?' she asked just before Fern lifted the lid.

'I'd pay for a speedy divorce. And then I'd take Jessie on holiday. Somewhere really fancy, like Bali or the Seychelles.' Fern eased open the box lid. 'Well, it's not money,' she laughed, taking hold of the silver, glittery card that was resting on the top. She opened the card and read aloud the words written inside.

Dear Dad,

It's Christmas Eve and I just wanted to wish you a very merry

Christmas. I find this time of year so tough without Sam. Thoughts of him are never far from my mind, no matter what the time of year. But Sam did love Christmas, didn't he? Do you remember how excited he used to get when he could turn the calendar page over to reveal December? He couldn't wait to charge down the stairs on Christmas morning and see if there were any presents waiting for him under the tree. I miss him so much. My heart hurts and there will always be a piece of it missing. Sometimes it hurts so much it feels like it all happened only yesterday. Is this the same for you?

As always, you remain in my thoughts. I'll be here should you ever feel ready to speak to me. Much love now, and always. Charlotte x

Fern placed the card down. Unable to control her emotions, she grabbed a tissue and cried into its soft pleats. Embarrassed by her outburst, she looked up at Edith, surprised to see that tears were also streaming down her cheeks. She handed Edith the box of tissues. 'Charlotte must have been Lockie's daughter. Sam's older sister, the one who was also out the day of the fire,' Fern said, picking the card up and reading it again. 'It feels awful to say, but I would never have left Jessie home alone when she was seven. They're still so young at that age.'

Edith blew her nose and threw the tissue on the fire, watching the fibres ignite and fizzle. 'Sounds like she and her dad didn't have the best relationship. Which is so sad because I know that he spent so much time alone.' Edith took another tissue and soaked up the tears welling in the corners of her eyes. 'I've walked past this house so many times over the past few years. I've never seen a car on the drive, or people coming and going. He must've been so lonely. And yet he had a daughter who wanted a relationship. It doesn't make any sense,' she explained. 'I'm glad that's it's not just me who finds all this so sad.'

'It is so sad, absolutely,' Fern agreed. 'I wonder if the accident drove a wedge in the family?' Fern rummaged in the box, the contents full of other handwritten cards, notes, and letters. She pulled out a few that Edith recognised immediately.

'Oh God. These are mine!' she exclaimed. 'These are the ones that I told you about. The ones I would push through on my way to work.' Edith could feel herself getting emotional, and she tried to conceal her face as she swept her hair to one side.

Fern sifted through the cards. 'Your kind gesture obviously meant a lot to Mr Sloan for him to have kept them alongside family memories,' Fern reassured. She selected another card and began to read it aloud.

Dear Dad,

I just wanted to wish you a very happy birthday. It's a big one this year for you. I just hope you're putting your feet up and taking it easy. As always, you remain in my thoughts. I'll be here should you ever feel ready to speak to me. Much love now, and always. Charlotte x

Fern shook her head. 'Mr Sloan was living here alone, struggling to cope with life, and yet he had family out there who were willing to help.'

With her bangles clattering, Edith reached out her hand and took hold of one of the letters from the box. 'This one looks important. It was sent via recorded delivery,' she noticed, examining the post office's pre-paid stickers on the envelope. She pulled out the letter and cleared her throat.

Dear Dad,

There are so many things I want to say, yet every time I have sat down to write this letter, my mind goes blank. The only thing that always comes to mind is how much I love you. Although it is exactly one year to the day that Sam died, I still can't make it through a whole day without crying.

Edith paused and wiped away her tears, unable to see the words on the page. She cleared her throat and continued.

Time has helped me to process things and to come to terms with everything that happened that day. I'm sorry that I let you and Mum down. And I'm sorry that it has taken me so long to tell you. But more than anything, I'm sorry that I wasn't there for Sam. I'll never be able to make things right. I'm the one that has to live with the decisions I made that day, and the consequences that followed. I have already lost Sam, and I don't want to lose you too. It would mean so much to me if we could meet in person, talk over the phone, or even just write to one another. At the time, me leaving home was the best thing for everybody. But I feel this is no longer the case. I need you in my life. You're my dad and I love you. Please let me know if you're willing to see me. And I'll be there. If not, I will continue to write to you so that you know I still care, and so you know that I have never given up on the hope of a reconciliation. I will always love you, Charlotte x

Fern and Edith were both overcome by a fresh wave of tears. They each took hold of their wine and took a sip, the warmth from the fire drying out their faces. 'I'm so glad that I didn't open the box by myself,' Fern commented, 'I would have felt even more upset had I been alone. It's just so sad. It's like something from a film.'

'It sounds like Charlotte blamed herself for what happened.'

Fern rummaged through the box, trying to see if there was a return address on any of the letters. 'Lockie must have had her contact details because she didn't leave it on any of these. Which is rubbish for me because it means I can't track her down. I wonder when the last one was sent.' Flicking through each card and letter, Fern searched for a date.

With two glasses of wine seeping into her bloodstream, Edith could feel herself relaxing. Cautiously, she held her hands close to the fire, warming her delicate skin in a way that felt so familiar. An aggressive flame hissed and spat, making her retreat a little. Sitting back, Edith wrapped her arms around her stomach for comfort.

'Are you okay?' Fern asked, picking up on her friend's sudden movement. 'You haven't burned yourself, have you?' she asked, concerned.

'No, I'm fine. It's just when I was younger, I didn't like fires, especially bonfires. I've been timid around open flames ever since.'

'I was always scared with Jessie at bonfires,' Fern recalled. 'She would always want to stand right at the front. She was fearless, even then.'

Edith took hold of one of the letters, allowing her gaze to fall on the heartfelt words. 'All this makes me want to try and make amends with my own family,' she revealed. 'Life is just too short not to give it a try.'

Fern looked up to witness the sad look that had appeared on her friend's face. 'Are you not close with your family?'

Memories from her own childhood made Edith want to burst into tears. 'No,' she began. 'I left home when I was young, and I haven't had a good relationship with my parents in such a long time.'

'I'm so sorry.'

Edith's gaze was drawn back towards the comfort offered by the familiar flames burning in the fireplace. Her thoughts became lost. For a moment, a tsunami of childhood pain came flooding back. 'It was my fault. I did some awful things. It was better for everybody that I left.'

'Where did you go?'

'I went to stay with a relative in Scotland. It wasn't meant to be forever. At least, I don't think it was meant to be a permanent move. But either way, I never went back home.'

'Do you ever speak with them?'

Edith shook her head. 'No. We just lost touch. My parents divorced and we all naturally headed in different directions. We just drifted apart, I suppose, and before I realised it, a decade had passed.'

Fern could see all the inner turmoil rising to the surface and pooling in Edith's eyes. 'It's never too late to try and make amends.'

Edith shook her head. 'I did try,' she sniffled. 'But it wasn't a two-way thing, and that felt even more hurtful.' With a tremble to her hand, she took hold of her wine glass and emptied the contents. 'I'm sorry for going on,' she apologised, drawing in a deep breath and wiping her eyes. 'We're meant to be celebrating you and all the amazing work that you've done with this house. You'll never want to invite me back at this rate.'

Fern admired the cosy snug that she had worked hard to create. 'If I'm being honest, it's nice to have some company. It's been lonely since I moved in, but now that the house is nearly complete, and more importantly, now that Jessie's room is finished, I might have some company soon.'

Edith caught a glimpse of Fern's vulnerability. 'It can take a while to settle into a new area. Have you met any of your neighbours yet?'

For the first time since the friendship between her and Florence had broken down, Fern felt like she had a friend to confide in. 'I went and introduced myself to Arthur and his wife, Olive, who live next door. They seem nice, but despite my best efforts, so far they've kept themselves to themselves, which is fine. And across the road, I've chatted briefly with Iris. She seemed friendly enough after our encounter in the café.'

Edith detected the hesitance in Fern's voice. 'I get the feeling there's more to the story.'

A nervous smile crept its way onto Fern's face, and she replied in a quiet voice. 'It's nothing really, just a weird feeling that I haven't been able to shake since moving here. I just get this feeling that someone's watching me.'

Edith looked taken aback. 'Who would do that?'

'There's nobody I can really think of. I did accuse Cooper, my ex-husband, but I'd like to think he has more compassion and sense than that. I'm probably just being silly. It's a big house, and with only me in it, I think it's sending me a bit crazy.'

Edith turned towards the window and listened as the tree

branches clattered in the wind, and she acknowledged that although it was a lovely house, it would be intimidating to live at Lunar alone. 'It is isolated up here. Why don't you put some security cameras up? Make yourself feel a bit more protected. Then you'd know if there's anyone snooping around.'

Fern laughed it off. 'It's probably nothing. I'm just not used to my own company. And you're right in what you said. It can take time to settle into a new area. I just need to find my feet, and I'll be fine.'

Edith giggled, feeling the effects of her second large glass of wine. 'I best start making tracks,' she said, knowing that it was getting late.

'Well, thanks for coming over.'

'No problem.' Edith placed her glass down. 'I'm so glad that you invited me. Anytime that you're feeling lonely, just call me. Chances are I'll just be sat watching something rubbish on Netflix.'

'What to do with all these?' Fern mumbled. Looking at the cards and letters.

'It's been nice learning a bit more about Mr Sloan. I think he was so misunderstood. Like we all are, I guess.'

Fern came across an envelope without an address, buried at the bottom of the box. 'This one looks different to the others,' she said, removing the contents. 'It's dated 2007, so it must have been written not long after the fire.'

'What does it say?' Edith questioned when Fern fell silent.

With the glow of the fire reflecting off her face, Fern looked up and read the letter aloud.

Dear Charlotte,

My life has fallen apart. I feel like I have no control and the bricks of my life just keep tumbling. I lost Sam, and there was nothing I could do about it. But I didn't try to stop myself from losing you, too. And now your mum has left. How did I get things so wrong?

I want to tell you to come home. But what is there to come home to? This house feels so empty. I would only be punishing you further if I asked you to return home. You deserve to be free. To be happy. And as your dad, there's nothing else in the world that I could want for you apart from happiness. No traces of that can be found here, at Lunar. At night, loneliness is all I have left. And that's all I deserve. When I can take no more, I fall into a deep sleep. Sleeping has become my saviour. I don't say this to seek pity. I have ended up existing in this house because of my own actions.

But I do often wonder where you are, who you're with and how you're getting on with your new life. If I was a better man, I'd pick the phone up and ask you these questions, or at least, tell you that I love you. Sometimes I feel like the toughest problems can be solved with the simplest of solutions. Maybe if I had the courage to send this letter, my problems would go away. I guess we'll never know.

As a man with no religious foundation, I have found myself turning to the Bible. So many of the teachings provide me with a great sense of comfort, none more so than Matthew 5:4: 'Blessed are they that mourn: for they shall be comforted.'

We were never very open with our feelings as a family, but I just wanted to let it be known that I love you, Charlotte. I always have done, and always will do.

Love, Dad

Fern placed the letter down with a heavy hand. Mr Sloan's words of loneliness became lodged in her mind and weighed down on her heart. It was like Lockie's feelings of loneliness were still clinging to the walls, and she couldn't escape his ghost.

'I can see how much this means to you,' Edith said, pressing her hand against Fern's. 'I'll help you to find Mr Sloan's daughter. She needs to have these, along with Sam's things.'

Fern stood up and walked to the bay window, looking at her

own reflection in the glass. She wondered if Mr Sloan had stood in the exact same footprint, feeling lost and alone. 'I just feel like I need to set him free. I feel like he's still trapped in this house.' She turned to Edith. 'There was obviously so much he wanted to say but nobody ever heard it, and I want to change that.'

The strength of the fire dwindled, and the raging flames dimmed to nothing more than a flicker. Outside, Edith could tell that the strength of the wind was picking up. 'I really had better get going,' she said. 'It's another early start for me tomorrow and I'm such a grinch if I don't get enough sleep.'

'Well, it's been lovely having you over. We'll have to do it again, only next time we'll have those pizzas.'

Edith grabbed her jacket and headed towards the front door. 'Absolutely. I'd invite you to my place, but my pokey little flat can't compete with this,' she replied.

'I bet its lovely,' Fern said, opening the front door, a flurry of leaves swooping round the porch in a frenzy. Like a pair of rolling dice, two thunderous clouds rolled in and erupted. Sheets of rain saturated the hardened ground, delicate flower petals scattering the floor like torn confetti. 'Take care getting home, its wild out here tonight,' she said, the wind scattering her hair.

'I will, and thanks again,' waved Edith as she scurried down the path, wrestling with the wind before making it to her car, regretting how much wine she'd drunk.

Fern locked the front door and began tidying, scooping all Lockie Sloan's letters and placing them back into the box. She grabbed hold of Dylan's hammer and instead of leaving it lying around until his next visit, she opened the door to the basement and made her way down the worn, disused steps. Switching on the light, she searched for his toolbox. The sound of the howling weather echoed through the basement as if it were a wind tunnel, and Fern heard dripping water. Concerned, she took a cautious step further into the room, trying to see if there was a leak. In the far corner, near the electricity panel, she caught sight of the precariously positioned coal skuttle that was capturing dripping water. Her heart fell to the floor. Her face flushed and her eyes appeared glossy. She sent a quick blasé message to Dylan, asking if he'd been the one who had positioned the coal bucket, or if he'd noticed the leak. Within seconds a reply came: *Hey. Didn't know there was a leak, sorry. I'll have a look when I'm next over.*

Fern took a hard swallow and peered around the room. Clambering over the boxes that were still cluttering the floor, Ferm made her way to the external door, pressing on the locked handle. She pushed down hard once, twice, and a third time, trying to satisfy her own neurosis. Paranoid and still clenching the hammer, she dashed back up the stairs and turned off the hallway and lounge light, plunging the house into a state of total darkness. Snaking the circumference of the room with her back pressed to the wall, she peered out over the dimly lit land. Through the side window, she scoured the garden for signs of movement. Her breathing became quick and shallow, and every slight noise caused her gaze to dart. Pressing her hands to the glass, she focused her attention on the clearing that she had uncovered deep within the shrubbery, sensing that someone could be stood watching her every move. The pelting rain continued to attack the garden with a volatility unusual for the summer. The blusterous wind struck through the dense foliage, and Fern felt like she was trapped in the eye of a storm. As the minutes passed, her heartbeat slowed, and the cape of apprehension wrapped around her body blew away with the wind. Her drunken eyes grew tired, so she curled up on the single chair huddled beneath a blanket, the hammer by her side.

13

Fern opened her front door and was greeted with an abundant collection of autumnal leaves that had settled in a haphazard nature across her moss-covered porch. A south-westerly wind had blown in an assortment of golden, orange leaves from the surrounding oak trees, the discarded foliage lining the moist wooden planks. Shining through the dark, dawn ambience that Lunar squatted beneath, vibrant shades of yellow could be spotted from the nearby mature sycamores. To perfect the cornucopia of colour, deep-red maple leaves completed the autumnal rainbow and paid homage to the musky time of year that had descended without apology over Aldebaran. Taking a moment to gather her thoughts after an unsettled night sleeping on the sofa, Fern gazed out over her garden and wondered how many leaves were yet to fall.

Stepping over the natural carpet of foliage, Fern made her way out of her front gate and headed down the main road. She jumped when a car whizzed past. The altered exhaust made a resonant, deep-sounding noise as the driver accelerated. Jittery, she looked over her shoulder to check that she wasn't being followed. Ahead of her in the distance, someone was approaching on the same side of the pavement. She held her breath and reached for her phone, fumbling to unlock the screen. A quick glance up confirmed that the man was clenching something in his hand. Her heart pumped faster at the thought that it could be a weapon. A long-handled kitchen knife was her initial assumption thanks to recent news reports focusing on the recent spate of knife attacks. Just as she was about to call for help, the passing stranger brushed past her. The stranger was in a hurry, not looking where he was going, his mobile phone still held in his hand.

With cold, shaking limbs, Fern pushed open the gate to her neighbours' house, Nebula.

'Hi. Thanks for coming over,' said Olive when she opened the front door. 'I didn't have your number. I thought that pushing a card through your letterbox was the next best thing. Every time I've nipped over, you've been out,' said Olive, indicating for Fern to follow her inside.

Fern stepped into the hallway. 'I've felt like a yo-yo this past few weeks. Coming and going so much that I made myself lightheaded. I'm just trying to get the house finished. And if that wasn't enough, I'm hoping to start work after having had a few months off,' Fern explained.

'What do you do for work?' Olive asked, leading her through to the kitchen.

'I make celebration cakes. Usually for birthdays and weddings.'

'Take a seat,' Olive invited, indicating to one of the island stools. 'And how is the house coming along?'

Fern cleared her throat and crossed her arms. 'The house is coming along nicely,' she replied, her voice wavering.

'That didn't sound very convincing.'

'The house is looking amazing. I'm so happy with how it's all come together. But in the process, I feel like I've lost my mind.' Fern rubbed her hands through her hair in a haphazard manner, the smile sliding from her face. 'Ever since I moved in next door, I've just had this feeling that someone's watching me,' she explained, 'and I feel like I'm actually going crazy,' she said, fumbling over her words. 'I think someone's actually been in the house without me knowing.' Fern blew out her cheeks before releasing the air and turning away to gather her thoughts. 'Actually, no. I *know* that someone's been in the house,' she corrected.

Olive drew in a slow, uneven breath, and her body froze mid-movement. 'That's awful,' she replied, noticing Fern's agitated demeanour. 'Have you called the police?'

Fern shook her head. 'No, not yet,' she revealed. 'It just feels like my life has been catapulted into the air, and I'm landing back down in one big mess. The police would look at me and sense the craziness.'

Olive balanced her walking stick and took a seat. 'Was anything taken?'

Fern's animated hands conveyed her sense of annoyance. 'No. That's the really odd part about it. Nothing has been stolen. Not that I can tell anyway. And nothing has been broken. Nothing has been vandalised. I think I'd have felt better *had* something been taken. At least then I'd have known why someone was doing it.'

'You should report it to the police so that there's a record.'

Fern flared out her hands. 'But what's there to tell? There's no sign of a forced entry, nothing has been stolen. It's just my intuition.'

'They might be able to do something. I'm not sure what. But if it was me, I'd be getting in touch with them anyway. You want to feel safe in your own home. 'Can I make you a coffee?' Olive asked, getting up and filling the kettle. 'I can make it Irish if that'll help with your nerves,' she said, a cheeky smirk spreading across her lips.

'Regular coffee would be great, thanks.'

'Do you have an idea of who would be stalking you, if that's the correct word to use?' Olive enquired.

Fern shook her head. 'I don't know,' she began. 'I lead a very uneventful life,' she confirmed, sitting upright. 'That was until my best friend had an affair with my husband. At that point, I guess my life automatically became quite eventful.'

'I'm sorry to hear that,' Olive sympathised, handing Fern her coffee. 'I bet you're wondering why I've asked you to come over,' she said.

'Your note didn't give much away, just that you wanted to have a chat,' she replied, spotting some scrapbooks resting on the island.

Olive hobbled across the room and lingered in the doorway. She listened and peered down the hallway before moving away when she heard Arthur moving about upstairs. She pulled on the handle, easing the door back into its frame. 'After you came over that day to introduce yourself, I couldn't get you, or Lunar, out of my mind,' she began. 'I've kept this secret for so long, Arthur's secret. But I feel like now is the time to talk about it. To talk about Sam.' Olive took hold of the books resting on the island and moved them in front of Fern. 'Arthur doesn't know I'm showing you these. But nonetheless, I thought you ought to see for yourself.'

Fern's heart jumped when Olive mentioned Sam's name. 'What are they?' she quizzed, confused. Her eyebrows pulled together in the centre of her forehead, wrinkling her skin.

Olive opened the first book. 'They're about an accident, or an incident. Whatever you want to call it. Something that happened at your house.' Olive's words sounded heavy with emotion.

The moment that Fern's eyes landed on the page, she looked up at Olive. 'When I found out how long you've lived here, I assumed that yourself and Arthur would have known about the fire.'

'I do,' Olive replied. 'I just wasn't sure if you knew about everything that happened that day.'

'I only know what I've read. A lady who lives further down the road, Iris Pepper, mentioned that something had happened about fifteen years ago, but wouldn't say what. So, I went to the library and found the newspaper reports,' Fern revealed, clearing the emotion clogged in her throat.

Olive took a seat next to Fern. 'So, you didn't know about any of this before you bought the house?'

Fern looked up at her neighbour and shook her head. 'The whole thing has really upset me. I find myself thinking about Sam, and I didn't even know him,' she explained, fighting back her tears. 'Can you tell me what happened that day?'

Olive pointed to the framed photo that was sitting on the island. 'Sam was such a special boy,' she smiled. 'He was so full of life and mischief. And he was always smiling. That's what I remember about him the most. His infectious smile.'

'Were you at home when the fire started?' Fern asked.

Olive looked down at her lap. 'I was away at the time. Staying with my sister in the Isle of Man. But Arthur was here. Alone.'

'Did he see what happened?'

'The night of the accident, I called him, as usual, to see how he was. But he didn't mention anything about the fire. He talked about the weather and what he'd had for tea that night. We chatted about the mundane. But he never mentioned the fire.'

Fern leaned in and admired the photo, her eyebrows rising. 'That's odd. How about when you got home? Did he talk about what had happened then?'

Olive shuffled on her seat, trying to find a comfortable position. 'I caught sight of the barn when I was driving up the lane. My stomach fell to the floor when I saw the damage because I knew that Sam aways played in there, especially during the long, warm summer months.' Olive paused, internally grappling with the memories as she voiced her experiences. 'After I'd taken my coat off and had a quick catch up with Arthur about my trip, I asked him what had happened to next door's barn.'

Fern could see how hard it was for Olive to relive the story. She watched how her neighbour rested her fingertips over the photo of Sam, the wrinkles around her eyes deepening. 'And what did Arthur say?'

'He said there had been an accident. A fire had broken out in the barn and Sam had been trapped inside. He knew Lockie and Elizabeth were both out at the time because he saw them arrive home, only to be greeted by two uniformed officers.'

'With living right next door, it must've been terrible for Arthur to witness it all unfolding.'

'Arthur isn't one to show much emotion. He's always been the same. He keeps things to himself. But I could tell how much it affected him. It was written all over his face. And when I tried to help and get him to talk about it, he said that he never wanted to speak about it again. He made me promise that I wouldn't bring it up. And so ever since that day, we haven't spoken about it. And if anybody ever asked me, I said I was away at the time, and didn't know any more than what was reported. People stopped asking after a while. It became old news to them. That was fifteen years ago.'

'I'm so sorry.' Fern held out her hand when she spotted Olive's tears.

'I've always wanted to be able to talk about it. To talk about Sam. Arthur knew how much Sam meant to me. The little lad was always popping over here because he knew I'd give him a few chocolate biscuits. And before he left, we'd always make sure there were no crumbs around his face so that his mum wouldn't cotton on.'

Fern studied the photo of Sam. 'It sounds like Sam was a joy to be around.'

'He really was. And not being able to talk about him has been so difficult for me. I feel like I've let him down, as though I didn't care about him. And nothing could be further from the truth. I don't think a day has gone by where I haven't thought about him.'

Fern reached over and put her arm around Olive, supporting her neighbour's frail frame. 'Sam would have known how much you cared for him. That's all you need to remember.'

Olive welcomed the comforting embrace. She relished the private moment to release all of her emotions. 'They say that time is a great healer, whoever they are. But I disagree. Time just gives you the opportunity to come to terms with the tragedy. Something so painful can never be healed.'

Fern released her physical gesture and sat back down on her stool. 'How did Arthur cope with everything that happened?'

Olive fidgeted with her heavy, gold wedding bands. 'Arthur

hasn't been the same since that day,' she revealed, before looking up to meet Fern's eyes. 'There's always been this look in his eye, a deep sense of sadness that I could see, even if others couldn't.'

'I can't imagine how hard it must have been.'

'And there was no escape from what had happened. In the days and weeks that followed, I would hear Elizabeth crying. Sobbing. I would be pegging out some washing and she'd be sat at the other side of the trees. It was the most heartbreaking thing to listen to. I could almost feel her pain in the air.'

'Were you good friend's with Lockie and Elizabeth?'

'Before that day, yes. We would spend time chatting with each other over a brew. She loved the garden, as do I. So, we always had that in common.' Olive's gaze became lost in her garden as she relived memories of old.

'And after the accident?'

'Arthur didn't want me going over there, and for the sake of our marriage, I agreed. I did go behind his back on one occasion, and even though I knew Elizabeth and Lockie were both home, they didn't come to the door.'

'Do you know what happened to Elizabeth?'

'Not that long after Sam died, I believe she became unwell and was taken away in an ambulance. She never came home. There were all sorts of rumours going around, and apart from Lockie, I'm not sure anybody knows what really happened to her.'

Fern allowed her attention to be drawn back to the photos of Sam. 'The reason I've been so interested in what happened is because there were personal items left behind at the house. Things that belonged to Sam, and I don't want to just throw them away,' she explained. 'I feel like I have this responsibility to return his belongings to his family.'

'I wish I could help you. But Elizabeth never talked about any relatives, and I never saw anybody visiting. There's obviously Charlotte, Sam's older sister. But she left home not long after the fire. I don't know where she went, but I've never seen her back here in Aldebaran.' Olive gathered the scrapbooks together and placed them back into the dresser drawer.

Fern swivelled on her seat to turn and look at Olive, the elderly lady now standing near the window, looking out over the garden. 'I know that Charlotte hasn't been back here. I found some letters that she wrote to her dad. And from what I could gather, Lockie didn't feel he was able to have a relationship with her. He felt she was better off away from Lunar. Away from all the terrible memories.'

'The fire destroyed that whole family. They were once so happy.'

Fern caught sight of Olive dabbing her face with a tissue that she'd pulled from her cardigan sleeve. 'I really appreciate you taking the time to share all this with me, I know it hasn't been easy.'

Olive turned around to face Fern and allowed the sun to rest on her face. 'I hope that there is some extended family out there. Sam's things should be treasured and handed to someone who loved him.'

Fern squinted, reluctant to divert her gaze, wanting to capture Olive's reaction to her next question. 'I went and visited Sam's grave,' Fern revealed in a quick breath. 'And I found a handwritten card, meaning that someone had visited not so long before. Did you leave the card, Olive?'

Her frail expression remained solemn. 'No, I didn't. I haven't visited the grave for many years,' Olive began. 'It seemed to get harder and harder each time, and I hated lying to Arthur. So, one year, I just stopped going, and I haven't returned since.'

'After everything that you've told me, I know this is probably a long shot, but do you think Arthur would talk to me about Sam? About the fire? Maybe he'd be willing to share his experience of that day. Anything could help me to track down some family.'

Olive got up and pushed her stool under the island. 'Arthur stands on the landing upstairs and looks out over your house every day. Without fail. And I know he's keeping secrets from me, which is terrible to admit because it's like there's a part of him that even after fifty years of marriage, I don't know. Maybe he will speak to you.'

Fern set aside her empty mug. 'Would it be okay if I tried?' she asked, getting up and walking towards the door.

'Of course. He's upstairs, I can hear him pottering about.'

Fern made her way through the hallway and up to the first floor. She spotted another photo of Sam, the framed picture hung on the wall. Seeing Arthur at the top of the stairs, she took a deep breath and calmed her nerves. 'Hello, Arthur,' she announced, reaching the landing. 'My name is Fern. I live next door. We met the other—'

'I know who you are,' he interrupted without turning to face his neighbour.

Fern watched ribbons of yellow smoke drift through the air when Arthur puffed on a cigarette. An ashtray on the windowsill was littered with old cigarette butts. The air felt heavy, and she noticed that Arthur's index finger was stained from the nicotine. 'How is my house looking?' Fern asked when Arthur remained silent. She took a step forward and stood by Arthur's side. Looking out over the golden landscape, she saw the farmers preparing the fields ready for the next year's harvest, the sun breaking through a collection of stubborn clouds. Her gaze then landed on her own patch of land. 'It doesn't look like I've done much from this angle,' she continued, her tone of voice light and engaging. 'But inside, I've made lots of changes,' she explained. 'It looks like a totally new house. You and Olive are welcome to come over any time.'

Arthur maintained his silent stance, his gaze focused.

'I like all of your photos,' Fern commented, looking around. She admired the wide array of wildlife photography on display. 'Did you take all these yourself?' she asked, hoping to draw him into the conversation.

The question didn't resonate with Arthur, and his silence continued. She turned back around and gazed out over Lunar. 'Do you remember the fire, Arthur?' she broached. Out of the corner of her eye, she saw the ingrained frown lines that had been carved into his face over time.

Arthur continued to suppress his voice.

Feeling uncomfortable at the awkwardness, Fern turned to leave and headed back down the stairs.

In a deep, bold voice, Arthur spoke. 'The fire is all I think about,' he began, continuing to look outside. 'The memories of that day are there when I open my eyes in the morning, and they're still there when I go to sleep at night. There's absolutely no escaping what happened.'

His words made Fern stop halfway down the stairs and she turned to look at Arthur, who was still standing on the landing.

'I know it must be difficult, but would you be willing to talk to me about your memories of that day?' Fern asked, walking back up the stairs. 'I'm trying to find out a bit more about the Sloan family and thought that you might be able to help me.'

'I can't help you. Not yet. I'm so sorry,' he apologised without looking at her. Arthur turned and walked into an upstairs room before closing the door behind him.

Fern peered out over her land, searching for answers to questions she feared may never be answered.

'Any luck?' Olive whispered as she walked up the stairs and joined Fern on the landing.

Fern shook her head and turned to look at Olive. 'He said he can't help me. Not yet. But I agree with you. I think he does have a deeper story to tell, you can see it in his eyes.' Out of the corner of her eyes, Fern caught sight of movement through the window. She squinted to gain a better view, watching as someone walked across her garden before pausing to peer in through one of the side windows. Fern's hands began to shake, and her face flushed as she tried to catch sight of the intruder, the person wearing a sports cap and baggy clothing.

'Are you okay?' Olive asked, noting Fern's change in demeanour.

'There's someone at the house,' she blurted, scurrying down the stairs. 'I must dash. Thanks Olive,' she said before careering down the stairs, pulling the front door open and running up the path.

Almost tripping over her own feet, Fern scrambled up the main road. Arching her neck, she looked towards her side window through the towering wall of trees, catching sight of the person as they turned to scurry towards the back of her house. Breathless, Fern bounded across her front garden and towards the back of her property, rolling her ankle as she stumbled. Panting, she burst into tears when she realised that she hadn't been quick enough, her back garden and patio vacant. Refusing to admit defeat, she continued to search every nook of the garden, and yet the person was nowhere to be seen. Fern fell to her knees in defeat. She cradled her face and cried, releasing a deep-rooted scream, just like the ones that had echoed from Lunar in a previous life.

14

It was a particularly dank evening in Aldebaran. A barrage of volatile clouds hung low and threatened to dispel an avalanche of torrential rain over the peaceful, sleepy village. The usual canopy of vibrant constellations had been put to bed. Not a single star could be spotted by eye, nor by telescope. Along the main arterial road, the sound of gushing water echoed beneath the surface like the resonance created by a distant waterfall. The hidden drainage system was still trying to disperse the remnants of a previous storm that had struck only hours earlier.

Spotting a break in the rain, Iris Pepper ventured outside and locked her front door. She side-stepped stagnant pools of water as she walked across the main road. Slow and steady, she made her way up her neighbour's dimly lit garden path, heading towards the house that acted like a beacon shining through the blustery, bleak evening sky. In anticipation of the next imminent deluge, she remained neatly tucked beneath her oversized golf umbrella. The waterproof parasol shielded her upper body the moment the heavens erupted as predicted. Her dainty feet squelched beneath a mudslide that had oozed onto Fern's pebbled path. The harsh conditions made Iris miss linking her husband's steady arm, and she wondered if she would ever come to terms with the fact that her Henry was no longer by her side. Iris minced as she walked. Her distorted gait made it look like she was suffering physically, and yet it was an emotional pain that caused her so much discomfort.

Lunar's shielded porch offered Iris some welcome relief the moment she climbed the slippery steps. The front door opened before she could even knock or reach out her hand and ring the bell.

'Hello, Iris,' welcomed Fern. 'Gosh, isn't it awful out there? Come inside and get dry,' she offered, holding the door open. 'I've been watching out for you. Had I checked the weather forecast, we could have rescheduled our little catch-up.' Just before she closed the door, a car tore down the road, the spray from the wheels causing a tidal wave to spill over the pavement.

'Here, let me take your umbrella,' Fern offered, taking hold of the dripping material and propping it up near the doormat, the water pooling on the floorboards.

Iris's body shivered beneath her clothes. 'I'll leave my coat on, if that's okay. I always feel a chill. Even in summer.'

'Of course. Let's go and get a warm drink,' Fern indicated towards the end of the hallway, through to the kitchen. She held out a seat for Iris. 'You sit here. I'll put the kettle on for us.'

Iris wrapped her padded, wax jacket around her slight frame. She took a moment to look around, trying to pick out areas of familiarity. 'I don't even recognise it in here,' she commented, peering around at the new kitchen. 'It's been such a long time since I've been in here. But I know that it never used to look like this.' The dotting of garden lights illuminated the patio area just enough for Iris to see the work that had been done. 'Elizabeth was always nagging Lockie about those crazy paving slabs. She hated them because the weeds would sprout faster than any flowers she planted.'

Fern poured the boiling water over the muslin teabags, relishing the moment of company that Iris's visit provided. 'It sounds like you knew the Sloan family well,' Fern commented, placing the drinks on the island, and taking a seat opposite Iris.

'I knew the family well, before the accident,' she admitted, her tone soft. 'But the fire changed all that. And I'm sorry for being so vague about the whole thing when we bumped into one another in the village that day. Having someone talk about the family after so long felt like a shock.' Iris took a tentative sip of her strongly-brewed tea. 'For the past however many years,' she began, her memory failing to work out the precise time scale, 'it's been easy not to think about the fire and the family. But now that you're here, and there's new life in this house. I guess it's bringing all my memories back to the surface.' Iris thought back to one of her fondest recollections of her time visiting Lunar. It had been a milestone birthday for Henry, and the Sloan family had decorated the front garden with balloons and bunting for him. 'Sam and Elizabeth had baked my lovely Henry this triple-layered chocolate cake. And little Sam couldn't stop teasing Henry about the number of candles they'd used.' Iris's face lit up when she spoke about her late husband. 'My Henry was brilliant with little ones. He had time for anybody.'

It moved Fern to hear Iris speaking so tenderly about her husband. 'I think the world could do with more people like your Henry. He sounded like a wonderful man.'

'He was one of a kind.'

Fern looked at her wedding ring finger. 'In a way, I wish I'd never moved here,' she confessed, internally grieving for the breakdown of her own marriage. 'I've never felt so alone since buying this place.'

Iris reached out her hand, an infestation of wrinkles decorating her skin like a crumpled piece of paper. 'I've been on my own for a long time, so I know what loneliness feels like,' she began, pressing her hand against Fern's. 'And you're not alone. You have me right across the road. And then you've got the birds for company, they'll never give you a moment's peace. And then, of course, we have the sound of the farmers for company, too. They seem to work longer hours as each year goes by.'

Fern smiled, acknowledging how many times she had already

sought comfort from the sound of the farmers and surrounding wildlife. 'Thank you, Iris.'

Iris sat back in her seat. 'Sometimes, I still forget that my Henry isn't here. I'll turn around and look for him, only to remember that he's gone,' she revealed, pulling her hand away and taking out a tissue, dabbing her eyes. 'I think most people would feel sorry for me and assume that I'm going senile. But they'd be wrong. I'm the one that feels sorry for them. I've experienced true love. Most people spend their whole lives searching for that type of companionship, yet never even come close.'

'I'm sorry,' Fern replied, looking up and spotting the glossiness clouding Iris's eyes. 'I invite you over, only to make you upset. What kind of neighbour am I?' she said. 'I'm hoping to make some new friends in Aldebaran. I don't want to put people off from wanting to come back.'

Iris took another slurp of her tea, wrapping her cold hands around the mug. She could hear the voices that had once bounced off the walls. 'I must admit, when you first moved in, and we bumped into one another that day, I was a bit standoffish with you, and again, I'm sorry. I couldn't bring myself to talk about the parts of my past that hurt the most.' Iris peered out at the garden. She remembered all the times that she'd launched Sam through the air on the tree swing that was once a prominent feature in the back garden. 'But I want to talk about the past. This house was once filled with so much laughter that I could sometimes hear the noise echoing down the road on a day when the wind blew in the right direction. I think it's about time some of that happiness returns to this wonderful patch of land. It's been long enough now,' she said, surveying the room again.

'Iris,' Fern began, placing her own mug on the counter. 'Would you tell me what you know about the Sloan family?' she asked. 'I obviously know there was a fire and I know that Sam died. I know that the fire broke out in the barn,' she began. 'But what I don't know is what happened after that day. What happened in the weeks, the months, and the years that followed? I've found all of these personal belongings that I want to place in the hands of someone who cares, and yet I'm having a hard time tracking anybody down.'

Iris savoured the collection of happy memories that rose to the surface like a sprawl of wild, spring daffodils in March. 'I spent so much time here looking after the children,' she replied, her gaze peering towards the ceiling. 'And the sound of Sam charging down those stairs always made my heart skip,' she recalled with tenderness. 'He was always scurrying about faster than I could keep up with. I was so scared that he'd come tumbling down and break his legs,' she explained. 'But that was just Sam's nature. He was always full of life and full of energy.' Iris unwrapped her jacket, the hot tea doing a splendid job of warming her up from the inside out. 'Elizabeth may as well have died in the fire, too,' she revealed. 'Because she never got over the tragedy. What mother would be able to come to terms with the death of their own child?' she questioned, her face grimacing at the notion. 'The moment the news was broken to Elizabeth that Sam had died, her hair turned white. It happened almost overnight. I've never seen anything quite so astonishing. And within a year, she was dead as well.' Iris lowered her gaze, the painful parts of her past raging like a stampede through her mind, leaving her emotions in tatters.

'Elizabeth has passed away?' Fern asked, her own expression bearing the weight of burden.

'That's what I think happened. Lockie said that she had taken an accidental overdose of sleeping pills,' Iris explained, shaking her head in doubt. 'But Elizabeth would have known exactly what she was doing,' she revealed. 'She wanted to be with Sam. There was no doubt about that. An ambulance rushed her to hospital, and she never came home. I never saw her again.'

Fern tried to digest the information, picturing in her mind which room Elizabeth had been in when she took her own life. The thought that another person had died at Lunar made her skin prickle. She felt a sinking feeling in her stomach at the thought that Elizabeth's body could have been found in the bathroom, the floor in there yet to be ripped out and replaced. Fern then pictured Elizabeth lying alone on the floor in the master bedroom, in the exact same spot where she now liked to sit and meditate as the early evening sun crept around to warm the room. 'And what about Lockie? What happened to him?'

'He never got over what happened either,' she revealed. 'He locked himself away in this big house for years and years. He kept himself to himself. He wanted nothing to do with anybody,' Iris said. 'And I tried to help him. I would knock on the door day after day. But he never answered,' she explained, taking in a sobering breath. 'And then one day, I shouted through the letter box that I wouldn't leave until he answered and so he came to the door. I could see the sadness that was drowning his eyes. It was heartbreaking.' Iris shook her head, trying to scatter the hurtful memories that clung tightly to her.

'Did he let you in?'

Iris peered down the hallway to where that conversation had taken place. She pictured the look in Lockie's eyes, and the way his body had been hunched over. 'No. He told me to leave him alone, and to never come back.' Iris looked out of the window, hoping that the change in scenery would help to dislodge the painful memories.

'Have you been to Sam's grave, Iris?' Fern asked, wondering if she was the one who had left the card.

'I attended the funeral, like a lot of the locals in the village. But I couldn't go back after that day. I find cemetery's such morbid, dismal places. And that's not what Sam was. He was a little boy full of life and laughter. And that's how I wanted to remember him.'

Fern cast her mind back to a conversation she had had with Olive next door. 'Didn't Lockie and Elizabeth have a daughter called Charlotte?'

Iris returned her attention to the table. 'Yes, Charlotte. She was a good few years older than Sam. She moved away from the area not long after it all happened. She went to stay with relatives, I believe. She never returned to Aldebaran either. Who could blame her? Her brother had died in a tragic accident. Her mum had committed suicide. And her dad had become a recluse.'

Fern gazed around the kitchen, trying to imagine how the Sloan family had navigated the space. 'It's just all so sad,' she commented. 'Did you know that Sam's room hadn't been touched since he passed away?' she questioned. 'When I moved in, all his toys were still in his bedroom. His bed was made. His clothes were left out. It's like Lockie was waiting for him to come home because he couldn't come to terms with the fact that he was gone forever.'

Iris began to cry like it was the day of the fire. Her sobs were heartfelt and deep like a child who had misplaced their favourite toy. The pain that had coursed through her veins fifteen years previous had once again awoken.

'I'm so sorry, Iris,' Fern apologised, this time holding out her hand, and pressing it against her neighbour's. 'I'm sorry to bring all of this up after so long. I should have known better.'

A warm smile spread across Iris's face. 'No matter how upsetting it is, it's nice to talk about the family,' she confessed. 'There were so many happy memories before it all fell apart for them,' she said. Iris wiped her nose, stuffing her tissue in her pocket. 'Nobody that remembers that day ever seems to talk about it. It's a taboo subject in the village. Always has been. It's like if people don't talk about it, then it never happened.'

'Did they ever find out the cause of the fire or how it had started?'

Iris nodded. 'They think it was started because of a cigarette butt,' she confirmed. 'And lots of people were questioned as part of the investigation, including myself and Henry,' she revealed. 'But nobody was ever arrested, which resulted in some local folk drawing their own conclusions about who was to blame.'

'And what was your conclusion?' Fern asked, sensing Iris had her own judgement.

'Arthur Aspey was a grumpy old man, even back then. He hated the noise that the kids made. Sam loved to play in the barn, which is obviously right next to his house. Arthur was also a heavy smoker.'

Fern's face grimaced at the news. 'Arthur Aspey?' she questioned, a sickening feeling brewing in her stomach.

Iris produced a small nod, leaning forwards with her elbows on the table. 'He never liked all the noise, and he was vocal about it, too. Elizabeth would tell me each time that he'd gone over and complained about the noise. But what could she do? Sam was just having fun and playing. The noise wasn't offensive in any way, and in my opinion, it was quite the contrary. I could have listened to the sound of his voice all day long.'

'I know that Arthur looks out over my house to this day,' Fern admitted. 'He stands at his landing window. His wife told me that he does it every single day.'

Iris folded her arms across her chest. 'That's odd behaviour from someone who has a clear conscience. I saw the police going to his house on numerous occasions following the fire. They only came to speak with myself and Henry once.'

Fern thought about what Olive had revealed about her husband and the secrets she suspected he was hiding. 'Surely nobody would deliberately start a fire that would endanger a child's life, or anybody's life, for that matter. Especially over something so trivial.'

'A friend of Sam's was also questioned by the police,' Iris recalled, sporadic parts of the puzzle drifting back like washed-up driftwood.

'Is that the boy who the papers reported was seen running?'

Iris nodded her head. 'I heard he was seen running away from the house. Away from the fire. I don't understand why someone would do that unless they'd done something wrong.'

'Maybe he was running to try and find help?'

'After Mr Aspey's house, mine is the closest property to Lunar,' Iris explained. 'And Henry was home that day. He was taking an afternoon nap in the conservatory. He was never woken up by someone banging on the door, or by the doorbell. He only stirred when the fire engines came blaring up the road in a convoy.'

'Did you know the boy? His identity wasn't revealed in the papers.'

'I didn't know him personally, but he was a local lad. He lived in the village. He was a few years older than Sam.'

'What was his name?

A vivid picture appeared in Iris's mind, the dark, bold features of the boy ingrained in her memories. 'Dylan. Dylan Wallace was his name. I've never forgotten it. He still lives locally, and from what I've heard, he's found himself on the wrong side of the police more than once. Nobody has much time for him in the village, and you wouldn't be a fool for understanding why.'

The tissue that Fern had been holding in her hand fell to the floor when her fingers released. She felt like the ground beneath her was crumbling, and she was free-falling. A second wave of betrayal struck against her already fragile heart.

'Are you okay?' Iris asked, getting up out of her seat and supporting Fern's body as it wavered. 'Are you feeling dizzy?'

In one quick move, a bolt of anger fired through Fern's legs, making her stand like a soldier. Planting her hands on her hips, she paced the room in disbelief. 'Dylan Wallace is the man who's been helping me to renovate this house,' she mumbled, her thoughts bouncing around in a chaotic jumble. 'He never mentioned knowing Sam, not once. And he never mentioned the fire. What kind of person does that? I don't understand. Does he think that I'd never find out? Does he think I'm stupid. Do all men think I'm stupid? I trusted him. I thought we were friends,' she ranted.

'You're no fool,' Iris announced when Fern crashed her body back down on the seat. 'I haven't known you very long, but I know the kind of woman that you are.'

Fern looked up at Iris, a sense of helplessness in her eyes. 'How have I ended up here, Iris?' she cried. 'Not long ago I thought I was happily married to my forever person. And now I find myself here, alone,' she said. She studied her kitchen, a room that she had created, a room that boasted postcard-worthy views, and yet deep down, it still felt far from the place she wanted to rest her head at night. 'I'm living in this house that has so much history, so many heartbreaking memories, and I feel like I'm falling apart, too.'

Iris remained composed. She sat up in her chair, like a judge about to deliver a sentence. 'Don't you believe in fate? Don't you believe that you're always being guided by a power so much bigger than yourself? You're here for a reason, Fern,' she began, indicating to the house. 'God knows that He can trust you with Lunar. He knows He can trust you to bring this house, this home, back to life. It would be such a shame if this place went to rack and ruin. How would Sam be remembered then? His legacy would be lost.'

Fern had never been religious. In fact, the church was something she had shied away from, unsure, even as an adult, where her religious compass fell. But Iris's words resonated and touched her heart, offering a sense of comfort amidst her turmoil. 'Thank you, Iris.' Fern stood up and went and sat beside her neighbour. 'Everybody needs someone like you in their life.'

'What are you going to do now?' Iris asked, reaching for her coat after noticing the time.

'I'm going to get some answers. That's what I'm going to do.'

Iris stood up, put her coat on and began to hobble towards the front door. She caught sight of the cupboard under the stairs. Vivid memories rushed back of how Sam would use the concealed cubbyhole as a place to hide, jumping out on her whenever she visited. 'That sounds like a wonderful plan.' She picked up her umbrella. 'I better get going,' she said, her heavy eyelids an indication of the late hour. The moment she opened the door, she was met with a strong wind, the strength whipping her fine hair into a frenzy. 'You know where I am if you ever need me. Don't spend too much time feeling lonely. Life is so short, and you're still so young. Get out there and find your Henry.' Iris popped open her brolly and stepped out into the storm.

'Let me walk across the road with you,' Fern insisted, grabbing hold of her coat. 'This wind could blow you away.'

'I'm a little too old to be flying through the sky like Mary Poppins,' Iris laughed, battling with her umbrella. 'You stay here. There's no point two of us catching a chill,' she insisted, pushing Fern back inside.

'Bye, Iris,' Fern shouted, watching her neighbour shuffle down the drenched path. Once the lights in Iris's house were illuminated through the windows, Fern shut out the howling weather and locked her front door. Behind the safety offered by the side window, Fern peered out over the deserted garden. She told herself that if Dylan, or anybody else, was thinking about sneaking around her property during the night, then this time, she'd be ready and waiting.

15

Unable to sleep, Fern had stirred long before the break of sunrise. Remaining buried deep beneath her winter tog duvet, she peered towards the window, failing to spot any traces of sunlight breaking through the cracks in the curtains. Feeling accustomed to the calls of her wildlife neighbours, Fern could only detect the early-morning chorus led by the pre-dawn singers, which she now knew included the local gang of robins, blackbirds and thrushes. She closed her eyes and urged herself to think of anything other than Dylan. But no matter how hard she tried, a gnawing feeling of anxiety brewed in her stomach at the thought of him sneaking through her home and then lying to her face. Pulling the duvet over her head, she listened to the cheery morning song delivered by the charm of chaffinches that were nesting close to her bedroom window. When the sound of the awakening main road competed with the birdsong, her impatience got the better of her, and so she bounded out of bed and got changed.

After forcing down a piece of toast accompanied by a strong cup of freshly-brewed coffee, Fern drove across the village and pulled her car up outside Dylan's house some time close to 8 a.m. She peered up and down the street and admired the row of well-presented, semi-detached Victorian houses. Fern hadn't been sure what to expect when she arrived, but this quaint, suburban street was not what she had imagined.

With apprehension still bouncing through her body, she looked up at Dylan's house. Every curtain was still drawn. The closed-off nature of the house filled her with a fresh bundle of jittery nerves. Dylan's van was parked outside the house, indicating that he was home. With a gentle footing, she stepped out of the car. She eased the door closed and tried not to alert any potential nosey neighbours to her presence. Slipping her phone back into her pocket, she stepped up to the front door and pressed her finger against the bell. She took a pronounced step back, leaving a safe gap between her and the front door. A chill clung to the air, the sharp, autumnal bite attacking her sensitive skin. Fending off what felt like a harsh bout of September shivers, she pulled her hat below her ears and her feet fidgeted like an army of ants.

It felt like an age before Dylan answered the door, allowing Fern time to peer over her shoulder, a skin of suspicion clinging to her body. The secluded side street remained deserted. Only a scraggy, jet-black cat offered her any company. The feline approached without hesitance, dancing around Fern's legs, its arched back wanting to be stroked. When no answer came, she rattled her knuckles against the door. It felt like the sound echoed all the way down the street. The noise was too alarming for the timid moggy and it darted, disappearing into the next garden, leaving Fern alone. A topsy-turvy sensation continued to swell through her body, an unsettling feeling that urged her to turn and leave. And yet despite her reservations, she reached out her hand and knocked again.

In one swift move, the heavy, grey door opened.

'Hi,' Fern greeted when she saw Dylan on the other side. 'I hope I haven't woken you.'

He took a quick glance at his watch. 'Hi,' he replied, a look of confusion appearing on his face. 'No. I was just in the back doing some washing.' Only allowing a narrow gap, he peered his head round the door. 'Was I meant to be doing some jobs for you today?' he questioned, pulling out his phone, scrolling through his work schedule.

Fern shook her head. 'No. I just wanted to come and have a chat. Would that be okay?' she stuttered, failing to make eye contact, and instead, glanced back at her car.

Dylan gazed downward, an unnatural stillness taking over his demeanour. 'You know, don't you?' he asked, lowering his head and putting his phone back into his pocket. 'I knew it was only a matter of time,' he said, his voice devoid of emotion.

Fern stepped closer. 'Can I come in?'

Dylan allowed the door to ease away from his grip. 'Sure,' he replied when the door opened fully.

Fern crossed the threshold and lingered in the hallway. The space felt cold, so she kept her head buried beneath her hat. A quick surveillance of her surroundings highlighted traces of everyday life, helping to make her feel at ease. She spotted a collection of what looked like family holiday photos lining the stairs. A miniature figurine of a cartoon duck holding a *Welcome Home* sign sat on a side table, along with a collection of supermarket coupons. An enticing smell of toast wafted through the air, accompanied by the warming scents of freshly-brewed coffee. 'Where should we go?'

'The lounge is through there,' he replied, indicating to the first door on the right.

Fern took the lead and walked through to the lounge. Her eyes immediately landed on a framed photo that was resting pride of place on the fireplace. 'This is Sam Sloan, isn't it?' she asked, taking hold of the picture to get a better look. 'I recognise those blue eyes and that playful smile.'

Dylan followed Fern into the room and took a seat. His fingers were interlinked, and he rested his arms on his legs. He wanted the opportunity to be heard, and for once, for someone to believe his side of the story. 'Yeah, that's Sam,' he confirmed. 'For what it's worth, I wanted to tell you who I was on the very first day that we met.'

Still standing, Fern's attention remained on the photo of Sam, his blue eyes sparkling behind the wooden frame. 'Then why didn't you tell me? You lied to me from the very start, Dylan,' Fern finally replied. She turned to face her friend, her face broken with emotion. 'You knew about the fire all along. You knew about Sam. You knew everything that happened at Lunar because you were there that day, weren't you?' she questioned, her sense of betrayal finding a strong voice. 'I trusted you.'

Dylan stood up and swept open the curtains. Having spent so many years hiding, he felt ready to confront his past head-on. The morning sunlight that was climbing above the horizon flooded in and illuminated the room, the warming rays resting on everything in sight. Dylan remained in the bay window, trying to find the correct string of words after his years of silence.

As the room was drenched in natural daylight, Fern spotted a few more framed photos that were positioned on the wall. She approached the photos to get a better look. Tears fell from her eyes in a steady stream, the moisture accentuating the dark circles that had settled themselves beneath her eyes. One of the captivating photos was of Sam. He was sat side by side with another boy on a brick wall, the sun making the lads squint. Their legs were dangling, their baseball caps positioned sideways on their heads, and both boys were pulling funny faces at the person taking the photo. 'Is this you next to Sam?' she asked.

Dylan sat back down on one of the single chairs. He lowered his head, like he was partaking in a private, silent prayer. 'Yes,' he confirmed, failing to look up.

Fern turned and took a seat. 'I thought we were friends, Dylan.'

He was quick to look up at Fern. 'We are. At least I hope we are.'

'Friends don't lie to each other,' she began. 'Friends are meant to have each other's backs. You know that I've been going out of my mind trying to find out what happened at Lunar. I've felt alone and vulnerable in my own home. And despite you knowing all that, you still didn't tell me what you knew. That's not how I want my friends to treat me. I've been dragged through enough this year by people who were supposed to care about me, and I've just had enough.' Fern's eyes were downcast and her chin low. She peered at her brown leather Chelsea boots, and wondered whose life she had accidentally stepped into, and when the unfamiliar journey would end.

The sight of Fern being upset made Dylan feel frustrated that he hadn't followed his instincts and been upfront from the very beginning. 'I thought that if I told you, you wouldn't hire me for the job. And although I knew it was going to be hard stepping foot inside the house again, I needed the job. I needed the income. And then we really got along. I liked your company and having you as a friend. I'd forgotten how amazing a close friendship can feel. I was scared to lose you.' Dylan lowered his guard and, for once, expressed his true feelings. 'I don't have many true friends, not anymore.'

Fern slowly eased her gaze off the ground. 'Well, we'll never know what my decision would've been, because you never gave me the chance,' she mused. 'You thought the worst of me. So why shouldn't I automatically think the worst about you?' She reached into her pocket for her car keys and readied herself to leave.

'I can explain,' he began, taking the first step to restore Fern's faith and rebuild the foundations of their crumbling friendship.

Flustered, Fern shrugged her shoulders with a sense of indifference. 'Then tell me honestly what happened that day. That's all I'm asking for, Dylan.'

Clearing his throat, Dylan looked up like he was facing judge and jury. He maintained strong eye contact. 'I didn't cause the fire that killed Sam,' he announced with confidence for his opening statement. These words rolled off his tongue with ease and familiarity because they were the exact same string of words that he'd told himself every single day for the past fifteen years. 'Sam was my best friend,' he added in support. 'Even though I was a few years older than him, it didn't matter. Not to us. We just had this special bond and liked hanging around together.' He paused and took a moment to compose his emotions, a bundle of raw feelings that he'd kept guarded for most of his adult life. 'But back then, when it all happened, everyone thought I was trouble. Especially Mr and Mrs Sloan,' he continued, now looking out of the window for inspiration.

Fern took a seat. 'Why did they think you were trouble?' she asked, encouraging Dylan to continue with his explanation when she saw his thoughts and attention drifting out through the open window.

'Because back then, we did some stupid stuff together. We played pranks and jokes on people, and to be honest, most of that craziness was my idea,' he confessed, thinking back on all the mischief that he and his best pal had caused in the village. 'I guess I was trouble, if I'm being honest.'

Fern held her breath, desperate to hear how the rest of Dylan's story would unravel. 'And what happened that day? The day of the fire.'

Dylan looked up with heavy eyes. 'Sam wanted to try a ciggy,' he revealed in one quick breath. 'And even though I didn't want to, he dared me to go and steal some from next door,' he explained, recalling the events of the day like it had only just happened. 'And we had always had this pact. If you were given a dare, then you had to do it,' he said in shame, lowering his head and running his hands through his thick, wavy black hair.

Fern heard the boiler kick into life, the radiators working to remove the stubborn chill that was still clinging to the room. She could see the barrage of genuine grief that was weighing down on Dylan's shoulders, and she wondered if he had ever had anyone looking out for him. 'What happened next?'

'Stupidly, I went along with it and snuck over to Mr Aspey's house. We both knew that he smoked, and that's where we could get our hands on some cigarettes,' he revealed, his stomach churning as the details were regurgitated. 'And it wasn't the first time that I'd snuck over to Aspey's house. I knew where I was going.' Dylan looked up at his favourite photo of Sam. His best friend was wearing a tattered Tom and Jerry t-shirt and a pair of well-worn, scruffy shorts. His heart ached at the memory behind the photo. He knew that right before the picture was taken, they'd both been out and bought second-hand BMX bikes with some money they'd earned from washing cars at the local village hall during the summer holidays. 'I grabbed the whole packet because I heard Mr Aspey shouting,' Dylan continued. 'And then I ran back to the barn where Sam was waiting for me,' he said. 'That's where we'd been messing about.'

'Then what happened?' Fern encouraged, adopting a nonjudgemental, sympathetic voice.

'Sam took one ciggy and lit it with some matches that he already had stashed in his pocket. And I ran back down the road to put the box back before Mr Aspey had time to figure out they were missing,' he explained, his words rolling off his tongue. 'But it took me ages because the old man was standing in his front room. So, I ducked out of sight and waited for him to leave.' Agitated, Dylan rolled his hands together like he was washing them with hot, soapy water. In his mind, he was attempting to wash away the pain that remained his constant companion. 'By the time I'd returned the packet and ran back up the main road, smoke was already coming from the barn.' Dylan's hands continued to fidget as a means of comfort, he couldn't help but roll his thumbs over the pads of his fingers. 'And then I heard the sound of Sam screaming.' Before he could stop himself, Dylan placed his hands over his face and sobbed. His unboxed swell of emotion gathered in his palms until his skin became saturated.

As the sole witness to Dylan's demise, despite some stubborn hesitations, Fern felt unable to resist offering her friend some compassion. She stood up and knelt on the floor by the side of Dylan's chair. She reached out and took hold of a tissue, placing it in his cold hand.

'The smoke was thick, and the flames were coming out of the

barn. I couldn't get inside to help him,' he revealed, stumbling over his words. 'The flames were everywhere, and I was so scared.' Symptoms of Dylan's post-traumatic stress disorder ignited, and he grappled with vivid flashbacks that landed him right back in the heart of the storm. 'I shouted to Sam that I'd be back soon, and I ran to find help,' he sobbed, his witness testimony mirroring that of his original police statement. Like in his nightmare, Dylan could hear Sam's screams with all the clarity of a twisted horror movie. 'I knew nobody was at home, so I ran onto the main road,' he explained, breathless like he was still running. 'Mr Aspey didn't answer his door, so I carried on running down the lane. I knocked at the house across the road, but the same thing happened. Nobody could hear me, or they weren't home.'

'So, then what did you do?' Fern asked, handing him another tissue.

'I carried on running until I found someone. Eventually, a car stopped. My words came out all jumbled. But the driver saw the fire in the distance and called for help.'

Fern rose to her feet and perched on the side of the seat, unable to ignore her caring instincts. She placed her arms around Dylan's shoulders, pulling him close. She believed every word of his story and, in her opinion, his heartbreak was impossible to fake or forge. Fern felt Dylan's body juddering beneath the weight of sadness, a strong, burly man brought to his knees. 'I'm so sorry,' she whispered.

'I was panicking, and I wasn't thinking straight, because obviously I should have run into the house and called for help myself. I just didn't think,' he explained, wiping his eyes. 'By the time the fire brigade arrived, Sam had stopped screaming,' he cried, a harrowing look evident in his eyes. 'The fire had burnt through the far end of the barn where Sam had been sat high up on the bales. It was too late to save him. I was too late,' he confessed, acknowledging his feelings of guilt that had finally found a voice. 'I wasn't quick enough getting help. I let him down.' Dylan got up and walked out of the room, closing the door behind him. The seat cushions retained a breath of warmth from where Dylan had been sat. The seat was scattered with damp, used tissues.

Wondering what to do, Fern stood up and walked through to the kitchen, the open-plan space generous with light now that Dylan had parted the curtains. Switching on the kettle, Fern looked in the fridge for some milk. The contents pulled further at her heartstrings. Half a block of cheese, a few stray carrots, and some dregs of milk were all the perishables on offer. Unable to help herself, she opened the cupboards. Nothing more than a few tins could be found, not enough ingredients to make a substantial, nutritious meal.

The door opened.

'Sorry about that,' Dylan apologised, finding Fern in the kitchen.

Startled, Fern turned to face him. 'I was going to make us a drink.'

Dylan felt embarrassed, knowing that, like his bank account, his fridge was running on empty. 'It's food shop day, so I think I'm out of milk.'

'Are you struggling financially?' Fern asked, concerned, unable to resist asking the obvious. 'I know when I took you on, you said you needed the money.'

Uncomfortable, Dylan walked back through to the lounge. 'Sometimes I have loads of work on.' He sat back on his seat, stuffing the used tissues down the side. 'But it's not always easy finding work, and I had a roommate who left unexpectedly and without paying what he owed.'

Fern turned off the kettle and took a seat on the sofa. 'I'm sorry for coming over here with such a harsh agenda,' she said, feeling guilty for questioning her friend's involvement in Sam's death. Although her instincts had recently been put under scrutiny, Fern knew deep down that her initial feelings about Dylan were correct.

'Don't worry. I'm used to people thinking the worst of me.'

Fern saw the vulnerability lurking in Dylan's eyes, a level of helplessness hard to fake.

'Do you really believe me?'

'I believe everything you've just told me. Why wouldn't I?' she replied. 'From what I understand, everything that happened that day was just a tragic accident.'

Dylan got up and wrapped his arms around Fern, savouring the tender moment as she reciprocated his unexpected show of affection. The longer the embrace lasted, the more he could feel his shackles of guilt surrendering their control. His breathing felt less laboured, and the constant stream of toxic noise running through his head silenced.

Fern freed herself from the hold so that she could look her friend in the eyes. 'You can't blame yourself for what happened. You somehow need to find a way to make peace with the past and let go of all this guilt that you're carrying around.'

Dylan hesitated before he spoke. 'The guilt has been unbearable,' he cried. 'Even though I knew that I didn't start that fire, and I did my best to save Sam, I felt like I should have tried harder to get him out. I shouldn't have accepted the dare. I shouldn't have left him alone to die,' he sobbed, lowering his head back onto her shoulder for support.

Fern took the weight of his upper body, his head buried into her neck. 'Dylan, the fire wasn't your fault. Sam's death wasn't your fault,' she repeated, making sure that he was hearing what she was saying. 'You have to start believing it. It was a tragic accident and Sam wouldn't want you to be so unhappy,' she said. 'You were his best friend, and he knew that.' She turned her head to look at one of the photos on the wall. 'Look at his smile,' she insisted, encouraging Dylan to look up. 'You can see from the photos how happy Sam was when he was with you.'

Dylan admired the photo that he'd looked at a thousand times. 'I thought about moving away. Making a fresh start. But it felt like I was leaving Sam behind. It would have felt like I was abandoning him again and I just couldn't do it.' He peered outside, spotting someone passing on the pavement. 'I felt anxious for so long after the accident because I could tell by the look in people's eyes that they blamed me. They believed that I'd started the fire and that I was running away so not to get caught.'

Fern noticed the way Dylan peered at the person walking past his house, and how he watched to see if they were going to approach his front door. She placed herself in his shoes and wondered how it must have felt to be wrongly accused of such a heinous crime.

'People didn't make it easy for me. They called me all sorts of names and I felt like an outcast. If it wasn't for my mum, I'm not sure what I'd have done. She's the only person who believed my side of the story. She never once thought that I'd done wrong, or that I was a coward.'

'I believe you, too,' Fern corrected him. 'How has it felt being back at the house?'

'It's been tough,' he sighed. 'That place is filled with so many memories. Good and bad. And when I heard that Mr Sloan had passed away, I felt relieved, even though I know that's a terrible thing to say. I spent so many years feeling terrified of bumping into him. Not that I ever did. I'm not sure he ever left that house.'

'You saw how rundown it was when I moved in. It didn't look like he had any real quality of life. If anything, I'd say he was extremely lonely. Do you know what happened to Sam's mum, and his sister?' she asked in hope.

Dylan shook his head. 'Not for certain. His family refused to talk or have anything to do with me afterwards. I heard rumours that Charlotte went to live with family somewhere. And I heard that Mrs Sloan passed away not long after the fire. I never spoke to any of the family after that day.'

'Iris Pepper, the lady who lives down the road, told me that Elizabeth took her own life. An overdose.'

Dylan lowered his head. 'After what happened, I can believe

it,' he said. 'Because the pain never goes away. Not really. You just learn to live with it,' he explained, recalling some of his own dark moments, and the time that he had thought it would be easier if there was no tomorrow.

Fern felt frightened by the way that Dylan spoke. 'Whenever you're feeling down, you can always talk to me. We're friends now, aren't we?'

The offer of support and friendship felt better than anything that Dylan had experienced in a long time. 'Thanks,' he smiled, almost lost for words.

'What was Sam like?' Fern asked, her eyes drawn to the photos of the little blond-haired boy with the enchanting smile.

Dylan's face lit up brighter than a thousand candles. 'He was so much fun to be around,' he began, smiling wistfully. 'There was never a dull moment. If we weren't playing on our bikes, we were out in the barn making up games and just messing about,' he recalled with fondness. 'That train track that was still on his bedroom floor,' Dylan revealed, 'we built that, together, the morning that he died.' Dylan's thoughts turned inwards, and he replayed that morning with sadness saturating his heart. 'It started spitting, so we came inside to keep dry.' Dylan turned to look at Fern. 'I only spotted the track because the door was left ajar one day when I nipped to the toilet. I wasn't snooping around or anything like that.'

'It's okay,' she replied, the look in her eyes conveying her level of understanding. 'I still have the train track. I packed it up and put it in a box.' She thought about what she was about to ask, wondering if it was the right decision. 'Would you like it? I'm sure that's what Sam would have wanted.'

'Are you sure?' he asked, touched at the kind gesture.

A warming sensation rushed through her heart. 'Absolutely. Come over whenever you're free and I'll show you.'

'Thanks so much, Fern, for everything.'

Fern thought about the puzzle she was trying to solve. 'That card I found at Sam's grave. Did you put it there?' she asked.

Dylan shook his head. 'I'm not a fan of visiting gravestones. I don't feel like I need to go to a cemetery in order to keep someone's memory alive. I think about Sam every single day, and my memories of him are alive in my mind, not buried out there.'

Fern's facial expression changed. 'Can I ask you something else?' She stood up and walked towards the window, looking out over the street that now boasted a bit more life. The black cat had returned, now sunning itself on Dylan's front step. Fern watched as a weathered post lady heaved her red trolley up the street like it contained ten tonnes of letters, her lips miming along to whatever was playing in her earphones. Turning her back on the world outside, Fern turned around when Dylan replied.

'Sure. Anything,' he answered without hesitation.

'Have you been to the house? I mean, when I haven't been home, or when I wasn't aware of it?' She bit her lip, hoping that Dylan would own up to having entered Lunar, finally squashing her suspicions, and feeling of vulnerability. 'It's okay if you did. I understand why you would have done it. And I'm not angry. I just need to know the truth,' she said, collapsing her body on the sofa in a show of desperation.

'I was never at Lunar without you knowing. I promise.'

Fern's heart sank faster than she could catch it.

'Why do you ask?'

Fern thought back. 'I just can't shake this feeling that someone has been watching me,' she explained. 'And I know you didn't really believe me when I said that someone had closed the lounge window that day, because it didn't look like anybody had broken in, but I knew that I left it open. And someone put a bucket in the basement so that it would catch dripping water.'

Dylan recalled one of Fern's messages. 'Is that why you were asking me about a bucket?'

Fern nodded. 'I didn't put it there, but someone did, and without me knowing.'

'You need to call the police.'

Fern released a heavy sigh. 'I don't think I do. At least not yet. I've come to the conclusion that whoever it was isn't out to hurt me. At least not physically. If that was their intention, they would have done it already. They've had the opportunity. I don't think that's their intention. It's just making me feel on edge, like I'm looking over my shoulder all the time. And anyway, there's no point calling the police because there's no actual evidence of any wrongdoing. There's no sign of a break-in. There's no sign of a forced entry. Nothing has been taken. It's just this feeling I have. My intuition.'

'Is there anything I can do to help? You've been there for me and now I want to do the same for you.'

'I want to figure out what's going on,' she blurted with frustration. 'I've come so far since leaving Cooper. I've bought a house and renovated it. I'm getting my business back up and running and making new friends,' she began to explain. 'I'm making a new life for myself, and I don't want to lose all that. I don't want to just let someone ruin my life all over again. I'm stronger now and I'm determined not to be scared. That's what it feels like. It almost feels like someone else is still living at Lunar, and I don't know who, or why.'

Dylan stood up and rolled up his sleeves, like he was preparing for a fistfight. 'I know Lunar better than anyone, and if there's something untoward going on, it's time it stops.'

16

Rain poured over Aldebaran like a monsoon, the sky above the village thick with heavy, charcoal clouds. Sitting snuggled up on the sofa in her lounge, Fern listened to the rain clattering against the windows, her steaming mug of coffee doing a fitting job of warming her insides. Alone, her mind wandered back to her old life. She pictured how she used to spend her Sunday afternoons, preparing Cooper's favourite homemade beef lasagne, which was always followed by an oversized mixed berry cheesecake. Surveying her surroundings and trying her best to make her new house feel like home, she put her feet up and wrapped the blanket around her body, just like she used to. Only now, the other end of the sofa was vacant. Just as she reached over to take hold of her book, darkness descended over the room, and throughout the entire house.

Submerged in darkness, she grabbed her phone and switched on the torch, illuminating the room. Standing, she peered out of the window and over towards the main road. A dotting of streetlights were still illuminated. Scrolling through her list of contacts, she pressed on Iris's number. Standing on tiptoes to try and catch a glimpse of her neighbour's house, she spotted that next door was also drenched in darkness.

'Hello,' Iris answered, a sense of curiosity in her voice.

'Hi, Iris. It's Fern from across the street,' she began. 'I'm sorry to bother you. I just wanted to know if you still have power over on your side of the street. My electricity seems to have gone out.'

'Nope. It's gone out over here, too,' she confirmed. 'It's been such a stormy day. The weather must have triggered something at one of the local sub stations. 'I was just about to call and report it,' she said. 'Why don't you come over and have a cup of tea with me? We can get some candles lit and ride it out together? Hopefully it won't be too long before it's back on.'

Fern had already vacated the sofa and walked to grab her coat, so thankful for the invitation. 'That would be great. Thank you so much. I'll be over in a few minutes.' Fern hid her head beneath her favourite pink bobble hat and opened the front door. An assortment of leaves and fallen foliage danced around her feet. The lightweight shrubbery got caught in the scrappy gusts swooping across the porch. With the torch on her phone leading the way, Fern navigated the short walk towards her neighbour's house. The main road felt unusually quiet. Eerie. When Fern opened Iris's gate, the creaking hinges fought to be heard above the downpour.

Positioned a little further up the main road, a car had been strategically parked for little over an hour. Nestled near some overgrown bushes, the vehicle's lights had been turned off, helping it to blend into the dark backdrop of the night. Charlotte spotted Fern walking across the road and enter her neighbour's house. The unexpected development made her unbuckle her seatbelt. Without overthinking what she was about to do, she flicked up her hood and stepped out of her car. Navigating the terrain with all the familiarity of a local, Charlotte crept towards Fern's empty house. With bold, confident strides, she walked up the garden path, stepping over the places where she knew deep puddles tended to form.

Taking out her keys, she climbed the porch steps and approached Lunar via the front door. She knew that she'd left the hatch doors unlocked on her previous visit, just in case when it came time to leave, she could do so via the basement. Shielded from the rain, she shook the stormy residue off her jacket and tamed her windswept hair. Emotionally drained, she no longer cared about being spotted. In her mind, Lunar was her home and part of her identity. That's where she belonged. The house and its history were a part of her. They couldn't be separated. With care, she placed her key into the lock, opened the front door, and stepped inside. Automatically kicking off an old pair of tatty trainers where a family-sized shoe rack had once been positioned, she headed barefoot straight down the hallway.

Knowing exactly what she'd come for, and where it might be, Charlotte stood in front of the cupboard under the stairs. Having discarded all her worries, all she thought about were laying her hands on the precious mementos once belonging to her younger brother, the items Fern suggested should be reunited with family. The moment that she reached out and clasped her fingers around the handle, the door fell ajar in her hand. Familiarity made her duck her head and watch out for the sharp hook that had always protruded in the top right-hand corner – the spot where her mum had once hung the dustpan and brush. Ducking, Charlotte reached in her hand and pulled the frayed piece of dangling cord, the single, pendant lightbulb illuminating the interior with a warm, subtle glow.

Taking to her knees, Charlotte leaned her body into the cluttered cupboard and began the search for her brother's box of possessions. With both hands, she removed the bulky items that were obscuring her way and placed them out in the hallway. Once she'd made a bit more space, she nudged her body further into the cavern, her intuition guiding her search. *I know it's in here somewhere, it must be.* Holding back her tears, a sense of desperation drove her search, her hands wading carelessly through the clutter.

The smell that permeated the enclosed space made Charlotte long for the past – an unidentifiable mustiness that brought back fond memories of her family, and her home. Sprawling her legs over a stack of crumpled boxes, Charlotte caught sight of a plastic box to her right. 'That's got to be it,' she announced. She reached in, grabbed hold of the box and heaved it back towards her body. Positioned directly beneath the glow of the light, she perched her body and rested the brimming box on her lap. Unclipping the handles, Charlotte removed the lid to reveal what she could already tell were the precious contents she had longed to find, the discovery making her cry and smile simultaneously. An inner radiance brought about a sense of calmness, and she arched her head. *Thank you*, she thought over and over.

One foot at a time, she ambled out of the hidden cupboard. With the box gripped firmly in her hands, Charlotte made her way upstairs and into the small bedroom. She placed the box on the bed and parted the new window shutters. The pitch-black ambience that still saturated the street told her that all the power was still out in the area. Welcome flecks of brightness filtered in through the open slats thanks to the positioning of the glistening, full moon. The darkened sky emphasised the brightness of the stars, and Charlotte recalled all the times in the past that she and her younger sibling had sat and stargazed side by side. Searching her memory, she tried to recall some of the made-up names that she and her brother had come up with for the different constellations they had inadvertently identified. 'Crazy bananas,' she laughed when the name came to mind.

Sitting on the new, single bed that had been placed on the far wall, Charlotte removed the box lid and took hold of the first item. She pressed Sam's red t-shirt to her cheek, relishing the feeling of the soft material against her skin. 'You wore this *all* the time,' she recalled, 'and even when Mum told you to put it in the wash, you still wore it the next day.' Charlotte admired some of the drawings that she recalled had once been displayed on the walls. 'You loved to paint, and you were so good at it,' she said, admiring Sam's eclectic use of colour. 'And we always knew when you'd raided your art box because we'd find bits of paint all over the house,' she said, remembering the day that their parents came in from the garden to find the entire kitchen table smeared with rainbow handprints.

Charlotte caught sight of the bear, the words *I love my sister* sewn into the fur, and it was like Sam had placed his hand on her heart. 'You kept it?' she cried, recalling all the times that Sam had been adamant that he'd chucked it away. With the bear pressed against her chest, she closed her eyes. 'I love you, Sam,' she sobbed, gazing at the bear through a trail of tears. Charlotte looked across the room to where Sam's bed had once been positioned and recalled all the nights that she'd read him a bedtime story, watching his eyes as they slowly closed.

'There are things that I want to say to you, Sam,' she began, addressing the bear. 'After we lost you, I was never given the opportunity to say how I really felt,' she explained, recalling the heartbreaking first few days and months that followed the fire. 'But now that we're both back under the same roof, back at home, I know that you'll be able to hear me. I know that you'll hear my words.' Before she continued, Charlotte sorted through her jumble of thoughts, making sure that she laid everything out.

'I need to say how sorry I am for what happened.' Charlotte turned her head and looked towards the sky, searching for her brother. 'I was meant to be the one looking after you,' she said through the lump in her throat. 'But instead, I left you alone,' she cried, allowing her tears to run free. With her chin quivering, she continued. 'I'm sorry for not being there when you needed me. I'm sorry for all the times that we got into an argument over silly little things. I'm sorry for not playing with you more. I'm sorry for all the times that I said you were annoying. I'm sorry for everything.'

Pleading for forgiveness, Charlotte continued. 'I'll never be able to forgive myself for what happened, but I need to know that you forgive me.' She lowered her head and held her arms in her lap. 'I've lost track of how many times I've felt like I don't want to be here anymore, and it's exhausting,' she cried, recalling each occasion when she'd considered taking her own life. 'I wish

I'd been the one trapped in the barn that day.' With the aching in her heart so unforgiving, Charlotte once again found herself seeking a way to end her pain. 'I punish myself every day for what happened, and I can't go on feeling like this,' she said, her voice cracking. 'Do you still love me?' she asked.

Charlotte closed her eyes and listened for a reply to the only question she needed an answer to. She waited, hoping to hear her brother's voice, and yet all she was met with was silence. 'I always think about you before I fall asleep, hoping that in my dreams, you'll come back to me, and everything will be okay.' Charlotte opened her eyes and expected to see her brother standing in his bedroom. When she was met with an empty room, she pressed her hands over her face to capture her disappointment. 'I've always told myself that if I could just come home, then everything would be alright. But I was wrong, wasn't I?'

Charlotte found a photo in the box of her and Sam in the back garden, the picture taken not long before his death. She held it close, scrutinising every inch. 'Please find a way to tell me that you still love me,' she said, blinking away her tears. Turning the photo over, she spotted a scribbled drawing of a butterfly and Sam's handwriting beneath. 'I remember how much you loved watching butterflies in the garden, and you always said that if you were going to be an animal, you'd be a butterfly, because you liked how colourful they were, and because then you'd be able to fly.' Placing the photo in her pocket, a flicker of light made Charlotte gravitate towards the window. 'The power's back on,' she muttered.

Her heart began to race, and panic set in. Scrambling, she put all the things back in the box and left it on the bed before scurrying across the room. 'I know I shouldn't be here, but I had to come back,' she said, opening the door. 'And even if I get caught, I don't care anymore. Being back here with you is all I've ever wanted,' she cried, trying to tear herself away from Sam's room. 'I've got to go, but just know that I love you,' she said, running out onto the landing and down the stairs. With her heart in her mouth, she paused at the bottom of the stairs when she heard footsteps approaching the front door. Panicked, she tripped over a box that she'd left in the hallway, falling flat on her face, her right cheek banging against the floor. Dazed, she scrambled to her feet, grabbed her trainers and plunged her body down to the basement. Ambling towards the external door, she fumbled to find her keys. The moment she pulled the door open, she heard a gasp from upstairs. She kept on running up the steps and rushed to push open the external hatch doors, before fleeing across the garden.

Back in the main house, Fern switched the hallway light on the moment she stepped foot through the door. 'Oh my God,' she said, witnessing all the things that were scattered over the floor. Lingering in the doorway, she listened. She noticed that the basement door was ajar. She edged further into the hallway and turned on the basement light. Through the silence, she could hear the rain, like a door or window was open. The noise drew her further into the cavern beneath the house. Stepping over the boxes, she paced towards the external door that was banging against the wall each time the wind tunnelled down the stairs. Peering up at the open hatch, Fern began to cry as she imagined someone running through her home. Inspecting the locks on both doors, she could see that nobody had broken in, the doors intact, and she mocked her own stupidity for not having prioritised getting the locks changed.

Ambiguous noises echoed and swirled around the ether. Like a standing target alone in the darkness, Fern felt like the walls at Lunar had eyes, and they had just opened. She had never entertained the idea before but in that moment, it felt like sleeping spirits had awoken. The energy in the air implied that those who had walked the land at Lunar previously had now risen, and the spirits were attempting to escape the torment of the past.

17

As Dylan pulled his van onto the driveway at Lunar, he noted how the blinds in every single window were closed. Perturbed, he checked his phone to make sure he'd arrived at the right time, wondering if his friend might still be in bed asleep. Confident he had the plan correct, he got out of his van and walked up the porch steps and tapped on the door.

'Is there a reason why your blinds are shut?' he asked when Fern opened the door.

She ushered him inside with a sense of urgency. 'Did anybody see you come in?' she asked, closing the door and locking it.

A concerned expression crept over Dylan's face, and he glanced around. 'I'm not sure. I don't think so. Why?'

Sitting herself on the stairs, Fern opened an awaiting box. 'Are you ready to help me?' she asked, revealing a collection of tiny cameras. She held one up to Dylan's face. 'And before you say that I've totally lost my mind, which at this point is a high possibility, just hear me out,' she said.

'Okay,' he replied with hesitance, looking in the box, a befuddled expression on his face.

'After what happened the other night, we know for sure that someone has been in the house,' she began, a newfound sense of reassurance in her voice. 'Well, next time it happens, these will capture everything,' she explained.

Dylan took hold of a camera. 'These connect to your phone, do they?' he asked, having heard about similar cameras before.

'Yeah, so all we need to do is dot some throughout the house,' Fern said with enthusiasm. 'If I can hide these in certain areas, the next time that someone is here, I'll see who it is on my phone.'

'Right?' Dylan questioned. 'But as soon as someone comes inside, they'll see them, won't they?' he questioned.

Fern shook her finger. 'No, because we're going to place them strategically,' she smiled. 'And look, they're so tiny, you'd never spot one. That's the whole point.'

'What will you do if you see someone?'

'Then I'll go to the police, and I'll have proof.'

Dylan could see the desperation in his friend's eyes.

Fern felt impatient for an answer. 'So, will you help me?' she asked, grabbing hold of the cameras.

'Of course I'll help you,' he agreed, picking up the box, eager to try and bring about a sense of peace to the troubled house and all those captured within its embrace. 'Where should we start?'

Fern walked into the kitchen. 'In here,' she said, peering around the space. 'You place one where you think it'll capture the best views, and then I'll walk in and see if it's obvious,' she said, walking out and closing the door. 'Let me know when you're done,' she requested through the door, taking out her phone and checking the app for the cameras. 'Once the motion detection function clocks a moving object,' she read, following the instructions on screen, 'the image will be sent to my phone with a notification. Wherever I am at the time, I can then log onto the app and see what's going on in real time.' She looked up, listening for movement in the kitchen. 'Cooper and I had a similar kind of thing installed for when we went away and left Jessie at home for the first time,' she recalled.

'Right, I'm done,' Dylan confirmed, opening the door.

Fern strolled into the room, her gaze moving from one area to another, her eyes scanning all the shelves and side units.

'Okay, this might actually work,' Dylan commented, pleased

that he'd managed to keep Fern searching for so long. 'You have to remember that this person won't be specifically looking for a camera. They'll be doing, well, whatever it is they're here to do,' he said, crossing his arms. 'So, this is promising.'

'Oh, it's there,' Fern finally announced, spotting the tiny camera on the top of a unit, sandwiched in between a selection of eggcups and other baking utensils.

'I've put it higher up, pointing down, because all this here is in a person's natural eyeline,' he explained, motioning with his hands in front of his eyes.

'Great, this is why I needed your help,' Fern smiled. 'Let's do another room,' she insisted, picking up the box and wandering through to the lounge.

'Why not put one in here?' he suggested, pausing in the hallway. 'If we can conceal another one high up,' he advised, pointing above the kitchen door, 'and face it this way, we'll capture anyone entering through the front door.'

Fern looked around. 'There are fewer places to hide it, though.'

Dylan walked up the stairs and reached up. 'What about here?' he suggested, holding the camera next to the smoke alarm. 'It blends in with the alarm, and the ceiling.' He peeled off the covering to reveal the adhesive strip and secured it in place. 'You'd never notice that,' he said, walking back down the stairs and standing at the front door. 'Your attention is drawn down the hallway.'

'Perfect,' Fern agreed, putting her thumb up.

Dylan strategically positioned another camera in the lounge, and two in the back room. 'So, what happens now?' he asked, lingering near Fern in the hallway.

'I wait,' she said, shrugging her shoulders. 'And hope that when this person comes back, which I'm assuming they will do, the cameras will capture their identity, and all this drama will finally be over.'

'Wouldn't it be easier, and safer, if you just get the locks changed?'

Fern gazed around at the home she had created, feeling emotionally and physically drained. 'I get where you're coming from, I'm just not convinced it'd stop there. I still wouldn't know who it is, and I'd be forever waiting for them to come back.'

Dylan looked up at the camera in the hallway. 'What if this person comes back when you're home? What would you do then? You'd be leaving yourself in such a vulnerable situation.'

Fern shook her head. 'Whoever it is could've hurt me before now,' she said. 'That's not their intention. I know it's not. This house is the draw, more specifically Sam, and I need to know why.'

This time, Dylan shook his head in frustration. 'You *think* they're here because of the house, but you're not sure.'

'True,' she admitted. 'Then what would you suggest?'

'If we're going off your theory, you need to leave the house empty for a bit. Give this person time to come in and do whatever it is they want to do.'

'And go where?'

'Go away. Take a mini holiday with Jessie. Go anywhere, but spread the word that you'll be away for a few days. Let next door know, let Iris across the street know. Let any of your friends know. Post it on your socials.'

Fern made her way into the lounge and thrashed open the curtains, letting in the light. 'You could be right, you know,' she agreed, peering outside. 'I don't think I need much of an excuse to escape this place for a few days.'

'Great,' he beamed. 'Keep me posted on progress,' he said, grabbing his coat off the bottom of the banister. 'I've got to dash. I have a job to get to.'

'Thanks, Dylan, for all your help. I really appreciate it,' Fern said. 'I know that being back here is hard for you, but without your friendship, I'd be lost right now.' She stood on tiptoes and wrapped her arms around him, relishing the feeling of security when he reciprocated the affection.

'Anytime,' he said, pulling away and walking towards the door.

'Ever since I completed the work here, other jobs have trickled in,' he smiled, 'and that's all thanks to you.'

Fern walked out onto the porch and peered around. 'I'll keep you posted on the situation here,' she shouted after him.

Outside in the barn, Charlotte pressed her ear to the old wood, listening in on Fern's conversation with Dylan. Once it sounded as though they'd stopped talking, she waited to hear the front door closing. When the expected noise failed to sound, she scrambled to the natural spy hole that'd emerged over the years as the wooden panels in the barn had warped. Unexpectedly, she watched as Fern approached the outbuilding, her eyes clouding with panic.

Like a bullet, she scrambled through the barn's interior, seeking somewhere to hide. She dived behind the mountain of cardboard boxes located near the door. With trembling hands, she fumbled to put her phone on silent, regretting the choice of pungent deodorant and perfume she'd applied that morning. Tucked away, out of sight, she listened as the sound of a key turning in the lock clattered, the hinges creaking.

Fern stepped into the drab interior, her neck sinking into her shoulders, cowering at the sight of all the dust and cobwebs. 'Hi, my love. How are you?' she asked, holding her phone.

'I'm good,' Jessie replied. 'Just on my way to class.'

'Guess what?'

'What?' Jessie replied, lackadaisical, her attention still with the group of friends that she was walking with.

'I'm taking you away,' she announced, her tone spritely.

Jessie paused and indicated for her friends to carry on without her. 'I'm about to go into class, Mum. What are you going on about?'

Fern looked at her watch. 'Sorry, I didn't realise the time,' she apologised, stepping further into the barn, the light from the open door casting shadows onto the pile of boxes that she had yet to unpack. 'I'm booking us a few nights away at this really fancy hotel in Oxford,' she boasted. 'It's a spa retreat. We leave tonight, if you're up for it.'

The thought of spending some time with her mum away from Lunar encouraged a smile to emerge on Jessie's face. 'Really? What's the occasion?'

Fern opened the first box, the ruffles of her wedding dress spilling out. 'I miss you,' she said. 'And I hate the fact that I don't see you that much anymore. I know that it's going to take time for you to feel comfortable here, so I'm not blaming you. I just miss you. That's why I thought a little weekend away would be the perfect treat, for both of us.' Fern ripped the tape off another box, searching for the Dior hand luggage she had bought for her last trip abroad.

With outstretched arms, Fern reached for a box resting just above Charlotte's head. Holding her breath, Charlotte closed her eyes and kept her body crouched like a frightened animal. Dislodged dust particles rained through the air and aggravated her stubborn asthma, and she could feel the onset of wheezing lungs and a rumble of coughs that were desperate to explode. Deep, thick swallows forced saliva down her throat, momentarily placating the tickle. Through prayer and will, she begged for Fern to leave; leave the barn, leave the house, and never return to Lunar, putting an end to her nightmare.

'Sounds great to me,' Jessie replied, excited by her mum's thoughtful gesture.

'Brilliant. I'll pick you up after college. We'll be there in time for an evening meal.'

Fern stuffed her phone back into her pocket, and with a careful touch, pulled out her bridal gown. The dress that had once meant so much to her now brought so many hurtful emotions to the surface. She pressed it against her body. It was the dress that she once hoped to pass down to Jessie, the dress that had accentuated every curve, the dress that had cost more than she and Cooper could afford at the time. Fern allowed her fingers to relish the soft fabric, and she pictured herself wearing it on her magical day, standing at the alter alongside the love of her life.

'I hate you!' she shouted suddenly, ripping the fabric with her hands, the delicate material tearing with ease. 'I hate you!' she repeated, so much anger spilling out in her words, her face red with rage. 'How could you do that to me?' she cried. Tatters of material scattered the floor, the dark, dusty interior soon speckled with flecks of white and ivory. The sequins shone like diamonds when Fern opened the door, and with a thunderous bang, slammed it shut behind her.

In one quick burst, Charlotte exploded from her hiding place and bent over on her knees, allowing a plume of coughs to erupt from her lungs. Burying her head in the tattered pieces of material to downplay the noise, she coughed and gasped for breath. Streams of tears fell from her eyes and, not for the first time, she prayed for the barn to take her life too.

18

The living roof at Flocks Hotel & Spa helped to blend the secluded building into the grassy undulations of the Oxfordshire landscape. From the moment that Fern had stepped foot inside the retreat's welcoming embrace and removed her coat, she had relished the feeling of anonymity. For the first time in weeks, as she merged herself amongst strangers, she didn't feel suspicious. Walking into the bustling restaurant, the relaxed expression on her face conveyed the feeling of freedom coursing through her. By the time she took a sip of her second glass of wine, she felt a million miles away from Lunar and the unsettling shadows that had been following her around.

Seated in a snug, corner booth in the hotel's high-end restaurant with Jessie, Fern savoured the moment of solace and relaxed. Her muscles released the tension that had been holding her body captive since her move to Aldebaran. 'This champagne chicken is delicious,' she commented, savouring the umami flavours. 'I've been living off microwave meals for too long. I need to start making an effort again and get used to cooking homemade meals for one.'

'You're checking your phone a lot,' Jessie commented. 'Is everything alright?'

Fern closed the surveillance app and released her phone, reluctant to let Jessie in on what was potentially unravelling back at home. 'Sorry, Jess. I've only just re-opened my diary, so emails and messages are starting to come through about potential orders. I'm supporting myself now, so every customer counts.'

Jessie felt relieved that she hadn't ordered the expensive lobster bisque starter followed by an 8oz sirloin steak, like she had initially intended. 'Are you worried about money?' she asked, taking a final bite out of her club sandwich.

'I'm not worried. It's just an adjustment. I haven't felt so independent since I left home and started university.' Fern took a sip from her oversized glass of wine. 'This place is amazing, isn't it?' She admired the impressive chandelier that hung above their table. 'If only I could get Lunar to feel so magical,' she said with a sense of sadness.

'The house is looking amazing,' Jessie replied, recalling the transformation that she was greeted by during her last visit. 'It feels homely, which is perfect. I don't want my home to feel like this,' she said, indicating towards the garish chandelier.

Fern reached out her hand and pressed it against her daughter's. 'You've no idea how happy that makes me feel. I know life hasn't been easy this past six months, and that my decision to buy Lunar added to our stress. I just wanted a place that you would call home.'

Jessie messed with her hair, tucking her stylish pixie cut behind her ears. 'I wasn't sure at first. The state of the house was a shock. But I love it now, and I definitely think that it's the right time for me to move in. If that's okay?' she asked. 'It's been great just popping over after college and having tea with you, but it won't start feeling like home until I actually move in.'

Fern couldn't hide her excitement and her face lit up. 'Of course it's okay.'

'Do you think Dad will be mad?'

'We'll talk to him together. I'm sure he'll just want you to be happy,' she replied, secretly relishing the fact that, for Cooper, the decision was bound to cut deep. 'There is something that I need to tell you about the house,' Fern announced, draining her glass before indicating to the waitress that she would like a refill.

'I don't like the sound of this,' Jessie said, her eyebrows raised. 'Have you found out that it's haunted?' she mocked.

'No, nothing like that, and it's nothing to worry about,' Fern was quick to offer reassurance. 'I found out from speaking to a few of my neighbours that there was a fire, about fifteen years ago,' Fern began. 'It was actually in the barn, not the house itself.'

A look of relief washed over Jessie's face. 'The expression on your face tells me there's more to the story.'

Fern looked up and met her daughter's gaze. 'When you found that photo in the kitchen, we wondered if it was the family who had lived at Lunar before us, remember?' she asked, buying herself a few seconds before revealing the truth.

'I remember.'

'Well, we were right. Mr Sloan and his wife had lived at Lunar with their two children. They had a daughter and a son, Charlotte and Sam.' Fern took a moment to pause while the waitress delivered the drink. 'Sam was trapped in the barn when the fire broke out, and he lost his life. He was only seven at the time.'

A deep furrow appeared in Jessie's forehead. 'That's so sad,' she commented.

'All the children's toys that I found in the house belonged to Sam, and I'm still trying to track down any family members so that I can hand it all back to them.'

'I'm glad we know what happened, and although it's a sad story, I feel better knowing the truth.'

'The house was so run down because Mr Sloan had been living there alone. My guess is he was still struggling to come to terms with his son's death.'

Jessie thought back on her first visit to Lunar. 'I wasn't sure I'd ever feel comfortable in the house,' she revealed, 'but it's unrecognisable now. It's bright, and warm, and clean, and inviting, and homely,' she explained, the list of compliments rolling off her tongue with ease. 'I can't wait to have my friends stay over.' Jessie tried to swallow a yawn, her eyelids feeling heavy.

'Should we head back to our room?' Fern suggested. 'It's been a long day. All that pampering was exhausting.'

Jessie grabbed her denim jacket and phone. 'I was hoping you'd say that. I'm shattered.'

Already feeling a little tipsy from the prosecco she'd drank during the afternoon massage session, Fern fumbled through the long, narrow corridors back to their room, holding onto Jessie's arm for support. 'I didn't think I'd had that much to drink,' she said, fumbling in her bag for the room key. When she held it to the receptor on the door, it repeatedly flashed red, denying them entry.

'It's a good job you have me,' Jessie mocked, taking hold of the card and opening the door. 'I'm putting my sweatpants on,' she said, throwing her bag down on the bed before reaching for her hoodie and tracksuit bottoms. 'I'm so tired.' Jessie crawled into one of the single beds and closed her eyes.

Fern pulled the covers around her daughter's body, like she had done a thousand times in the past. 'Goodnight, my love,' she whispered, delivering a gentle kiss to her daughter's forehead. 'I'll be back soon. I'm just going to go and have one last drink in the bar while I catch up on a few work emails.'

Fern ruffled her hair and applied a fresh layer of gloss to her lips before grabbing her bag and heading back out into the hotel's maze of corridors, navigating her way to the bar. 'Double rum and coke, please,' she ordered, taking a seat on one of the bar stools. 'Plenty of ice,' she requested as an afterthought, feeling a little flushed.

'It's last orders,' the bartender advised, placing the drink in front of Fern.

'Perfect,' she smiled, crossing her legs and swinging her body round. The entire bar was empty, herself and the bartender the only people left in the room. She savoured the moment, allowing the fiery, copper liquor to mull in her mouth before she swallowed it. When she heard her phone vibrate on the bar, she saw that a notification had come through from her new security app. The motion detector at Lunar had identified movement. Fumbling, she logged into the app, opening the real-time footage on her screen. Through an intense, cold stare, she drew the phone closer to her face. She squinted, desperate to bring the blurred screen into focus.

'Anything else before I close up?' the bartender asked, removing Fern's empty glass.

Without looking up, she shook her head, refusing to take her attention away from her phone. The bartender walked away. As he went to pull down the shutters and dim the lights, he tried to ignore the pang of pity that flashed through his mind for this lonely, drunk woman that was hunched over his bar. As he turned to try and encourage her to call it a night, he was met with a vacant stool. Fern had disappeared and the room was empty.

Feeling flustered, Fern found herself searching for a quiet spot to sit down. Each social area that she stumbled across had already dimmed their lights for the night. Unwilling to risk disturbing Jessie in their shared bedroom, she headed outside. Sheltering beneath the wooden gazebo that swept across the entire front of the hotel, she sat at one of the tables overlooking the private lake. Engrossed by the surveillance, the world beyond her phone failed to exist. She failed to appreciate the decorative crisscross pattern created by the festoon lighting that illuminated the hotel grounds, or the array of nocturnal bugs that fluttered and danced near the dangling bulbs. Having opened her list of contacts, Fern dialled Dylan's number. A noise in the distance made her look up, and she tried to decipher the collection of ambiguous shadows that the festoon lights were reflecting across the surface of the still lake, her suspicions and shadows returning with vengeance.

'Hi,' Dylan said when he answered his phone.

'There's someone in the house,' Fern spluttered in response, breathless. 'And I'm watching him right now,' she confirmed, opening the surveillance app on her phone for a second time.

'What? Who is it?' Dylan asked without taking a breath. 'How did he get in?'

'I can't see his face,' she said, 'but the camera in the hallway has just picked him up.' Fern failed to feel the chill that was rolling in across the exposed landscape. Her nose turned red, and her eyes stung each time the breeze swept across her face. 'He's wearing a black bulky parker. The hood's covering his face. He's just stood there. He's not doing anything,' she narrated. 'I didn't see how he got in.'

'Have you called the police?'

Fern's befuddled, drunken mind struggled to process what was happening. 'No. I called you,' she confirmed. 'Oh, God. He's moving. He's heading towards the kitchen now,' she announced, her words slurred. 'My screen's gone blank. What's happening? Why can't I see him anymore,' she rambled, anger and frustration flowing through her words.

'I don't know, Fern. I'm not there. Hang up and call the bloody police,' he said, failing to understand why that hadn't been her first call. 'Someone has broken into your house, so just call 999 before he leaves.'

'Oh, I can see him now. The camera in the kitchen has picked up his movement. He's looking through my kitchen cupboards,' she said, moving the phone closer to her face again so that she could try and see his facial features. 'What's he doing? I don't understand,' Fern's skin crawled at the sight of someone invading her personal space. 'I knew I wasn't going mad,' she mumbled to herself, crying.

Dylan turned up the volume on his phone, the sound of Fern's voice becoming faint. 'What did you say?'

Fern cleared her throat and adopted a decisive tone. 'I knew I wasn't going mad. I knew someone had been watching me,' she cried. Her tears were thick and heavy with fear as they tumbled off her cheeks.

'You need to hang up and call the police.'

Gripped, Fern studied the way the person navigated her kitchen with ease and familiarity. 'I want to see who it is. I need to know, Dylan,' she said, refusing to divert her attention. 'This is the psycho who's been in the house before. It must be,' she explained, still scrutinising the figure on her screen.

'How do you know?'

'It's pitch dark in there, Dylan, and he's walking around without bumping into anything. It's like he knows the layout. He already knows where everything is.'

Dylan turned off his television and pulled himself off the sofa. 'It doesn't make any sense.'

'He's walking out of the kitchen,' she explained, waiting for another camera to detect his shadow. A black and white fuzzy screen appeared on Fern's live footage. 'The screen's gone blank again. Why? What should I do?' she said, the impatience in her voice turning to panic.

'He could be leaving, and you haven't called the police,' Dylan said with equal frustration, pacing his lounge with heavy stomps. 'Should I go over?'

The live feed reappeared. The footage captured the person lingering in the front room. 'He's in the lounge now,' she announced, jumping in her seat the second the image flashed on screen.

Dylan ran his hands through his hair, and he sat back down, his fraught nerves putting him on edge. 'What's he doing?'

'I'm not sure, the camera's only picking up part of the room and I can only see his feet. He's sat in the single chair, Dylan. Just sat there, like it's his house, like it's his seat and he can come and go as he pleases.' Fern willed the person to move and come into view. She tried not to blink and ignored the stinging sensation stabbing at her eyeballs. Her breath was becoming scrappy as her heart pumped and her extremities shook as she tried to anticipate what the man's next move.

'Fern. Please call the police. This guy could be dangerous.'

'Wait. He's moving,' she snapped, making Dylan jump at the other end of the line. 'He's walked back into the hallway.'

'What's he doing? he asked, realising that his suggestion to call the police was being repeatedly ignored.

'He's just stood near the bottom of the stairs. I still can't see his face and it's so frustrating.' Without realising it, Fern's legs continued to bob up and down on the spot and she failed to notice that the battery on her phone was running low.

'And he isn't breaking anything? He's not stealing anything?'

'No. He's just standing there, Dylan. He doesn't seem in a rush, and do you know why? It's because he knows that I'm not home. He knows that I'm away.'

'Who did you tell about your plans?'

'Not many people, really. Cooper, and Iris Pepper, my neighbour across the street. But I did put it on the social media account for my business, so anybody could have seen it.'

Dylan grabbed his car keys. 'I'm going over there. You've said it yourself before, you don't think he's dangerous. I can confront him and put an end to all this craziness.'

'No. Absolutely not. I'd never forgive myself if something happened to you. I don't think he's dangerous, but if you take him by surprise, who knows how he'll react.'

'I know that house better than most people, Fern. I can sneak up on him before he even knows that I'm there.'

'Wait,' she whispered, making a shushing sound. She watched as the person made their way up the stairs, their hand navigating the banister. 'Did you hear that?'

'Hear what?' Dylan asked, turning up the volume on his phone until it reached the maximum.

'Listen,' Fern said, urging the noise to resonate again. 'The screen's gone blank. Why didn't I put camera's upstairs, too?' she said, the benefit of hindsight making her kick herself.

'What did you hear?'

Fern failed to respond, but Dylan could hear her laboured breathing at the other end of the line. 'What's happening? Talk to me, Fern,' Dylan asked when the line remained quiet.

'Shush,' she insisted just as the live footage flicked back onto her screen. 'She's back downstairs.'

Dylan held his breath and waited, failing to pick up on Fern's choice of pronoun. Gripping his car keys, he contemplated ignoring his friend's orders and making the dash up to Lunar.

Fern watched the person reappear back in the lounge, live images flicking on her screen. Tears rolled from Fern's eyes the moment she watched the stranger pick up Sam's teddy from the fireplace. The sound of bracelets jangling against one another echoed with familiarity down the line, making her cry harder. 'I left one of Sam's teddies on the fireplace. That's what she wants. That's why she's there. It all makes sense now,' Fern cried, pressing her free hand over her eyes and shaking her head with sadness. She watched how the person held the precious, soft teddy close to her face so that the fabric brushed against her skin. Then came the final confirmation as the intruder turned to the left, her face now in full view of the hidden camera.

A stabbing pain attacked Fern's heart the moment she realised that she'd suffered another bout of betrayal. Waves of sadness clouded her eyes, and she pulled her gaze away from her screen, unable to watch the heartbreak anymore. Her head hung low, and the disappointment fell like a boulder from her shoulders.

Dylan could hear Fern's breathing becoming more laboured down the line. 'Fern, please talk to me. What's going on?'

Fern drew her attention back to her phone. She watched as the person took a seat on the sofa, and flickers of familiarity shone through the darkness brighter than a perfect cut diamond. 'I know who it is, and why she's there,' she confirmed. 'I can handle this by myself, Dylan, and I don't need you to do anything. There's nothing to worry about and I'll call you when I'm home. Thanks again for everything.' Fern hung up the phone and turned it off. Sitting back in her chair, she looked out across the lake. Her emotions tumbled and turned like the changing wind. One minute she felt angry, and the next minute she felt so much sadness that she could barely draw breath.

19

Having dropped Jessie off with Cooper on the way home from their spa retreat, Fern pulled up to Lunar, alone. For the first time since purchasing the former farmhouse, a comforting sense of stillness swept through her body when she looked up and admired her home. The sun had already crawled upwards from the East, and Fern sat and watched as it hovered on the horizon. She admired how the sun shone behind Lunar, a flurry of light setting the vista on fire. Flickers of light sept through the backdrop of majestic trees, and a myriad of autumnal colours shone like nuggets of gold. In that moment, just as a warming slither of sunshine reflected off her face, she made peace with Lunar, and its deep-rooted history. The longer she sat in silence, appreciating the present moment for all that it was, the more she felt her fears dropping away, reminiscent of falling leaves during autumn's crescendo.

Continuing to peer up at her home through a fresh pair of eyes, Fern finally started to feel an emotional connection to the property. As Lunar's new custodian, she pictured how pretty the garden would look come springtime when new shoots started to flourish through the dense undergrowth. She imagined Jessie spending time at the house during the long, summer months, the prospect filling her heart with joy. And she pictured how she herself might spend time stargazing at Lunar during the clear, frosty winter evenings.

Opening the car door, the thought of being alone at Lunar no longer felt intimidating as she walked towards the front door without hesitation. Placing her key in the lock, she felt ready to face Lunar's history, understanding that it was time to set old ghosts free. With a gentle push, she eased the door open. Not a sound could be heard, and she knew that the person who had visited the previous evening had long since departed.

With her suitcase still lingering in the hallway and with her coat wrapped around her torso, Fern set about lighting the fire. After just one night away, the rooms at Lunar felt particularly prickly. Every lingering trace of warmth had been consumed by the high ceilings and exposed gaps in the floorboards. A penetrating, hostile chill encouraged Fern to hustle, and she brought together all the essential ingredients to build a fire. Accommodating her request, the flints soon ignited, the cast iron grate containing the coals as they warmed and turned from ash to a vivid reddish orange. Just as she placed the fire guard across the hearth, she heard an unexpected knock at the door.

'Hello, Arthur,' she greeted when she opened her front door. 'Is everything okay?', she asked, concerned.

'Hello, Fern,' he replied. Like he was standing to attention, Arthur's frame appeared rigid, his hands by his side, one gripping a walking stick.

An awkward silence presented when Arthur didn't say anything else.

'Is Olive okay?' Fern asked, noting the worrisome expression on her neighbour's face.

Arthur peered over to the barn, and then looked back at Fern. 'We're both fine, thank you. I'm here because I'm ready to talk to you. That's if you're still interested in knowing more about the Sloan family,' he said, his knuckles white from clenching his walking stick.

Fern opened the door wide. 'It'd be lovely to have a chat,' she smiled, indicating for him to enter. She moved her travel bag out of the way that still needed to be unpacked. 'You've only just caught me. I've just returned home from a night away with my daughter.' Noticing how unstable Arthur appeared on his feet, Fern offered to assist. 'Do you need any help?'

'No. I'm fine, thank you. It just takes me longer to get about than it used to.' The moment that Arthur stepped foot inside, a flood of memories tumbled behind him. He paused in the hallway. 'Gosh, I wouldn't even think that this was the same house,' he commented, peering around at the vibrant interior. 'When Lockie and his family lived here, there was a big cuckoo clock right here,' he explained, pointing to the wall near the lounge. 'And it would scare me to death if I just happened to walk past it on the hour,' he smiled, the memory particularly vivid.

'There were a lot of things left behind, but I don't recall seeing a clock,' Fern replied. 'Shall we take a seat in here?' she asked. 'It's a lovely room for capturing the sun at this time of day.' Fern indicated for Arthur to follow her into the lounge. 'Please, take a seat.' Fern sat herself on the sofa, allowing Arthur to sit on the single chair nestled near the window, the seat closest to the fire.

Arthur eased himself into the chair, allowing the padded cushions to support his frail frame. He glanced outside. 'It's so strange seeing the barn from this angle,' he commented, arching his neck to look across at the outbuilding. 'For so many years - what feels like a lifetime, actually - I've stared at it from the other side of the trees, up there from my landing window,' he pointed.

Fern's bouncing knee indicated her nerves. 'Can I get you a drink? Tea, or maybe a coffee?'

'Do you know the one thing that birds don't like?' he asked, ignoring her question, consumed by his own trail of thoughts.

Fern shook her head. 'Cats?' she smiled. 'And fast dogs, I imagine.'

'Birds don't like noise. They're ever so timid, and the slightest noise scares them away.'

Unsure where his trail of conversation was going, Fern remained quiet, allowing her aloof neighbour to elaborate.

With his gaze still locked on the barn, Arthur continued. 'And when I was working professionally as a photographer, or even just taking photos in my garden for my own personal pleasure, noise was my nemesis.' Arthur brought his gaze inside until it landed on Fern. 'Children make a lot of noise,' he said. 'And sometimes I'd sit for hours in my garden, poised with my camera ready to capture the shot - the money shot, as they call it in the business - and then the Sloan kids would head outside to play. And just like that, the birds would be gone,' he said, clicking his fingers in the air.

Fern observed the glossiness that had appeared in Arthur's eyes, his wrinkles more prevalent whenever he frowned.

'I remember when my daughter was growing up. My husband and I would often say that we could hear her before we saw her,' Fern sympathised when Arthur stopped talking.

'Over the years, the noise coming from this house all blended and it sounded the same. Screams of excitement. Screams of adventure. Screams of fun. Screams of fright. Screams of pain. It all sounded the same. Noisy,' Arthur explained. 'And at the start, never having had children myself, I would go running over whenever I heard these screams. You see, I was worried that someone had hurt themselves. I'd then see the children chasing after each other with water guns, or goodness knows what, and saw for myself that the screams were all just part of their excitement.'

Sensing that Arthur's story was finally unfolding, Fern perched her body at the end of her seat.

Arthur adjusted the heavy-rimmed glasses that were wedged on his button nose. 'And that day was really no different.' He bowed his head, losing himself in the memory, in the noises, and in the pain. 'I'd been waiting for the money shot all day — for weeks, really. I knew that there was a willow tit nesting in this area.' Arthur looked up to meet Fern's awaiting gaze. 'Willow tits are very rare in these parts. They have like a sooty-black cap and a black, untidy bib, so quite distinctive in appearance,' he explained with enthusiasm, his facial features sparkling with the talk about birds. 'So, I wanted the shot.' He allowed his gaze to drift back out towards the barn. 'And that afternoon, I'd been ready with my camera all day. I was staked out in the garden under my makeshift bird hide, waiting for this illusive feathered creature to make an appearance.' Arthur paused and allowed himself a moment to gather himself. 'And just as the little fellow landed in my garden, a scream as loud as I've ever heard made it disappear in an instant.' Taking out his handkerchief, Arthur dabbed his face and removed any remaining sparkle lurking in his eyes. 'I was so furious that I dropped my camera and stormed off inside. I put some music on and turned the volume right up. I was intent on making my own noise for a change.'

'Then what happened?' Fern encouraged, sensing the pain that Arthur was grappling with. 'What happened once you came inside?'

Arthur watched the roaring fire that was now warming his face. His thoughts became lost in the pyramid of flames, the smell and the sight of the smoke triggering the trauma that had consumed him for more than a decade. 'Sam's initial scream that day was unlike anything I'd ever heard before. It just sounded different. But, because I was so annoyed, so angry, and so frustrated, I turned up my music to drown out his constant din, instead of running over there and checking that everything was okay,' he confessed, his eyes now full of tears and remorse. 'I had all the windows shut, so I didn't smell the smoke at first. And although I did hear somebody knocking at the front door, I assumed they were playing tricks on me. So, I just sat back and ignored it,' Arthur drew in a deep breath, pushing air past the ghosts and demons that had lived inside him for fifteen years. 'It was only when I heard the blasting sound of sirens that I turned the music off and stepped outside to see what was going on.' Arthur raised his arms in the air, his stick falling to the floor. 'It was like a volcano had erupted,' he described. 'I just couldn't believe what I was seeing.'

Fern stood up and went over to the window where Arthur was

sitting. She picked up his stick and perched herself on the floor by his feet, handing him a box of tissues.

'The smoke was nasty stuff; thick and black,' he described, 'and it was pouring out from one side of the barn. That's when I knew he wasn't screaming because he was having fun.' Arthur looked down at Fern. 'Sam was screaming in fear.' The moment the words left Arthur's lips, his body winced, like the ghosts from his past were clawing at him. 'Sam was screaming because he was trapped inside by the fire, and I had ignored his cries for help.' Arthur gazed out at the barn that, for fifteen years, he had wanted to tear down with his bare hands. 'I allowed Sam to suffer. It was my fault that he died that day.'

Not knowing what to say, Fern stood up and sat on the chair arm. Placing her hand around Arthur's frame, she cradled his shaking body. She felt Arthur lean into the embrace, her upper strength supporting his weakening figure.

Arthur couldn't stop the constant stream of tears that were falling onto his lap. 'I watched them trying to get him out, trying to save his life. But the fire was too strong. It was too overwhelming. And they just couldn't get to him in time,' he sobbed, spluttering through his words.

Fern sat back down on the floor, looking up at her frail neighbour. 'Sam's death wasn't your fault, Arthur,' she reassured. 'It was just a tragic accident,' she reached out and held his hand, holding it tight so that he could feel the pressure. 'Had you known what was going on, of course you would have helped straight away. But you didn't know. It was just a terrible accident that nobody could have anticipated.'

Arthur thrashed his head. 'I heard his screams. I heard him dying. And I chose to turn my music up and ignore it. And why? Because I was more bothered about some stupid shot that I'd missed out on.'

'Arthur, listen to me,' Fern begged, manoeuvring her head until she reestablished eye contact. 'You weren't to blame for

Sam's death. You just weren't,' she protested. 'I've read the news reports. I've spoken to people about what happened that day. It was just an accident. Sam was messing about with cigarettes and matches without knowing the dangers. It wasn't your fault. It was an accident. A tragic accident.'

Arthur looked out over the barn again, his breathing beginning to regulate. 'After that day, I found myself standing on the landing window watching that wretched building. I felt paranoid, and needed to make sure that it wasn't on fire again. I felt the need to constantly check that there was nobody trapped inside. I needed to make sure that I hadn't missed someone else's cries for help. And as the days turned into weeks, and weeks turned into months, and months turned into years, I couldn't stop myself. It became an obsession, and it still is.'

Fern shook her head at the torment evident in Arthur's eyes. 'The fact that you've lived with these feelings of guilt for so many years is heartbreaking,' she began. 'It's almost like you lost your life that day, too.'

'I've tried to make peace with it. I desperately wanted to come to terms with what had happened. But there was no escaping the memories. I can see this house from my windows. I had to pass the barn if I wanted to go out anywhere. So, in the end, I just shut myself away from the world. It felt easier that way. I didn't have to talk about it to anybody. I only saw Olive, and she respected my wishes and never asked me to talk about it.'

'I know it's hard to talk about, and it brings back a lot of difficult emotions, but I'm so grateful that you chose to talk to me. I didn't know anything about the fire when I bought the property,' Fern replied. 'And at first, I felt intimidated by this house. It felt scary to me. Hostile even. But the more I've learned, the more I've come to realise that, at one time, this house was a loving family home. That's what I want to cherish. That's the legacy of Lunar that I feel responsible for upholding.' Fern crouched before the fire and stoked the coals, distributing the wealth of warmth until the flames settled into a gentle burn. 'Arthur, do you know what happened to Lockie and Elizabeth?'

Arthur eased back into the seat, his posture becoming more relaxed. 'I tried my best to support Lockie over the years. I wanted to be there for him, as a friend. No matter how hard it felt, I would make myself come over here and see if he wanted anything, any food, any company. But I wasn't welcome in this house, not anymore. That was made clear.'

'You were friends, weren't you?'

Arthur nodded. 'We were good pals for a long time.'

'Did he say why the friendship was over?'

Arthur winced in his chair, his arthritic hips causing pain, and discomfort. 'A few months after the fire, I came over again to check up on him. He didn't answer, but the door was unlocked, so I let myself in. I found Lockie sat in this very room, right there,' he pointed. 'The room was dark, cold and dismal,' he recalled. 'And I could tell that the rest of the house was in the same state of disarray.'

'And what did Lockie say?' Fern asked, trying to picture that day in her mind.

Arthur sighed. 'He didn't even look me in the eyes. He just told me to leave. He told me to never come back. So, that's what I did.'

'What about their daughter?'

'Charlotte moved away. She went to live with a relative, as far as I know. She never returned to Aldebaran.'

Fern added another shovel of coal to the embers. 'And what about Elizabeth?'

Arthur took a moment before replying. 'One day, not long after the fire, she came over to see me.'

'Why? What did she want?'

'She wanted me to get her a supply of painkillers,' Arthur revealed. 'She couldn't bear the thought of leaving the house to go shopping. Or to go anywhere. And she couldn't ask Lockie because she didn't want him to know how desperate she was feeling. Their marriage was strained after they lost Sam. I could see that. They used to come and go together all the time. Or even just spending time in the garden together. They were soulmates.'

'Did you get her the pills?'

Arthur shook his head. 'No, I didn't,' he confirmed. 'I offered to get some help for her. I offered to take her to the doctors or to get someone to come to the house. I offered to do anything. But I couldn't bring myself to do that knowing her intentions.'

Fern recalled the conversation that she'd had with Iris and Dylan, knowing that Elizabeth had passed away not long after the fire. 'I've heard that Elizabeth passed away.'

Arthur fidgeted in his chair with discomfort. 'I got a call from the hospital that day. They said that Elizabeth had been asking for me, and nobody else,' he explained. 'So, I went and saw her.'

'What happened?'

'She attempted suicide by taking an overdose. She'd somehow managed to get her hands on extra painkillers despite me refusing. But she survived. It wasn't her time,' he said, shrugging his shoulders. 'And when I went to see her, she said that even though they'd managed to save her life, she wanted people to think that she'd died.' Arthur made no attempt to wipe away the stray tears that were cascading down his weathered face.

'What?' Fern questioned, confused. 'Elizabeth faked her own death?'

'She told me that the only way she could carry on, the only way that she could deal with life, was if she could be someone else. She wanted to leave everything behind so that nobody would know her. She didn't want anybody knowing what had happened to her, or to Sam. And she asked me to help her. She made me promise.'

A look of confusion spread over Fern's face. 'Surely people asked about her? And what about Lockie? What was he told?'

'Elizabeth never returned to Lunar after that day. She just disappeared. She went and started a new life somewhere, and Lockie let her go.'

Fern looked around the impressive room. 'And Lockie stayed here, alone?'

'He did. He continued to hide himself away in this big house. He never spoke to anybody, as far as I know, and he survived by getting everything delivered to the house. He certainly never went anywhere. And by living the way he did, he didn't have to face people, or their pity.' Arthur pictured Lockie and saw the haunting expression that was always lodged on his neighbour's face. 'Rumours did the rounds, obviously. But nobody knew what had happened to Elizabeth apart from myself, and Lockie. So, it worked. And as time went on, people asked fewer and fewer questions.'

'Do you know that Sam's room was preserved, if that's the correct word?'

Arthur looked confused. 'What do you mean?'

'When I got the keys to this place, the small bedroom at the front of the house looked untouched. The bed was still made. Sam's toys and clothes were scattered about. It was like his room hadn't been touched since the day of the fire.'

Arthur bowed his head. 'I knew that Lockie never got over Sam's death. That was obvious. When I would look out from my window, I could see Lockie sitting in his chair. So, I knew that he was alright. But like I've said, he wouldn't let me in. No matter how hard I tried. So, I didn't know about the situation upstairs.'

'Because of the things that were left behind, I've been trying to find any relatives of Sam's so that I can pass the things back.' Fern took out her phone. 'Do you know who this is?' she asked, showing Arthur a photo that she had of Edith.

He took hold of the phone and held it close to his eyes. 'No, should I?'

'Her name is Edith Preston. She lives and works in the village. For reasons that I still don't understand, she has connections to this house, specifically connections to Sam, I think.' Fern thought back to the live camera footage, and the way that Edith had navigated the interior with familiarity. 'She's a friend of mine, or was a friend, or still is a friend. I'm not quite sure yet,' Fern revealed. 'She's been here a few times, but she never mentioned having any connections to the property or the Sloan family.'

Arthur took another look at the photo. 'The only people I know who have connections to this house are Charlotte and Elizabeth.' Arthur looked up at Fern. 'Charlotte had very dark features and pale skin. Her hair was curly and a deep shade of brown. She wore thick glasses that dominated her face, and odd clothes that made her look a little strange, but her smile was warm, and gentle.' He looked back at the photo. 'Even with the number of years that have passed since I last saw her, I don't see any traces of familiarity here.' He handed Fern her phone. 'And it's definitely not Elizabeth. That I'm certain. And Elizabeth wouldn't have come back to Aldebaran, not without letting me know. The only contact she's had with me over the past fifteen years is a Christmas card each year, always signed *Much love, ES*.'

Fern's heart skipped. 'Do you have an address for her? Or a contact number?'

'I don't. She never wrote a return address on the envelope or left any phone number.' Arthur could feel his nerves tumbling through his stomach at the thought of what he was about to reveal. 'There is something I haven't told you.'

Fern looked up and spotted a fresh wave of turmoil wash over Arthur's face. More creases developed on his wafer-thin skin, ageing him in an instant. 'What is it?' she asked.

Arthur closed his eyes to contain his tears. Shutting out the image of Lunar's transformation meant that he was able to see the room as it had been the day that Lockie Sloan had passed away. 'I knew Lockie's daily routine, and it never wavered. I'd been keeping an eye on him from afar for so many years,' he began, opening his eyes. 'So, I knew that day that something was wrong.' Pressing his fingers over his eyes, he felt like he was once again standing next to Lockie Sloan's dead body. Arthur's skin came alive, and he felt cold to the core. The sense of loneliness and isolation that had greeted him that day came back to haunt him, once again wrapping its suffocating embrace around his fragile bones. 'Olive and I came over,' he continued, removing his hands and looking at Fern. 'We found Lockie slumped in his chair. His body was cold. His limbs were lifeless, and we knew that he'd passed away.'

Fern wanted to be able to erase the grief that she could see was causing Arthur so much pain. 'Oh, Arthur. I'm so sorry,' she consoled. 'I had no idea.'

'We called 999, but it felt like a lifetime before anybody came,' he explained. 'So, I remained by his side until the ambulance arrived. I didn't want him to be alone anymore. Nobody deserves to die alone.' The warmth from the open fire helped to remind Arthur that he was no longer immersed in the harshness of that day. The feeling of Fern's hand pressed against his helped to pull him back into the present moment. 'Next to his chair, I saw an envelope with my name written on the front,' he said, pulling out an envelope from his inner jacket pocket at handing it to Fern. She turned it over to reveal the name Charlotte scrawled on the front. 'Lockie knew that I watched him. He knew that I'd be the one who would find him,' he explained. 'And his last wish was for his daughter to have this.'

Fern flipped the envelope over and saw that it was sealed. 'A letter?' she questioned.

'I'm guessing so, but I haven't opened it,' he replied. 'Lockie trusted me, and now I'm trusting you,' he explained, lowering his head. 'You're already trying to find Charlotte or Elizabeth, so I'm hoping you'll be able to track them down much faster than I could.'

Fern held the letter in her hand, knowing that it was another piece of the Lunar jigsaw puzzle that she was trying to solve. 'I'll do my best.'

'This house has drained the life from so many people,' Arthur said, getting up and taking hold of his walking stick. He took one last glance at the room before walking into the hallway and towards the front door. 'It would be nice, if only in a small way, if there could be a happy ending after so much tragedy.' Arthur opened the door and stepped onto the porch. 'Thank you, Fern,' he began, turning to face the house one last time. 'It feels nice to have you as my new neighbour.' Arthur looked up at his landing window, the window that had held him prisoner for so many years. 'It's time for me to make peace with this place,' he added, taking in a large breath and filling his lungs with a fresh sense of optimism. 'I know that I don't need to keep watch anymore.' Arthur made his way down the steps and onto the gravel path, Fern by his side for support.

'It's now time for me to keep an eye on you,' she said as he made his way down the path. 'That's what neighbours are for.'

Fern watched as Arthur made his way home, and she felt the baton changing hands. She rested the letter in her palm, acknowledging its importance and finding herself overcome with the sense of responsibility to track down Sam's family and fulfil Lockie Sloan's dying request.

20

In the heart of bustling Aldebaran, Fern positioned herself across the street from the café where Edith worked. She took a seat on one of the benches that offered the best view of what was occurring at the heart of the quaint eatery. Sheltered beneath a mature horse-chestnut, Fern wrapped her coat tight to fend off the seasonal chill snapping at her body. Once settled in her secluded location, she took out her phone and made a call.

'Hi, Dylan,' she said when he answered the phone.

'Hi. How are you?' he asked, downing his tools and deciding now would be the perfect time to take a coffee break.

'I'm good. Jessie and I arrived home yesterday, and I know that we spoke briefly last night, but I just wanted to say again how sorry I am for the way I cut you off the other night,' she apologised, keeping her eyes firmly set on the café. 'And please don't be mad at me for what I'm about to say.'

'You still haven't called the police, have you?'

'How did you know?'

Dylan produced a long, heavy sigh that fell like a dead weight from his lips. 'I just knew,' he declared. 'I think you're crazy. This supposed *friend* of yours broke into your house. Friends don't do that. You need to call the police and tell them everything.'

Fern went quiet with nerves.

The silence told him that she still hadn't changed her mind. 'I'm a real friend. So, tell me this woman's name again, and where she lives, and I'll call the police for you. Then it's nothing to do with you.'

From her vantage point, Fern's eyes followed Edith's every move. Watching how she interacted with customers, Fern observed how her friend prepared an order, and how she behaved when she thought nobody was looking. 'Her name is Edith Preston. I don't know where she lives because she's never invited me over to her place.'

Dylan paced and released another heavy sigh, swearing beneath his breath. 'Shouldn't that have been a warning sign? The fact that she's never invited you over to her house?'

'Dylan, it's not like I've known this woman for years. We're talking a handful of months,' Fern protested. 'And I admit, when I moved here, I was lonely. I was feeling really isolated and generally in a very dark place mentally thanks to the breakdown of my marriage,' she said in one long breath. 'The very fact that Edith was so nice to me, and made me feel welcome was all I needed to want to be friends with her. I didn't think to do a background check.'

'And have you done one now?' he asked, his fingers already scrolling through various social media platforms looking for an Edith Preston.

'Have I what?' she whispered when someone took a seat at the other end of the bench.

'Trawled the internet to find out who she *really* is?' he said, like it was obvious.

'She's not on social media. Not that I could find anyway.'

Dylan could feel his frustration mounting. 'That's another red flag. Who isn't on social media? Even if it's not to post details about their own lives, people create accounts just so that they can stalk others.'

With a pair of sunglasses obscuring her eyes, her hair uncharacteristically scooped back into a sleek ponytail, and one of Jessie's winter denim jackets wrapped around her frame, Fern felt reassured that even if Edith happened to glance over in her direction, her identity wouldn't be obvious. 'There's a connection to Edith and Sam, Dylan, and I need to know what it is. Going to the police isn't going to help me find out any of that information,' Fern revealed. 'And I hate to say this because I already know what your reaction's going to be, but I feel sorry for her. To have the guts to enter someone's house means she must be desperate. She hasn't stolen anything. She hasn't tried to hurt me. So, I need to know what she wants.'

Dylan shook his head and placed his free hand over his face. 'You feel sorry for her? She's made you feel uneasy, and worse than that, Fern, this crazy woman pretended to be your friend when, all along, she's been lying to your face.'

Fern watched how Edith applied some lip balm, pressing her lips together to smooth in the moisturiser. She watched how Edith restocked the cake counter, making sure that all the cookies, cupcakes and cream cakes were well presented. Fern smiled as she watched Edith offering a child a free sweet from the glass jar, and how she offered the little girl a high five. 'She doesn't look crazy, Dylan. She looks normal, whatever *normal* looks like.'

'Have you got a photo of her? I wonder if I'd recognise her. I've never been to her café. But this village isn't exactly big, so you'd think that our paths would've crossed at some point.'

Fern sent the photo that she'd shown Arthur. 'Have you got it?' she asked. 'I found this picture of her on the café website.'

'Why are you whispering? Where are you?' Dylan asked, hearing background noise.

The person that had been sitting at the opposite end to Fern got up and left, allowing her to speak in a normal volume. 'Don't get mad,' she began. 'But I'm sat outside her café. I'm watching her right now. What does this say about me? I'm the one who's stalking now.' Fern peered around, a sudden sense of paranoia rocking her composure.

Dylan produced a theatrical groan, and his tension was audible. 'You're playing a dangerous game.'

'She doesn't know that I'm here. All I'm doing is watching.'

'Why don't you just go and confront her in the café? She wouldn't act crazy in front of customers. That'd be bad for business.'

'I'm not sure I'm that brave. I'm not a confrontational kind of person.'

'Then why are you watching her? What's that going to achieve?'

Fern wasn't exactly sure what she was hoping to uncover but felt that she had to do something. 'Have you looked at the photo?' she asked, changing the subject.

Dylan opened the message and peered at the image of Edith. 'Long, blonde hair, pretty and has a good sense of fashion. If I didn't know that she was a stalker, I'd say that she looks cute.'

'Can we please stop calling her a stalker?' Fern watched Edith go about her afternoon in the café, serving one customer after another, smiling, and chatting like she didn't have a care in the world. 'You knew the Sloan family, Dylan. Think,' she encouraged. 'Edith must have been connected to them in some way. How about Sam's friends in school, in his class, or maybe in the village? Did they have any other neighbours back then?'

'I was older than Sam, remember? So, I'm not too sure about his classmates, but I don't remember him being good friends with any girls. And I don't recall the name Edith,' he said, his forehead crumpling as he tried to cast his memory back. 'Sam was a boy's boy. He wasn't interested in girls. He thought they were annoying.'

'What about family? Any cousins? Aunties?'

'Not that I know of. But I'm not sure, Fern. We're talking fifteen years ago, and I've tried to block most of it out,' he confessed. 'Sam and I just used to pally about after school and on weekends. We didn't speak about his genealogy,' he explained. 'His mum and dad didn't like me much, and Charlotte was fifteen or sixteen at the time. I can't remember exactly how old she was, but older than me. And she was always out with her own friends.'

Fern detected the strained tone of Dylan's voice. 'I'm sorry that all this is making you think about the past. I'm just confused,' she said. The autumn sunshine filtered down over Fern's face, the surrounding trees boasting shades of amber, blood orange and yellow, the leaves falling each time a gust of wind ripped through the branches.

'Let the police be confused. This is what they're paid to do.'

Fern bent down and pretended to tie her shoelace the moment she saw Edith grab her coat and head out onto the street.

'I can tell you're moving. What's happening?'

'I'm following her,' Fern revealed, getting up and tracing Edith's steps.

Dylan shook his head and rubbed the base of his neck. 'Fern, be careful,' he warned.

Fern crossed over the road, allowing more space to grow between her and Edith. 'I know what I'm doing,' she said. 'She's not heading to my place. We're heading towards the opposite end of town.'

Dylan's mind raced. 'Maybe she lives over that way and she's just on her way home?' he questioned. 'I'm trying to think what else is down that end of the village. The post office? That bakery at the end of Harker Street?'

'We've already passed both of those,' Fern replied, a sense of vulnerability creeping into her mind when she spotted Edith turning down a secluded side street. 'She's heading to the railway, I think.'

'She could be commuting. Maybe she doesn't drive?'

Fern walked a bit faster. 'I don't think so. She keeps looking at her watch. She's rushing. I can tell by her pace.'

The railway station came into view, both platforms bustling with commuters. Fern tried to blend into the crowd and peered up at the screen, trying to process all the unfamiliar place names.

'Are you still there?' Dylan asked when the line went quiet.

'Yeah, sorry. I'm just trying to figure out which train is arriving next.'

'Don't get on,' Dylan requested. 'You could be heading

anywhere, and you don't have a ticket, which could get you a fine,' he warned. 'Just walk away. Take some time to think about what you want to do next. We can come up with a plan together.'

In the distance, Fern spotted the train approaching, the squeal of the wheels sounding when it navigated the sharp curve in the track. 'It's here,' she mumbled, her flighty hand movements causing her to drop the phone. The clatter made people turn and look. Shielding her face, Fern turned her back and bent down to pick up her mobile. 'Are you still there?' she asked, noticing the cracked screen.

'What's happening?'

'I just dropped my phone and made everyone look at me,' she said, turning back around to look for Edith. The train drew up to the platform and came to a complete halt. The doors swung open and intermittently beeped. 'She's getting on. What should I do?' Just as the doors began to close, Fern jumped and slipped herself through the narrow gap.

'Don't get on!' Dylan shouted.

Fern made her way through the carriage and spotted Edith taking a seat in the distance.

Dylan listened to the sounds emanating down the line. 'You're on the train, aren't you?' he asked, hearing the conductor's overhead announcements.

Fern took a seat a handful of rows behind Edith. The train pulled away from the station and sped down the tracks. 'I am,' she revealed. 'I'm sat a few rows behind her on the opposite side,' she whispered when the carriage fell quiet. 'She keeps looking at her watch. I'm sure she's meeting someone. I want to know who.'

The high-speed train passed a handful of stations without stopping, unfamiliar scenery whizzing past Fern's window. The further out of town she ventured, the more nervous she felt. Her muscles twitched beneath her clothes, and she thought about Jessie. 'What am I doing?'

'I'm here. It's okay. Just keep talking to me,' Dylan said, sensing

Fern's nervousness in her heavy breathing. 'At the next stop, get off, go home, and call the police.'

The train began to slow down, and Edith stood up. She turned to look in Fern's direction. Pretending that she was fixing her shoe, Fern bent down until Edith passed. The smell of Edith's familiar perfume sank into her senses, making a surge of adrenaline pump through her heart. 'She's getting off,' Fern whispered as Edith brushed past her. Standing behind another passenger, Fern also prepared to depart.

'Where are you?' Dylan asked, already thinking about grabbing his car keys and making his way to Fern.

'I'm not sure,' she replied, trying to see which station they were approaching.

'Just be careful,' Dylan begged.

'We're at Bloomfield,' Fern confirmed the station as the sign came into view. The doors swung open, and Fern disembarked. She kept herself a handful of paces behind Edith, snaking her way through the stream of commuters. 'She's almost running now,' she commented, struggling to keep up.

'What's at Bloomfield?' Dylan asked, trying to think if he knew of any connections to the nondescript village.

With the phone still pressed to her ear, Fern followed Edith through a maze of side streets, trying her best to memorise the route. They emerged a few moments later onto a quaint cul-de-sac. A cluster of houses sat snugly around a central grassy island, where a few kids were playing with a well-used ball.

'Wherever she's going, I think she's arrived,' Fern announced, shielding herself behind a wall just before entering the secluded nook. She watched Edith in the distance as she took a seat on an empty bench.

'Where are you?'

Fern peered around. 'Just on some estate. There's nothing here but residential houses.'

'Is she meeting someone?'

'I don't know.'

'What's she doing now?'

'She's taking a hat out of her bag,' Fern narrated, still spying from afar. 'And now she's just looking at her phone.

'And there's nobody else around?'

Fern peered at all the houses, looking for any signs of life. 'There's just some kids playing football.'

'Does it look like a rough area?' he asked, trying to build an accurate picture in his mind.

Fern admired the well-maintained gardens and the array of new cars dotting the driveways. 'No, it seems nice,' she said. The sound of a car in the distance made Fern turn her head. 'I think there's a car approaching,' she said, her voice full of intrigue.

A white BMW 4 series pulled up to house number eleven. It was a house with a double garage and an impressive oak porch. The nicest house in the semi-circle cluster, in Fern's opinion. 'A lady's getting out of the car,' Fern explained, 'and Edith looks upset,' she continued, noticing how her friend kept wiping her eyes. 'She's just staring at this woman.'

'Can you get a good look at her face?'

Fern watched as the woman carried bags of shopping into the house, before reappearing and collecting some more. 'She's probably my height-ish. Short, grey hair that's tucked behind her ear,' Fern began. 'At a guess, I'd probably place her as late-sixties.'

'I wonder what the connection is. Is Edith not going over to talk to her?'

Fern shook her head. 'No, she's just watching.'

'Take a photo of the woman and send it to me,' Dylan requested.

Fern put her phone on speaker and opened her camera. 'Okay. I'm just waiting for her to come back outside,' she commented, bracing herself and zooming in on her camera, ready to capture the image. 'She's coming back out now,' Fern confirmed, pressing the button and capturing a few photos. 'They're on their way to you.'

Fern pressed the phone back to her ear just as a message notification buzzed. 'Oh my goodness. Edith has just sent me a message,' she announced, looking up to make sure that Edith was still sitting on the bench.

'What does it say?' Dylan asked, waiting for the photos to load.

'Finishing work soon. Thought I'd stop by your place on my way home.... Lots of leftover cake to share. Will you be in?'

'She's lying to you, Fern,' Dylan opened his messages and clicked on the images. The colour drained from his face. He sat upright in his chair, the packet of biscuits that'd been perched on his lap fell to the floor. 'I know who the woman is. I'm sure of it,' he announced, zooming in on the woman's pixelated, blurred face.

'Who is it?'

'It's Elizabeth Sloan.'

Fern felt her heart pounding against her chest. 'What?' Fern could feel herself getting upset. The thought of finally tracking down a member of Sam's family felt overwhelming. 'Are you sure it's her?'

Dylan nodded but didn't reply. The shock stole his words. He could see flickers of Sam coming to life before his very eyes, his childhood friend having inherited the lion's share of his mum's mannerisms.

'Dylan? Are you still there? Talk to me.'

'Yeah, it's her, Fern,' he confirmed, feeling sick at the shock of it all. It was like he'd come face to face with a ghost. 'Elizabeth died not long after the fire,' he said, confusion saturating his memories.

'No, she didn't. That's just what she wanted people to believe.'

'What? How do you know?'

'Arthur Aspey told me. He came over to my house yesterday.'

'And he told you Elizabeth was alive and well?'

'He told me that after the fire, Elizabeth wanted to start a new life. She wanted to go somewhere where nobody would know her, or know what had happened to Sam.'

'I can't believe it. Everybody thought she died.'

Fern put her phone on speaker and began to walk away.

'What are you doing? I can tell that you're walking.'

'I'm heading home,' she said, a lightness to her step. 'Now I know where she lives, I know that I can return Sam's things to his mum, where they belong, and I can get some closure on this whole story that I've been drawn into.'

'And what about Edith?'

Fern opened her messages and began to reply to her friend's text. 'I'm just replying to her now,' she began. 'I'm telling her that I'm out tonight.'

'Why do that?'

'Because I have this niggling feeling that she'll still come over, just like she has been doing. Only this time, I'll be waiting for her.'

21

Lunar remained draped in swathes of darkness. The clear, crisp night sky allowed a cluster of constellations to twinkle, the seven stars of The Plough particularly visible as Fern gazed up from where she was standing in her back garden. In anticipation of the evening to come, she arched her head and sought strength from a higher source that, even though she didn't fully understand, she could sense was there in spirit. In a moment of vulnerability, she closed her eyes and asked for guidance and protection through her storm. The shadows and ambiguous noises that emanated from the surrounding fields ignited a feeling of apprehension that began to rattle through her body. She looked at her watch, then drew in a deep breath. The anticipation of Edith's arrival heightened the collection of nerves that were now visible in her body language. Agitated, she paced the patio in a bid to regain her poise. She puffed on a cigarette for the first time in thirty years, recalling how the sensation had once served to settle her nerves. With her sense of hearing heightened, every slight noise stole her attention.

She peered to her left towards Arthur's place. The sight of the new frosted glass on Arthur's landing window only added to her nervousness. The privacy window meant that Arthur could no longer look down over his neighbour's property. And although initially Fern had found his behaviour intrusive, she now realised that she had sought comfort from her neighbour's watchful eye.

His daily presence had offered her a sense of reassurance, and tonight, Fern had never felt more alone.

'I'm beginning to think that you were right. This was a bad idea,' she said when Dylan answered the phone. She headed back inside, the whites of her eyes shining through the darkness that dominated the entire house. 'I'm scared of the dark,' she confessed.

Dylan glanced at his phone, seeing the late hour. 'It is a bad idea, but you can still change your mind. Turn some lights on.'

'No, I want to see this through. I need Edith to assume the house is empty and that'll only happen if the lights are switched off.'

'Then why don't you just call the police and have them waiting there with you?'

Fern crouched herself in the corner of the kitchen behind the internal door. 'She's not dangerous, Dylan. I know she's not. I don't want to ruin her whole life by getting her arrested. I just want to understand why she lied to me. I want to understand why she's so interested in this house, interested in Sam.'

'You could be waiting all night. She might not even turn up.'

With the radiators having already turned off, Fern began to feel a chill, and her bottom felt numb from sitting on the cold, hard floor. 'I've been waiting in the dark for nearly two hours. I'm not giving up now.' Fern glanced out of the kitchen window, wondering when her life had become so unfamiliar, so turbulent. She hated herself for craving the stability found in her old life, a life she had turned her back on.

'Did you know that it's Sam's birthday today?' she asked, recalling the dates etched onto his gravestone. 'That's another reason that I think Edith will come here tonight,' she added, resting her head against the wall. 'If she has connections to this house, connections to Sam, then today will have particular poignancy.'

Dylan fell quiet for a moment and checked the date on his phone. 'I'd actually forgotten about his birthday,' he confessed. 'How terrible is that?'

Fern was quick to reply. 'It's not terrible, Dylan. Life just moves on. You haven't forgotten about Sam. You still think about him *all* the time. That's all that matters.'

'Why don't I come and be your backup?' he suggested, hating the thought that his friend was placing herself in danger.

'I don't want her to feel like we're ganging up on her. It's going to be confronting enough. And besides, I *really* don't want to put you in harm's way.'

'I haven't had a friend like you since Sam,' he confessed.

'You're a good person, Dylan, and you could have loads of friends. You just don't give people a chance to get to know you.'

Feeling himself getting upset, Dylan changed the subject. 'How long are you going to wait up?'

'I'm not sure. Midnight maybe.'

'I just get a bad feeling,' Dylan confessed, his level of anxiety making him realise how much Fern had come to mean to him.

'I'll be okay,' she reassured. 'Once I speak to her, I'm sure everything will be okay,' she said, trying to convince herself.

A noise outside made Fern go quiet.

'Are you still there?' he asked, hearing Fern's heavy breathing.

'I'm just going up stairs. I thought I heard a noise outside,' she spluttered.

Dylan flapped his arms in the air. 'Aren't you better staying downstairs so that you have a way of escaping?' he said, exasperated.

'Too late now,' she said, breathless. 'I can get a better view from up here,' she replied. She paced from room to room, peering out of the upstairs windows, watching for any signs of movement. A noise coming from downstairs pulled Fern's attention away from the window, and she held her breath, listening. 'She's here. I knew she'd come,' she revealed, hearing a clattering noise coming from the basement, knowing that it was the cluster of pans that she had purposefully left on the floor. 'Got to go,' she said before hanging up, putting her phone in her pocket.

With slow, careful paces, Fern crept across her bedroom floor.

She tucked herself behind the open door, her warm breath firing out into the chilly, nighttime air. With her heart in her mouth, she heard the basement door creaking as it swung open on its rusty hinges. The confirmation of Edith's arrival made her feel sick to her stomach. She pressed her back against the wall and closed her eyes. Panicked, she wondered if she had enough time to send Dylan a message, asking him to come over after all. With shaking hands, she reached in her pocket for her phone, the sound of footsteps in the hallway downstairs making her stop. She peered through the gap in the bedroom door, blinking incessantly. The bulging vein that ran the length of her forehead pulsated and her face turned ashen as she anticipated what was to come.

The bottom step on the stairs creaked beneath someone's weight, the noise echoing through the silent house. Fern held her breath and listened to the sound of someone climbing the stairs. A shakiness rumbled through her legs, weakening her limbs. The moment that Fern heard Edith's bangles jangling, she knew it was her. Edith made her way across the upstairs landing and towards the small, front bedroom.

'Please don't be scared,' Fern announced, slowly moving out from behind the door and positioning herself on the landing. She held out her hands in a show of surrender.

Edith remained in the doorway to the small bedroom, twisting slowly to face Fern. Although awash with tears, Edith produced a meek smile. Her shoulders sank and she felt an undercurrent of relief trickle through her veins. She wasn't crying because she'd been caught. She wasn't crying out of fear. Her tears fell at the realisation that it was over. Her time at Lunar was over.

Fern kept her hands outstretched. 'I'm not angry with you, Edith. I just want to talk. I want to understand what's going on. I want to help.'

Edith lowered her head. Her tears continued to fall like a heavy downpour, landing in pronounced pools on the wooden floorboards. 'Please, don't come near me,' she mumbled the second that Fern took a step closer. Having craved empathy, comfort, and understanding for a large part of her life, Edith knew that if Fern offered her any semblance of compassion, her tears may never stop falling. 'I don't deserve your kindness or understanding,' she added, unable to look at Fern.

'Okay,' Fern replied, stepping backwards. 'Please just sit down and talk to me. I want to help you, Edith. You're my friend, or at least that's what I'd hoped when I first met you. I wanted nothing more than to be your friend.'

Edith raised her head and met Fern's eyes. The glow of the moon shone in through the landing window. 'And I wanted to be your friend. I've come to know you well over these past few months, and you're such a kind soul,' she explained. Her face scrunched, like she was grappling with something. 'But despite all that, I just couldn't forget what you've done to me,' she cried, her eyebrows pinching to a point. Edith allowed her body to slide down the doorframe. When her bottom reached the floor, she pulled her knees close to her chest.

'What have I done to you?' Fern questioned. She sat herself on the top step of the landing and rested her arms on her thighs. 'I don't understand,' she said, shaking her head, bewildered.

Edith lifted her head to make eye contact with Fern, her gaze focused. 'You took this house away from me.'

'What do you mean?'

'This house should belong to me, not you. And it was going to be mine until you came in and placed a higher offer. An offer that I couldn't match, or beat. The sale had already been agreed. I felt like the house was finally mine. And then everything changed.'

Fern thought back to the day of the sale. She recalled the conversation with the estate agent, learning that an offer had already been accepted on Lunar. 'You wanted to buy this house?' she questioned, never once having given any thought to the person she outbid.

'I did buy it. My offer was accepted, until you came along,' Edith cried.

Fern shook her head. 'I'm so sorry,' she apologised. 'I didn't know you at the time.' Fern felt her phone buzzing in her pocket and chose to ignore the incoming call. 'Had I known you back then, had I known that you wanted to buy this house, I would have stepped aside and walked away.' All the feelings associated with that difficult period in Fern's life came rushing back. 'I was going through such a tough time. I was desperate and I was alone. I knew that I could afford this place and it was in the perfect location to start a new life for myself. So, that's the reason I placed the higher bid.

Edith's skin turned blotchy. Her eyes became wet and dull, saturated with a lifetime of sadness. 'Everything was going to be alright once I came home.'

The pieces of the puzzle still weren't slotting into place. 'What do you mean, once you came home?' Fern asked, moving to the other end of the step, edging herself closer to Edith.

Edith wiped her face before replying, unable to stop herself from sobbing. 'You still don't know who I am, do you?'

Fern saw the way that Edith peered into what had previously been Sam's bedroom. 'I'm guessing you were related to Sam in some way, or you were one of his friends,' Fern replied, empathy in her voice.

Edith lowered her head and produced a slow, disapproving shake. 'I wasn't his friend,' she commented. 'I was his *best* friend.'

Sensing the deep-rooted feelings of loss that were still showings signs of dominance, Fern said the only thing she'd want to hear if the roles were reversed. 'I'm so sorry for your loss,' she expressed. She leaned across and handed Edith a handful of tissues.

Edith cried harder in response to the grief that she still felt so greatly. 'I miss Sam so much that it hurts,' she cried, placing her hand over her heart, willing the feelings of anguish to leave her body, and finally allow her to take a guilt-free breath.

'Did you and Sam go to the same school?' Fern asked, trying to gain a greater understanding of Edith's situation.

Edith closed her eyes and clasped her arms in a self-soothing gesture, waiting for her pain to subside. 'Sam was my little brother,' she revealed through shallow breaths and a quiet, subdued voice. For the first time in years, Edith felt overcome with emotion the moment her truth found a voice. For so long, she had wanted to keep his memory alive and share with people that Sam Sloan was her brother. It was a secret she'd been hiding since her return to Aldebaran, and now the truth was out.

Fern's jaw fell. 'What?' she asked, the revelation almost knocking the wind from her.

Edith peered long and hard into what she had always known to be her little brother's bedroom. 'The night before Sam's fourth birthday,' she began, a slow smile spreading across her face, 'he had gone to bed early. And once he'd fallen asleep, I crept into his room and filled this whole space with helium balloons,' she explained, gesturing with her hands how they'd hung from the ceiling. 'And when he woke up in the morning, I just remember hearing this scream of excitement tumbling down the stairs.' Edith closed her eyes so that she could see Sam's smile. She could recall the way that his eyes had sparkled that morning, full of excitement and joy. Becoming lost in the memory, Edith could smell the scent of the strawberry and mint shampoo that Sam used to wash his hair with.

'So, your name isn't Edith Preston? Your real name is Charlotte Sloan,' Fern asked.

'Charlotte Edith Sloan. When I got married, I decided to go by my middle name.'

Fern slotted all the pieces of the puzzle into place until ambiguity made way for clarity. 'Now I understand why you wanted to buy this house.'

Edith looked through the darkness at Fern. 'This isn't just a house to me. This was my home,' she cried. 'This is the only place that I feel close to Sam,' she added, her tears trickling down her face, the moisture seeping into the corners of her mouth as she spoke.

'Why didn't you tell me?' Fern cried. 'I would have understood,' she added, wiping her own eyes with a tissue. 'Do you know how intimidating it feels knowing that someone is watching you?'

Edith stared at the floor and her chin quivered. 'I'm so sorry. It was never my intention to scare you. When I saw you moving in, I thought I'd be able to deal with it. I wanted to be okay with how things had turned out. But no matter how hard I tried to come to terms with it, it felt like Sam was being taken away from me all over again,' Edith explained, her chest juddering beneath the weight of her erratic breathing. 'And I couldn't bear the thought of losing this place. I was scared of letting go of my final connection to Sam.'

She took some keys from her pocket and slid them across the floor. 'These belong to you now,' she confessed.

'What are they?'

'They're my old set of keys from when I lived here.'

'I don't understand why your dad didn't leave this place to you in his will. You're his daughter, after all.'

'I have an idea why, but now he's gone, I guess I'll never know the truth.' Edith sifted through some of her cherished memories of her dad. As each memory surfaced like a sprouting seed, she did her best to remember the time in her life that she knew Lockie had loved her more than anything. A wide, genuine smile appeared on her face when she thought about the way that her dad had once looked at her, and the way that he hugged her, making her feel precious.

'When I was younger, I was so close to my dad. He was everything to me. Whenever I felt sad, or upset, or scared, I would go to him for advice. Always him. He had this ability to make everything better.' Edith paused. Looking to her left, she peered into the room that had once been her bedroom. She pictured the way that she and Lockie would crouch on the floor with a bath towel over their heads. Beneath torchlight, they would read bedtime stories together. 'But after the fire, everything changed.' She took a deep breath, bracing herself for what she was about to admit. 'My mum and dad had left me in charge the day that Sam died. But because it was scorching that afternoon, I nipped to the shop to buy ice creams. Mum and Dad told me not to leave the house, but I thought I knew best, so I did it anyway.' A stream of tears and erratic breaths prevented Edith from finishing what she had wanted to say. All the years spent grappling with grief had sapped her strength, leaving her body drained. And although she had never confessed it out loud, all she wanted to do was sleep forever. 'It was my fault that Sam died. I left him alone.' Edith pressed her head into her knees and wrapped her arms around her legs.

Fern reached out and passed Edith another tissue. 'I'm so sorry,' she consoled, putting her own feelings aside. 'I can't even begin to understand how hard it's been for you.'

The touch of Fern's hand pressing against her back encouraged Edith to look up. 'After the fire, my dad couldn't even look at me. He never said the exact words, but I knew that he blamed me for what had happened to Sam. They both did. And they had every right to. Had I stayed home that day like they asked, Sam would still be alive.'

Fern could see the same level of grief in Edith's expression that she'd witnessed in Dylan and Arthur. 'You can't continue to blame yourself. Sam wouldn't have wanted you to be so unhappy.'

Edith looked at the spot in Sam's room where his bed used to be positioned. She pictured how they'd both snuggled beneath the single duvet whenever there was a storm. 'I've tried to forgive myself, but it's so hard,' she cried, releasing a weighted sigh. 'I thought that being away from Aldebaran would help. So, after the fire, I left home and went to stay with some relatives. It was the best thing for everyone, and I never spoke to my parents again.'

Fern handed Edith another tissue.

'I did try to keep in touch with my parents, but it was just too hard for them, which I understood. And when I eventually moved back to Aldebaran a few years ago, I came here and tried to make amends with my dad. But he didn't want to know. He told me to leave him alone.'

'How did you find out that he'd passed away?'

'I got a call from the hospital. My name must've still been listed on his record as a next of kin. After the house sold, I remembered that I still had the keys,' she explained. 'And after the first time that I let myself in, it was never my intention to keep coming back. But I was so shocked at the state of the house.' Edith got up and walked into the small bedroom. 'I couldn't believe that Dad hadn't touched this room. It felt like I'd gone back in time. It felt like Sam was still here. And for a moment, it was like the fire had never happened, and I didn't want to lose that feeling.' Edith stood in the window and peered out. She looked up at the darkness, picturing how she and Sam would stargaze.

Fern stood up and joined her friend at the window. 'I just wish you'd told me,' she said. 'Had I known all of this, I would have sold this place to you straight away. I would've walked away.'

Looking down, Edith's gaze became unfocused. 'Why haven't you called the police?'

A look of empathy appeared on Fern's face. 'I knew that you didn't want to hurt me. I soon understood that this was never about *me*.'

'I'm so sorry for all the trouble I've caused you,' she began, her body shaking as she sobbed. 'It's something else that's all my fault.' Edith cupped her face in her hands.

Fern wrapped her arm around Edith's shoulders. 'The fire was an accident, Edith. Nobody wanted Sam to die that day. It was nobody's fault.'

Edith turned and initiated an embrace. She allowed her face to bury itself into the crease of her friend's shoulder. 'I've waited fifteen years for someone to tell me that it wasn't my fault,' she cried. 'I can still see the flames and smell the smoke,' she sobbed. 'The memories of that day haunt me everywhere I go. There's nowhere for me to escape, no matter what I do.'

Fern pushed Edith away so that she could look her in the eyes. 'You loved Sam, didn't you?'

Edith nodded slowly, her tears falling away as she did.

'And you didn't leave him alone that day wanting something bad to happen.'

This time, reminiscent of a child's innocent gesture, Edith shook her head and her bottom lip protruded.

'So, enough,' Fern said, gripping Edith's upper arms. 'Sam didn't die because of you. He died in a fire that was started by accident.'

Edith lowered her head, failing to believe she had played no part in her brother's death.

'Look at me,' Fern encouraged, making eye contact. 'You've got to forgive yourself. It's *time* to forgive yourself.' Fern walked towards the bedroom door and switched on the landing lamp, casting a warm, safe glow over the dark space. 'Wait here. I won't be a minute.'

Edith watched as Fern disappeared. In a moment of reflection, Edith could hear the way that Sam had once shouted her name, the tone of his voice always etched with excitement. She remembered the way they would both race up the stairs, each one wanting to be the first to reach the top. With a warming smile, she pictured the way that they had both hidden under their parents' bed, reaching out with their hands to grab their mum and dad's feet, making them jump with shock. Her skin tingled as she relived Christmas Eves gone by, remembering how she and Sam would sleep in the same bed for that one magical night, trying to stay awake to catch a glimpse of the festive man dressed in a red coat and black boots. With the light resting on her face, Edith savoured the memories that, for the first time in years, didn't feel overshadowed with guilt.

'Here we are,' said Fern, bouncing up the stairs. 'I found this in Sam's room. It was buried beneath his duvet. I know how much it'll mean to you.' Fern reached out and passed Edith the huggable-sized chocolate teddy bear, the soft toy that had the words *I love my sister* stitched onto his midriff.

Reaching out her hands, Edith took hold of the bear, recalling the day that she'd given it to Sam. 'I couldn't believe it when I set eyes on this,' she began, feeling its fur, her eyes gazing in wonder. 'I was going away on an adventure school trip, and Sam was so upset. He was only maybe four at the time,' she recalled. 'He was distraught at the idea that I wouldn't be home to read him a story at bedtime.' Edith smiled when she told the story, recalling Sam's face when he unwrapped the present. 'So, I bought him this bear. I told him that he could sleep with it at night, and that it'd be like I was there with him, until I got home,' she commented, peering around his bedroom. 'When we bickered, he always maintained that he'd got rid of it.'

'It was tucked up in his bed, so it must've meant a lot to him,' Fern replied, relishing the moment of tenderness that she had been able to provide for Edith.

'There's something else I want to give you,' Fern began. 'Let's go and sit down,' she suggested, leading Edith through the house and into the lounge. They both sat on the sofa, their knees pointing towards each other. Fern took the letter out of her pocket. 'Arthur Aspey was the one who found your dad,' she began. 'And he'd left him a letter.' Fern handed the envelope to Edith. 'Your dad wanted to make sure that you got this.'

Trying to prevent herself from crying, Edith held the envelope in her palm like it was a precious stone. 'What is it?'

'I'm not sure. I'm guessing it's a letter for you.'

Edith and Fern both looked at the letter, both equally nervous about its contents.

'If it's okay with you, I'm not going to open it right now. I'm not sure I'm emotionally strong enough to cope with what it might say.' Edith slipped the envelope into her jacket pocket. 'It was hard enough reading those cards that my dad had kept in Sam's room.'

'I understand. Open it whenever you're ready. I'll always be here if you need to talk.'

'You really mean that? After everything that I've put you through?'

'Of course. I'd still like to think that we're friends. You're welcome here anytime, especially if it helps you to feel closer to Sam.'

Edith stood up and walked towards the window. 'I've learnt that I don't have to be here to feel close to my little brother,' she turned around to face Fern. 'Sam will always be in my heart, and my memories can never be taken away from me. It's time for me to leave Lunar in the past and focus on building myself a happier future. That starts by forgiving myself.'

'If there's anything I can do to help, you know you only have to ask,' Fern offered.

To pave the way on her journey of forgiveness, there were certain bridges along the route that Edith knew needed rebuilding. 'There is something I really want to do,' she began, pulling together the pieces of her plan. 'And if you'd be willing, I'd be so grateful if you would help me.'

'Of course,' Fern nodded without hesitation. 'Anything.'

Having once entered the house unlawfully via the basement, shielding her identity beneath a hood, Edith made her departure from Lunar across the threshold she had crossed a thousand times, her head raised to the sky. A familiar array of constellations sparkled in a show of support, the clouds dispersing to reveal the twinkling gems. With Sam's teddy tucked deep beneath her coat, Edith walked away from her childhood home cherishing the only memory she cared to carry, the memory that would act as a guiding light along her journey of forgiveness.

22

With a jumble of skittery nerves making their way through her body, Fern turned onto the cul-de-sac where she knew Elizabeth Sloan lived. She pressed the mute button to silence the radio, doing her best to creep down the street without alerting anyone to her presence. With the engine turned off, she sat and looked up towards Elizabeth's house. A pang of guilt that she couldn't shake wedged itself to the core of her conscience. She knew that she was about to open a box of painful memories for Elizabeth, events that had long since been put to bed.

Questioning her moral compass, she took out her phone and called Dylan for support. 'Hi,' she said when he answered his mobile. 'I've arrived,' she added, keeping her eyes fixed on the house across the road.

'Do you know what you're going to say to her?' he asked.

'No idea. My mind keeps going blank and I'm not even sure if it's the right thing to do anymore.' Fern watched the way that Elizabeth pottered about in her kitchen, watering the pots of herbs that were on display before closing the window. 'She's singing and smiling like she doesn't have a care in the world. She looks happy, Dylan. Happiness that I'm about to destroy.'

Dylan drew upon all his memories of Mrs Sloan. 'She adored Sam, you could tell by the way she looked at him. So, from afar it might look like she doesn't have any cares in the world, but

I bet thoughts of Sam are never far from her mind, even now, fifteen years on.'

Fern sought comfort from the sun that was pouring in through her windscreen. Like she often found herself doing at home, she admired the way that a blue tit bobbed about on a delicate tree branch, its blue, yellow and green feathery hues reflecting in the sunshine. 'But if she had really wanted to keep Sam's belongings, wouldn't she have made the effort to go and get them herself? Maybe she doesn't want the painful reminders. Maybe she'll shut the door in my face,' she said when the tiny bird fluttered away.

'Maybe she will. Maybe she won't. But unless you go and ask her, you'll never know what her reaction would've been. How could any parent not want to keep such precious reminders?'

Fern glanced at her reflection in the rear-view mirror. 'You're right. I at least need to give her the chance. That's what I set out to do when I first found Sam's things. And now that I'm here, I need to see this through. I'd never forgive myself otherwise.'

'You're doing the right thing,' he encouraged.

Fern watched as Elizabeth reappeared in the kitchen with her coat on. 'I think she's getting ready to leave. A man is walking out now and getting into a car. I'm assuming he's her partner, or husband.' Fern scooted down in her seat, trying to avoid being spotted. 'She's home alone. Now's my chance.'

'Then go, before you change your mind. Call me the second you're out,' he said before hanging up.

Checking herself in the rear-view mirror for a second time, Fern applied a fresh layer of lipstick before turning off her phone and opening the car door. The air felt chilly, encouraging her to zip up her coat and flip up the collar, preventing the breeze from reaching her naked neck. Fuelled by a prolonged and purposeful intake of breath, she darted across the road, knocking on the door and taking a step backwards.

The door opened immediately.

'Hello. Can I help you?' Elizabeth asked, clutching her handbag and keys.

Caught off-guard by the prompt response, Fern spluttered. 'Oh, erm, hi. Are you Elizabeth Sloan?' she asked, feeling her cheeks flush. With a sense of awkwardness, Fern cleared her throat and took a step back.

All traces of natural blush drained from the woman's face. Her eyes widened, and she felt her throat constrict. She peered out, checking if anybody else had overheard the question that Fern had poised. 'Who are you?'

'My name is Fern. You don't know me. I've recently moved into a house called Lunar in Aldebaran.'

Trying to contain the look of surprise that had crept onto her face like a disease, Elizabeth forced a smile. 'My name is Mrs Orton. You must have the wrong house. I'm sorry,' she apologised, closing the door.

In a brave, bold move, Fern held out her hand to prevent the door from closing. She took a step forward and wedged her foot in the narrow gap. 'I'm not here to cause any trouble. I just want to talk to you about Sam.'

The woman's face crumbled, and the depths of her eyes became vacant. Like a ghost had just settled above her grave, a penetrating chill swept across the woman's body. After so many years of hiding the truth, just the sound of someone saying her son's name made her want to fall to her knees and weep. Like every last bit of oxygen had been taken from her lungs, the woman fought for her next breath.

Noting her reaction, Fern placed her hand on the woman's arm for support. Like Fern had predicted, the box of memories had been sprung open. 'Are you okay? Would it be okay if I came in for a minute?'

The woman looked unsteady on her feet. She glanced at her watch, and then allowed the door to fall open. 'I'll just need to make a call,' she replied, taking off her coat and hanging it back on the rack. Grabbing her phone, Elizabeth indicated towards the lounge, the room overlooking the manicured front garden. 'Please, go and take a seat. I won't keep you a minute,' she said, disappearing down the hallway.

After taking off her shoes, Fern stepped inside the cosy, family home. The interior felt warm against her skin, and the carpet beneath her feet felt soft, a freshly hoovered pattern still ingrained into the beige weaves. The aroma of freshly brewed coffee and toast hung in the air, and on every wall, family photos were displayed with pride. Some of the photos had been taken on holidays, whilst others were of funny, unintended moments of mishap that had, by chance, been captured on camera.

'Sorry about that,' Elizabeth apologised, walking into the lounge. 'I was just about to leave to meet a friend. Had you called a few minutes later, you'd have missed me altogether.' She took a seat at one end of the three-seater sofa, indicating for Fern to sit at the other.

'I'm so sorry for just turning up like this, Elizabeth,' Fern apologised, perching herself precariously at the end of the cushion.

'My name is Lizzie. I haven't been Elizabeth for a very long time,' she corrected, uncomfortable being referred to by the latter. 'I'm not sure why you're here, or what you want from me,' she said, her words unintentionally leaving her lips with a sharp edge.

Fern thought through all the things that she had practiced in her mind. 'I bought your old house, Lunar, after Mr Sloan passed away,' she began. 'And I was surprised to find some personal items had been left behind. It's been my intention to try and return the belongings to a member of the family.'

Lizzie gazed out of the window. Firsthand experience with grief had taught her to breathe through the pain until it began to loosen its suffocating grip. Taking hold of the locket that rested near her heart, she rubbed the metal between her fingers in an attempt to self-soothe. 'Lockie's belongings?' she asked with hesitance. Since the day that she had turned her back on her husband, and

Lunar, Lizzie had hoped and prayed that Lockie had managed to move on with his life and forge happiness out of the darkness that had engulfed the house. 'As you can see,' she added before Fern had time to reply. 'I've remarried,' she explained, indicating to the photos.

Fern admired the photos but failed to see any reminders of Lizzie's previous life. 'You look very happy,' she said, taking time to study each photo, searching for evidence of her life at Lunar. Fern cleared her throat before asking her next question. 'Would it be okay if I showed you what I found?'

Lizzie stood up and walked towards the bay window, crossing her arms in an aim to protect her emotions and shield her heart from further pain. 'I don't need any reminders of my ex-husband,' she said, anticipating what Fern was about to reveal. 'That's part of my past.'

Fern witnessed a sombreness that saturated Lizzie's eyes. 'As I said, I'm not here to cause trouble. I just want to talk.' Fern reached down and took hold of her bag, pulling out some of the items she had uncovered at Lunar. 'The day that I got the keys to my new home, I was shocked at what I found,' she began, taking hold of Sam's precious brown, highland cow soft toy. 'Like this, for example,' she explained. 'This was obviously a cherished comforter. It didn't feel right to just get rid of it.'

Lizzie took a seat next to Fern and, with a delicate hand, took hold of the soft toy like it was as precious as a newborn baby. Her eyes glossed over. 'This was Sam's absolute favourite teddy. He went everywhere with it until he was about five. And even after that, although he didn't carry it around with him all the time, he snuggled it every single night.' In the blink of an eye, Lizzie crumbled. The threads that had been holding together her demeanour severed, leaving her deflated.

Fern rummaged in her bag, handing her a tissue. 'I'm so sorry. I wasn't sure if coming here was the best thing to do. It's just, as a mum myself, I wouldn't have forgiven myself had I not tried my best to return these things to Sam's family. I treasure everything of my daughter's.'

'How old is your daughter?'

Fern smiled. 'Jessie is seventeen. She's just started college.'

Without even having to think, Lizzie replied. 'Sam would have been twenty-three.'

A painful silence hung over the room.

'I only found out about the fire after I'd moved in,' Fern explained, breaking the tension. 'And when I saw the items that had been left behind, the *way* it had been left, I knew I had to do something other than just throw them away without a care.' Fern reached into her bag, pulling out Sam's pyjamas, a medal from sports day, and a photo frame that she had found at the side of his bed.

Lizzie took hold of the pyjamas. She felt the material between her fingers, picturing how Sam had once looked wearing them, his dainty feet getting caught because they'd been too long. 'What do you mean, the way it had been left?' she asked, looking up at Fern once the words had had time to register.

Fern cleared her throat and made herself look Lizzie in the eye. 'The small bedroom at the front of the house was still a child's bedroom. The bed was still made. Clothes and toys were still laid out. It felt like it hadn't been touched in years.'

Lizzie cried at the image Fern had described. 'You mean Sam's bedroom?' she asked, already knowing the answer. She broke down into a flood of tears, her face awash with grief. Despite the passing of time, Lizzie could still recall every detail of Sam's bedroom. 'That afternoon, before Lockie and I went out, I'd told Sam to tidy his room. But he never did. Sam was always too busy playing, or riding his bike, or kicking a ball,' she explained through a pained smile. 'Are you saying that Lockie hadn't disturbed Sam's bedroom for all these years?'

Fern nodded her head, picturing the cold, dusty room that she had unearthed. 'It didn't look like it'd been touched in a long time,' she began. She reached into her bag and took out her phone. 'I took a video when I first moved in. I wanted to capture the memories before I removed everything and started decorating.'

She pressed play and handed the phone to Lizzie.

With one hand pressed over her mouth, Lizzie watched the footage. Each time she blinked, a fresh stream of teardrops escaped from her eyes. 'It was just how Sam had left it that day,' she uttered, spotting the train track on the floor that he'd been playing with. 'I remember all of his pictures stuck to the wall,' she said with fondness, 'and each day when he came home from school, he'd have another that he'd stick to the wall.' Lizzie continued to shake her head, overwhelmed with disbelief. 'How could Lockie have lived like this for so many years?' she cried. 'This is why I had to leave, otherwise I'd have been the same. I would never have been able to move Sam's things. I would never have been able to forgive myself for what happened.'

Fern thought back to what Arthur had told her. 'I spoke with Mr Aspey recently. He and his wife still live next door to Lunar,' Fern confirmed. 'He explained the nature in which you left Aldebaran.'

Lizzie tore her attention away from the screen. 'Arthur was the only person, apart from Lockie, who knew the truth about what happened the day I left Lunar,' she revealed, maintaining eye contact. 'I didn't fake my own death or anything so calculated. But I did allow people to come to their own conclusion.'

'It must have been so hard,' Fern consoled, 'leaving everything behind.'

Lizzie took a minute to compose herself. She peered out of the window and reminded herself of how far she'd come in her journey to live alongside the stubborn ghosts that accompanied grief. 'It was hard to leave, but I just knew that I would never be able to forgive Lockie for encouraging me to go out that afternoon,' she began. 'I wouldn't have been able to forgive Charlotte, my daughter, for leaving Sam by himself,' she continued, wiping away her tears. 'But more than anything else, I knew that if I stayed at that house, I wouldn't have been able to forgive myself,' she cried, hiding her face in her palms, cradling the fresh wave of pain that had taken over. 'Before I left that day, I told Sam that I'd be home in time to tuck him into bed. And I wasn't. I broke my promise to him,' she said, looking up at Fern. 'He was only seven. He didn't deserve to die. I was his mum. I should have been there to protect him. I shouldn't have left him home alone,' she cried with the same intensity that she had done fifteen years previously. Fern moved over and wrapped her arm around Lizzie, allowing their heads to press together like they were lifelong friends.

'I've come to learn a lot about the fire, and what happened at your house that day. And I know that what happened was an accident,' Fern whispered. 'Nobody wanted it to happen, and you weren't to blame. Neither was Lockie. And neither was your daughter. You all loved Sam. That afternoon was just a tragic accident.' Fern pulled away, looking Lizzie in the eyes. 'You have to forgive yourself,' she said, just like she had told Arthur, Dylan and Edith.

'You must think that I'm an awful person, leaving everything behind the way I did.'

Fern shook her head. 'No, I don't think you're an awful person. I think you were struggling to come to terms with the death of your child, like any parent would. You did what you thought was best. Nobody can criticise you for that.'

Lizzie peered at the footage on Fern's phone again, looking at Sam's bedroom. 'I didn't need to take anything from the house to remind me of Sam because he's with me every day, in my mind, and in my heart,' she revealed, pulling open the rose-gold, heart-shaped locket that was hanging around her neck. 'Sam is here, with me, and he always has been. There hasn't been a day that has gone by in the past fifteen years that I haven't thought about him.'

Fern looked closely, admiring the tiny photo of Sam. 'His eyes were so blue, weren't they?'

'Blue eyes and blond hair. He was a real charmer, and he quickly learned that his cheeky little smile could get him out of all sorts of trouble. People adored him. Everyone adored Sam.'

'I can't imagine how you coped afterwards,' Fern said and, not for the first time, welled up at the tragedy.

'More than anything, after he passed away, I hated the way people looked at me. They would give me this awful look of pity. Everyone I came into contact with in the village felt sorry for me, which I understood. But I already felt sorry enough for myself. I couldn't handle everyone else's grief, too. It felt so all-consuming. And I knew that if I was going to leave Aldebaran and try and start a new life for myself, I couldn't bring that level of pity with me. I knew that if I was going to have any chance of finding happiness again, I needed to leave the past behind me. But I was never leaving Sam behind,' she cried. 'He came with me.'

Lizzie admired the photo of Sam that Fern had found in his bedroom. 'There were so many times that I wanted to go back to the house after I left. But I just couldn't bring myself to face it all again,' she explained, holding the items in her lap. 'These things are so precious, and I often wondered what Lockie had done with all of Sam's belongings.' Lizzie took a moment to hold back all the emotions that she could feel were threatening to break the dam that she'd shielded behind for so long. 'When I was told that Lockie had passed away, I just wanted the house to be sold. I couldn't deal with the thought of going back there and facing it all over again. I never thought for one second that any of Sam's things would still be there, not after so long.'

'Do you still speak to your daughter?' Fern asked with hesitance.

Lizzie shook her head. 'We haven't seen or spoken to one another for years,' she revealed, such a deep level of sadness etched in her voice. 'After losing Sam, we were fighting a lot and life became unbearable for all of us. So, in the end, we all agreed that it'd be better if Charlotte went and stayed with my sister in Scotland. She needed the opportunity to be able to smile again, and I couldn't provide that for her, especially at Lunar. I had spiralled into a deep state of depression and was barely able to function. I wanted a better life for her. I wanted to set her free from everything that we were going through.' Lizzie thought back to the day that she'd said goodbye to her daughter, and how she'd wanted to run after the car instead of letting her go. 'The day she left Aldebaran was the last time that I saw her. We didn't speak over the phone. We didn't see one another. And now here we are, fifteen years later. My sister always gave me updates. She'd tell me how well she was doing and that's all I needed to know. I knew that she was happy. I didn't want to jeopardise any of that by selfishly trying to have her back in my life.'

Fern cleared her throat to ensure her words would be heard first time round. 'Your daughter isn't happy. She's really struggling.'

Lizzie looked up to meet Fern's gaze. 'What do you mean? How do you know?'

Fern drew in a deep breath. 'Your daughter is back in Aldebaran. She has been for a few years.'

Lizzie's eyes widened and her gaze became unfocused. Her posture stiffened as tension became visible in her muscles. She shook her head in disbelief. 'Charlotte is back in Aldebaran?' she questioned, a lump rising in her throat.

'I became friends with her when I moved to the village. She goes by the name of Edith now. Edith Preston,' Fern began. 'She married some time ago, but has since divorced. She decided to use her middle name when she moved back to Aldebaran, so people didn't know who she was. She wanted to be able to make a fresh start. Much like yourself, I suppose.'

Lizzie couldn't hide her sadness. Standing, she walked to the window, trying to conceal her face. 'She's really living back down here in the Cotswolds?'

'She is,' Fern confirmed. 'When our paths crossed, I was going through a tough time personally, and her friendship meant a lot to me.' Fern paused, trying not to get emotional as she relived the story. 'I only found out her real identity a few days ago.'

A look of shock and sadness dripped from Lizzie's eyes. 'How does she look?' she asked, picturing the teenager who she had said goodbye to.

Fern couldn't hide the truth. 'She looks vulnerable. Fragile. Edith needs support. She needs love. She needs understanding. She needs her mum.'

'I can't believe she's come back.'

'She's actually been here, too, to *your* home,' Fern revealed.

'What? Really? When?'

'She was last here a few days ago. She wants to have a relationship with you, she's just scared of rejection. She came home searching for comfort, searching for help. She hasn't been able to forgive herself for what happened to Sam and still bears the responsibility for what happened.'

'If she knows where I live, why didn't she come and knock? Why didn't she let me know she was back?' Lizzie broke down like a bereaved parent learning of a loss. 'I lost my son. I never wanted to lose my daughter as well. She's all I have left.'

'Edith needs to hear that. She feels like you've moved on with your life and she doesn't know where she fits.'

'I think about her and Sam every day. They're my children. Nothing means more to me than them.'

'I was hoping that you'd say that,' Fern smiled with relief. 'Edith wants you to come to a little event she's planning on hosting at a café she owns in the village. She's only invited a few people, and her hope is to try and build bridges, and of course, take a moment to remember Sam.'

Lizzie drew in a deep breath and felt a weight pressing down on her chest. The thought of facing her past terrified her, but without hesitation, she replied with a wistful smile. 'I'll be there.'

For any stargazing enthusiasts, the conditions at the peak of Aldebaran were perfect. During his daughter's childhood, Lockie had taught Edith everything he knew about astronomy. Not long after celebrating her sixth birthday, the year she had unwrapped her very first telescope, Lockie sat his daughter down. He outlined the magic set of conditions that were required for a perfect night of stargazing. On that occasion, Edith had been far too interested in looking through her new telescope to take note of any astrological theorem that Lockie had to offer. But as the years passed, and the more she sat out with her dad, the more she became enthralled by the complex workings of the majestic night sky.

Tonight, as Edith took to her usual place on a patch of land her family had come to know as the landing, she recalled everything that her dad had once preached as gospel. She could see that the sun had set low enough below the horizon, and that the crescent moon wasn't shining bright. Her extremities told her that it was a crisp, clear winter's night, with bouts of frost biting at the surrounding blades of grass. It was the kind of evening where Edith could see particles of her own warm breath firing through the atmosphere. As far as she could see, the vast expanse of the night sky was free from cloud cover. And through her keen eye, she could tell that the transparency was good because there was minimal dust or humidity to muddy the twinkling celestial city. Tonight, had Lockie been sitting next to her in his rightful place, his eyes would have shone brighter than the mighty star of Sirius.

With care, Edith opened the crossbody bag that was draped across her chest and pulled free the unopened envelope left for her by her late father. Sniffling due to the chilly temperature attacking her senses, her cold fingers peeled apart the glue. With the tips of her fingers, she reached inside and pulled free the paper concealed within. Playing tricks with her senses, a waft of her dad's Dior aftershave drifted through her nostrils, making her turn to check that he wasn't standing by her side. The nostalgic smell released a swell of tears that, thus far, she had managed to restrain.

With her phone acting as a torch, Edith shone the light over the letter, highlighting the first line: *I'm sorry*. Pressing the letter to her chest, she closed her eyes and allowed a well of tears to fall from her face. Overcome with guilt, she tormented herself at not having done more to help her dad.

She was startled by the sound of footsteps approaching her from behind.

'Only me,' Fern announced, waving her hand and shining her phone torch through the darkness like a lighthouse. 'I know you said that you wanted to be alone up here, but I had this feeling that you'd need some support. So, here I am.' Fern took a seat beside Edith. Unbeknownst to her, she had seated herself in what had been Sam's spot on the landing. She took a tissue from her pocket and passed it to Edith.

'Thanks,' Edith cried, accepting the tissue and offer of company. 'I didn't realise how hard this was going to be.' She glanced at the letter, fearful of any potential hurtful words contained within. 'Dad would bring me and Sam up here all the time,' Edith reminisced. 'He would teach us about the stars and constellations in a way that made it all sound so magical. He had this way of bringing things to life, and Sam and I would always love the long winter months because they were some of the best for stargazing.'

Fern looked up. 'I only wish I knew what I was looking at,' she mused, trying to form patterns with the stars that came to life before her eyes.

Edith's eyes sparkled and her face shone in a way she hadn't experienced for a long time. 'Can you see that cluster of three stars?' she asked, pointing. 'Those three stars make up Orion's belt.'

Fern wasn't sure exactly what she was looking at. She just knew that all the twinkling dots that she could string together looked like the prettiest daisy chain of diamonds. 'I think I see it.'

Feeling like the letter was burning a hole in her hand, Edith looked at Fern. 'Would you read it aloud for me?' she asked, handing the letter to her friend. 'And once you start, please don't stop. No matter what it says. No matter what my reaction is. I just need you to keep on reading and rip the plaster off.' Bracing herself, Edith crossed her legs, placed her hands in her lap, and waited for Fern to commence.

With a sense of duty, Fern straightened out her torso and pressed her shoulders back. Holding her phone over the letter, she cleared her throat and began, not stopping until she reached the end.

Dear Charlotte,

I'm sorry.

I could say these two words to you a thousand times and it still wouldn't convey the true extent of the sorrow that I feel. And if you take nothing else away from this letter, please always know how deeply sorry I am. For everything.

Writing a letter seems cowardly, but at this stage in my life, I have run out of options. There are things I need you to know, and with my health declining, I fear that my time to make amends is running out. I can physically feel that my body is shutting down. I'm so tired and each day has become a battle that I no longer have the energy to fight.

I've done some terrible things in my life and made some awful mistakes. As a result of these errors in judgement, I feel deeply ashamed of the man that I have become. And even though I will go to my grave having not forgiven myself, as I search my heart for answers, the only thing that really matters to me is your forgiveness.

Losing Sam the way we did was a tragedy that, to this day, I've never managed to make peace with. I've been unable to forgive myself for the role that I played in the events that unfolded that day. I was to blame for what happened. Nobody else. Just me. And if that decision wasn't bad enough, I made another terrible mistake after Sam's death.

I let you go.

I allowed you to leave home instead of wrapping my arms around you and holding you so tight that I could have felt your heart beating against mine. I should have offered you comfort. I should have been your shoulder to cry on. I should have been there for you. But the main thing that I should have done was to tell you that Sam's death wasn't your fault, and I should have kept telling you this until you believed me.

You weren't to blame for what happened, Charlotte. You never were. I'm so ashamed to admit it, but at the time, I wanted to believe that it was your fault. I needed someone to blame. I didn't want to accept that my decision had led to Sam's death. But that's what happened. That's the truth that I am now able to admit. I was the parent that day. Not you. I was responsible for Sam. Not you. And I'm so sorry for ever making you feel otherwise. After Sam died, I should have loved you even more than I already did. I should have cherished the love that I still had in my life, but instead I pushed you away.

I know that over the years I've done what I can to give you the best start in life financially, and I hope that the money has made a positive impact on your life. I hope you'll understand my reasons for not leaving this house to you in my will. The bricks and mortar at Lunar hold nothing but a storybook of painful memories, and it was my intention to set you free from that burden. I want more for you than a life living on the very land that caused our family so much pain. I have forced myself to live a solitary life at Lunar for such a long time, and this isolation has served as my personal form of punishment. Please don't continue to punish yourself. You have suffered enough. We all have. If I want anything for your future, it's for you to make peace with the past. You will never forget Sam, and he will always be in your thoughts. But you don't need to be at Lunar to remember him, or to feel close to him. I've lived in this house since the day Sam died, and it's never made me feel any closer to him. I feel most connected to him when my eyes are closed, or when I'm outside looking up at the stars.

How I have missed stargazing with you both over the years. Some of my fondest memories are the times that I would sit out on the landing with you and Sam by my side. Do you remember how we used to make up funny names for the constellations? I remember you would often speak about having a star named after you. In this letter, you will find documents detailing just that. There is also a star up there named after Sam.

Love to you always,

Dad.

Realising that she hadn't stopped to take too many breaths, Fern allowed her lungs to expand as a flood of fresh air gushed into her system. She looked at Edith, who was sobbing. Shuffling her bottom closer to her friend, Fern snuggled herself right up beside Edith and wrapped her arm around her body. 'You're going to be okay,' she reassured, waiting until the sobbing eased and for Edith to catch her breath.

'My dad died alone,' she cried. 'How could I have let that happen? I should have kept trying until he agreed to let me in.'

'Your dad was trying to protect you. That's what parents do. He wanted you to be happy.' Fern could feel Edith's body juddering as her emotions continued to pour.

'I wanted to tell him that I loved him.'

Fern thought back to the night they uncovered the contents of Lockie's treasured wooden box. 'And you did. In those cards that we found. You told him how you felt, and he knew that you loved him.'

'I've waited for so many years for my parents to tell me that it wasn't my fault.'

'And you need to start believing it,' Fern encouraged, releasing a silent prayer of gratitude to Lockie for having left his daughter such a perfect gift, the gift of freedom.

'It's just going to take time,' Edith replied as her father's words penetrated the layers of guilt that had formed like armour around her heart. For the first time since she had returned to her hometown, Edith noticed that she didn't feel fragile, or broken. She could feel the pieces of her heart knitting together, and her tears had subsided, allowing for a smile brighter than a morning sunrise to break through. She cast her gaze back to the speckled night sky. 'I did always want a star named after me. I can't believe he remembered. And now I have one,' she smiled, pondering which tiny spec in the galaxy Lockie had chosen for her. 'Thank you for doing that for me,' she added, taking hold of the letter and scanning the words again.

'My pleasure. Are you ready for tomorrow night?'

'I wasn't. But I am now, thanks to my dad.'

24

THE COLLECTION OF ARTISAN BUSINESSES THAT WERE SCATTERED along both sides of Aldebaran high street were beginning to bed down for the night. Retailers could be seen closing their shop shutters. Café baristas hustled to bring in outdoor tables and chairs before the heavens opened. A cluster of last-minute shoppers darted in and out of shops before they were met with locked doors. Uncharacteristically, Edith's café had been closed all day. A small, scribbled note had been stuck to the window, notifying customers that a private event was taking place, and that the café would re-open for business the following morning.

In the snug studio flat that sat above the café, Edith remained in front of her bathroom mirror, her feet planted to the spot. Even though she'd been positioned in front of a hairdresser's mirror for over three hours during a morning appointment, she still couldn't quite come to terms with the sight of her new reflection. For well over a decade, Edith had warmed to her new persona, hiding her old, familiar identity behind a façade consisting of heavily applied makeup, long strands of straightened, bleached blonde hair, and a pair of contact lenses.

Back in the privacy of her flat, she glided her fingers through her curly, chestnut hair with a gentle touch. She recalled how, as a child, she had loathed her abundance of natural curls, begging her mum to straighten it after each wash. Through fresh eyes, she admired how her new hairstyle once again framed her face, her natural bundle of curls bouncing off her shoulders, tickling her ears.

With nothing more than a dab of tinted moisturiser applied to her cheeks, and a light layer of cherry lip balm on her lips, Edith gazed harder at her new reflection like she was being reunited with an old friend. With all the delicacy of a butterfly emerging from within its chrysalis, Edith reached out for her new prescription glasses and placed them on her face. The tawny, round frames completed the final part of her physical transformation. She arched her head and continued to gaze into the mirror. Tears trickled down her face when the person staring back felt familiar. She reached out her arm towards the mirror and gently touched her reflection.

Outside on the high street, the sound of chattering voices pulled her away from the mirror. She peered down from the living room window, seeing that some of her guests had already begun to arrive. Tearing herself away from the window, she dashed back to the bathroom, grabbed her phone, and switched off the light.

On the pavement, Fern stood in front of the closed café door. 'Hi,' she announced when Dylan joined her.

'Hello,' he replied, giving Fern a hug before looking at the café. 'I'm a bit nervous about all of this,' he declared, looking at the invitation he had received from Edith. 'I'm still not sure what *A night for Sam* will involve.'

'It's Edith's way of trying to build bridges with people that she cares about,' she began. 'I just hope that her mum comes,' she said, peering up and down the street, searching for Lizzie's familiar figure.

Dylan pressed his hand down on the handle, the door falling open. 'It says we should go in,' he said, turning to face Fern.

Fern took one last glance up and down the street. 'Yeah, let's go inside,' she agreed, 'for all I know, Lizzie might have had a last-minute change of heart.'

Dylan and Fern entered the welcoming embrace of the snug café interior. 'Oh my goodness,' Dylan announced, clasping his hand over his mouth, his eyes darting from one thing to another. 'I'm assuming the café doesn't always look like this?' he asked, walking up to one of the photos of Sam, trying to see where it was taken.

The sight of the café also took Fern's breath away, a plume of tears surfacing before she had time to blink. As she arched her head, she admired the array of black and white photos hanging from the ceiling, each one a photo of Sam, his beaming smile lighting up the sullen room that was lit by candlelight. On the walls, a gallery-worthy collection of canvases had been displayed; below each, a little handwritten note offered a caption. 'Sam was always climbing trees,' Fern read aloud, reading the note below the photo of Sam perched high up a mature oak tree.

Dylan spotted a photo of him alongside Sam sat on a wall. *Best friends*, read the caption. Dylan could feel his emotions getting the better of him. Without having to search his memories to recall the specific details of the photo, his memory immediately placed him right back to that point in history. 'This photo was taken right before we finished school for summer,' he explained with fondness. 'We were talking about what we were going to do over the holidays, and we decided that we were going to wash cars to earn some extra pocket money.'

Fern walked over to where Dylan was standing, placing an arm over his shoulders. 'Are you okay?'

Dylan wiped his face and, with a quaking voice, replied, 'It's so nice that Edith recognises how close me and Sam actually were. That's all I've ever wanted.'

At that moment, the café door opened, and both their hearts leaped to their chest.

'Hello,' announced Arthur Aspey, poking his head around the narrow gap in the door.

Fern got up to assist her neighbour. 'Hello, Arthur,' she greeted, holding the door open so that he could enter with his walking aid. 'Lovely to see you.'

'I wasn't sure I had the right day when I saw it was all closed up,' he said, pulling the invitation out of his bag and taking another look at it, holding the card closer to his eyes.

Fern closed the door. 'It's definitely the right day, Arthur. I think Edith closed the café today so that she could prepare for tonight,' she announced, indicating to the café's interior.

Arthur caught sight of all the photos, inducing such a strong stream of emotions that he felt unsteady on his feet. He reached out and linked Fern's arm for support. 'Goodness me,' he said, not knowing where to look first. 'Just as I remember him,' he whispered, recalling the way that Sam's smile had shone.

'Come and sit down,' Fern suggested, assisting Arthur to a table. 'Arthur, do you remember Dylan? He was Sam's best friend.'

Dylan stood up and reached out to shake Arthur's hand. 'Hello, Arthur.' Once pressed against his skin, Arthur's hand felt cold, his handshake weak. 'It's been a long time since I last saw you.'

A pang of guilt spread over Arthur's face when he came face to face with Dylan, someone Arthur had once thought had started the fire. 'It has been a long time,' Arthur replied. 'You were just a young lad when I last saw you.'

'I wonder when Edith will arrive?' Fern asked, checking her watch and making small talk when a gap in conversation emerged.

Nervous, Dylan cleared his throat. 'I owe you an apology, Mr Aspey,' he began, fidgeting with his invitation and avoiding eye contact. 'I'm sorry for all the times that I caused you trouble,' Dylan began, lowering his head, ashamed of his childish behaviour. 'At the time, I thought it was funny to knock on your door for no reason, or to make lots of noise when both Sam and I knew you were in your garden,' he admitted. Dylan looked up and met Arthur's gaze. 'I didn't know any better at the time, but I've grown up a lot since then, and I know better now. So, for that, I'm sorry.' A wave of relief flooded through Dylan's body the moment he confronted his past, a lightness appearing in his heart.

Arthur offered up a warm smile in reciprocation. 'You weren't doing anything wrong. You and Sam were just being kids,' he replied. 'I was always too caught up with my work. It was all that mattered to me back then,' he said, shaking his head, wishing that he could go back and do it all over again. 'But after that dreadful day, when the silence I craved finally came, I missed all the noise and commotion. I missed hearing the rumbles of laughter as you and Sam played in the garden, and in particular, I missed hearing the sound of Sam's voice. What I wouldn't give to hear him one last time.' Arthur glanced up at one of the photos of Sam, recalling how his clothes always looked a little dishevelled, a sign that he'd been climbing a tree, or playing in the fields. 'He was one of a kind, and I miss him to this day.'

'I miss him, too,' Dylan agreed, filling a pause in the conversation when he spotted Arthur's emotions getting the better of him. 'I miss him every day, actually, and I often wonder what he'd be doing now.'

A moment of honesty encouraged Arthur to speak the truth, and he looked up and waited to catch Dylan's gaze. 'For a long time, I blamed you for what happened that day,' Arthur confessed. 'I saw you there and drew my own conclusion.' Arthur lowered his head and took a moment to think back to that day.

'I didn't start the fire, but I did give Sam the cigarette,' Dylan revealed, loathing himself, still, for the part that he had played in the tragedy. Transported back in time, Dylan could hear Sam screaming in his mind, a sound that, no matter how hard he had tried, he could never free himself of. 'I saw the fire. I saw the smoke, and I tried to get him out by myself, but I just couldn't. The flames were too intense to make it past the door.' The nauseating smell of smoke drifted through Dylan's senses like it was still infusing the air, fifteen years later. 'So, I ran to get help.'

Listening to the emotion in his words, Fern reached out her hand and took hold of Dylan's, squeezing it tight, offering him the compassion and understanding that he had always craved.

Arthur had also been transported back to the day of the fire and asked a question he had always wanted to know the answer to. 'Did you knock on my door?' he asked, a sickening feeling brewing in his stomach at the anticipation of Dylan's reply.

Dylan nodded. 'I did. But you had music on. You mustn't have heard me, so I just kept running.'

An immense feeling of regret rocked through Arthur's body, his shaking hand releasing grip of his walking aid.

'Oh, let me get that for you,' Fern said, jumping up to grab the stick.

'I did hear you knocking that day,' Arthur confessed, 'but because you'd knocked so many times before, and then ran away, I thought it was just another trick. So, I ignored it and turned up my music.' A haunting feeling of regret infested Arthur's mind like a disease, and the expression lodged on his face reflected his state of inner turmoil. 'Had I answered the door, I could have called for the fire brigade straight away, and they would have arrived sooner. Maybe they'd have been able to save Sam's life.'

The creaking sound of a door opening made all three of them look up, turning their heads to face the back of the café.

'Hello,' announced Edith, her shadowy figure lingering in the safety provided by the doorway.

The moment she stepped into the light, Dylan and Arthur felt like they had come face to face with a ghost.

Fern got up and approached Edith. 'Wow, I *love* this,' she said, feeling Edith's hair. 'You look completely different,' she added, giving her friend a hug, unable to get over the transformation.

'This is who I really am,' Edith revealed, peering down at her own frame. 'I've been hiding for so long and pretending to be someone that I'm not.'

'Well, I think you look fabulous.'

Edith blushed. 'Thanks for coming,' she replied, peering into the café, noticing that her mum hadn't arrived. 'I'm so nervous,' she revealed, doubting the gesture she had extended to those estranged from her past.

Fern took hold of Edith's cold hands. 'Don't be nervous. Dylan and Arthur are so lovely, and they're both here for you.' Fern turned around to look back at where the guys were still sitting. 'I'll break the ice,' she smiled, guiding Edith through the café.

Dylan and Arthur stood up. 'Hi,' Dylan greeted when Edith and Fern approached.

Fern cleared her throat. 'Dylan. Arthur. This is Edith, Sam's big sister.'

'Hi,' she replied, offering up a meek, unstable smile. 'Thank you for coming tonight.'

Dylan couldn't help but gaze at Edith, and in his mind, it was like he had travelled back in time and was now stood in front of the girl he had once known so well. 'Thanks for inviting me,' he said through a shaky voice.

'You sit down. I'll get us all some drinks,' Fern offered when she sensed the tension in the air.

Edith took a seat alongside Arthur. 'It's been a long time since we all saw each other, hasn't it?' she commented, unsure how to initiate such a delicate conversation.

Arthur relaxed and sat back in his chair. 'I remember those biscuits you used to bake with your mum,' he smiled, recalling how delicious the warm, crumbly biscuits had tasted. 'They paired nicely with a strong cup of milky tea.'

'I remember those, too,' added Dylan, recalling how wonderful the house had smelled when anything was baking in the Sloans' oven.

Edith relaxed her shoulders and allowed herself to release the pangs of anxiety that had been stirring in her stomach since the day she had posted the invites. 'Sam liked chocolate chip cookies the best,' she commented, relishing being able to talk openly about her brother for the first time in years.

Fern arrived at the table carrying a pitcher of lemonade and a handful of glasses. 'Here we go,' she announced, pouring everyone a tumbler, and then sitting down herself.

'This is the furthest I've ventured out of the house in a long time,' Arthur announced. 'My Olive isn't feeling too well, so unfortunately she couldn't make it tonight.'

'I appreciate you all making the effort to come and see me,' Edith said, summoning up the courage to say what she had to say. 'For such a long time I've tried to hide who I really am, Sam's sister, because I couldn't forgive myself for what had happened,' she explained, looking down at her lap. 'But I don't want to do that anymore,' she confessed, taking in a breath. 'I'm proud to have been Sam's sister, and although it isn't easy, I want to be able to talk about him, to celebrate his life and to keep his memory alive.'

Through the flickers of burning candlelight, Fern caught Edith's gaze and offered her an encouraging smile.

'I haven't been able to forgive myself for what happened that day either,' Dylan replied, voicing his own insecurities. 'I have always blamed myself for what happened to Sam.'

A moment of silence developed, and although you couldn't see it, feelings of guilt and sorrow hung heavy in the air.

'I also blamed myself for Sam's death,' Arthur added.

Acting as an impartial mediator, Fern aided the conversation. 'I have come to know all of you since I moved to Aldebaran, and the one thing I have learned is how much you all loved Sam.' Fern looked at each person in turn as she continued to speak. 'Sam wouldn't have wanted any of you to be unhappy. You should all be proud to speak about the memories that you each shared with him.'

Another moment of silence developed in the café, Fern's words echoing off the walls.

'Whenever Sam came over to my house, he was always so curious about all my photos,' Arthur added. 'He wanted to know where each one had been taken, and he loved nothing more than having a go at taking some photos himself.' He reached down to take hold of his bag and pulled out some pictures. 'After Sam passed away, maybe a good handful of months later, the film in my camera ran out. So, I got it developed, and this is what I found.' Arthur handed out some photos to the others seated around the table. 'He took all of these himself, without me even knowing,' he revealed.

Rumbles of giggles ricocheted around the table. Dylan admired a photo that Sam had taken of his muddy shoes propped up on one of Mr Aspey's pristine, white pouffes. 'This was Sam all over,' Dylan announced, his attention becoming lost in the pictures. 'A bit cheeky.'

Edith relished the unseen photos, drinking in every detail of her late brother. 'I love this one,' she smiled, turning the picture around so that the others could see. 'He was taking a picture of himself in front of a mirror, and look,' she added with enthusiasm, 'you can just about see how much he's smiling.' Edith picked up her glass. 'I'd like to make a toast,' she began, waiting for the others to join her in raising a glass. 'I just want to thank you all for coming tonight,' she continued, taking a deep breath. 'It's taken me a long time to come to terms with the fact that I wasn't there for Sam that day,' she added. 'I loved him so much, and I now feel proud and privileged to say out loud that Sam Sloan was my little brother. I won't hide who I am anymore. If anybody has something to say to me about what happened that day, then that's okay,' she cried. 'And I'll be keeping this photo right here,' she explained, indicating to the large photo of Sam that was displayed on the wall. 'Because it will encourage my customers to ask me who he is.'

Just as they all clinked glasses, the café door opened.

25

Everyone turned in unison to face the café door. Edith's heart pounded and she took hold of Fern's hand for support. 'Is it my mum?' she whispered, waiting for the person to appear.

Along with a gentle swoosh of cool evening air, Lizzie walked in, and like a stranger, she lingered in the safety of the doorway with a notable sense of hesitation as her companion.

Fern released Edith's hand and stood up. 'Hiya, Lizzie,' Fern welcomed, continuing in her role as mediator. 'Please, come on in,' she encouraged, checking that there was nobody else outside before closing the café door. 'Are you okay? I'm so glad that you decided to come.'

Lizzie cleared her throat, her hand movements jumpy. 'I'm so nervous,' she whispered, trying to secretly spot any familiar faces amongst the intimate gathering. Hidden beneath the subdued flickers of light offered by the dotting of candles, Lizzie's dream materialised before her very eyes. Like a magnet, her gaze was drawn to the young woman who she instantly recognised as her daughter. Lizzie had always wondered how this moment would feel, and yet despite years of anticipation, it felt better than she could have ever envisaged. Through a wide grin, an unwavering maternal bond made Lizzie's eyes shine, her facial features coming to life. She reached out and took hold of Fern's hand, wanting to make sure that the moment wasn't wrapped up as a dream.

'Are you ready to come and meet everyone?' Fern asked with a reassuring smile.

Lizzie nodded and took a deep breath, sensing that someone was approaching them both.

'Edith, this is Lizzie, your mum,' Fern introduced when Edith approached the door.

Edith's heart skipped beneath her chest in a way that she had forgotten was even possible. She felt like a child again, looking up and desperately trying to gain her parents approval and forgiveness. In a silent prayer, she asked to uncover the kind of love that had once radiated from the person who she cherished the most. 'Hi,' she said, looking at Lizzie. Even though she'd recently seen her mum from afar, up close, the woman standing before her appeared different. Edith had forgotten how her mum's nostrils tended to flare whenever she was upset. She had forgotten how her long eyelashes fluttered each time she blinked, and how she would blow loose, wispy strands of hair out of her face instead of fixing them with her hands. Up close, Edith was taken aback by how much her mum had aged. A series of fine lines scattered Lizzie's face, and the skin around her eyes puckered at the corners, a sense of fragility evident in her demeanour.

Lizzie burst out crying and she swooped her hands up to cover her face the moment she caught sight of her daughter. 'Hi,' she replied, her face broken with tears. Through her saturated eyes, Lizzie admired Edith's familiar, soft features. With a delicate touch, she reached out and felt her daughter's hair, recalling how soft and smooth it had been as a child. 'I'm so sorry,' Lizzie whimpered, shaking her head with sorrow. She didn't know what else to say, knowing that words alone were unable to erase the pain of the past.

Edith wrapped her arms around her mum, allowing Lizzie to melt into the unexpected show of affection, nuzzling her face into Edith's warmth.

Fern walked away and re-joined the table, giving the mother and daughter duo a moment to themselves.

Lizzie pulled herself away and placed her hands at each side of Edith's face. 'I'm so sorry,' she repeated, watching how Edith was crying, her eyes closed. With the tips of her fingers, she brushed away her daughter's tears, just like she had done so many times in the past.

'I'm sorry, too,' Edith replied when she opened her eyes, finding herself stood before her mum for the first time in fifteen years. 'I'm so glad that you're here.' The pair continued to savour the embrace, an embrace that felt warm, familiar, and safe to both. 'I've missed you so much,' Edith confessed, recalling all the moments during the past fifteen years when she had craved her mum's advice and guidance.

Lizzie produced a tender, genuine smile. 'I'm here now, and I'm not going anywhere.'

'Do you promise?'

Lizzie looked deep into Edith's eyes. 'I promise. It's you and me again, just like it always used to be.'

Edith could feel the eyes of the others watching from afar, themselves waiting for their moment to meet Lizzie. 'Let me introduce you to everyone,' she said, taking hold of her mum's hand and guiding her towards the table. 'Everybody, this is my mum.' Edith pointed to each person as she made the introductions. 'This is Mr Aspey, our old next-door neighbour. And this is Sam's best friend, Dylan Wallace. And, of course, you already know Fern.'

Arthur stood up, his emotions just about being contained beneath the surface. 'Hi, Lizzie,' he smiled, the pair sharing a meaningful hug.

'Hello, Arthur,' she replied. 'You're looking well,' she added, noticing that, despite the passing of time, his eyes had retained their sparkle.

'It's all that fresh air I get sitting in my garden,' he replied. 'It's so lovely to see you again. It's been far too long. My Olive is at home, she's not feeling well today, but she can't wait to have you over for one of those chats that the both of you used to enjoy.'

Lizzie beamed at the memory of her and Olive chatting in the garden, the pair fluttering away the long summer months while the children darted like butterflies around them. 'That would be wonderful.'

Dylan stood up, waiting his turn to greet Lizzie. 'Hello,' he welcomed.

'Blimey, time really has passed me by,' she smiled, noticing that Dylan was now a good foot taller than she was. 'It's good to see you again,' she offered, resting her hand on his arm. 'It's crazy to think that Sam would have been your height now,' she mused, taking a moment to look around the café, drinking in all the images of her fallen son. 'This place looks wonderful,' she commented. 'Is this your café?' she asked, looking at Edith.

'It is,' she confirmed. 'I've had it for a few years now.'

Lizzie and Edith took a seat next to one another.

'I'm so glad that you came and found me,' Lizzie smiled. 'We have so much to catch up on.'

'I don't even know where to start,' Edith replied, trying to recall all the major life events that had happened since the day she had left the family home.

Fern took the opportunity to stand. 'Why don't we go and have a closer look at some of these pictures and leave you two to it?' Fern suggested, looking at Arthur and Dylan.

'Great idea,' Dylan agreed, helping Arthur to his feet.

Fern, Arthur and Dylan wandered to the back of the café, perusing the photos before huddling together around a snug table, chatting and giggling like they were all old friends.

Lizzie turned to face Edith, taking hold of her daughter's hand. 'You look so well,' she beamed, relishing the fact that she could also see flickers of her son shining through her daughter's eyes.

Edith spotted the creases that were covering the back of her mum's hands and regretted all the time they had lost. 'You look really well, too,' she replied. 'I was so nervous about tonight. I wasn't even sure that you'd want to come after all these years.

There's so much history. So much has happened.'

Lizzie looked down at her hand as she cradled Edith's. 'I have so many regrets, and not trying to find you earlier is one of my greatest. But if there's one thing that I want you to know, it's that I love you, Charlotte, and I always have done.'

The warming touch of her mum's hand sent shivers coursing down Edith's spine. 'It's so strange to be called Charlotte again,' she replied. 'I've used my middle name for such a long time now,' she admitted.

'I'm sorry,' muttered Lizzie, realising her mistake.

'Don't be,' Edith smiled. 'It's taken me a long time to come to terms with who I am, but I'm now proud to be Charlotte Edith Sloan. She's no longer someone I'm trying to escape.'

'No, I'm sorry for—' Lizzie began to correct, building the courage to look her daughter in the eye. 'I'm sorry for everything,' she began, a deep sense of sorrow saturating her words. 'I've wanted to say this for so long, and I'm ashamed that I haven't found a way to do it sooner.' Lizzie maintained her daughter's eye contact. 'I'm sorry for everything that happened that day,' she explained. 'I'm sorry I left you and Sam alone. I'm sorry that I blamed you. I'm sorry that I couldn't cope with life afterwards. I'm sorry that I made you feel unloved and unwelcome. I'm sorry that you left home. I'm sorry for not keeping in touch. I'm sorry for not finding you sooner. I'm sorry for all of it,' she said, the words rolling off her tongue. 'I never forgot about you, or Sam, and I've thought about you both every single day.' Lizzie broke down, all her feelings of guilt, regret and grief spilling out through her words. 'I've wanted to say sorry for such a long time, I just never knew where to start, or if you'd even hear me out. I thought you were happy, and that's why I haven't tried to find you. I didn't want to ruin the new life you'd made for yourself.' Lizzie's body trembled beneath the weight of grief and regret that she'd been carrying around for so long.

'You loved me and Sam so much, and we both knew that more

than anything,' Edith explained, recalling all the fond memories from her childhood. 'You told us that you loved us every single day, multiple times a day, and we used to have silly little fights about who loved each other the most. Do you remember?' she asked, failing to wait for a reply before continuing. 'And you always loved spending time with us, either playing games, or reading, or baking, or helping us with homework.' Edith paused to catch her breath. 'You were a brilliant mum, even when I was moody, and rude, and unwilling to listen to your advice. You were always there for me.'

'But I wasn't there for you when you really needed me the most.' Lizzie's emotions poured through her words.

Edith felt ready to release any lingering feelings of resentment. 'I did need you, but I also understood your reasons for wanting to escape from it all.' Edith thought back to the day that she left Lunar. 'I felt relief the day that I left home because it was so hard watching you and Dad, and I couldn't do anything to help. I was adding to the problem because I was a reminder of what had happened.'

'Putting you in that car was one of the hardest things I've ever done,' Lizzie admitted, recalling the day like it happened yesterday. 'I didn't want you to leave, but I also knew that I couldn't look after you in the way that you needed.'

'I knew that you and Dad blamed me for what happened,' Edith replied.

Lizzie grabbed hold of both of Edith's hands in a manner that conveyed she would never let go. 'I did at the time. But that's because I was looking for anyone else to blame apart from myself,' she revealed, momentarily closing her eyes, trying to shield herself from the internal pain stabbing at her heart. 'But all along, I knew that *I* was to blame for what happened to Sam. *I* shouldn't have left you two alone that day. *I* should have been there to look after you both. *I* was the reason that Sam died,' she explained, opening her eyes and allowing the tears to roll down her face. 'I ignored my instincts and went out anyway and left the two of you alone. You were only kids. You needed me there. There was nobody to blame that day apart from myself.'

'I think we all blamed ourselves for what happened to Sam,' Edith replied. 'You blame yourself for going out with Dad. I blamed myself for leaving Sam alone. Mr Aspey blamed himself for not raising the alarm sooner. And Dylan blamed himself for giving Sam the cigarette,' she explained, offering up everyone's explanation. 'And yet nobody was to blame. With help from Fern, I've come to realise that.'

'I'm so sorry for ever making you feel like it was your fault,' Lizzie said with sincerity.

'I'm sorry, too,' replied Edith, mother and daughter wrapping themselves within an embrace that neither one ever wanted to let go.

'I wish I'd tried harder to make amends with Dad before he died. There are so many things that I'd have said to him.'

Lizzie admired her daughter, and how she'd developed into such a beautiful young woman. 'No matter what happened, your dad loved you,' Lizzie began. 'That night, during our anniversary meal, Dad was talking about how proud he was of you. You remind me so much of him.' When Lizzie scratched her cheek, Edith noticed her mum's wedding rings.

'Are you remarried?'

Lizzie looked down at her left hand. 'I am,' she beamed. 'Ralph makes me so happy. I'd love it for the two of you to meet, he's heard so much about you.'

'Of course. I'd love that,' Edith replied, relishing how happy her mum appeared, and for the first time since Sam's death, she believed that she would also come to experience happiness.

Fern got up and approached the table. 'How about we get going and leave you two to it?' she asked. 'I think you've got a lot to catch up on.'

Lizzie looked up, dabbing her saturated face. 'Before you go, I have something to share with you all, if you wouldn't mind staying for just a few more minutes.'

'Of course,' Fern replied, indicating for Arthur and Dylan to join them.

Lizzie stood up and faced her audience. 'I was going through some of the colouring books that Fern found in Sam's room,' she began, looking over at Fern. 'And I came across this,' she explained, pulling out a book from her bag. 'It's a little note that Sam wrote. I'm not sure exactly when, there's no date, but judging by the writing, I'm guessing that it was written not long before he died.' Lizzie flicked through the pages until she came across the one that was littered with Sam's words.

Waiting with eager anticipation, Edith, Arthur, Dylan and Fern all sat in silence, listening for what Lizzie was about to say next.

Lizzie cleared her throat before starting. 'My name is Sam,' she began, her emotions already threatening to erupt despite having read the letter to herself dozens of times in the past twenty-four hours. Upon hearing Lizzie's first four words, lumps appeared in everyone's throats. They had all longed to hear Sam's voice, his turn of phrase, and now their dreams were coming true. 'I live in a village called Aldebaran. My house is big, and it has a barn that's good for playing in.' Lizzie paused, wanting to do Sam's exact words justice. 'I live with my mum and my dad and my sister. She's my best friend,' she continued, turning to look at Edith and reaching out her hand when she could see her daughter was struggling to contain her tears. 'My big sister buys me ice creams from the shop up the road and she reads stories to me at night. I'm a bit scared of the dark but that's a secret.' Lizzie turned to look at Dylan. 'Dylan is my other best friend. He's older than me but I can ride my bike just as fast. He is fun and he makes me laugh. We do pranks on people and get into trouble.'

Fern reached out and wrapped her arm around Dylan's shoulders, pulling her friend closer to her body, his head momentarily resting against hers.

After a short pause to allow Sam's sentiments to be absorbed, Lizzie continued. 'Mr Aspey lives next door,' she read, turning to look at Arthur. 'He likes to take pictures and sometimes when he isn't looking, I use his camera,' Lizzie smiled. 'I like taking him cookies that me and Mum have baked because I get to eat more with him.' Arthur released any lingering feelings of guilt that his body was holding onto and allowed feelings of contentment to flood through his heart.

With everyone still reeling in Sam's words, Lizzie turned to acknowledge Fern. 'A few words of my own,' she began. 'I wanted to thank you, Fern, for taking the time, and the compassion, to handle Sam's things with such care. You have returned his precious memories to us and allowed his voice to be heard after so many years.'

Choked with her own emotions, Fern cleared her throat and replied. 'When I first moved into Lunar, I found it hard to understand how I could ever find happiness again. And yet happiness is what I've found. I was never fortunate enough to have met Sam for myself,' she replied. 'But he's a little boy that I will always hold close to my heart, and whilst I'm living here in Aldebaran, at my lovely home, Lunar, I just wanted to let you all know that you're welcome to visit anytime. I hope that you can all take comfort in the memories of Sam that you find at my house. I consider you all friends now, and even though it hasn't been under the best circumstances, I'm so grateful to have met each one of you.'

'Let's cheers to that,' Dylan initiated, making sure that everyone had a glass. 'Here's to new friendships, and to keeping the memory of Sam alive.' Dylan raised his glass into the centre of the table. 'To Sam, who we will never forget.'

FIFTEEN YEARS EARLIER

PART ONE

A STRAY, TABBY FELINE SNAKED THROUGH THE LONG-STEMMED shrubbery decorating Lunar's impressive front garden. The prowling cat disturbed a patch of delicate, sky blue Borage flower heads, making the stems dance. Despite the cat's commotion, unperturbed, a drift of bees continued to scatter particles of pollen amidst the stillness of the hazy, late spring afternoon. Bathed in swathes of comforting sunlight, Elizabeth Sloan looked out over her back garden from where she was standing in her bedroom window. She caught sight of her son's abandoned candy red BMX bike on the lawn. Sam was nowhere to be seen, which she thought was odd because even if he couldn't be spotted, the sound of his voice still managed to travel from all corners of the property.

'How strange,' she commented, turning back to face the room. 'I can't hear Sam.'

Perched on the end of their bed, Lockie continued to fasten the laces to his fancy shoes. 'He's played outside all day. I bet he's downstairs crashed out on the sofa.'

'How does this look?' Elizabeth asked, standing in front of the full-length mirror. 'This is the fourth dress that I've tried on, and they all feel a bit tight around my hips,' she grumbled, peering at her silhouette from every angle hoping to catch a more flattering reflection. 'I can't remember the last time I wore a dress.'

Lockie pressed himself against his wife's back and delivered a trickle of tender kisses to the nape of her soft neck. 'It's been forever since we went out without the kids.'

Elizabeth turned around and kissed him on the lips. 'Should we just order a takeaway instead? I don't like the thought of leaving the kids home alone. We could rent a film, and all have popcorn afterwards. It'll be a real treat.'

Lockie shook his head and stuffed his hands into his trouser pocket in a show of frustration. 'Charlotte's sixteen now. She's old enough to take some responsibility for herself, and for Sam. It's only going to be for a few hours. It's not like we're leaving them by themselves overnight.'

'I know it won't be for long. But I'll worry. They aren't used to being left alone. We've never done this before. Not once.' Elizabeth wandered back to the window, peering out to see if she could see or hear her son.

Lockie reached for his jacket and huffed with irritation. Elizabeth's reluctance to leave the kids took the edge off his excitement. 'It's not every day that we'll be celebrating our twenty-year wedding anniversary,' he began. 'So, come on, let's go. The kids won't even notice that we've gone.'

With reluctance and a heavy heart, Elizabeth reached for her handbag and jacket. 'I'll just go and speak with Charlotte to make sure that she's alright. Then we'll get going.'

She walked across the landing to her daughter's room and knocked on her door. 'Can you turn that down a bit?' she asked. When no reply came, she let herself in.

'Can you knock next time?' Charlotte snapped when she spotted her mum standing in the doorway.

'I did knock, but your music's so loud you didn't hear me.' Elizabeth walked further into the room and swung open the curtains. She looked out of the window to see if Sam was at the front of the house. 'Why do you like sitting in the dark? It's not normal, Charlotte. It feels so depressing in here. No wonder you feel miserable.'

Lying on her bed and rolling her eyes, Charlotte reached out and turned the volume down by a single notch. 'Did you just come to have a go at me, or do you actually want something?'

Elizabeth performed a little pirouette in the middle of the room. 'What do you think of my dress?' she asked, allowing the material to swoosh around her feet.

Charlotte's facial expression remained unchanged. 'I wouldn't wear it. But it looks okay on you.'

Elizabeth moved Charlotte's legs so that she could perch herself on the end of the bed. 'I'll take that as a compliment.'

'It wasn't meant as one.'

Brushing off her daughter's snarly, teenage attitude, Elizabeth changed the subject. 'Dad and I are off out now, so you're in charge. Do you remember the rules?' she asked, raising her eyebrows in the hope that her daughter had digested their earlier conversation.

Charlotte looked towards the window, hating the fact that the sun was pouring into her room. 'Why do we have to have rules for every single thing we do? This family is ruled by rules.'

'Rule number one,' Elizabeth continued, holding up a finger. 'You're not allowed any friends over,' she confirmed. 'Rule number two. No leaving the house under any circumstances,' she continued, holding up another finger. 'Rule number three. No fighting or bickering with Sam. If he needs anything, he'll be coming to you. So, be nice to him. Rule number four. Don't leave Sam by himself. You're responsible for him tonight. You're his big sister, so act like it.'

Charlotte interrupted Elizabeth. 'How many rules are there?' she exhaled, already bored by the conversation and dismissing the rules as unnecessary. Her mum's words were drowned out by thoughts of the treats she was going to buy from the shop.

Elizabeth held up another finger, much to Charlotte's annoyance. 'Rule number five. Don't answer the door to strangers. Just ignore it, and they'll go away. And rule number six. Call us if there are any problems, and we'll come straight back. We're only going out for a quick something to eat. The restaurant is about twenty minutes away, so we're close by if you need us. I've written down the details and left them near the toaster.'

'I think we'll cope without you,' Charlotte said sarcastically.

Elizabeth stood up. 'I'll go and tell Sam that we're going, okay?'

Charlotte cranked up the volume on her alternative choice of music, failing to answer her mum.

Elizabeth strolled into Sam's room. She shook her head when she saw the complete disarray it had been left in. Sam's part-built train track covered most of the floor space. His bed covers were in a crumpled mess, and most of his clothes were draped over his chair or piled up in the corner of the room in a dirty heap. Elizabeth quickly made his bed, tucking some of his teddies underneath the duvet.

'Everything okay?' Lockie asked, appearing on the landing.

'Sam must be downstairs,' she said, closing the door before Lockie saw inside. She headed downstairs so that her husband would follow. 'Charlotte is in her room, as you can hear,' she added, pausing at the bottom. 'And I've gone through all of the rules with her, not that she was paying any attention.' Elizabeth listened for Sam, knowing that she could usually hear her son before she could see him. She peered her head into the lounge, surprised when she saw that the room was empty. 'He must be outside,' she said, peering down the hallway and sensing that Sam wasn't in the house. 'Maybe he's in the barn,' she said, arching her neck so that she could see through the side window. Sam's bright BMX was leaning against the outbuilding wall, the door ajar. 'He must be. His bike's there.'

Lockie gathered his wallet and keys, eager to leave. 'I'll get the engine started,' he said, walking outside. 'Otherwise, we'll never leave, and we'll end up being late for our table reservation.'

Elizabeth also headed outside and made her way round to the barn. Side-stepping over Sam's fallen bike, she opened the side door.

'Hi, Mum,' Sam announced. He jumped down off the towering bales that were located at the far end of the rustic building.

'Be careful, my love,' Elizabeth shouted. Her heart leapt into her mouth whenever she saw the way that Sam flung himself around like he was some kind of superhero. 'We don't want any broken bones. The summer holidays will be here before we know it, and you wouldn't want to be stuck inside with a cast on your leg, would you?'

Sam kicked some stray straw that'd come loose when the bales were being moved. 'I'm always careful,' he groaned.

'I'm your mum, so I'm just asking you to be extra careful.'

'Playing on the bales is fun,' he giggled, his red t-shirt full of mud, his holey shorts covered in dried-on dirt. 'I hope the farmer always keeps the hay in here. It'd be boring without them.'

'Listen, Dad and I are off out now,' she said, ushering him over so that she could give him a goodbye hug. 'Come and give me a big love before I go,' she insisted, crouching down and indicating with her arms for him to accept her embrace. 'Your sister is in her bedroom. So, if you need anything, you know where to find her.'

Sam bounced over and flung his arms around his mum in a genuine show of his enduring affection. 'How long will you be gone?' he asked, hiding the box of matches that he'd taken from the kitchen and had clenched in his hand.

'We won't be long. We're just going out for some tea. Do you like my dress?' she asked, standing and doing another twirl.

'It's very girly,' he replied, unable to remember his mum ever wearing a dress. 'Can I come too? I don't want to stay here by myself.'

Elizabeth's heart melted at the sight of Sam's big blue eyes. She crouched back down and wanted to do nothing more than take him with her. 'You can come out with us next time,' she promised, kissing the back of his hand, his skin smelling of the outdoors. 'We're going to a fancy restaurant tonight. I don't think they'd have chicken nuggets or fish fingers on the menu. And anyway, there's popcorn in the cupboard, and because I'm not here, you can eat as much as you want,' she smiled, winking.

'Okay,' Sam replied, placing the box of matches into his pocket and grabbing a bouncy ball, throwing it to the top of the stacked bales.

'Be a good boy for your sister. And remember, no friends over while we're out, especially not Dylan. You can watch whatever you want on TV and eat popcorn instead.'

Sam nodded in agreement, already knowing that he wasn't in a TV-watching mood, not when the weather was so warm.

'And tomorrow, we'll have a fab family day. Maybe we could go to that trampoline park that you like. The one that has the drop slide and climbing wall near the entrance. What do you think?'

'Can Dylan come with us?' he said, producing his signature, sparkling smile. It was the smile that melted Elizabeth's heart. It was the smile that always meant that Sam would get his own way.

'We'll see,' Elizabeth smiled, blowing a stream of kisses and opening the door. 'Bye, my love,' she said, walking away. 'See you soon. I'll be back to read you a bedtime story.'

Outside, just before joining Lockie in the car, Elizabeth picked a few stalks of lilac cuckoo flowers. Having forgotten to wear any earrings, she slipped the stalks behind her ear, pinning them in place.

'Are you ready?' Lockie asked when she got into the car, failing to notice the floral decoration to her hair. 'I was about to come and get you.'

Elizabeth found it difficult to concentrate, her thoughts still firmly placed on Sam. The thought of him playing alone in the barn pulled at her heart strings, inducing feelings of guilt. 'Sam really wanted to come with us. I could tell that he was upset,' she said, hoping that Lockie might still have a change of heart.

Unperturbed, Lockie buckled his belt. 'Sam can come with us next time,' he confirmed, starting the engine.

With a sinking feeling stirring in her heart, Elizabeth watched the house fade into the distance as the car pulled away. Internally, she kicked herself for failing to stand her ground with Lockie, hating the way that she tended to go along with whatever he thought was best. 'Next time, we're hiring a babysitter,' she stated as fact. 'And I don't care what Charlotte says. Until she starts to show some maturity, I'd feel more relaxed leaving someone more responsible in charge.'

'Okay. Next time, we'll get a babysitter,' Lockie agreed, just to placate his wife. 'But let's just enjoy tonight while we can.'

Elizabeth gazed up at the canopy she knew so well. 'It's meant to be a full moon tonight,' she commented, trying to distract herself. 'I wonder if we'll get an influx of stargazers.'

Back at Lunar, Sam watched from the barn. He waited for his mum and dad's car to disappear. The moment the vehicle left the driveway, he ran out to grab his bike and headed for the main road. When he heard a car approaching over his shoulder, he peddled faster to try and race the speeding vehicle, his legs tiring as the car whizzed past, the sound of the engine blaring in his ear. Out of breath, he stopped and turned around, noting how far away from home he had already cycled. In the distance, he spotted the vibrant shade of yellow that he knew was Dylan's bike frame and began to wave to catch his friend's attention.

Peddling back towards home, Sam shouted. 'Dylan, can you play?'

Dylan stopped and turned around upon hearing his name being called. When he saw Sam on the main road, he also peddled back towards Lunar.

'Are your mum and dad not here?' he asked when he reached the house, spotting that the car wasn't there.

'They've gone out,' Sam replied. 'Can you stay and play? Should we go in the barn?'

Dylan looked up at the house, knowing that Elizabeth and Lockie didn't much like it when he and Sam played together. 'Yeah, let's go. But don't tell your mum and dad that I was here without their permission.'

'Before we go to the barn, can I show you the train track that I started building this morning?' Sam asked with a sense of pride, a few drops of rain starting to fall.

The two boys abandoned their bikes and charged towards the house, running up the stairs before bouncing into Sam's small bedroom. 'Look, I even have a working turntable,' boasted Sam, providing a demonstration. The two boys crouched on the floor together and, without needing instruction, continued to assemble the train set. The sound of the noisy, battery-operated trains failed to disturb Charlotte, who was still locked away in her bedroom, blaring music.

'Should we close the curtains?' Dylan asked. 'Then we can see if the lights in the tunnel are still working.'

Sam scrambled over the track and knelt on his bed to reach the curtains. Embarrassed, he grabbed the teddy that was resting on his pillow, the words *I love my sister* stitched onto the front. He stuffed the bear under his duvet before Dylan noticed.

'Let's go down to the barn,' he suggested, abandoning the train set and charging back down the stairs. Dylan followed, leaving the train set scattered half-finished across the floor.

Outside, the rain had stopped. Basking beneath the warm, spring sunshine that shone with exuberance, a bustle of bees bobbed about on the array of flowers that decorated Lunar's front garden with all the pride of a flower show entry. 'Run!' Sam shouted and screamed when he spotted a few stray bees, the buzzing sound of their wings causing him to dart across the paved path.

Wanting to beat Sam to the barn, Dylan darted across the

flower beds to take a shortcut, the sound of his screams travelling over into next door's garden. 'Race you!' he shouted. Without realising, Dylan's clumsiness had made him disturb a pile of leaves that Sam and his mum had gathered the previous winter. Tucked beneath the makeshift shelter, a secret prickle of hedgehogs were starting to emerge from hibernation, something Sam had been waiting to witness during the long, drawn out winter months.

'I won!' Sam announced, breathless. 'And I didn't even cheat,' he said, failing to notice the mess that Dylan had made during the impromptu race.

The two boys snuck inside the barn and climbed up to the top of the bales. Sitting with their backs against the wall, the warmth being absorbed by the barn roof soon made them feel hot and sweaty.

'What should we do now?' Dylan asked, spotting a ball. 'Basketball?'

Sam scrunched up his nose. 'It's too hot for that.'

The unusually hot weather that had continued to burn over Aldebaran for the previous few weeks meant that everything in the garden was dry, and brittle, the trickle of rainfall doing little to hydrate. The sun had scorched the grass, turning it a pale shade of brown.

'We could get out the hose to cool down.'

'Why don't we do dares?' Sam suggested with a wicked smile.

Dylan shook his head. 'Nah,' he groaned, not wanting to land himself in trouble.

Ignoring Dylan's refusal, Sam continued with his idea. 'I dare you to sneak next door and take Mr Aspey's box of cigarettes.'

'Why don't we go and make a ramp for the bikes instead?' Dylan suggested, loving nothing more than riding his yellow mountain bike.

'You can't turn down a dare,' stated Sam. 'It's the rules, remember?' He took out a box of matches from his pocket, striking one, the flame igniting instantly. 'And we should see what it's like to suck in the smoke. I've seen Arthur do it loads of times. It looks pretty easy.'

Dylan wasn't in the mood for dares, knowing that he was already on a last warning with his mum for staying out too late the previous evening. 'If I get caught, my mum will be raging. She's already said that she'll lock my bike in the shed if I get into any trouble today.'

'You too scared?' Sam sniggered, knowing that whenever a dare involved Mr Aspey's house, it was extra risky.

Annoyed, Dylan stood up in a huff. 'No, I'm not scared,' he protested, scrambling down and making his way outside.

Not long after Dylan left the barn, the side door opened. 'I'm going to the shop to buy us some ice creams. I'll be back in a minute, okay?' Charlotte announced, standing in the doorway, failing to smell the matches that Sam had been playing with.

'Can I come, too?' he asked, stuffing the matchbox back into his pocket and shuffling down on his bottom until he reached the ground.

Charlotte sighed, knowing that it was bad enough that she was breaking the rules. 'No, you stay here and play. I won't be long,' she said, closing the door, her decision final.

Sam sulked back to the top of the bales and sat back down, waiting impatiently for Dylan's return. He took out his box of matches and with only two left, struck one with confidence to ensure that it ignited. Seeing how long he could hold it before it threatened to burn his fingers, Sam accidentally dropped the match while the flame was still burning.

The barn door burst open.

'Here you go,' Dylan said with excitement. He climbed back up to where Sam was sitting and threw him the box of cigarettes. 'It stinks in here. How many matches have you been lighting?'

Too distracted by the cigarettes to spot the ignited, fallen match, Sam flipped opened the box and took one out. He inspected both ends, wondering which part to put in his mouth. 'Let's light it,' he said, getting out his last match from the box.

'You can light it, but I don't want to. I'm going to run and put these back before he notices,' said Dylan, grabbing the box and jumping back down.

Before Dylan had even left the barn, Sam struck the last match. The flame ignited and developed into a steady burn. With the cigarette pressed between his lips, Sam sucked until his cheeks produced dimples. He held the match over the end of the cigarette until the tobacco smouldered. The moment that he inhaled, he dropped the cigarette and started to cough. With a bout of toxic smoke infiltrating his lungs, Sam struggled to catch his breath, his asthmatic lungs wheezing.

The ignited cigarette landed and nestled itself amongst the bales. Still caught up in a coughing fit, Sam lost his balance. His leg became wedged between two stubborn, weighty bales that were pressed together like a sandwich.

Within seconds, the cigarette that Sam had dropped caught fire, the bales closest to the ground quickly igniting, and the flames spread. Towards the back of the haybales, established flames began to emerge where the discarded match had begun to singe the kindling.

The growing flames caught Sam's attention, making him release a scream so high-pitched, it could have broken glass.

'Dylan!' he screamed, his facial features becoming washed away with a plume of thick, heavy tears. He yanked on his exposed thigh, trying to free his foot from his trainer in the hope that it would aid the release of his trapped leg. It was no use. Realising he was stuck, a look of fear crept across his pallid face. 'Help!'

Despite Sam's incessant screams, nobody came. Within minutes, thick, toxic billows of fumes filled the barn. The initial delicate vapour tendrils quickly developed into one thick, colossal cloud. With one hand over his mouth and nose, Sam spluttered after each breath he stole from the jaws of the fire. Originating from the pit of his stomach, he released another bout of piercing screams when the flames snaked dangerously close to his trapped body. The sound of his cries penetrated the barn structure until the terrifying noise made it beyond the walls of the prison inferno. The strength and direction of the wind carried the harrowing sound of Sam's shrieks across the garden, the noise falling upon the deaf ears of nothing but a rogue, dubious cat and a collection of docile wildlife awakening from hibernation.

Weakened physically, the heat from the aggressive blaze made Sam cower his face. Within minutes, the entire space was dominated by a series of hungry flames in search of sustaining fuel. Silenced beneath the fire's ruling authority, the intensity of Sam's screams diminished. 'Mum,' was the last audible word to leave his parched lips, the sound tailing off as his voice lost strength and he swallowed more suffocating stems of smoke. The moment the fumes took permanent residency in his lungs, the toxicity of the gasses killed any remaining traces of oxygen fighting to keep Sam's body alive.

His limbs lost rigidity and became limp. Suddenly, he stopped struggling. He lay his head down on the makeshift straw pillow and closed his eyes like he was asleep.

PART TWO

Unawares that a fire had erupted, Dylan returned the cigarettes and closed Mr Aspey's gate. He ran back up the main road towards Lunar, eager to hear Sam's thoughts on the cigarette. The sight of flames pouring from the top of the blazing barn sent a surge of panic through his body. The stench of smoke drifting through the air made him feel the burn of bile in the back of his throat, and a hard thud penetrated his chest.

He ran back to the property and towards the direction of the barn. Dylan scrambled across the garden, searching for his friend who he assumed would be shielding himself from the fire. 'Sam, where are you?' he shouted in desperation when he failed to lock eyes on his friend.

Panting in defiance of the smoke, Dylan threw his body over the garden shrubbery until he reached the side of the barn. Without testing the handle for heat, he pulled open the side door. An avalanche of blackened smoke lashed across his face. The intensity of the flames made him retreat and shield his eyes from the inferno. A shudder swept through Dylan's entire body when he heard Sam's voice, a weak mumble breaking free from inside the heart of the beast. 'I'm going to get help, Sam!' he shouted through the blaze. The tears flooding Dylan's eyes soon disappeared beneath the heat emanating from the scorching inferno, his eyeballs stinging when the smoke got to them.

Panicked, Dylan tripped over his own feet in his bid to reach Lunar. He burst into the house like a fighting bull released into its arena. 'Charlotte!' he screamed as loud as his lungs allowed. He lunged his body in and out of every room but failed to find Sam's older sister. 'Charlotte!' he shouted again, his hysteria making him forget which rooms he'd already searched.

'Help!' he called out to anybody who might be nearby. He charged out of the house and back onto the road, his feet pounding on the pavement. The main throughfare remained unusually quiet. He barged through Mr Aspey's gate and stumbled up the porch, tripping over his own feet again. With clenched fists, he banged on the front door with both hands. 'Help! Help!' he shouted, and yet nobody came to his rescue. His eyes widened and prickled in protest to the smoke that had now embedded into the pores of his delicate skin. His shuddery breaths were barely able to escape due to the tightness in his chest.

Inside his house, Mr Aspey was seething. The sound of children screaming had scared away the birds he had been trying to capture on camera, and he'd wasted all day trying to get the shot that never came. He turned up his music when he heard that the children were still shouting. A grimace spread across his face at the assumption that he was being pestered. Infuriated by the disruption and assuming that he was once again on the receiving end of more cruel pranks, he ignored the banging on his door. With every window closed, Arthur settled himself into his favourite seat in the lounge and put his feet up on his sizable pouffe. With a recently brewed cup of tea in his hand, he savoured the moment of rest while his favourite selection of country music songs blasted in the background.

Outside, Dylan careered back onto the main road, his panic sending him hysterical. He caught sight of the flames that were rising into the sky, the type of flames he'd only ever witnessed at bonfires. 'Somebody help!' he shouted before charging through another garden gate. While banging on Henry and Iris Pepper's door, he peered across the road at the blaze, his face contorted in cries for help. No answer came, so he ran back onto the main road and threw himself in front of a passing car.

With the alarm raised, Dylan and the man he'd waved down ran back to Lunar. As the man searched the house for the owners, Dylan grabbed the hosepipe attached to the side of the house and dragged it across to the barn. He turned the mechanism until water started to fire. Breathless, he attempted to open the door, but the flames were too intense. 'Help is coming, Sam!' he cried, noticing that he could no longer hear his friend screaming. 'I'm here, Sam. The fire brigade will soon get you out. Just hold on.'

Within minutes, Dylan heard the deep hum of an engine roaring up the main road. He abandoned the hosepipe and, along with the man who had stopped to help, waved to make sure that the firefighters spotted them. Out on the street, people had started to gather. The flames and the sight of smoke had begun to draw attention.

'He's in there,' Dylan cried the moment a firefighter jumped down from the cabin. 'He was at the back,' he spluttered, exhaustion making him fall to the floor. Without wasting any time, the fire officer indicated with his hands where he wanted his awaiting team to focus their concerted efforts. Within seconds, two fire fighters held a red hose in place and pumped water over the burning barn, the iridescent crescent of a rainbow appearing as the sun continued to shine through the powerful jet stream. The fountain of water sprayed into the air until it clashed with the flames, and a battle commenced between the two elements.

After a few moments, the fire officer approached Dylan. 'My name is Flynn. What's your name?' he asked, crouching down to Dylan's level and lifting the shield on his helmet.

'Dylan,' he replied, looking over, waiting for Sam to appear. 'Have they found him yet?'

Fire officer Flynn placed a hand on Dylan's shoulder, trying to divert his attention away from the blaze. 'Dylan, who's in the barn?'

'Sam. He's my friend,' he cried, wiping his face with his sleeve, his dishevelled appearance testament to his heroic efforts to save his best friend's life.

'Is there anybody else in there?' Flynn asked.

Dylan shook his head. 'No.'

'How old is Sam?'

Dylan looked over Flynn's shoulder, waiting for a firefighter to walk out of the barn carrying Sam over his shoulder, just like he'd seen on television programmes. 'Seven.'

Flynn looked over to the house in search of an adult. 'Dylan, do you live here?'

He shook his head, keeping his focus firmly set on the barn.

Flynn continued with his line of questioning. 'Where are Sam's parents? Are they home?'

Dylan shook his head again. A stirring sensation in his stomach made him feel like he was going to vomit. The stench of smoke clogged in his nostrils. 'They went out.'

'Do you know where?' Flynn was met with another shake of the head. 'Is there anybody else home?'

'Sam said his sister was home,' he recalled. 'She was playing loud music,' Dylan added, remembering the din coming from Charlotte's room when he and Sam had been upstairs playing with the train set.

Flynn stood up. 'Wait here for me, Dylan. I'll be back in a minute,' he requested, before walking over to the van and instructing a colleague to enter the house.

Dylan remained crouched on the floor like a wounded soldier waiting to see his fellow comrade rising like a warrior from the burning ashes. It felt like he was waiting for hours. And still there was no sign of his best friend. Through a constant stream of tears, Dylan watched how the hoses drowned the raging flames until the fire was brought under control. After the flames were smothered and the fire was completely extinguished, all that could be seen were ripples of smoke seeping into the sky. Dylan turned to look at those people who were standing on the pavement, wondering why one woman was crying. He looked at her harder, wondering if she knew Sam. The stench of smouldering embers made some of the onlookers feel sickened to their stomachs. Unable to watch any longer, a handful of bystanders decided to move on, concluding the fate of the fire for themselves.

But Dylan refused to move. Before making his way home to tell his mum all about what had happened, he wanted to see Sam and make sure that his friend was okay. With still no sight of Sam, Dylan noticed that the initial hive of activity had calmed. The firefighters were no longer scrambling for equipment or shouting commands. There seemed to be lots of people in uniform standing around, not doing much apart from talking.

'What's happening? Where's Sam?' he asked when Flynn returned. 'Why have they stopped?' he questioned, still unable to see his friend. 'Why are they putting stuff away?' he shouted before standing up. 'Have they found him?' Amongst the huddle of firefighters, Dylan caught one man looking at him, a sad expression on his face. 'Don't stop yet!' he yelled. 'You need to rescue my friend,' he cried. 'I'll show you where he is.'

Flynn reached out his arm and prevented the distraught boy from walking away. 'Dylan, where do you live? I need to call your parents.'

Dylan didn't hear Flynn's question. His attention was now focused on what was happening at the side of the engine. Puzzled, he watched the firefighters put away the hoses and remove their helmets. He noted how they had all stopped talking. The garden felt quiet, despite their being lots of people huddled in close proximity.

'Dylan, where do you live?' Flynn repeated.

Without looking at the firefighter, Dylan muttered his address. 'Is Sam okay?' he then asked.

In the distance, Dylan heard a siren. From his vantage point, he watched an ambulance and police car pull onto the drive and park alongside the fire engine. 'Why is there an ambulance? Is Sam hurt? Can I see him now? I need to talk to him.' Dylan felt his stomach churn. A stabbing pain shot through his insides, and he crouched over to be sick, his skin clammy and flushed.

Flynn indicated to the police officer when she got out of the car. 'Dylan, I need you to go with this special officer. She's going to take care of you until your parents arrive.'

'Hi, Dylan. My name is Sally. I'm going to sit with you until your mum and dad arrive, if that's okay with you?' she explained, placing a hand against his back. The police officer guided Dylan to her car, helping him to take a seat in the back. She sat alongside him, arching her body so that she was facing him.

'Am I in trouble?' he asked once inside the car.

'No. We just want to have a chat with you when your mum and dad get here, that's all,' she said, her voice quiet and tender.

Dylan peered out of the window and watched the police put up a tent at the side of the barn. 'What's that for?' he asked, watching the tarpaulin being erected.

Sally diverted his question. 'What year are you in at school?' she asked, trying to pull his attention away from the unfolding crime scene.

Dylan looked behind him, seeing that a fresh set of people had gathered on the main road. He spotted Charlotte trying to push her way through. 'That's Sam's sister,' he said, trying to open the car door, relieved to see a familiar face, hoping that Sam had been with her all along.

'The doors are locked,' Sally confirmed, adding to Dylan's fraught nerves.

'I need to talk to her,' he protested, still pulling on the handle trying to escape.

'The officers will talk to her. You don't need to worry about anything,' Sally reassured.

'Is Sam okay?' Dylan asked in a moment of bravery, turning to Sally so that he could capture her expression. When no reply came, he repeated the question. 'Is he okay?' Pools of despair deeper than an ocean welled in Dylan's eyes when he was met with an expression the officer couldn't mask.

Sally reached out her hand and took hold of Dylan's. 'I'm not sure,' she replied, her arms capturing Dylan's upper body when it collapsed into her waiting embrace.

Outside the car, Charlotte walked past the commotion and onto the chaotic land at Lunar. 'What's going on?' she asked nobody in particular. *Where's Sam?* she thought to herself in a moment of terror, panicked by the sight of all the emergency services. Flynn walked over to meet Charlotte, guiding her away from the chaos and in through the front door of the house. 'Where's Sam?' she asked aloud, looking around for her little brother. 'Sam?' she shouted up the stairs, expecting to hear his voice, or witness him bounding down the stairs in his usual haphazard fashion.

'Charlotte, where are your parents?' Flynn asked.

'They went out for a meal.' She peered through the side window to the barn, seeing that one whole side of the outbuilding had been ravaged by fire. She began to cry when she spotted Sam's abandoned bike lying on the lawn. She turned slowly to face Flynn. 'Where is my brother?' she cried, looking the firefighter right in the eyes.

'Which restaurant are your parents at?' Flynn asked, his tone calm. 'I need to get in touch with them.'

Charlotte handed Flynn the number of the restaurant that her mum had left and then went and stood by the lounge window that was closest to the barn. She watched and waited for Sam to appear, expecting him to come running in from outside with a tale to tell, like usual.

Moments later, Flynn returned having spoken to the restaurant manager and confirmed that Mr and Mrs Sloan had left some time ago. 'Your parents should be home soon,' he confirmed. 'Why don't you come and wait in the kitchen with me?' he encouraged, trying to usher Charlotte into a room where she couldn't witness the scene unfolding at the side of the barn.

Unresponsive to his request, Charlotte remained planted to the spot where she had been standing, still searching for her little brother. She chose to ignore the sickening sensation that was twisting through her insides like poison. Despite her instincts telling her that something awful had happened, she chose to believe that Sam was safe, and instead, she focused her thoughts on how she was going to explain the fire to her parents.

Outside, about a five minutes' drive away, Elizabeth and Lockie turned onto the main road that led directly into Aldebaran. The familiar hills that depicted home came into view in the distance. 'Have you seen all the smoke?' Elizabeth commented, spotting the sinister ripples rising over the horizon. 'I wonder what's gone on?'

'I don't know, but the stargazer's won't be out in their droves if it doesn't clear by nightfall,' Lockie commented, recalling that it was set to be a full moon. He turned to look at his wife. 'Thanks for a great evening. It's been amazing,' he beamed. 'We should do this more often,' he suggested, reaching out to rest his hand on his wife's exposed thigh.

'It has been lovely,' Elizabeth commented, still gazing up at the smoke. 'But I've missed the kids,' she confessed, failing to mention that she hadn't been able to stop thinking about them all night. She had even made an excuse that she was too full to manage dessert, just so that they could return home sooner. 'I hope that Sam's still awake,' she said, peering at her watch. 'Then I can give him a goodnight kiss.'

The moment their car approached the driveway to Lunar, Elizabeth and Lockie spotted the collection of emergency service vehicles stationed on their land. Simultaneously, their hearts dropped the second they saw that the collage of smoke decorating the sky had originated from their barn. The gaggle of onlookers still lining the pavement gawped at the couple as the car turned onto the drive. Elizabeth always admired the vibrancy of her front garden whenever she turned onto her driveway. But not today. Today all she could see were billows of grey smoke and flecks of ash trickling through the air like poisoned confetti, the dark, dusty residue landing on the delicate petals of her favourite cuckoo flowers.

'Oh my God. What's happened?' she said, her face losing all traces of its natural blush. A bout of nerves rumbled through her full stomach, making her want to vomit. 'They're all looking at us,' she mumbled, trying to hold back her tears when she saw the collection of saddened faces staring at her sympathetically. A spate of fear stole the breath from her lungs and she gasped. Composing herself, she and Lockie got out of the car and watched as two uniformed police officers approached their vehicle. The lilac flowers that had been tucked behind Elizabeth's ear all evening fell to the floor.

'Are Charlotte and Sam okay?' she asked before the officers could speak. Elizabeth diverted her gaze into the distance, searching for her children. She spotted Sam's abandoned bike amongst the chaos, the distinctive red paintwork also tainted by fallen fragments of smoulder.

'Hello. My name is Kate, and this is my colleague, Officer Peters. Are you Mr and Mrs Sloan?' the police officer asked.

Elizabeth ignored the question and looked towards the barn. She saw that smoke was still seeping from the far end, the exact location where she had left her son. Her face turned angry. 'Where are my children?' she asked, watching as various members of the emergency services gathered near the white tent that had been erected at the side of the barn. Blue and white police tape encased the outbuilding like a security belt, restricting access.

'We are,' Lockie finally announced, answering Officer Kate's initial question. Lockie took hold of his wife's hand and entwined his fingers around hers. Her skin felt perishing against his, and he could feel a nervous tremble in her hand.

'Would you please come inside with me?' Kate asked, indicating towards the house.

Elizabeth released her hand and thrashed it through the air. 'Just tell me where my children are,' she demanded.

'Please, let's go inside,' Kate insisted as she and her colleague continued to walk towards the house, leaving behind the prying eyes of onlookers.

With reluctance, Elizabeth and Lockie were escorted into the house. The moment she stepped foot through the door, Elizabeth noticed that Sam's trainers weren't lying scattered on the floor like usual. Compared with the commotion outside, inside it felt quiet, and the television wasn't blasting at the volume it normally did when the children were in control. There was no sound of stomping feet coming from the upstairs bedrooms, and there was no racket drifting down from Charlotte's speaker. Through Elizabeth's eyes, a sense of hostility and emptiness had invaded her home, sensations which made her stomach drop to the floor. A sickening taste of apprehension gave her the chills, and she was already punishing herself for having left the children alone.

Once in the kitchen, Kate advised them both to take a seat. The door was secured back into its frame by Officer Peters, who proceeded to take his position at the table, at one side of Elizabeth. Kate seated herself at the opposite side of the table, next to Lockie. A box of tissues had already been placed in the centre of the table.

The unfamiliar patten on the tissue box didn't go unnoticed to Elizabeth, and she knew that they had been placed there by someone else's hand. With her fingers fidgeting in her lap, Elizabeth didn't take her eyes off Kate's soft features. In particular, she paid close attention to the positioning of the officer's lips, trying to anticipate the words that would follow. At the same time, Elizabeth continued to listen for any noises coming from upstairs, desperate to hear Sam and Charlotte's voices, or the sound of their stomping feet.

Officer Kate cleared her throat and prepared herself for the shattering news that she was about to deliver. Despite her extensive experience, notifying family members about the death of a loved one never got any easier. The nauseating feeling in the pit of her stomach told Kate that she was about to destroy someone's world.

'We received an emergency call earlier on this afternoon,' she began, stating the facts. 'We were notified by a member of the public that there was a fire at this address.' Kate's tone remained steady, and calm, her eye contact never wavering. 'Emergency services arrived on the scene and a team of firefighters worked hard to put out the fire that was found to be contained to your barn.'

Elizabeth and Lockie remained silent. They both dived headfirst into an ocean of prayer and drew upon an inner faith that they had previously abandoned. At sporadic intervals, Elizabeth forgot to breathe. She felt suffocated by the barrage of information being thrown in her direction. Every single one of Kate's words became clogged in her throat, making her desperate to escape and pop up for breath.

'We also received confirmation that a young boy was trapped inside the barn,' Kate confirmed.

With selfish motivations, Elizabeth willed Kate to continue with her explanation, and reveal that it had been another boy who had been trapped in the barn. Anyone but her own son.

Unable to meet the eyes of a mother about to be bereft, Kate diverted her gaze for the briefest of seconds. 'And we now believe that the boy was your son, Sam.'

The moment that Sam's name left Kate's mouth, Elizabeth felt a stabbing sensation penetrate the core of her heart. She pressed her hand against her chest, trying to soothe the initial stinging that was tearing apart her vital organ until it felt like only tatters remained. Every trace of joy and peace fell off Elizabeth's face.

Like a statue, Lockie remained frozen. The world around him ceased to exist. He couldn't hear any distant noises or the sound of Kate's foot as it tapped nervously against the hard, tiled floor. He couldn't smell anything, not even the distinctive perfume his wife had sprayed liberally only hours earlier. The metal clasp on his watch was pinching at his skin, and yet he felt nothing. The shattered state of his internal emotions made him feel like he was riding a terrifying rollercoaster that he wanted to depart, only he was strapped in with no way of escaping.

Despite Elizabeth's crumbling demeanour, Kate knew that she had to continue to deliver the news. She dragged the next string of devastating words from her mouth. 'Despite the best efforts from the firefighters, it is with great sadness that I need to inform you that they were unable to rescue your son. Sam passed away earlier this afternoon.'

A drowning silence engulfed the room and, for a moment, for all those beating hearts contained within the kitchen, it felt like the world had ended.

Slouched in her seat, a withered shadow of her former self, Elizabeth fell apart one piece at a time. Her eyes clouded and filled with deep wells of sorrow. Inside her body, a grief-choked scream was gaining momentum, waiting for its moment to erupt. She prayed that Kate would find herself mistaken, that the police radio might bleep with an announcement that her son was, in fact, alive.

After a few agonising seconds, Kate attempted to offer her initial words of condolence. 'I'm very sorry for your loss,' she said, reaching out to offer a physical show of sympathy.

Elizabeth immediately retracted her hand. She jumped out of her seat and, with all the eagerness of a hare escaping capture, she bolted out of the door. On her hands and knees, she scrambled up the stairs.

'Sam? Sam? Where are you?' she shouted, pushing open each door in turn, searching frantically to find her missing son. A pent up, haunting scream clawed its way through Elizabeth's body until it found a voice. The sound exploded from her throat and pierced the silence, startling everybody in the room. Beyond the kitchen window, a flutter of unsuspecting house sparrows scarpered from their resting place, intimidated by the erupting shriek.

Outside, beyond the front garden to Lunar, the remaining cluster of onlookers fell silent the moment that Elizabeth's scream broke through and echoed amid the lingering breeze. The haunting sound failed to lose strength as she continued to scream with more protest than an innocent soul being sentenced to death.

Down the hallway in the lounge, Charlotte's entire body jumped when she heard the sound. In that moment, she knew deep down that her little brother was never coming home. In a form of self-defence, she blocked out the sound of her mum's hysterics and placed her hands over her ears. She didn't cry. Instead, she thought about how life was going to be as an only child. When the family went on holiday and hired bikes, she'd no longer have Sam to ride tandem. During the easter festivities, would there still be cakes to decorate and treasure hunts to enjoy, like there had been every other year? Who would play swing ball with her in the garden? Who would eat her marshmallows? Sam had always loved the billows of whipped cream and stack of marshmallows that accompanied steaming mugs of hot chocolate at Christmas time. Who would she talk to in the car while her parents listened to the country radio station she detested? Who would she read stories to at nighttime. Who would be her stargazing companion? Who would she love unconditionally, and who would love her back?

Running back down the stairs when Sam was nowhere to be found, Elizabeth pulled open the front door and charged outside. She ran towards the smouldering barn. 'Where is my son?' she shouted. A barrage of awaiting police officers prevented her from gaining access to the building despite the best efforts of her thrashing limbs.

Elizabeth's reaction to the devastating news dragged Lockie out of his own state of shock, and he ran outside after his wife. 'Elizabeth!' he shouted, running over to the barn, grabbing hold of her arms and releasing her from the officer's grip. He eased her body to the ground and shared what would be his last ever tender embrace with his wife. 'I'm here for you,' he whispered, holding his wife tight to prevent her from crumbling.

Elizabeth thrashed herself free from the embrace. 'You made

me leave,' she shouted, pulling herself away from his affections. 'I told you that I didn't want to go out. I told you that I didn't want to leave them alone. But you made me do it anyway,' she cried, banging her hands against Lockie's chest before running back into the house and up to Sam's room. Officer Peters went to Lockie's aid and bent down, helping him to his feet like he was injured. Shoulder to shoulder, Officer Peters guided Lockie back inside the house, sheltering him from the eyes of the world; eyes that were burning into his back and leaving behind an intangible sheaf of sorrow.

Elizabeth slammed Sam's door and sat in the corner, the exact spot that he used to sit whenever he had landed himself in big trouble. With her knees pulled to her chest, she buried her face, shutting out the world she no longer cared to be a part of.

'Tell me it isn't true,' Elizabeth begged when the door opened, and Officer Kate appeared. 'Tell me that Sam is okay.'

Kate closed the door and sat on the floor next to Elizabeth. With their arms touching, Kate peered around at what she could tell had been Sam's bedroom. 'I'm so sorry, Mrs Sloan,' she announced gently, admiring the photo of Sam in her eyeline. Kate supported Elizabeth's frame as her body began to crumble. 'I'm so sorry for your loss.'

Elizabeth already knew that no amount of support was ever going to help her come to terms with the death of her son, a death that, in her eyes, could have been avoided had she only stood her ground. The guilt that she would come to carry for the rest of her life had already begun to take hold.

Kate heard a message come through on her earpiece radio, telling her that Charlotte was asking to see her mum. 'Your family need you, Elizabeth. Your daughter is downstairs and she's asking to see you. She hasn't been told what's happened.'

Walking as though she was half asleep, Elizabeth was guided downstairs and into the lounge where Charlotte was waiting.

The second that Charlotte locked eyes on her mum, she ran

over and flung her arms around her waist, burying her broken face into her mum's chest. 'What's going on?' she cried. 'Where's Sam?' Her tears penetrated the material on Elizabeth's dress. 'I'm so glad that you're home,' she added when her mum didn't say anything.

Charlotte continued to hold onto her mum, waiting for her affection to be reciprocated. Although Elizabeth placed her arms over Charlotte's back, the embrace wasn't delivered with any true level of sincerity.

'I'll give you two a minute. I'll just be outside if you need me,' Kate advised, closing the lounge door.

Sensing her mum's reluctance to engage in the embrace, Charlotte pulled away. 'Where's Sam?' she asked again, still hoping that she had somehow got the story all wrong, and that her little brother was safe. 'The police told me to stay in here.'

With her daughter looking deep into her eyes, waiting for an answer, Elizabeth was forced to say the words out loud for the first time. 'Sam is gone,' she began, shaking her head when she heard her own words. 'He died in the fire,' Elizabeth confirmed, allowing her gaze to drift outside until it landed on the barn. The words left blisters in Elizabeth's mouth as they left her lips.

Charlotte shook her head and refused to believe her mum's words. 'Is he not out on his bike somewhere? Has he not snuck off to Dylan's house without telling us? Maybe he's scared to come home because he knows he'll be in trouble.'

Despite knowing it was wrong, Elizabeth allowed herself to unleash her grief onto her daughter. 'You tell me where Sam is. You should know, because I left you in charge,' she cried, momentarily feeling better once the weight of her blame had been shifted.

'I only left him for a few minutes while I went to buy us some ice creams,' Charlotte defended.

'You left Sam by himself, and now he's gone!' she shouted, an ugly twist to her mouth. Elizabeth released an uncontrollable stream of sobs that rocked through her whole body, and she crumbled into a heap on the floor, already hating herself for placing the blame elsewhere.

Charlotte crouched on the floor alongside her mum, wrapping her arms around her in the hope that she could prevent her from breaking. 'I'm sorry, Mum. I'm so sorry.'

'Please, just leave me alone!' Elizabeth shouted, thrashing her arms before running out of the room and back up the stairs. She scrambled into the bathroom and opened the cabinet, grabbing hold of the paracetamol packet, and shakily forced a few down her throat, keeping the rest of the packet clenched in her hands. She scurried into Sam's room and tucked herself into the foetal position on his bed, immersing herself in his world and seeking comfort from the scent that lingered on his clothes. With Sam's favourite soft toy tucked beneath her chin, she hugged the little highland cow and waited for his return. Swathes of consuming denial wrapped around her body, telling her that if she waited for long enough, her patience would be rewarded, and Sam would return to the embrace of her awaiting arms.

The sound of Elizabeth's constant sobs echoed through the quiet house. Downstairs, having spoken with the officers about what would happen next, Lockie prepared himself for the grim task of having to identify his son's body. He watched through the lounge window as the gathering of emergency services slowly dispersed, leaving behind nothing but a pile of saturated embers. A smoky stench continued to trail through the air, serving as a devastating reminder of the fire that had stolen his son's life. With the day ending, and daylight turning to dusk, the ever-blackening sky drowned out the sight of any smoky remnants.

When the last vehicle pulled away from his land, Lockie headed outside. He told himself that he just needed to get some air, but deep down, he wanted to search for Sam himself. He looked in every crevice that his son had once used as a nifty hiding place, like the secret nook behind the woodpile, only a colony of scurrying woodlice and a clutter of spiders to be found. He foraged amongst the undergrowth that linked the chain of cherry trees, Sam's lonesome swing swaying in the breeze. Lockie checked beneath the garden furniture just in case Sam had nestled himself amongst the jumble of chairs and table legs, uncovering nothing but an empty juice carton and crumpled crisp packet. Seeing that it was a clear night, perfect for stargazing, Lockie headed to the landing. The clearing in the neighbouring field offered perfect astronomical views and had always been Sam's favourite spot to use his telescope. With bated breath, Lockie made his way through the makeshift clearing and stepped out into the open field. Sam wasn't there, but evidence of his previous visit remained embedded into the land. With his size three feet, Sam had stepped in a muddy patch, the soles of his shoes leaving behind a pronounced footprint. Crippled with sadness, Lockie sat down and released his own sea of sorrow, knowing that soon he would need to return to the house as a father of an only child. In a moment of denial that he prayed would never end, Lockie closed his eyes and pretended that he was sat stargazing with his son. He could hear Sam's voice and could feel the softness of his son's skin as their hands pressed together. For a moment, life once again felt complete, and he fought to keep his eyes closed for a few more precious seconds. Shaking, and with the chill of the night now attacking his skin, with reluctance, Lockie opened his eyes and turned to face Lunar.

The only place left for him to check was the barn. Dragging his feet, Lockie walked back towards the house and ducked below the police tape, stepping inside the damaged outbuilding. The interior remained drenched in darkness with only a faint flicker of light emanating from the house. Inhaling the pungent, smoky fumes made Lockie wretch, and he couldn't help but hunch over at the waist. Once his coughing and spluttering subsided, he raised his head and cried in the face of his demons. He could hear Sam crying. He pictured how his son would have been trapped in the bales, the flames rising around him. Upon recalling the conversation he'd had with Elizabeth earlier on that day, and the forceful way that he had insisted they leave the children home alone, Lockie hung his head with guilt.

Being in the barn brought Lockie to his knees. He failed to register that the ground was still saturated, and his trousers soaked up the cold, black residue. A sudden loss of breath added to the internal pain that Lockie could feel had begun to gnaw at his heart. His vision became blurred the more his eyes grew wet with grief, and a bout of penetrating chills coursed through his weakened limbs. The glow of the full moon reflected over Lockie's fragile, lone silhouette. The longer he remained kneeling, the more it appeared as if his shadow had been swallowed by the broken land at Lunar. With the soft ground acting as his kneeler, Lockie closed his eyes, turned to God, and prayed for a miracle.

The End

LUNAR